"What do you see with your lion's eyes, Etienne La Marque?"

He turned to her, his gaze unreadable in the shadows. Valerie longed to reach out and touch his face, to put her hands on him and ease the ache of his accidental caress.

To touch him.

"You have the eyes of a lion," she whispered. "It is a formidable animal. Powerful." She didn't know where the words came from, but she could not bring herself to stop them.

"Yet within a pride," he said, his voice low, "the lioness is the predator to be most feared."

She clamped down upon a rising sob. Tears pressed behind her eyes. She blinked them back.

"I am angry. At what he did to me. To you," she said. "And I want to go home."

"You will." In the darkness, his voice curled around her like an embrace.

SWEPT AWAY BY A KISS

KATHARINE ASHE

AVON

An Imprint of HarperCollinsPublishers

AVON BOOKS
An Imprint of HarperCollins*Publishers*
10 East 53rd Street
New York, New York 10022-5299

Copyright © 2010 by Katharine Brophy Dubois
ISBN 978-0-06-196562-3
www.avonromance.com

First Avon Books paperback printing: August 2010

Avon Trademark Reg. U.S. Pat. Off. and in Other Countries, Marca Registrada, Hecho en U.S.A.
HarperCollins® is a registered trademark of HarperCollins Publishers.

Printed in the U.S.A.

10 9 8 7 6 5 4 3 2 1

To Georgie.
They are all for you, but this one is especially.
And to my husband, the model for all my heroes.
Thank you both from the deepest place in my heart.
The ocean sings there for you.

Swept Away by a Kiss

Prologue

Paris, France
1799

Fourteen years old? She is merely a child." Steven Ashford did not bother concealing the puzzlement in his rough whisper.

His companion, dark as the night, chuckled despite the stench of sewage and the ankle-deep puddles of the alley in which they hid.

"Ah, but the child foretells the woman," Maximin murmured. "When she grows to be that woman, I will seek her out again and I will make her mine."

Brow creasing, Steven tried to discern the set of his friend's features through the curtain of rain. Maximin must be hoaxing. Steven couldn't imagine otherwise. At eighteen, Steven never failed to attract female attention. A few years earlier he had barely discovered whiskers on his jaw before women became impatient to introduce to him the manifold pleasures of the body.

Love, they called it.

At first he willingly complied. But within months the thrill of his adventure in physical love had paled in comparison to the endeavor that captured both his body and heart. Now, with that heart pounding in anticipation so loudly he could barely hear the rain slanting around him, Steven marveled at his friend's folly.

"You are a fool, Maximin." He shook his head. "Girl or woman, I haven't time for diversions like that, or the desire to—" His voice stilled.

The man they awaited appeared in the mist of rain-flecked lantern light at the alley's end. Steven steadied himself, sensing Maximin's same ready tension.

The caped figure strode down the narrow street, his tricorne ladling tiny waterfalls in three directions. Then, as though aware of danger, he paused.

"Who is there?" The downpour consumed his cultured accents. He continued forward more slowly, peering to either side.

Steven swallowed. His thumb slipped forward on the ivory hilt of the blade in his palm, tilting the tip upward.

"I know you are there," the man said into the flickering silvery black. "What do you want? Money? I will give you as much as you need if you allow me safely past. On my honor, I promise it as one citizen to another."

Steven smiled ruefully. Men in positions of power never believed they could be harmed. Stillness streamed through his veins, cool and stealthy as a midnight ocean breeze. He stood, coming shoulder to shoulder with Maximin in the deluge. They moved into the center of the alley, one behind, the other in front of the politician. Maximin nodded. Steven's lips curved again, this time in anticipation.

"We have no wish for your money, Monsieur Representative," Maximin said.

The politician's gaze darted between them, but his voice remained confident. "Then what do you want?" His hand moved to the sword hilt at his hip.

"Why, Monsieur Citizen," Steven replied in equally refined tones, "justice, of course."

As one, he and Maximin stepped forward to claim their demand.

Chapter 1

Boston, Massachusetts
May 1810

THE RIGHT HONBLE.
THE EARL OF ALVERSTON
DERBYSHIRE, G.B.

Dear Valentine,

I have been childish. I have been selfish. I have been every kind of fool. But I have now had enough of that sort of thing, and enough of exile. Dearest brother, you, at least, forgive me. I am coming home.

Your Unfaithful Sister,
Valerie

Chapter 2

Breathe," Lady Valerie Monroe whispered into the flutter of breeze curling down the hatchway. The wooden stair gleamed with fresh polish, inviting. Beyond the open hatch above, the azure sky seemed infinite.

Setting her foot upon the lowest step, Valerie drew in a tentative breath. As though encouraging her, a current of briny air rushed down the hatchway, tangling in the sable locks escaping her bonnet, beckoning her aloft.

She propelled herself up the steps onto deck. Risking her milky complexion, she tilted her face into the late-afternoon sun spill and gazed up through lacy rigging into the heavens. The mingled scents of crisp salt water and acrid tar teased her nostrils. Gruff male voices rose through the tumult of activity across deck and on the quay beyond. Valerie filled her lungs and a smile split across her lips.

"I can breathe again." Caught up by the wind, her words sounded like a prayer.

She moved to the deck rail. On the dock below, sailors and tradesmen hustled about wharfed vessels, shouting in as many languages as colors billowed from lofty masts. A choir of brawny workers heaved crates and barrels onto her ship. Her gaze followed the procession of men and merchandise aboard, traveling aft, then up to the main-mast's tip rising high above the roofs of the dockside buildings.

A sigh trembled in her throat. In moments, at the whis-tle of the boatswain's pipe, the Dutch merchantman would embark for Portsmouth. For England. Home.

Valerie's starchy American cousins worried about her sailing alone across the Atlantic on a merchant ship. But Valerie didn't care a fig about the crossing. Her only thoughts were for her destination. Two interminably long years had passed since she'd last teased her beloved brother, Valentine, or embraced her dearest friend, Anna; last run barefoot through a velvet Derbyshire meadow; last tickled her lips on champagne in a Mayfair mansion; last truly lost her breath dancing in the arms of a gentleman.

Two years of searing guilt. Two years of alternating heartache and tedium.

"Now I am free," she murmured, imbibing the heady sea air like a tonic. Free of numbing misery. Free to make a new start.

Her gaze slipped across deck and over the motley group of sailors making ready to set sail, boys and wizened elders, Dutchmen and ex-slaves, all weathered and wiry with sea-worn strength. Settling into her cabin earlier, she had overheard Cousin Abigail instructing the captain to clear the deck of idle sailors when Valerie came above. It would not do, Abigail whispered, for an Unfortunate Incident to occur during the crossing.

With a giddy breath, Valerie laughed at the recollec-tion. Abigail was a pea goose. With the earl dead, what use did Valerie have any longer for common sailors . . . or under grooms, or junior footmen?

The sun slipped behind the dockside warehouses, casting burnt shadows upon the bay. Soon they would be under way. Soon she would be with her loved ones again. Valerie worried her lip between her teeth. When she stepped off the ship in England, Valentine and Anna would greet her warmly. They might be the only ones.

A whisk of wind grabbed a lock of hair and sent it scampering across her sight. Firmly willing away her unwanted thoughts, she drew the dark tress aside.

She froze.

Ten yards away upon the dock stood a man dressed in a black gown and a high-collared cape. Only the sharp edge of white at his neck relieved the grim costume. He held a black hat in one hand. As the breeze pulled at its broad brim, gold glimmered upon his finger.

Valerie stared. The black-clad stranger was no country vicar or city bishop—pale-skinned, limp-wristed, and altogether distasteful. Despite his priestly garb, this man positively radiated masculine heat.

Her lashes fluttered as her gaze traveled down his habit. The shape of the ebony robes and the hat were distinctive, the breathtaking male shape beneath just as alluring. A Jesuit stood before her, one of the legendary, despised race of priests people uttered such thrillingly barbarous stories about. Handmaidens of the pope, missionaries to jungle savages and plains bandits alike, they dressed like natives and even worshipped with them.

Valerie knew ample, lurid details about the fraternity's members. She was not likely to forget such titillating knowledge, or how she acquired it. Sneaking into the library late at night to read about the scandalous clerics had earned her one of the earl's most chilling reprimands to date. She had been only fifteen. The iciest chastisements came later, culminating in her journey to Boston. To exile.

Valerie narrowed her eyes against the gathering dusk. Her girlish imagination had once conjured up a mysterious figure just like this, a man of privilege and power who nevertheless bore a heathen's heart past redemption.

But Valerie was no longer a girl, and the sight of this very real Jesuit's broad shoulders stretching his mantle taut stirred in her an entirely womanly appreciation. Captivated, she continued staring as an urchin scurried toward the priest and grasped him around the knee.

The child's dusky face looked as grubby as the rags draped over his bone-thin frame. But without hesitation the priest swept back his elegant cloak and bent. An object passed from the boy's fist into the man's palm—a slip of paper, perhaps? The priest's hand enclosed the tiny one, and his other stole across the matted twists of the boy's hair in a captivating gesture of approval, or possibly affection. He stood to his full height again, and the urchin ran off.

"Lady Valerie!" The anxious call of Valerie's maid sliced into her reverie.

The priest turned and looked directly at her. His eyes flashed gold in the failing light. A frisson of recognition skittered through Valerie's belly. Her breath caught.

She did not know him. She would certainly remember if she'd met him before. At a distance he appeared handsome, all teak skin and ebony-clad masculinity cast in the slanting rays of sun. But the sense of familiarity clung, spreading to her throat and chest.

Disturbed by the absurd impression, she tried to look away. But his gaze held hers like a silken grip. For an instant, as though in a dream, she seemed to look out of someone else's eyes at the solitary figure at the water's edge.

Her maid's footsteps sounded upon the planking. Peculiar panic darted through Valerie. She wrenched her gaze from the priest.

"Yes, Harriet?"

The maid bobbed a curtsy. "Mr. Raymer says the ship is ready to get under way. He wants your company."

"I will be there shortly." Smudges of purple stained Harriet's gray cheeks. Valerie frowned. "Harriet, you look unwell."

"A touch of the megrim is all, miss." The maid wrung her hands.

"You better go and have a rest. I don't want you laid up below deck all month for taking the first day too quickly."

Wanting to turn again toward the quay—and the priest—Valerie dampened the urge. He was exactly the sort of inappropriate man she once eagerly sought out. But she had changed. Two years of grief had seen to that. Not even a handsome, mysterious stranger could inspire her to recklessness.

Besides, she didn't have anyone to shock with that sort of behavior any longer.

She ushered her maid back to the hatchway. Harriet descended to the cabin, and Valerie started aft toward the captain's observation deck. But an odd warmth gathered between her shoulders, tugging her back. Taking a quick breath, she turned.

Not far along the quay, a cluster of sailors rested from the press of last-minute work before the sun's disappearance. A scraggly dog picked around their feet for bits of discarded tobacco. But where the Jesuit had stood was nothing but the worn wood of the dock and, beyond, the darkening lap of water in the bay.

He had vanished, just as Valerie's unease at making this journey to England had disappeared. Instead, a spark of excitement sizzled through her, and her blood, so cold for twenty-four months, hummed with warm anticipation.

* * *

Valerie.

The name rustled through Steven's consciousness. A memory followed, words sung into the fire smoke in his grandfather's gravelly voice.

Strong. Her heart is strong. Your path will cross hers and you must choose which road to tread. But only one will lead you home.

Valerie.

Valor. Strength.

His grandfather had said much more. Steven tried to recall it as he strode down the quay in the hush of early evening. But his thoughts were already full of the project at hand. He hadn't the leisure to muse on futile prophecies. His destiny did not matter. Steven respected his grandfather, but he never much cared for the notion that a man couldn't create his life for himself.

Steven's future had not been predestined, after all. The Natchez blood running in his veins alongside the blue of the English aristocracy saw to that. He could have easily spent his lifetime as a pell for men of pure lineage, scorned and beaten for being born a lesser mortal. But he hadn't. Only ten years old, he'd fled England and forged another future for himself.

No, Steven did not believe in prophecy, even when it involved a beautiful woman. He didn't believe in fate either. A man's future should not be determined by his parents' blood, or by the color of his skin as so many believed.

Including the villain Steven now hunted.

On silent feet he slipped into the warehouse. The note the boy had passed him indicated this as the meeting place his contact preferred. The building echoed dank and cool after the long winter and smelled of brine. Scanning the high-ceilinged chamber stacked with barrels and crates, Steven's gaze went to the shadows, to tiny windows, other possible escape routes—the usual perusal for such a meeting. He wished he had a sword at his side, regretting the disguise he had donned so long ago it seemed like a second skin and made bearing a sword impossible.

His strength and agility would have to do. At least today he would not be required to brandish a weapon. A man never knew, though. Not when lives and gold and power were at stake, as always in the world of the slave trade.

Steven drew a slow breath, trying to quell the peculiar expectation stirring his senses. Anticipation over the imminent meeting didn't cause it. He knew what was to come. For two years he and Maximin had planned everything carefully. This meeting would merely confirm a final detail. Nothing about it worried Steven now.

But . . . *Valerie.*

A coincidence. Women all over the world bore that name. He'd even shared a bed with one years back if he remembered correctly, and hadn't given it a second thought.

But this English noblewoman, she stared at him so fixedly, as though she knew.

Steven shook himself. She knew nothing. She was a complete stranger, and she would remain one despite the journey they were about to share, a journey that would not proceed as the beautiful Englishwoman imagined. Not if everything Steven arranged came to pass.

Footsteps scuffled upon the sandy floor. A man appeared in the dim light of a lantern.

"Angel?" he whispered. His gaze skittered around the building, searching for Steven in the shadows.

"I am here," Steven said, managing not to cringe at the alias given him years earlier. He still thought it was ridiculous. If the men and women working for him truly knew him, they would have named him much differently, no doubt more like the name his mother's people had offered him.

"Expect them in four days, Father," the man said.

Four days, long enough to sail past the American naval barricade and still remain within the pirate Bebain's territory. Perfect.

"Thank you, my son." The priestly words slipped easily off Steven's tongue. He had played the part for so long, it barely took effort.

Recalling the English beauty's wide, direct stare, Steven wondered briefly if pretending to be a priest would be quite so easy for the next four days.

Chapter 3

Good heavens, not again," Valerie muttered, setting a basin beneath her maid's chin. How a person could be so ill, so many times, while the ship moved in such calm waters, Valerie could not fathom.

"I'll be better in a trice, my lady," Harriet moaned, falling back onto her cot.

Valerie rinsed a cloth in water laced with her own lavender oil and placed it upon her maid's forehead. Back in Boston, Cousin Abigail insisted Harriet would make a fine companion for the crossing. Valerie should have known better. The girl's dull temper did not suit her, but Abigail thought of Harriet as a steadying influence on her wild English mistress.

Valerie snorted inelegantly, patted her maid's hand, and rose.

"Rest now, Harriet. I am going above deck for a bit, but I will be back soon."

"But, milady, you can't. Your cousin—"

"My cousin does not have any say over my comings and

goings any longer. No one else does either." The words slipped over Valerie's tongue like sweet wine. "We have been aboard nearly three days already and I simply must be free of this cabin. No one will notice if I poke my head above without you."

Harriet groaned again. Valerie tucked the ends of her shawl under her elbows and ducked from the chamber. A few steps along the gun deck took her to the hatchway and up into the bright morning.

The Dutch barque was broad and solid, its square sails filled with wind driving it eastward. Scattered sailors worked unhurriedly beneath the early summer sun. A trio of boys at the deckhouse door chased a tune from a pair of mouth organs and a pillbox accordion. The music danced across the decks, mingling with the roll of water carved by the ship's stern and the white-tipped ocean swells.

She did not see the captain at his usual post on the upper deck and looked toward the prow. Her lashes fanned open. Another passenger stood at the forecastle rail, his black-clad shoulders and back to her. But his virile, robed figure and proud stance were unmistakable. The Jesuit.

Beside him, the navigator, a hoary old seaman, fiddled with some sort of tool. His hands seemed anxious on the instrument. The priest spoke, and snatches of phrases skittered to her on the afternoon breeze.

French?

She shouldn't be surprised. A Dutch ship was bound to carry other foreigners, even passengers whose nations were at war, like England and France. Boston had its fair share of monarchist émigrés from France's war-torn colonies. Perhaps this priest with the broad shoulders was an aristocrat driven abroad by the Revolution. Or maybe he simply sought the adventure that came with a missionary's vows in America.

A crease formed in Valerie's brow. Flight from the

dangers of revolution she could appreciate, but not that other sort of sacrifice. She would never understand how a man could deny himself intimacy in hopes of securing divine love. In Valerie's experience, human love was hard enough to win.

The navigator reached beneath his coat and pulled out an envelope. As though he expected it—just as with the boy on the dock—the priest drew it from the older man's fingers and slipped it into his sleeve. The sailor's face filled with relief.

Valerie's eyes narrowed, her pulse quickening. The envelope must contain something of great value to cause the navigator to react like that.

"Welcome atop, Lady Valerie," a voice boomed across deck. "It is a glorious day."

Valerie pivoted to greet the shipmaster. "So glorious, Mr. Raymer, that I have come up without my maid. Unfortunately she is ill. May I impose upon you for company?"

"Certainly. In such fine weather, no one should cower below. Please join me for some refreshment."

Valerie accepted the master's outstretched arm and he led her aft. Beneath a sturdy awning, a table was already set with tea and biscuits. Shaking her head at the proffered chair, she leaned against the rail and looked below at the waves splashing against the ship's broad sides. The salt air sank deep into her lungs.

Untying her bonnet ribbons, she removed the hat. Her hair worked free in the breeze and she sighed at the glorious sensation. She had been so proper and well behaved living with her cousins. But she was not in England yet, and she didn't have anything to hide aboard this ship. None of the sailors would notice if she acquired a freckle or two as penalty for her minor transgression. And aside from Harriet, no one else aboard would care a fig if she went without her bonnet. Certainly not a French priest.

The captain regarded her with bashful appreciation as he filled a teacup for her. Valerie smiled over the rim at the Dutch sailor. She liked his affable, fatherly air, a quality the earl had entirely lacked.

"It's a shame your servant has taken ill in such a fine wind," he said. "Fortunately, we are not likely to see truly inclement skies. You chose a good season to sail."

"Don't you think there is any chance of a storm, Mr. Raymer?"

"When Beauty ventures into the open, not even Neptune dares produce an errant wave to drive her below deck." The fluid French words caressed Valerie's senses. She swung around to face the priest.

This time she hardly noticed his Jesuit costume. He was, quite frankly, astonishingly handsome, nothing like the stiff, pallid noblemen who pandered to her in London and Boston since her come-out four years earlier. The priest's perfect masculinity appeared like an artist's rendering of a man carved from rich marble—the angle of his strong jaw, the sensuous curve of his lips, the aristocratic cast of his brow. Unfashionably long, sun-gilded hair curling around his collar and impossibly high, sculpted cheekbones lent him an exotic air. A rakish air. Dangerous.

Valerie lifted her gaze. His flame-laced, amber eyes glowed with amusement and the arrogance of a confident adversary.

Her heart stumbled. She righted it and tilted up her chin.

"You flatter me, *monsieur*."

"Flattery tends to mislead, *mademoiselle*. I prefer the truth." Rich, warm, and startlingly seductive for a cleric, his voice curled into Valerie's belly, tightening it.

"The truth? I suppose that is a necessity of your vocation," she quipped, trying to overcome her unexpected reaction.

"Rather, personal proclivity." His mouth curved up at one edge, a mouth God had clearly spent great time and care fashioning.

"I see. I didn't know men of the cloth were allowed that."

The curve turned into a grin.

"On occasion. Dependent upon good behavior, of course."

"Of course." A smile tugged at Valerie's lips too. She stifled it. His words teased, but the fiery spark in his eyes remained. He was not flirting with her. He seemed to be challenging, though she couldn't imagine why. Of course, the French were an overly proud people, especially when they thought they were winning a war.

The captain looked anxiously between his passengers, no doubt recalling Cousin Abigail's dire warnings. But he needn't worry. Valerie was through with unsuitable dalliances and foolish escapades, even if her cousins did not believe it. And even if, at the particular moment, her own senses did not seem to believe it either. But she'd always chosen willing partners in her crimes of passion. A Catholic priest speaking of good behavior did not exactly fit the model, no matter how breathtakingly handsome.

As on the quay in Boston, he returned stare for stare. But something unsettling was happening in his eyes. The gold glint grew deeper. Knowing. Valerie's insides quivered.

He knew she had just dismissed him out-of-hand.

No. He could not read her mind. She blinked to dispel the vision.

A lion's eyes gazed back at her.

Valerie's blood seemed to rush toward stillness. As a girl she had seen a real lion at a London menagerie. The priest's slow, penetrating gaze mimicked the magnificent animal's. It seemed to warn her that she, always the predator before, had become the prey.

Startled by her absurd musings, she wrenched her attention to the shipmaster.

"I suspect good behavior is a quality Mr. Raymer values in his sailors," she managed. "Don't you, Captain?"

"Yes indeed," Raymer said with a splutter of relief. "But please forgive me for neglecting my duties as a host. Lady Valerie, allow me to present to you Father Etienne La Marque, late of the Louisiana Territory. Father, this is Lady Valerie Monroe."

La Marque bowed, bending his lean frame deeply as though in mock reverence. The wooden beads tucked into the sash around his waist clacked against the crucifix at the end of the chain.

"So then, *monsieur*," she said, wishing she could shake herself free of his curious effect, "on this voyage should we expect to encounter the dreaded sea god himself, or some of his nereids?"

"Perhaps a stray mermaid?" A half smile flickered again at his lips. "One can only hope, my lady." He seemed genuinely amused now. But, for heaven's sake, mermaids? Did priests truly flirt? "Naturally," he added with a Gallic shrug, "such encounters depend upon the route we sail."

Raymer chortled. "Lady Valerie is bound for Portsmouth, Father. The Earl of Alverston will meet her there." The captain announced the noble connection with undisguised pride.

The priest tilted his head. "Family, my lady?"

"Yes. I have lived with my American cousins for two years and am anxious to return home to my brother's estate. Mr. Raymer has kindly taken me and my maid aboard at the last minute, although I suspect he left valuable cargo behind to accommodate us."

"Yet none so precious, I daresay," the priest said.

Valerie silently exhorted her foolish knees not to turn to jelly.

Raymer chuckled gruffly again. "Nothing is as valuable as human cargo, Lady Valerie."

"Good heavens, Mr. Raymer. Cargo?" She laughed, but her hands went cold. She had been weaned on caustic wit, and as the daughter of a peer she always knew her worth lay in her lineage and dowry. She willfully flouted that for years, but now that she was trying to make a new start of it, the captain's comment cut too close to the quick.

Her gaze slipped to La Marque. His smile had vanished.

The gaff fluttered, setting up a sudden racket, and the heavy boom slipped sideways. Raymer's expression sobered and shifted to the mizzenmast. A sailor hurried over and the captain stepped aside to speak with him, his thick legs sturdy as the deck tilted. Valerie steadied herself, and her gaze slid back toward La Marque.

The ship rolled, pitching Valerie forward. Her palms met solid muscle beneath cassock, hard and lean. Fingertips and palms alive with instant feeling, she pressed against him to steady herself. He grasped her wrists, and Valerie swung her head up. Awareness, delicious and thrilling, jolted through her. Flame sparked in his eyes. The heat of his body reached out, enthralling and forbidden. Valerie swallowed through the thickness in her throat. His gaze shifted to the motion at her neck, stroking like a caress.

She tugged her hands away, grabbing on to the rail for support.

What on earth was happening to her? She'd spent two miserable years in her cousins' home, bored senseless with every gentleman they paraded before her, and now a handsome Frenchman's brief touch overset her? *Ridiculous.*

If the earl were alive, he would say, *Typical.* Society would no doubt agree.

"Mr. Raymer keeps a well-ordered ship," she said hastily.

"It is in his interest to do so." The priest's voice sounded hard.

Valerie's gaze snapped up. "The captain is a fine gentleman," she said uncertainly.

"Raymer is no different from all other merchants, my lady, gladly ferrying whatever he can to increase his wealth."

That seemed unjust. The Dutchman was so kind and fatherly.

"I think you are ungrateful, sir. Here you are taking advantage of a man's hospitality, then abusing him for it?"

"If I am indulging in that sort of behavior, at least I am in good company." La Marque's brow lifted and he looked pointedly at her bonnet swinging from her elbow on its ribbons.

Valerie's eyes shot wide. *Fustian.* She should not have removed the thing in Mr. Raymer's company. It was an insult to the gentleman. And now the priest was chastising her for it like some stuffy Almack's patroness.

His eyes glinted. Valerie lifted a palm to her warm cheek and sucked in a breath. She never blushed, not involuntarily, at least. And she never quailed like this with men, not even very handsome men.

"You are not offended," he said, his gaze gentling with humor. "You are trying to decide how to respond, but you have no real quarrel with me, though you wish you did." A hint of a smile played at the corner of his lips again.

Valerie's throat tightened. How did he seem to know her already? He couldn't possibly, as he couldn't have read her mind earlier. Could he? Perhaps priests had some special knack for that sort of thing. But it was more than that, a familiarity she could not shake off, as though he truly did know her.

A flurry of wind curled off the main course and across Valerie's lips, stroking her cheek. La Marque stood close enough for her to imagine his scent—delectable man and a hint of limewater. His golden gaze seemed to darken, and hunger ground in Valerie's belly, deep and tingling.

Too deep. And, in point of fact, somewhat south of her belly.

She blinked to clear her senses again. She should not allow him to flummox her. She could do this. It was only mild flirtation, after all, and with a priest, for pity's sake. It could be amusing. He seemed clever, and he was lovely to look at. Added to that, she would do anything to avoid spending hours alone dwelling upon her uncertain future.

She lifted her brows in mock disapproval.

"Is this some sort of examination, *monsieur*? Have I failed or passed it?" Of course she could do this. It was what she had always done best, after all.

Aside from seducing inappropriate men.

Chapter 4

Steven allowed himself a grin. This woman was as willful as her touch was heated, and exquisite from her sparkling eyes to her lithe, beautifully curved body and regal bearing. In the brisk breeze, her gown clung to her intoxicating figure as though reveling in contact with her flesh. Her loosely bound, dark hair strayed against her full lips, unwilling to be tamed by pins.

"Upon what in God's great creation, *mademoiselle*," he replied, "could I wish to examine you?"

Her ocean-colored eyes danced and she took a visible breath, tightening the confection of expensive silk across her high, perfectly rounded breasts. She did not reply, openly considering him instead. Steven stood immobile, bearing down upon his stirring arousal as her gaze slipped along the length of his cassock. Her lashes fluttered, a flicker of desire simmering in her eyes.

She cleared her throat, finally lifting her gaze. It shone warm but peculiarly clouded, as though something more than desire troubled her.

Not what he had expected. Not welcome either. Her desire he could accept. He had been the object of women's desires for years and never paid it much attention. But he didn't like her confusion. Confusion in a willful woman invariably became curiosity, and the bonnet hanging at her elbow showed how much she respected convention.

Steven did not have room in his plans for a curious, unpredictable woman. Especially not one with eyes the color of the turbulent sea.

He should not have sought her out. He had managed to avoid her for three days, taking his dinners alone rather than meeting her in the captain's quarters each evening. Something drew him, though, some ineffable lure. Now that he had made the mistake of speaking with her, however, he might as well play the moment in a manner that would fulfill her expectations.

Taking her gloved hand, he raised it near his lips, bowing again and hoping the courtly gesture would put her at ease.

Her fingers went rigid. Instead of a coquettish glimmer, her eyes swam with need, a world waiting to come to life. Vibrant and raw, the emotion in her gaze constricted Steven's chest.

He had misjudged her. Willful, beautiful, yes. Desirable, without doubt. But not a jade or even a coquette. Perhaps twenty-one, yet still full of youthful passion, Lady Valerie Monroe was precisely the sort of bride Steven's aunt continually encouraged him to take. The sort who would make a perfect viscountess.

Steven did not want his viscountcy, the title he had unexpectedly acquired years earlier. And he certainly did not want a viscountess. Not ever, and especially not now when he had a job to complete that he'd been planning for months. A notorious slave trader ran amok in the Atlantic, greedy for the vast fortunes won trafficking since Britain had declared the trade illicit three years earlier. With each shipload of men and women that Clifford Hannsley, Fifth Marquess, sold illegally at western ports, another bag of gold passed into his insatiable hands, gold that helped him influence kings and princes.

Hannsley, however, had the bad luck of long ago making himself Steven's childhood nemesis. Steven was determined to destroy his old rival or die trying. He had no space in his life for a noble title or the trappings that went along with it.

Valerie's fingers tightened around his.

"Will you say something poetic now?" she asked, her sweet voice slightly unsteady and hurried. "Men always try to say poetic things when they halt just shy of kissing a woman's hand."

Steven stared, heat surging through him. Clearly he had been at sea far too long. No woman's touch had ever gotten him hard so quickly, her voice stealing into his lungs like the musky smoke of incense. It must be the enforced celibacy. Though that failed to explain the sharp familiarity of her touch.

Beautiful, willful, desirable . . . familiar.

A distraction from his purpose.

"Do they?" he managed to reply with credible evenness.

Her rose-hued lips curved into a playful grin, lips far too shapely to be used solely for speaking. She nodded.

"Oh, yes. Typically about flowers." Her cheeks dimpled, but her gaze stayed firmly in his, as though it cost her effort to appear amused.

"Flowers?"

"Of course." Her tone hinted at strain. A man less skilled in reading subtle cues might not notice that, or the delicate flickering of the gold-rimmed cameo pinned to her bodice disturbed by her heart's quick, hard beats.

"To what purpose, I wonder," he said, slipping the pad of his thumb over her knuckles.

The cameo flickered faster.

"To describe the woman as a flower. To make amends for whatever he said wrong, or simply for not kissing her." She bit her soft lower lip.

"How remarkable." He should stop this. "What sort of flowers?"

"I would think a Frenchman, of all people, would know that. But perhaps . . ." Her gaze slipped to his chest, taking in his priestly garb once more. Her eyes came up again, the same vibrant need in their sea-blue depths. "A lily, tulip, rose, what have you."

"I begin to think, my lady," he said slowly, "that you are no prosaic flower. Rather you are like cool rain after an overly warm summer day."

"Good heavens, *monsieur*, rain?" Her eyes glimmered too bright. She spoke quickly. "Not a red, red rose, or a velvet tulip touched with dew? I don't know whether to be impressed or disappointed by your originality. But I appreciate your effort. Fate has been unkind to you, I am afraid, to have crossed your path with a poetically jaded woman." She laughed, a brittle cascade of false pleasure.

Steven had enough. She didn't want this inane banter and neither did he. Not after what she had just said about fate, his path, and her. His grandfather's words resounded in his head, her fingertips pressing warmly to his palm, as though some part of her might steal within him through such a simple channel.

He released her hand.

"I pay no attention to fate, *mademoiselle*. Only to fortitude."

"Fortitude?" Her gaze met his squarely, a question in their expressive depths.

"Forgive me, Lady Valerie, Father." Raymer came toward them. "I am terribly sorry to have abandoned you for so long. The quartermaster needed me to— But that would not interest either of you, of course." He offered Lady Valerie his arm.

She tucked her hand into his elbow.

"That's quite all right, Mr. Raymer. Monsieur La Marque and I have just discovered a shared dislike of poetry. He has quite diverted me, really." Her voice sounded nearly steady.

The captain smiled at her and patted her hand. "Would you like a tour of the ship, my lady?"

Her gaze flickered to Steven again.

"Very much, thank you."

"Good afternoon, Father," the shipmaster said, and bowed. She sketched a curtsy, and the pair walked away. Steven watched after them, the graceful sway of her hips holding his gaze.

She called him *monsieur*. Not Father.

He rubbed a palm over his face and took a deep breath. One more day until they caught up with the ship that would take him away from this woman. One more day, and counting.

Storms rocked the ship.

In her dream, Valerie knew she dreamed. She tried to wake herself.

Thunder and rainfall on the deck above sounded quick and staccato, like the clattering of booted feet. Safe within, she heard the dolphins, alongside bow and beam, springing high on silver-laced wings, reaching, stroking the midnight ether, warning her in frantic voice.

Valerie tugged at the bed linens to cover her ears. She struggled and pulled again but some force held her still. She pushed. A hand gripped her arm.

Crashing into wakefulness, Valerie flung the hand away and bolted from the bed. Harriet tumbled to the cabin floor, fingers pressed to her mouth, eyes wide with fright.

Hurried footfalls still thumped upon the deck above—real, not a dream. Shouts rose, and the sharp snap of a revolver. Valerie's heart slammed against her ribs.

Gripping her maid, she dragged her into the narrow space between the cot and deck. With a terrified whimper, the girl pressed inside the crevice and Valerie threw the bedlinens over the opening. She reached for her gown and slid it over her shift, pushing her feet into half boots, drawing her hair into a hasty knot, then wrapping her hooded cloak about her. Hesitating for only an instant, she reached into her traveling trunk, grabbed a short, sliver-thin knife encased in red leather, and tucked it into her cloak pocket.

The wild pattering of footsteps above stopped. Only the lapping of water against the ship's hull and muffled voices upon the deck disturbed the stillness.

The merchantman's guns were quiet.

Valerie opened the door and peered into the lamp-lit emptiness of the captain's day cabin. The door to the gun deck gaped wide. Beyond, the hatch cover above the stair yawned, but not a breath of moonlight shone down the opening. Dread skittered up Valerie's spine. Any girl reared in the English countryside knew what a new moon meant, that postilions and gatekeepers could not see the swift advance of thieves until it was far too late.

For a terrible moment, she stood rooted to the deck floor. Then she straightened her shoulders. She would rather be taken fighting than cowering like her terrified maid. Gulping down another breath, she sent herself up into the night.

Torches lit the deck. No broken bodies littered the deck, no sign of scuffle at all. The merchant sailors were trussed to barrels and rails, a few groaning, but no blood anywhere. A sleek little craft rested upon the water not far distant, its crew members busy transferring the Dutch trader's lighter cargo to their own ship.

Valerie searched for Mr. Raymer, finding him strapped to the helm on the poop deck. Mouth gagged, his eyes opened wide.

A massive arm swung around Valerie and dragged her backward. Before she could reach for her knife, an enormous fist trapped her hands and pressed them against her midriff.

"Remain still," a deep voice at her ear rumbled in French, "and you will not be harmed."

Small comfort coming from a man who could clasp both her hands in one of his. Footsteps approached.

"What do you have there, Zeus?" a sharp voice said. Valerie's captor turned her around to face the questioner.

The man's lined face was lean, almost like a caricature. Deep-set eyes gleamed beneath pencil-thin brows, and a shock of peppery hair rose high upon his forehead, sliding in a slick trail to his shoulders. His mouth widened into a grin.

"Ah, how marvelous," he exclaimed. "A pearl nestled amongst scabby oysters. We've won an unexpected treasure."

Valerie shivered as the pirate's pale, glittering gaze ran over her. He could see little of her cloak-wrapped body now, but he would undoubtedly see much more shortly. She clamped her mouth shut, resisting the nausea rising in her throat.

"Come now, beautiful lady, do not succumb to modest vapors so soon," he said lightly. He raised his fingers beneath her chin, forcing her to meet his gaze. "So much of the evening remains to be enjoyed, no?"

Despite herself, Valerie trembled. It seemed that her

giant, silent captor held her more gently, but she must be imagining it.

"Captain!" a sailor called from across the deck.

"Ah, Mr. Fevre, my true and worthy mate." The pirate captain gripped Valerie's arm and pulled her around.

"We have subdued him, and the ship is loaded." Fevre cast only a brief glance at her before he spoke. His shoulders were stooped, and his eyes shifted anxiously from face to face. A patch of dark moisture spread across the front of his trousers. Valerie looked away quickly.

"Good," the captain clipped. " Show me."

Reluctantly, it seemed, Fevre gestured aft. A pair of sailors led La Marque forward from astern. Bound with ropes, he seemed almost pale beside the black- and brown-skinned men flanking him, like all the pirates except the captain, including the massive, inky-fleshed arm encircling her shoulders.

"Magnificent," the pirate captain purred. "Take him to the ship and go back yourself, Mr. Fevre." He turned to Valerie again, eyes glimmering feral. "I will return when I finish here."

Valerie's mouth went dry. As Fevre turned to follow orders, La Marque's softly assured voice cut the velvet darkness.

"You do not wish to burden yourself with this woman, Captain."

Drawing Valerie's cloak from her shoulders, the pirate halted and turned to the priest. Irritation twisted his grotesque features.

"On the contrary, she is no burden to me whatsoever. You, however, should take care not to cause me more trouble, my little priest. I have already made sufficient allowance for you, and I will not make more." He gestured to the guards. "Away with him."

The captain motioned for Valerie's captor to release

her. Zeus's huge arm slid away, and the pirate ran his fingers across her jaw. She pressed down upon her terror.

"She is unmarried," the priest's voice again crossed the deck. "And she is of noble blood. Her family will not like to learn you have trifled with her. You will find yourself in greater trouble than you wish."

The Jesuit's guards stopped at the edge of the ship. It seemed amazing, and foolhardy, for them to disobey their captain. But everyone knew pirates were a democratic lot. Perhaps the Jesuit knew his game well enough.

The buccaneer master laughed.

"What do I need fear—me, Gaston Bebain—of some idiot, effeminate English lordling?" Bravado colored his voice. He twisted a lock of her hair around his thumb, then rested his clawed fingers upon her cheek. Valerie resisted the instinct to jerk away.

"Soft, like China silk," he murmured. "But you say she is unwed, my clerical friend? This intrigues me. I assumed she was the wife of our stalwart old master here." He laughed again, gesturing toward the Dutch sailors. He dropped her tresses and turned from her as though she were of no further interest to him. He considered the Jesuit again, frowning.

"The sad truth is that I have no use for an innocent aboard my ship. She would do me little good like that." His voice was conversational. Valerie shivered. She understood that tone and the abrupt shifting of attitudes. Bebain was mad.

He approached the priest, a thoughtful expression upon his face. Frustration stirred in Valerie's trembling limbs. How could La Marque remain so calm and still, as though her fate weren't being spoken of in terrible terms on a ship likely to be sunk in short order? Why didn't he speak again, convince Bebain not to harm her, or all of them?

Her fists clenched as her tight throat constricted.

"For God's sake, Etienne, do something."

"Etienne! Etienne?" the captain purred. "We are employing Christian names with the English beauty, are we, Father? How charmingly intimate."

The priest remained silent, his gaze hard.

"Hm, I suppose you know something about her unwed condition, after all. From personal experience, my friend, or can you convince me otherwise that she is—hm, how shall we say?—maladroit for my use?" Bebain spoke as one man to another, as though discussing the merits of wines or cigars. Valerie's blood slithered with ice.

"She is untouched, well protected since the moment she came aboard." Etienne's voice mimicked the pirate's casual tone. Then it dropped deeper, suggestive. "She would not serve a man of mature tastes well."

Bebain stood immobile, as though listening for a whispered suggestion, a lap of water, a ripple of sail to tell him what to do. Abruptly he released a shout of laughter and grabbed Valerie by the arm, dragging her across deck. Halting before the priest, he pushed her forward and she fell against the Jesuit's chest. With his hands tied behind him, Etienne did not move. Valerie wrenched away.

"What?" roared Bebain with indignant laughter. "You do not approve of my solution, pretty one?" He pressed a hand into her back, gripping Etienne's shoulder and drawing them together until her brow tapped the Jesuit's chin.

"This is ideal, don't you see? A virgin and a man of the cloth. The perfect Paradise." He laughed, a jackal's bark, and clapped his hands. He bent to speak near Valerie's ear, his breath caressing her neck like a snake's scales.

"We will construct an Eden-garden schoolroom, my lovely innocent. I, naturally, will play the starring role, the Serpent. And if I understand our clever cleric well enough, he will prove more useful to me than I first imagined. I suspect I will not have long to wait before you are delightfully prepared to join me in my less sanctified confessional. And if you do not comply, I will kill you both."

He stepped back and raised his arms theatrically. "Thanks be to God for the blessing of sacred priesthood."

His laughter shrilled through Valerie, washing her limbs with renewed tremors. As her giant guard reached for her, she thought she heard him exchange quiet words with Etienne. But when she looked toward the priest, he had already turned away.

Chapter 5

The pirates carried Valerie onto their ship, tying her up away from activity. Exhausted and stunned, she barely heard the sailors' shouts, the hissing and sliding of the lines, and the night wind hollowing out the sails.

When her chin fell to her shoulder, she roused jerkily, forcing open her eyelids. Through the crisscrossed lines at the rail the shadow of the merchant ship loomed. Lanterns lit and sails furled, it sat peacefully in the glimmering water, receding as the corsair gained speed.

Tears of relief prickled in Valerie's eyes. The pirate captain had spared Raymer's ship. It seemed an unexpected mercy, especially from a madman who thought she was of no use to him as a virgin.

In moments of risqué London gossip, Valerie had heard that some men only enjoyed their pleasures with women of extensive experience, birds of paradise, opera singers, widows. Bebain, it seemed, was that sort of man. But his solution to finding a virgin was to provide her with an education before taking her for his own use. And her instructor was to be Etienne La Marque.

Whether this lesson was meant as a punishment or prize for the priest, Valerie couldn't imagine. Etienne was probably worth ransom. But whether Bebain kept him for money or some other reason, before he released the priest, he was going to shame him.

Or, perhaps, reward him.

Shaking, Valerie clamped her mouth shut to gathering sobs. Nothing, no matter how dreadful, could be worse than the living numbness she had endured for two years. She must remember that, whatever occurred.

When activity upon the ship quieted, its swaying movement lulled her to sleep again. She awoke to morning sunlight pressing through her eyelids. High above, a clear sky framed heavy white sails. She shifted and her arms erupted in pain. Struggling to sit, she tested her bonds.

Footfalls sounded upon the planking beside her, and she twisted around. Two men blocked the sun. The giant from the night before stood in his bare feet a head taller than the man beside him, who was lighter-skinned and finer-featured than his companion. His ears, fingers, and wrists glittered with gold, and he wore a bold sash of red and black cinched around his waist.

He peered at her intently, then the two sailors spoke to each other, their speech sounding vaguely French. The giant, Zeus, came toward her. Valerie tensed.

"Do not be afraid." He crouched and reached for her hands, untying the ropes, to Valerie's astonishment.

She pulled her arms forward and rubbed gingerly at her wrists and shoulders.

"Why shouldn't I be? This is a perfectly horrid situation. I would be a thorough widgeon not to be out of my mind with fear right now."

A glint of amusement flickered in the other sailor's eyes.

Quick anger smothered Valerie's fear.

"You think this is amusing?"

The beringed man did not reply, but Zeus murmured, "The Angel will not harm you."

Valerie shook her head. Sleep must still be clogging her ears. Surely the fellow did not mean Bebain? She looked from one inscrutable face to the other, and the giant grasped her hand to help her rise.

Valerie took a deep breath, squaring her shoulders.

"What will happen to me now?"

"A chamber has been prepared for you," the beringed man said. "Come with us." Something commonplace about his tone dulled the edge on Valerie's anger and alarm. She went with them across the deck.

The ship's topside reflected wealth and order. Rope coiled upon the sparkling boards in perfect spirals, barrels were symmetrically arranged to port and starboard, and metal and woodwork brightly reflected the morning sun. The sailors worked with methodical discipline. However disordered he was in mind, Captain Bebain kept an extraordinarily neat ship.

Valerie followed her escorts down a steep, narrow stairwell onto the corsair's gun deck. The modest chamber they entered near the stern end, forward of the captain's quarters, boasted one small window starboard. A beautifully woven rug covered the floor between a collection of fine furniture bolted to the deck: a small table and wooden armchair, a carved Indian chest, and a surprisingly large, iron-framed bed made up with white sheets and a dyed indigo woolen blanket. Several framed oil paintings decorated the walls.

Valerie's stared. The pictures depicted naked women and men joined at mouths and hips. In one, the man's face was lodged between the woman's thighs.

She dragged her gaze away. Zeus had disappeared, and

the gold-ringed man stood alone at the threshold. His eyes twinkled.

"*Monsieur*—"

"Maximin."

"I would like some food, please." Valerie pressed her hand to her growling belly. Again, the pirate's coal-dark eyes smiled. Sore from head to foot, and weak with hunger, Valerie felt her thin veneer of composure dissolve. "Why are you looking at me like that?" she snapped.

"You are a beautiful woman. It pleases me." No hint of malice or even desire colored his tone, merely simple male appreciation.

"Well, I hope it pleases you enough to inspire you to bring me some food."

He grinned again and gestured to the wooden chest.

"Use whatever you find there. Call Zeus if you want anything." He closed the door. A key turned in the lock.

Valerie washed with a basin and small pitcher of water upon the table, then opened the chest. The aroma of sweet sandalwood tickled her nose. Among a stack of surprisingly fine men's linen shirts were a simple maid's frock and an ivory lace garment apparently intended as a night rail. Valerie considered the flimsy piece, then stuffed it into a bottom corner of the trunk.

She unfastened her gown, slipped it over her head, and draped it across a bedpost. Turning down the bedcover, she climbed in between unexpectedly dry sheets. She studied the scandalous pictures until her eyelids drooped.

When Valerie awoke, the giant brought her bread, hard cheese, and wine. As he retreated, she called out, "Zeus?" He paused at the door. "That is your name, isn't it?"

He nodded, his expression benign.

"Did someone give you the name, or did you choose it yourself?"

His expression did not alter.

"My master named me."

"Were you born in America?" Valerie's stomach howled with hunger so greatly that the meager rations he brought looked like a king's feast. But since waking she had devised a plan. All men could be manipulated. A woman only needed to know what a man most valued or despised to get what she wanted from him. At one time Valerie had known her father's aversions better than her own. She had put the knowledge to good use often enough.

"No, miss. They took me from my home when I was a boy." Zeus's stance remained solid in the door frame. Not a muscle flickered upon his face. But he did not leave.

Valerie's confidence edged higher.

"I wonder that they dared. A man of your impressive stature and strength . . . You must have been a strapping lad."

He turned toward the passageway. Valerie's heart fell into her stomach. Clearly this man could not be cajoled with flattery. Her thoughts flew. "I wonder if you can help me, Zeus."

His massive shoulder shifted, his chin tilting toward her. Valerie seized the signs of interest.

"I am not accustomed to being alone, you see," she said, a hint of quaver in her voice. "My maid usually attends me, or—or a gentleman friend," she stammered, allowing the full force of maidenly fear to shine through her eyes. She was frightened, for sure. But maybe if this man believed her to be on the verge of hysteria he would agree to help her.

His brow furrowed.

"Perhaps—" she stuttered. "Perhaps, if some companion could pass the time with me, so that I would not always be thinking of—of—" She broke off, her gaze entreating. "Would you stay for a bit and talk with me?"

"I must remain outside."

"Oh." She laced the single word with disappointment. "Then may I have something to keep me busy? A deck of cards? Perhaps a book would help."

Valerie revised her plan as she spoke. Of course a man torn from his family and homeland while still a child would not respond well to an aristocrat's helpless misery, no matter what her circumstances. Instead of pathetic, she should act vulnerable and determined. Anyway, she *was* determined. Determined to wrest her way out of this captivity by any means necessary.

Zeus nodded. She had won a victory, if only a tiny one. Valerie released her breath slowly.

When he left, she dove into the simple food and drink. Revived, she paced around the little chamber, but the activity did not relieve her agitation. No doubt Bebain would soon call for her. She must prepare herself for that, and for whatever else would come.

Her stomach roiled.

She shook her hands free of tremors and went to the window. The colors of sunset, violet, fiery orange, scarlet, and fuchsia, swept across the western sky over the reflecting sea. With an odd thickness, Valerie's heart fluttered.

She could end the horror before it began, she supposed, staring at nature's riotous canvas spread before her. They would undoubtedly take her above deck again. If she went docilely, the pirates might become accustomed to her timidity. They would not expect it when she pulled away and flung herself overboard. It would be as easy as spending pin money to give her life to the sea rather than the madman who captained this horrible vessel.

She stepped back from the window.

She had never taken the easy path before, and didn't know what it would be like to do so. Only four days ago, after all, she had been ready to put herself at the mercy of the unforgiving *ton* to regain the company of her loved ones.

She would still do it. She would see this nightmare through and somehow make it back to England. She longed to feel her family's embraces and know she was finally home, loved.

The door opened behind her. Throat tightening, she swung around and met the priest's golden gaze. He stood tall in the cabin doorway, his wrists shackled together, and abruptly she understood her frustration with him the night before. Even bound, Etienne La Marque emanated an aura of slumbering power. Small wonder she had imagined he could save them.

The sailor Maximin stood behind him. He unfastened the irons around Etienne's wrists and handed over the oil lamp. The priest stepped across the threshold and the door closed. A key slid in the lock.

"Good evening, *mademoiselle*." He rubbed his wrists, drawing Valerie's gaze to the action. He had strong hands, long, beautiful fingers. Hands that could hold a woman just as she wanted to be held.

Valerie's breath stuttered, and warmth collected in her middle. What would it be like to have him touch her, and not because someone forced him to?

"Are you unharmed?" His lion eyes watched her, their expression unreadable.

"I have been left to myself all day," she managed.

"I didn't know where they took you last night. I am relieved you are well." He fastened the lamp into a clasp upon the table. He looked around the cabin, his regard coming to rest on the armchair. "May I?"

He made the request prosaically enough, but Valerie suddenly saw his weariness, and something else, a slight darkening along his jaw and another over his eye. Bruises.

They must have beaten him when they took the ship, yet now he seemed more concerned over her safety than his discomfort.

She gestured with a jerky motion toward the chair. He lowered his lean body, the grace of a great cat in his motions, a lion's regal elegance.

Valerie swallowed. "I napped most of the day. Did they let you sleep?"

"They did not." His gaze swung up. "Until now."

Chapter 6

She followed his gaze to the bed, the bed he probably considered merely a piece of furniture upon which a man slept. She took a steadying breath, shoved back her shoulders, and crossed her arms.

"Then you should sleep. Have you eaten?"

"Yes. I have been fed. Like an animal. I hope you fared better."

Valerie nodded and turned again to the window. The light had faded entirely from the sky. She drew the shutters to and clasped them. Warmth gathered between her shoulders and upon the backs of her hands, strange and stirring, dipping into her middle. She pivoted and met Etienne's gaze. The amber depths of his exotic eyes shimmered with heat. Untamed and hungry. *Like an animal.*

Valerie foundered, desire tangling through her limbs and belly. He swallowed visibly, with a slight movement of his head, as though he wished to turn away. But their gazes held.

Finally his voice came deep and quiet into the stillness.

"You understand what Bebain intends for you and me."

"Yes." To her shame, the word came out like a whisper.

Silence stretched between them.

"If I am to be of any use to us in the days ahead in es-caping this prison," he said, "I must be rested. You too. But neither of us will sleep well if forced to sit in this chair all night."

She nodded.

"We are agreed, then." He stood, and his powerful pres-ence in the confined space flooded Valerie's senses. She held her breath as he reached through a slit beneath the sash of his dark robe and drew out a small, worn book. He placed it and the string of wooden beads upon the table. In mute anticipation Valerie watched him remove his cloak and lie down on the mattress. His eyes closed, and within moments he seemed to sleep.

She stood motionless. She had been in tight quarters with handsome men, mostly of her own making, but she'd never before felt so dizzyingly overset. Perhaps because this time she played someone else's game, a game much more serious than any she had ever devised.

She glanced at the table. The battered gold lettering upon the book's cover read *Écriture Sainte*, *Holy Bible*. She ran her fingers over the softened leather binding, tracing the letters and teasing the frayed, colored ribbons tucked within the pages. She considered the beads but did not touch them. Settling back in the chair, she let her gaze slip to the priest's supine figure.

In repose, his face was as perfect as in animation. Her pulse quickened and her gaze slid down the length of his body, leisurely inspecting the breadth of his shoulders, his narrow hips and muscular legs stretched straight atop the counterpane. Upon the ocean, it seemed, beauty was not reserved to spectacular sunsets.

Trying to ignore her heartbeat's unevenness, she opened the Bible.

Steven awoke before dawn, as was his habit at sea. Of course, he usually met the sunrise in his own cabin. He'd never spent a night in this one, the cabin Maximin used when both of them were aboard. But that had not been the case during many months of hard work on land and other men's ships to get them to exactly this place.

Not exactly this place, in truth. The woman should not have been taken prisoner. Steven had hoped to avert that, but he hadn't been quick enough to warn Maximin. He also expected her to hide, a patently foolish assumption, he realized too late.

Still, he and Maximin were close to their goal. If they played this final charade right and succeeded in gaining the confidence of the sailors Bebain had brought on board, the madman's mania could work in their favor.

They had not planned their first mate's betrayal. But Fevre's duplicity brought them a wonderful treasure. When he falsely sold the *Blackhawk* to Bebain, he hadn't counted on Maximin returning from his journey to the coast so quickly. As Steven's partner insinuated himself into the crew, pretending to be one of Fevre's men instead of the opposite, the mate had not said a word about it to Bebain. He was terrified for his life from both Maximin and Bebain.

That was all Maximin had been able to whisper to Steven in the few minutes they had to speak since coming aboard his ship. But it was enough. Fevre's treachery was an unexpected boon. He did not know the identity of Bebain's aristocratic employer, the man Steven and Maximin truly sought to ruin. With the appropriate encouragement, the pirate would surely give up information about the Marquess of Hannsley's other ships, perhaps even names of contacts at trading ports.

Yes, all was going well.

Except for the one inconvenient detail.

Steven knew without looking that Valerie had not lain down upon the bed. His gaze sought her across the tiny chamber.

She was curled into the chair, her legs tucked up beneath her and head bent awkwardly against the chair back. Her half boots were arranged neatly upon the pine planking, but the tangle of skirts about her ankles betrayed her failed attempt at orderliness. Her eyes moved swiftly beneath closed eyelids, her brow taut with anxiety. A few locks of dark, glossy hair strayed across her forehead and exposed cheek, and she breathed heavily, the bodice of her sheer gown straining against the fretful inhales. She trembled.

Reaching for the blanket, Steven eased off the bed and bent over her.

His knee exploded in pain.

He staggered back, knocking his elbow hard against the bedpost and landing on the edge of the iron frame. Damping his instant flash of anger, he looked to his attacker.

Ready to spring from the chair, Valerie stared back at him from across the few feet separating them, her foot that had kicked him poised above the floor. A tiny, razor-sharp knife sparkled in her clenched hand. Her eyes, the centers wide and black, showed frightened wariness.

Her gaze shifted and fixed upon the blanket, and awareness dawned upon her lovely face. She lowered the knife, but only slightly.

"What are you doing?" Her voice was rough with sleep.

Steven pulled himself to a sitting position on the edge of the bed. He laid the coverlet beside him and rubbed at his knee.

"Covering you up," he replied in French, the language he had made his own from the time he was a child, long before his grandfather warned him to mend the ragged edges of his life. "You were trembling."

She didn't like the sound of that. She frowned, and her free hand ran up her other arm as she shivered, but she did not speak or lower the knife further.

"You have a powerful kick, my lady," Steven commented, keeping his voice dry. From the depths of sleep she had awoken to defend herself as though trained to do so. Her spirit of defiance went deep. She'd had to fight for herself at an early age, it seemed. "Where did you learn to do that?"

"Learn? Nowhere." She blinked and straightened her graceful shoulders, shaking off the remnants of slumber. "But my brother gave me this. At the time I thought it was a rather dramatic gesture." She studied the knife and slowly turned it around in her hand, then returned her gaze to Steven. Her grave, sea-blue eyes challenged. "He had been at war by then, you see."

In the guise of Etienne La Marque, Steven had taken insults from Englishmen so often he barely noticed now. He gestured to the knife.

"You may feel free to put that away."

"Oh, may I?" She was fully awake now. "So silly of me. I suppose now that I am safe with you I can relax my guard, is that correct?" She slid her other stockinged foot onto the floor, exposing a slender calf and neat ankle. The knife remained high. "I am so relieved to know that, Father."

Chapter 7

S teven stilled. "I believe you know you can trust me not to harm you," he said quietly.

Her long-lashed eyes lit. "I don't know anything of the kind, Monsieur le Prêtre. Your words last night did not particularly comfort me, although they certainly assured that madman. I have no idea what you may or may not consider advantageous to your situation. For all I know, this entire thing could have been planned from the start. Certainly your lack of action in trying to save us when there was opportunity makes me think you never intended to."

"Opportunity?" Steven asked, the incredulity in his tone perfectly sincere. Regrettably. "Three men ambushed me in my cot, beat me, and tied me up before I had awakened fully. How might that constitute opportunity, I wonder?"

"You might have fought then. You should have tried to rescue Raymer, and me." Desperation laced her words.

"You should have at least made an effort. You might have done something."

Steven regarded her calmly. "I am a priest, my lady, not a pirate. What would you have had me do to our captors, exorcise them?" He cocked a brow. "I hardly think that would have sufficed."

A reluctant smile pulled across her lips. The transparent play of emotions across her beautiful, sleep-chased face delighted Steven. And aroused him. She was remarkably lovely, sitting all rumpled and slightly confused. Lovely enough to forget his purpose.

Standing, he moved to the window and unlatched the shutter. Damp morning air slid across his skin, scented with salt. The faintest touch of gray stained the eastern horizon. It would be morning soon, time to get to work. There were at least a dozen men aboard whose loyalties he was not certain of yet. Mutiny at high sea was a perilous thing when a man did not know his enemies from his allies.

"I am sorry," she said into the silence of creaking boards and lapping water. "You must have been as helpless as I was once we were surrounded."

Steven glanced at the blade still clasped in her palm, and his mouth crooked to one side. "More helpless, make no doubt of it."

Sliding the knife back into its slender sheath, Valerie grimaced and lifted a hand to her neck. In the dim light, her throat shone smooth along the graceful curve of her chin and cheek. Steven dragged his gaze away.

"You must sleep in comfort now," he said.

Awareness flickered in her eyes, along with renewed wariness. She did not trust him. And well she should not.

"Please, let us be allies, Valerie," he said, using her name for the first time since entering the cabin the evening before. He hadn't wanted to utter the word, as though in doing so he would bring his grandfather's prophecy into the confines of their tiny cell. "Please, you must trust me." The irony of his words cut at Steven worse than any knife blade could.

Her lashes flickered. Not accord, but acknowledgment.

"It is almost daylight," he said. "I will take the chair while you sleep."

"You think he will call for us?"

"I have been ordered to serve an ill sailor. But for now, sleep heals all wounds." He glanced at his abused knee. A tiny crease appeared in Valerie's cheek.

She let him usher her to the bed. For some time she lay stiff and silent, her gaze restless. But eventually she slept. Steven settled into the chair to await the dawn.

She ran. Despite the water collecting around her ankles, she made headway. But the birds followed, pursuing her with dark wings and red faces. Vultures, the American kind, hunting her. But vultures only hunted the very young and weak, and anger filled her because she was neither.

Another bird hovered in the sky, black and full-winged. A hawk, drifting languidly upon the currents of wind at a distance, waiting to see if she would escape the others. Waiting and watching her from afar.

Etienne was gone when she woke. Valerie rapped upon the door and called for Zeus. He brought her thrice-brewed coffee and a bowl of thin porridge. A slim volume with the words *Batailles Maritimes* embossed on the brown binding lay upon the tray. She thanked her guard, investing her words with a touch of grateful fragility. He lingered a moment longer than necessary.

When he left, Valerie scrubbed her face with water,

scouring away the look of dependent helplessness. Then she washed her simpering mouth clean with bitter coffee and gave herself a short scold. The giant felt sympathy for her. Her ploy was succeeding so far. She should be satisfied.

Grateful at least for the window and the view of the endless ocean, she ate and read, the knot in her stomach tightening with each passing hour. At midday Zeus brought more food but this time Valerie could not stomach it. Instead, she asked him for needle and thread, then settled down in the chair. It took her hours to alter the maid's frock to fit her. But the final product satisfied, and she donned it, glad to have a change of clothing.

She had just tied the sash made from the gown's hem beneath her breasts when Zeus opened the door. Wrists loosely bound, she followed her guard to the upper deck. Bebain stood upon the bridge with his first mate. Unlike the night before upon the merchantman, Mr. Fevre seemed at ease.

The pirate captain turned a fulsome smile upon her.

"Dearest lady," he cooed. "I hope your accommodations are to your liking?"

"They are tolerable."

"Good, good." He fingered the edge of her sleeve. "I wish above all else for you to be happy here." He gestured toward the seascape. "This, pretty child, is my kingdom. Of this and all we have passed, I am lord." He regarded her briefly, smiling. She stared, sickly mesmerized by the way his fleshy nostrils quivered. "I am master over it, as I am master of these men whom God put on Earth to serve me." He paused, scanning his immaculately ordered vessel. "And they serve me well, no?"

Without waiting for her reply, he clipped, "Let us go," grasped her forearm, and tugged her forward. He paused mid-step, kneading her bare flesh. Valerie held her breath.

"Hnh," he finally grunted. His gaze slid away and he drew her with him amidships.

"I am a civilized man," he resumed. "I do not care for having slaves aboard my ship. So I hired these freedmen for their labor, men who once were slaves, you know." They approached the mainmast, its sun-bright sails now easy with wind. He paused beside the giant stem of wood and caressed an iron manacle attached at shoulder height. "But they remember whence they came. And if they forget, often I remind them. This keeps them particularly loyal to me, and obedient." The last few words he enunciated carefully, as though instructing a small child.

Valerie stood frozen, her gaze locked upon the mast. Beneath Bebain's hands, dried blood ran in dark streaks to the mast's base, coloring the thick, coiled lines of hemp with rusty remains. Horror sluiced through her as she took in the sparkling clean boards of the deck at the foot of the mast. Of the entire well-scrubbed ship, this altar to its master's cruelty remained filthy with the stain of violence.

"You are not pleased with my treasure?" Bebain clucked in displeasure. "No matter, I have other delights aboard my palace with which to amuse you."

Alarmed by his quick change in humor, Valerie tensed. The pirate's pale stare narrowed.

"But you are not yet ready," he snapped. "Zeus, I do not need you. Mr. Fevre will help me escort our guest to her quarters."

The first mate stepped forward and took up the ropes at Valerie's wrists. As they crossed the deck he collected another thick coil. Bebain followed, Valerie's blood curdling with fear as they went below to the cabin. By the time they reached it, her hands shook uncontrollably.

"Here we are, my sweet," Bebain said with a wide-lipped smile as they entered her prison cell. He turned to his mate and gestured impatiently to Valerie's gown. "Remove that monstrosity. Then tie her."

Valerie jerked back, pulling free of Fevre's hold.

"Oh, do not distress yourself needlessly, pretty one," Bebain soothed. "I do not intend to harm you. How could I, my dear, when I wish you to be happy here? No, no. I only wish to offer some inspiration to our pure and noble cleric." His fingertips trailed across her cheek as Fevre moved behind her. Grasping her jaw with a taloned hand, Bebain lifted a dagger to her throat and pressed the flat of it into her windpipe.

"Now be a pet while we prepare the good father's temptation."

The unfamiliar guard towered beside Steven nearly as tall and broad as Zeus. It did not bode well. It suggested that Steven's faithless first mate stepped cautiously now that he was betraying both his masters. Fevre must be truly frightened to employ this kind of brawn against him. He should be. His trip to the stockade approached with each hour.

But Steven needed more time. He'd spent most of the day locked in the lazarette, tending a sick sailor. Ezekiel suffered from a tumor and hadn't long to live. As master of the ship, Bebain should act as physician for his crewmen. But he had passed on that duty to Fevre, and Fevre did not have any taste for men even weaker than himself.

Steven offered Ezekiel what comfort he could. He was so accustomed to the role of priest by now he performed it with ease, and meant every word he said. Confined to the sickroom, though, he had no chance to talk with many of Bebain's sailors, and he did not see Maximin all day, which concerned him. They had matters to discuss, not the least of which was how to manage to keep Valerie safe while staging Bebain's defeat.

And this change of guard worried him.

He preceded the sailor across the gun deck to Maximin's cabin. The lumbering guard turned the latch without unlocking it first.

Not locked?

Steven swung around. The sailor slammed a heavy fist into his chest, yanking the ropes from his wrists. The door swung shut, grazing Steven's shoulder, and the key ground in the lock.

He turned. Prickling heat spread across his chest.

Trussed in ropes, Valerie reclined at the head of the bed, legs spread, feet tied to either footpost. She wore only a thin shift, ruched to her thighs. Ropes twined between her legs and around her hips, climbing in intricate knots up her body to coil around her neck. A strip of rough cloth between her teeth pulled her lips back. From beneath lowered lashes, she stared at him, shame and pain mingled in the sea-colored pools.

Fury barreled into Steven's senses, turning his stomach. He crossed the space in a stride. She tilted her head to look up at him and the ropes creaked around her neck.

"Don't move." He clenched his fists, for the first time in years aching to use them upon a man. "Did he hurt you?"

She held his gaze steadily, willful denial brimming in her gaze now.

He took a tight breath and reached toward her.

"I am going to remove the gag."

She blinked once, deliberately. Steven took it as assent. Dropping to his knees, he reached for the rag tied around her jaw. Her sable hair whished across his knuckles, soft and silken. Biting back upon his unwanted spark of arousal, he worked the knot loose and drew the cloth away.

"That was not tied tightly," she rasped, meeting his gaze from a foot away, awareness clear in her ocean eyes.

"As intended, no doubt," he replied. "Did he—"

"No." She swallowed with obvious discomfort, the red marks tapering from her lips dipping into a grimace. She seemed on the verge of saying more, then closed her mouth.

Steven sat back upon his heels.

"And tomorrow morning?"

"He was vague." Her brow lowered. "He mentioned punishment."

Pressing down upon his anger, Steven did not need to study the complex series of knots spread across Valerie's body to know how long it would take him to unbind her, and to understand what Bebain hoped to accomplish with this sick game.

"Punishment if you remain bound," he said, silently damning the priestly guise that encouraged Bebain's insane imagination. "When did he do this?"

"Two hours ago. Or three." For the first time, Valerie's voice quavered, hinting at the desperation hidden behind her direct gaze.

Steven rose to his knees, forcing a calm to his movements he did not feel. He scanned the elaborate system of knots wrapped around her body.

"Where is your knife?"

"In my shoe."

He moved to the clothing piled upon the chair, and bile rose in his throat. The madman tied a woman like an animal, yet folded her garments neatly for reuse. Steven drew the tiny weapon from the lining of the costly leather boot and turned back to the bed.

"This will not be of use on most of the knots. They are too close to your skin." Watching her pale face, he sat at the foot of the bed and grasped the rope stretching from her ankle to the post. He set the knife to it.

"No." Her voice was rough. "Don't use it. Then he will know I have it."

Steven regarded her steadily, a rush of sharp heat sweeping through him. Valerie's body tensed against the bindings. Color dusted her cheeks. She craved freedom, but from much more than these tethers. She would not let this setback cow her into submission or carelessness. Desire curled in his blood, mixing with respect and fresh anger.

He pushed aside the sensations.

"I should have thought of that."

"Why?" She scanned his clerical robe. "Are you accustomed to concealing knives from pirate captors?"

He lifted a brow and returned to his task. "I will break the glass on the lamp. It will appear I used that to cut the rope."

"Clever," she murmured. "Perhaps you are a dab hand at deception after all, despite your avowal the other day."

Steven did not respond. He could not. He'd told her he preferred the truth, but everything he let her believe about him was a lie.

He cut into the rope. It was slow work.

"It is a very small knife," she finally said, quietly this time.

"It will do."

"I never imagined it would ever be of any use, and now I have employed it twice in a single day."

He felt her gaze upon his back as he worked, like a touch. The blade was thin but sharp. The rope snapped and Valerie curled up her leg, her bare skin brushing across linen. Ignoring his heightened pulse, Steven moved to the other side of the bed and set to the bonds attached to the footpost there. In a minute, the sliced rope slipped through his hand. She drew her knees together.

"And for the rest?" she asked.

He turned to face her, unsurprised at the upward tilt of her chin. A brave woman, Valerie Monroe, and infinitely more seductive in her defiance than any man's warped fantasies could render her with ropes and gags.

Steven studied the complex network of twists and loops. A lynch knot wound about her neck, interwoven with another rope. That one, doubled back upon itself, crossed her shoulders, twined between and beneath her breasts, around her hips, and finally restrained her wrists against her abdomen in repeating knots. All lay flush against her body. To untie or even cut each tether, the one before it must first be loosened, or the succeeding knot would tighten and, working its way up, grip her neck like a noose.

Steven drew in a long breath.

"He has contrived a series of lynch knots. Not impossible to unravel, but each connected to the next, beginning at the top. This will take some time."

"That's all right. I have no other engagements this evening."

Steven met her candid gaze. In the gathering twilight, her eyes glowed the color of storm-tossed waves. One slender, dark brow perched higher than the other. He allowed himself a muted grin.

"No names yet upon your dance card, my lady?"

"Not yet, though I still have hope." Her lashes fluttered, but guardedness flashed beneath the pretended coquetry. "Valerie—"

"Please begin now." Without any movement, she seemed to straighten her shoulders. "The sooner I am free of these, the better."

Undeniably seductive.

"I will have to touch you."

She held his gaze in silence. Steven wanted nothing more than to cup her cheek in his palm, pass his thumb across her abused lips, and speak soothing words. But the longer he returned her look, the faster the heat rose in his blood, spilling through his limbs, rocking him with long-suppressed need.

He bit down upon it, forcing his senses to obey and shifting his gaze to the ropes, bonds like shackles holding her captive. They represented everything he despised, everything dark and evil in the world. Nothing like the feeling of life and hope this woman's spirit sparked in him.

He moved forward on the bed. Bebain had situated her in the center of the mattress, her shoulders leaning against the intricate headboard. Silently Steven cursed Maximin for purchasing the fancy iron piece months ago in Philadelphia. If he had chosen a bed more like Steven's—solid mahogany—Bebain could not have arranged her upon it so provocatively.

It didn't matter. The madman would have contrived another way to display her enticing curves and creamy skin. But Steven did not need Valerie lying upon her back, clad only in a sheer silk shift, to become aroused. That morning she had been half asleep and pointing a knife at him, and he had gotten hard so fast watching her she might as well have been Aphrodite.

Now was no different, despite the ropes and Steven's resolution to remain in control, at least upon the surface. Sometimes the Jesuit habit's loose skirt did come in handy.

Taking care not to touch her skin, he pressed his fingertips into the first knot at her collarbone and pried. Fashioned of cured hemp, the rope flexed, strong but malleable. He would free her from her bonds eventually.

Whether he would do so before she fainted from lack of oxygen he couldn't be assured. Beneath his hovering hands, her breasts rose and fell with quick, short breaths. Steven pinned his gaze on his task, not allowing it to stray to the exquisite mounds brazenly defined by the tight bindings.

"Say something." Her voice came as a bare whisper near his cheek, her breath caressing his skin.

"Relax."

"Easy for you to recommend."

"Not so." Most assuredly not.

"More distortion of the truth, Father La Marque? I suspect nothing ever ruffles your composure."

The knot sagged open. Steven turned to the next one. Lace tickled the base of his palm. As suited a wealthy English noblewoman, she wore an elegant shift, with scalloped straps caressing her graceful shoulders and finely figured embroidery edging the neckline. A tiny satin rose nestled at the alluring shadow between her breasts, hinting at concealed beauty. It was a garment fit for a princess, even a princess made of steel rather than the satin Valerie appeared to be upon the surface.

The second knot slipped free, but not enough to unfasten the tie binding her to the headboard. His fingers followed the loosened rope between her breasts to the next lynch. She sucked in a breath, tightening the fabric over her flesh. Dusky pink circles pressed up under the white silk.

"Why did you go to live with your cousins in Boston?" Steven didn't know if he asked the question to quiet her nerves or his. The back of his hand brushed the inner swell of her breast. A quiver radiated through her. Heat pooled in his groin, insistent.

"The earl sent me." Her voice sounded flat. Steven suspected his would be rough if he spoke. He nodded, fixing his concentration upon the twist of rope tucked against her ribs.

He wanted to touch her, to cover her slightly raised nipple with his tongue and tease her arousal to a hard peak through the thin veil of silk. He could not, for so many reasons. The most vital was not even his priestly pretense, or that it would satisfy Bebain's wishes.

The ropes held Steven's desire in check. When he took a woman to bed, he wanted her free, unfettered to touch him just as he touched her. These wrappings, intended to make Valerie into a gift he could not refuse, repelled him even as the woman within them set his body on fire.

"Your brother, the earl?"

"No."

A peculiar frisson of warning skittered through Steven.

"Husband?" He didn't think he had mistaken it, but perhaps she was a widow. Plenty of Englishwomen her age lost husbands to the war.

"I am not married." As though reading his thoughts, she added, "Nor have I ever been married, as you correctly informed Bebain the other night." Her voice was tight, as though she still harbored anger for the things he had said to dissuade Bebain from taking her.

"I thought we dealt with that this morning. And you were not offended that I assumed your innocence." She felt spectacular against his skin, the soft weight of her breast yielding to the pressure of his fingers as he worked at the knot splayed flat against her ribs.

"That is the second time you have presumed to know my tolerance for offenses," she murmured.

He glanced up. He shouldn't have. Her lips were parted and damp, the tender redness faded at the edges. Her eyes shone like lit coals, beckoning.

Only a man with a fool's destiny would resist the invitation.

Chapter 8

I presumed correctly upon both accounts, didn't I?" Low and husky, Etienne's voice skimmed across Valerie's senses like whiskey upon the tongue, flooding her with eagerness. His touch shimmered through her flesh until her thoughts muddled. The stiffness of her limbs and soreness of shoulders and back faded away beneath his regard.

"Perhaps." He did not need to know any more about her, certainly not whether she was a virgin. Few among the *ton* would believe the truth if she told it anyway, and it could not possibly matter to this man either way.

He held her gaze, his hand warm against the underside of her breast and immobile. He had halted his efforts at untying her. Valerie's belly tightened, the sensation shivering outward. Her nipples prickled.

"Etienne," she whispered, not knowing what she intended or even wanted beyond freedom from her bindings. Not the frustrated craving coursing through her now. How could she want that? She had changed. She was not the same foolish girl she had been for so many years.

The sound of his name seemed to recall him to his task. He dropped his gaze and finished with the knot. A muscle flexed in his hard jaw. The rope slackened, his grasp slipped away, and Valerie took in a deep, free breath.

"Your father sent you to America, then," he said, returning to his questioning as though nothing had passed between them.

But nothing had, except in Valerie's famished imagination.

She nodded. Etienne's gaze trailed her stomach to her hands, strapped palms-down against her abdomen. Valerie pressed her knees together, the chunk of hemp at the crux of her thighs digging into her flesh. She shifted her hips to ease the pressure, and the line at her neck twitched tight.

Concern lit his tawny eyes. She wanted to ask what he meant to do next, but her tongue would not form words.

He touched one finger lightly to the twine around her wrists.

"This must wait for the rest."

Valerie understood. She had understood even as Fevre tied the knots while Bebain watched, a smile of glee stretched across his narrow face as he anticipated the Jesuit's agony and her shame. Bebain wanted her hands trapped until the last, so Etienne would be forced to unravel all the other bonds. He did not want her to be able to free herself.

But even as Bebain's evil grin had clotted her blood, Fevre's touch had not bothered her. As he fashioned her grim harness with unsteady hands, she suspected his fear of Bebain overwhelmed everything else and that he did not take any pleasure in the activity.

Valerie doubted the priest would enjoy undoing what Fevre had done. He brought his rigid gaze to hers. He did not want this. He might find her attractive, but he was not a man to be easily swayed from his convictions.

She parted her legs, drawing in a breath.

"Just do it, and end this," she clipped, taking refuge in her loathing for Bebain. If she concentrated her thoughts upon the evil delight the pirate captain took from imagining his captives' misery, she might be able to distract her nerves.

Etienne reached for the cords below her hips. The knot shifted against Valerie's most tender parts, and heat erupted inside her. She tried to breathe slowly, to remain still as he grasped the tether and pried at it. She fixed her gaze upon his hand, hoping that watching his deliberate actions would cool the tendrils of fire racing from her core through her belly and limbs.

It did not. The sight of his strong hands between her thighs sent shivers of turmoil through her body. She wanted him to turn his attentions away from the rope. To touch her. She ached for it so badly she bit down upon her lips to stop herself from begging him to.

Etienne's fingers grazed her. Valerie's body flinched within, a sting of pleasure so intense a gasp shot from the back of her throat. Her eyes flew wide. But he did not seem to note it. She wrenched her gaze away, hoping he could not see the sweet, sudden throbbing of her flesh, so powerful that a moan gathered in her chest. Was it all inside her, or could he observe what he did to her and hate her for it? Hate himself?

She forced herself to look, sucking in tiny gasps of air. Sheer fabric bunched between her flesh and the knot, the silk obviously damp. Etienne's beautiful, long fingers were white with strain as he dug into the hemp.

Wrapped in confused, heady need, Valerie lifted her gaze past the taut angle of his jaw to his beautiful mouth. His lips were a thin line, his brow creased.

"I am sorry," she whispered.

"For what? That you boarded the wrong merchantman in Boston? That sadistic madmen sail the Atlantic?" His voice was tight, his accent thicker than usual.

Valerie's insides shook with the strain of holding her legs still. It tortured him to touch her this way. His words and posture made that clear, but her body didn't seem to care. She struggled not to press into his touch, to make the brief shock of delicious pleasure come again.

"I have never apologized to a man before."

"I don't doubt it."

She bit the inside of her mouth.

"I know this is impossible, but you needn't insult me."

"It was not an insult."

The knot fell loose. Etienne drew his hands away, exhaling audibly. Valerie's gaze shot to his. He did not look at her, setting to work upon the ropes at her wrists. The perfunctory caress should not affect her more strongly than what had gone before. But somehow it did. In stunned silence she lost herself in his confident touch upon the backs of her hands and the insides of her wrists, all pretense of her self-control slipping away. Bathed in intimate heat, she ceased breathing.

He finished, drawing the tethers from around her neck and hips. She gulped in tides of air and struggled to a sitting position. Hands striped with red marks and trembling, she smoothed her shift over her thighs and tucked her feet beneath her, her entire body aching.

Etienne stood and turned to the window. He passed a palm over his face in a distracted gesture. His broad shoulders and back remained stiff, stretching the black fabric taut.

Guilt seared Valerie, irrational, but painful all the same.

"Thank you."

"Don't." The curt word cut across the small room.

"You could have refused."

"And left you to his promised punishment tomorrow?" He looked over his shoulder at her. "What sort of man would that make me?"

He was not saying what he wished. The heated glint in his amber eyes and the abruptly tempered tone of his rich voice told her so. She wished she knew the words to make him speak what he truly felt. But he held himself in harsh control again, impenetrable except for his entrancing eyes.

She gathered herself to stand upon wobbly legs, grasping the headboard for support. Etienne unclasped the top buttons of his robe, then reached for the lamp and unhinged it from the table. He snuffed the flame between his fingers, plunging the cabin into shadows. Flexing her feet and arms to restore feeling, Valerie heard him separate the metal casing and oil dish from the bulb, then strike the glass upon the table. It broke with a dull clank.

"Valerie." Etienne's voice came unexpectedly quiet in the dark. "I fear I have not been as careful of your sensibilities as I should tonight."

Valerie swallowed down her choke of astonishment.

"I understand."

"I suspect you don't, in point of fact. But that does not excuse me."

"I have put it behind me already," she said, gripping the headboard, praying he could not hear her heart's raucous pounding. "You will too, soon enough."

"Now who presumes to know the other?"

He meant to ease the tension, but Valerie's hands still shook. She took another full breath and words stumbled out.

"I don't know anything. I only hope."

A long silence stretched between them. In the shadows, Valerie felt the intensity of his gaze upon her, watchful and waiting.

"Are you all right?" he finally asked.

After a moment, she nodded. He gestured toward the bed. "You should rest now. Will you be able to?"

Stepping over the ropes tangled upon the floor, Valerie lowered herself onto the mattress. She pushed the woolen blanket to him. Opening the coverlet, she slipped stiffly beneath, but she could not lay her head upon the pillow.

In raw relief, she heard Etienne speak again, his voice now an easy rumble.

"Tell me about your mother, Valerie. No doubt you inherited your beauty from her."

A peculiar tightness gripped her throat. Men had often complimented her on her looks. None ever did it so meaningfully. It did not matter that Etienne asked hoping to shift her thoughts from the events that had just passed and the horrifying hours she remained bound and gagged, alone and helpless. She wanted the distraction, the reassurance of old memories to soothe her and to calm the confused desire racing through her.

"I am like her in appearance, if only that." She tucked her hands beneath her cheek and turned onto her side to look at the priest. He lay upon his back, still as burnished bronze in the nearly faded light. "She died when I was a girl."

A long silence reached through the cool night air as the ship rocked upon the ocean's mild surface. Valerie sensed it for the first time since returning below deck. How, during all those hours trapped, hadn't she felt the sea's lulling rhythm?

"I see," he finally replied.

Her throat thickened.

"What do you see with your lion's eyes, Etienne La Marque?"

He turned to her, his gaze unreadable in the shadows. But he did not speak. Valerie longed to reach out and touch his face, to put her hands on him deliberately and ease the frustrated ache of his accidental caresses on her body. To connect with another human, another body and heart and soul bound into one.

To touch him.

"You have the eyes of a lion," she whispered. "It is a formidable animal. Powerful." She didn't know where the words came from, but she could not bring herself to stop them.

"Yet within a pride," he said, his voice low, "the lioness is the predator to be most feared."

Valerie's throat closed. "I am not fearsome."

"You are strong, Valerie. It is the very meaning of your name. Fortitude."

She clamped down upon a rising sob. Tears pressed behind her eyes. She blinked them back.

"I am angry. At what he did to me. To you," she said. "And I want to go home."

"You will." In the darkness, his voice curled around her like an embrace.

The midnight street blazed livid with fire. Black clouds billowed from the barricade fashioned of wagons and chairs, shop marquees and bales of straw. Her nostrils clogged with the smoke of burning flesh. She choked, gagging, and collapsed upon her knees. Her hair tumbled about her, obscuring her vision. She lifted a hand to brush it away, and her palm came up from the ground painted thick with blood.

A strong grip seized hers, slipped, clamped around her sticky fingers, and jerked her up. Reflected in his tawny eyes, the flames of a thousand bonfires caressed the silver stars with wild unconcern.

Chapter 9

An unfamiliar sailor brought Valerie breakfast. Fevre stood behind him at the door, his stance edgy as he took in the discarded ropes. Then he instructed the other man to gather the ruined bindings and follow him out.

She paced the cabin until Zeus appeared to take her above deck. The midday sun shone bright again, startling after the dim lower deck. Valerie filled her lungs with salty, fresh air and threw back her shoulders. Sailors cast her glances as she crossed the deck. She returned them, but each snatched his gaze away. Bebain held his crew with a tight rein of fear. She would not find any allies atop, that seemed certain.

Reclining at a table spread with a lavish lunch upon the quarterdeck, the pirate captain inspected her. He stood, brushed flakes of biscuit from his pristine pantaloons, and set down his goblet of wine.

"How did you enjoy your adventure yesterday, little one? More importantly perhaps, how did our fine holy man enjoy it?" He trailed a sharp fingernail along her jaw to her bodice.

She turned her face away.

"It is to be like that, then, is it? He refused to speak of it too, the coward. And I know of your clever trick with the lamp glass." He leaned toward her again, seeming to study her face. "I needn't have bothered, eh? Ah well." He sighed theatrically and shrugged. "So I am still waiting. Growing giddy with impatience, yet still waiting. Hasten your education, my girl. Perhaps I will invent another adventure to inspire our saint, shall I? We shall see, my beauty." His fingers slid from her shoulder and curved around her breast with proprietary ease. Willing herself not to shy away where he pressed into skin rubbed raw from the ropes, Valerie set her jaw.

At dusk, when another unfamiliar sailor admitted the Jesuit to their shared quarters, she no longer felt so resigned. After hours alone to muse upon her plight and grow more anxious imagining the pirate's next attempt to subjugate her, Valerie's hope had become firm resolve.

As Etienne sat and removed the Bible and beads from his cassock, she rehearsed in her mind everything she had planned throughout the afternoon. She didn't much like the strategy, but it offered her only chance at survival on her terms. If she waited for someone to save her out of the goodness of his heart, she would be aboard this cursed ship forever. And eventually, whether he considered her prepared according to his standards or not, Bebain would take her to his bed. Or kill her.

She could not employ Zeus's help. He seemed immovable. In any case, her conscience would not allow it. She would not use a man to secure her freedom who had his stolen while still a child. She had only briefly seen Maximin atop this morning and hadn't spoken to him. But something about his knowing grin told her he would not fall prey to manipulation. Not sufficiently to risk his life for her, at least.

No, she could not depend on the crew for her escape.

That left the priest.

He called them allies, but Valerie needed more than an ally to help her escape Bebain. She needed a devotee, the kind she had depended upon for countless escapades in her past, using the unstinting loyalty of boys and men so blinded by their lust for beauty and wealth they did not know a thing about who she actually was.

With her juvenile heart hungry for attention, she had cared about each of them in her own way, admiring them for one thing or another. But she had not loved them, at least not the way they professed their love to her. For two years she suffered over how she had behaved with willful, spoiled disregard for other people's hearts. In her Boston isolation and grief, she promised she would never use another person that way again.

Now, however, her desperation swelled to panic. She could lie to Etienne and tell him she felt hopeful. But her skin crawled with terror imagining the pirate captain binding her to his bed the next time, and to his ship the same way he bound the sailors aboard. She saw the blood-caked mainmast and determined that one final time she must have a man's devotion, someone who would bend to her will no matter what it meant to him.

She slid her gaze along the length of Etienne's cassock, across his broad shoulders, to his face. Her breath stilled. He stared at her impassively again, golden eyes diffident. But his jaw was tight with control.

Valerie knew that look now. And she knew that although this man might have chosen a career in the church, he was not a celibate by nature.

The night before, he had wanted to touch her, perhaps as much as she wanted him to. His relief when he finished unbinding her told her that. But she would not let him resist any longer. She could not escape Bebain without help. If her fate meant having her body used for a man's pleasure, she might as well arrange it to her advantage.

She took a fortifying breath and opened the lid of the sandalwood chest.

"There are some fine garments here, Etienne. You should look them over." A gentleman's linen shirt topped the pile. She caressed it with supple strokes.

"A man of the cloth has few material needs, Valerie," he said easily enough, but a subtle tension had entered the chamber. Valerie's heartbeat raced as she casually folded over several garments to uncover the lace night rail. Her hands arrested upon it for an instant. She pulled back as though surprised.

"Oh. I—" She bit her lower lip, her cheeks warming. Anna had always teased Valerie about her ability to blush on command, *only* on command until she met Etienne La Marque.

Anna would not tease her now.

"I—I cannot imagine what this is intended for," she said prettily.

"Can't you?"

Ignoring his flat tone, Valerie drew the night rail from the trunk and draped it across her lap.

"Perhaps it is some sort of undergarment." She fingered the filmy lace bodice. "Or perhaps not." Her gaze flickered upward.

Her eyes shot wide. Etienne's gaze raked her with heat. Unlike the night before, he did not bother masking it. But something else simmered within the fiery depths of his eyes, something familiar and real, that same uncanny awareness of shared understanding she had seen on board the merchantman. Her breath halted, alarm and confusion tangling through her.

Gaze locked on hers, he stood and took a step forward. Reaching down, he curved his fingers tight around her hand holding the night rail and pulled her up. The power radiating from his body dizzied her, urging her to close the tiny space between them. His breaths came taut as his fingers entwined with hers, twisting the seductively soft silk between them, like twined rope but this time binding them together. His golden skin emanated the scents of sea and man and the faintest hint of lime. He filled her senses, his grip unyielding.

Heady with longing, Valerie tilted up her chin. He bent his head and drew her to him, trapping the silk between their bodies, pressing the back of her hand to his chest, his fist nestling between her breasts.

Aching for him, need singing through her breasts and pooling between her legs, Valerie parted her lips, no longer playacting. Far too late, she realized she never had been.

Chapter 10

Don't, Valerie." His breath grazed her brow. Her heart tripped as his hand gripped hers tighter, jamming her knuckles into his hard muscle. "Don't do this." His voice was rough. His chest rose, brushing her sensitized nipples. "I told you already, I will be your ally. I swear you will not be harmed. Do not look for more assurance than that."

Shame rushed through her, prickly and wretched. Smothering the alien emotion with anger, she yanked her hand away. The night rail fell to the floor.

Etienne picked it up and placed it in the trunk. He leaned back against the table, folding his arms across his chest. He took a deep breath before he spoke.

"If it helps to hear it, I don't blame you."

A sensation like humiliation, cold and wrapped in confusion, settled into Valerie's midsection. She cast him a sharp look.

"You'd better not. Hypocrisy is particularly unappealing in a priest."

Etienne laughed, the sound resonating with open honesty in the tiny chamber.

"Oh, come now, Valerie." The corner of his sculpted lips lifted. "You are a beautiful woman. I would be dead not to notice that." He paused. "Or to want to touch you."

The coil inside Valerie tightened. Weak-limbed, she sank onto the edge of the bed, unable to meet his gaze and hating herself for it. Frustration and bewilderment warred inside her.

"Isn't priestly training supposed to drive that out of a man?"

"Suppress it, perhaps," he murmured. Her gaze slid up. He met it with frank acknowledgment. "Desire is not so easily defeated."

Did he know how he affected her, or was this tumult of feelings hers alone? Men could so easily separate lust from emotion. She had known that for years. Why did she think this man should be different?

"Are you teasing me now?" Her voice was not entirely steady.

"Of course not," he said, tilting his head. "I am trying to express sympathy."

Unbidden, a chuckle bubbled up in Valerie's throat, and like salt in water, her anger dissolved, along with her plan to seduce him. With a few honest words and a lifted brow, he had disarmed her. No man had ever disarmed her. Except the earl. But this felt so different. It felt good.

As though marking the end of the conversation, Etienne sat on the chair and removed his boots. Valerie remained still, waiting as her heartbeat slowed, fixing her gaze upon his profile. The lamplight set his unique features in relief. She held back a sigh. In point of fact, he was the beautiful one. Heaven must have resounded with riotous laughter when God called this man to be a Catholic priest. How she ever thought herself clever for trying to tempt him, she didn't know. Dozens of women had probably tried before, only to fail like her.

He shortened the lamp's wick. He had arrived in the cabin with another lantern, brought from wherever he spent the day. Bebain, she mused, seemed peculiarly generous as a captor. Generous and cruel.

Valerie licked her dry lips, pressing her palm into the cool bed linen.

"You have promised now, you know."

"Hm?" He sounded suddenly tired as he set his boot down.

"You hadn't promised before. Now you have. You are honor bound to help me."

Waiting for his reply, Valerie resisted the weakness seizing her again. Staring at him was a strange and delicious torment. Sweet, painful, and ceaseless.

"I am a man of my word, Valerie," he said, his voice quiet but firm. "I will protect you. Whatever comes, remember that."

"Whatever comes?"

He turned, and his gaze rested upon her in the hint of moonlight. "Whatever comes."

She stared at his eyes, searching their amber depths. Only the barest trace of heat remained, cloaked in warm, lucid sincerity. She closed her eyes. She was not dead. And she was not vowed to celibacy. Etienne promised to protect her from Bebain. But Valerie had no idea who would protect her from her own foolish heart.

"Why did your father send you to Boston?"

The question hit Valerie with unexpected force. During two years abroad, she had never spoken of it. Her cousins in Boston knew, of course. Most of the *ton* did as well. There were plenty of witnesses to the event, and gossips loved scandal. But Valerie had never told anyone the story about her escapade that night at Vauxhall Gardens, not even Anna.

"I eloped with an impoverished Italian violinist. Briefly," she added, certain that of all people, this man did not care. He hoped to engage her in conversation so she would relax and sleep. He considered her a responsibility.

"It came to nothing," she added, "which was for the best. I only did it—" If she could not tell a priest, for pity's sake, she might as well give up all hope of ever conquering her regret. "I only did it to anger the earl, so that he would pay attention to me. As punishment, he sent me to Boston. To be rid of me."

Steven stared at the beauty on the edge of the bed, her eyes glimmering with the barest hint of starlight filtering through the window, and his veins ran with anger, directed at a man he had never met. He bit down upon the harsh words that came to his tongue. To suit his priestly role, he had been doing the same for years. But it had never proved so difficult. What sort of man would condemn his own daughter, a girl of Valerie's spirit, will, and heart, to a foreign land for the sort of indiscretion she spoke of? It smacked of cowardice.

"Why do you call him by his title?" He kept his voice even.

"I never called him Father, except when my mother was still alive." She paused. "I will never have the opportunity to again. He and my eldest brother died in a carriage accident just after I reached Boston."

"Why are you returning home now, after so many months?" He didn't know why he asked. In a few short days she would be on a packet headed for England, safe with her own kind.

Steven's work among the crew had progressed swiftly

today, despite his confinement to the infirmary under the close watch of the burly guard. But several of his men had come through the sickroom, supposedly checking on their ill mate, but mostly to convey messages to him about Bebain's sailors. One by one they were turning away from the pirate. Only a handful of Bebain's men were not accounted for yet. By tomorrow, they would be.

After Steven settled matters concerning Bebain, he would send Valerie on her way.

"I was ready to leave America," she said softly, finally stretching out upon the mattress. She cradled her arm beneath her head. "I miss my brother and Anna dreadfully."

"Anna?"

"A friend. Nearly my sister." Her eyelids fluttered closed. His attempt to calm her was having its effect. She cupped her cheek in her hand, and a sigh of falling slumber escaped her lips.

She did not stir when Steven laid the blanket over her and brushed a stray lock of hair from her cheek.

He watched her, his blood rushing like waves in a coming storm. No matter how he willed it, he would not rest. Not with success so close at hand, albeit only in this preliminary round. Once they bested Bebain, he and Maximin had much more work to do before they achieved true victory.

But even if this part of their plan was not nearly complete, Steven still would not be able to sleep with Valerie's ripe, enticing body inches away. For years, self-discipline had been his closest companion. But he was not by any means made of stone, as yesterday's enforced contact with her barely clad beauty proved.

Rising carefully, he went to the chair. His glance flicked to the open chest and the lace night rail lying atop the pile of clothes. She was as bold as a woman with twice her life's experience. But at moments she seemed like nothing more than a frightened girl. Desperation had driven her to do what she had tonight. And desire.

Steven took up the man's linen shirt tucked beneath the lace and lowered himself into the chair. He sat motionless, watching her, relieved that Bebain remained disinterested in her.

Soon it would be over. She would return home, reunite with her family, and marry some respectable English lord. If she chose her husband, she would no doubt select one who could appreciate her strength of spirit. But Steven did not know her brother. Perhaps he would give her to a man ill suited to her.

Rubbing his hands over his eyes, he silently scolded himself. It did not matter to him whom Valerie wed. Let the drawing room biddies bother themselves with those sorts of concerns. His worries had nothing to do with that sort of domestic nicety.

She lay upon her side, her form graceful under the thin blanket. Beneath smooth lids, her eyes moved, busying their mistress in a shadowed reality. She had dreamed heavily the past two nights, as well. Steven's grandfather believed in the prophetic power of dreams, another lesson in destiny Steven gladly ignored.

Valerie's breathing quickened, and her face pinched. Her dreams distressed her. If they were anywhere else, if the threat of Bebain's peculiar, jaded interest did not hang over her head, Steven knew what he would do. He would lie down behind her, wrap his arms around her delectably curved body, and stroke her shining hair until she stopped dreaming and slept undisturbed. He longed to do that innocent thing.

He never could, no matter how chaste his intentions.

Because those intentions would remain chaste for mere moments. Once he put his hands upon her, he would sweep them up her slender waist to her young breasts and tease them to arousal, to peaks tighter and darker than her stirrings of awakening the night before. He would set his mouth upon her neck, tasting her as she stretched willingly, allowing him freedom upon her silken skin, along her throat where flesh became tender, feminine beauty. His hand would move reverently over her rounded hip, between her thighs, and she would welcome his touch.

She wanted him as much as he wanted her. When she watched him and her heart beat rapidly, the fluttering fabric across her breast betrayed her, the delicate flush in her cheeks, the moisture on her unconsciously parted lips. And when he touched her last night, she had gone damp with need for him so quickly he barely managed to pull away.

In the moment the ropes had come off and she was free, with nothing between her need and his, Steven experienced the first flash of panic in his life. He didn't even remember what he said to her then, only that he spoke to keep his hands still, to bolt his feet into place on the opposite side of the cabin. It had taken every ounce of his willpower to resist her, and again tonight.

He hadn't much willpower left to spare.

He forced himself to focus on the shirt in his hands, to study the fine fabric and tiny stitches, its clean-washed texture. Maximin's latest purchase at port, no doubt, probably Portuguese. It would do. Steven liked his mother's people's way of keeping clean, and he could no longer bear Europeans' slatternly habits.

He had spent ten years of his childhood in that other world. Valerie's world. But he hadn't given it much thought since then, except on the day nearly five years ago that he received the letter from his uncle's solicitor. His solicitor now. Of course, his aunt's letters occasionally reminded him of that distant place. She never suggested he should return, though; she knew him well enough to realize he never would. His steward was an honest, capable man, and Steven had a lifetime of work to do here.

He unfastened the buttons of his cassock and the shirt beneath, then pulled the garments over his head and hung them upon the bedpost. He'd worn them for so long, the shirt bore the imprint of his body, just like his buckskin breeches. Men of the cloth, be damned. Steven fully appreciated the basic material comforts, including clean clothes and baths.

Taking up the linen towel, he dipped it in the basin of fresh water. He ran the damp cloth over his skin, cleaning away salt and sweat. Bebain probably supplied the water for Valerie, wishing her to be as neat as possible when he finally took her to his bed. It was the sort of thing the fastidious madman would value.

The thought slid through Steven's blood like ice. He glanced at the woman whose fate currently obeyed Bebain's erratic will. She lay completely still as before, but her half-lidded eyes shone like obsidian in the hint of lamplight, her gaze trained upon him. She met his look unflinchingly.

Then her gaze shifted downward.

Chapter 11

The caress of her hungry stare seared Steven's skin and beneath it, swallowing his breath like a hurricane wind. Heat swept through him, surging into his groin. In mute ecstasy, he watched her discover his scar. Her brow creased, her gaze traveling the length of the jagged relic of Steven's youth, from his waist to his ribs.

She must see the swift pounding of his heart, the flush of his skin everywhere her gaze lingered. He was unmasked, as he had not been in years. Decades.

Need burned rough and urgent in him as her gaze stroked, her lips parted, tiny sighs escaping as her breasts moved with deeper breaths, each moment sheer agony for him.

He could not speak. Could not make his mouth form the words that would end it, that would drag her away from this submerged passion that blazed between them, reminding her that he was not a man to be tempted. That he was a man who could not be tempted.

Struggling, he opened his mouth to speak firm, clear phrases, anything, as he had done for years with ease, playing his part.

Her gaze dipped, and his futile efforts disintegrated.

He ached. Ached with the pressure of hard heat, ached knowing he could do nothing about it, could not stop her from looking or her eyes from widening in female awareness, could not stop himself from needing her with every drop of his blood. He was not a celibate by any means, but he had never wanted a woman with this craving, this pain.

But alongside the pain, he was unbound beneath her scrutiny, heady almost. He had hidden his desires for so long behind disguises, seeing after other people's problems and needs. Her bright gaze stripped him of pretense, delving into his soul as deeply as it sank beneath his skin. For a precious, intoxicating moment, he felt free.

His hands shook. Trying to contain the tremors, he drew the linen shirt behind him and shrugged his shoulders into it. Not trusting his unsteady fingers, he pulled the garment across his chest and waited.

Valerie's hooded gaze slipped back to his. For a moment she stared at him through long lashes. He held his breath.

Her eyelids dipped, and closed.

Steven remained motionless. Minutes passed, hours. He didn't know, did not care. He watched her, hunger in his hands and mouth as he drank in her beauty, her sable hair, her lusciously curved lips he could practically taste upon his, imagining them upon his body. Need streaming through his veins, he traced the graceful line of her neck, the delicate angle of her jaw, the creamy satin of her skin.

He was a damned fool.

She'd only been awake for a minute, perhaps not even that long, but he was trembling. Steven could not remember the last time he trembled from something other than cold, and even then he had been very cold indeed. He could so easily go to the bed, take her into his arms, and give her pleasure for every pleasure he took in return. He could succumb to temptation.

He would not. She was beautiful. But he was not a man to be swayed from his course by beauty alone.

He fought to ignore the voice in his head insisting that more than her beauty beguiled him. He had known many lovely women in his life. None was as quick of mind and resilient of spirit as this willful yet wary woman. In a few short days she had revealed to him more of her nature than perhaps she intended, and Steven was troubled he had so easily been drawn in, as easily as a moth to a bright flame. Many men before him must have yielded to temptation with this woman, to touch her and to give their hearts over to her.

It would be so easy. Like the man she had spoken of, perhaps, and others. The wiles she had practiced upon Steven earlier were not new to her.

He did not fault her for it. A young woman of her status lived a stultified existence, a life that would drive Steven as insane as Gaston Bebain if he were forced to live it. That life must cinch at Valerie's lively spirit as effectively as the ropes upon her body had the night before. She had learned to use that body to wrest some adventure from life.

He, however, could and would resist her enticements. Within hours he would fulfill his plans, and she would again be upon a ship bound for England. His work would continue and she would become nothing but a memory.

As he buttoned his shirt with unsteady fingers, the thought brought with it no comfort.

She must have dreamed it. The vision she had seen in the midnight dark could not be real.

Shivers glistened up Valerie's back as her eyes opened

to the gray light peeking through the cabin window. She did not move, the ship swaying her body as she stared at the empty chair.

He had the shape of a god.

Some tiny sound had awakened her. She had watched the water glint off his skin as he bathed, golden in the glow of the lamp, and she hadn't even considered looking away.

Then his slow lion eyes discovered her seeking regard. Heat spiraled in her as her gaze traveled across his lean, muscular body, the long, angry slash of the scar stabbing her with alarm. She traced the dark line of hair descending beneath the waistline of his breeches to the thick bulge below, and her insides turned to molten honey.

When he drew the shirt around his body, her gaze had caught a glimpse of a black stain upon his forearm. But the sleeve covered it quickly. He'd paused, and in a half-dreaming sleep as she met his gaze, the indescribable longing returned, skimming beneath her skin and twining into her most intimate places.

She fell asleep with the longing unanswered and the image of Etienne's warm, lucent eyes imprinted upon her dreams.

Now, with daylight filtering through the window, Valerie clung to the bed, willing sleep to return, her breaths short and body throbbing. But the ship moved roughly, and footsteps clustered upon the deck above. The night, and the vision it had brought, dissipated.

She was straightening the bed linens—in which, it seemed, her cabin mate had not slept—when the door opened and Zeus gestured her forward, the familiar length of rope in hand. Fashioning the binding into a loose knot around her wrists, he looked unusually grim.

"What is happening, Zeus?"

His massive hand rested gently upon hers, his brown eyes weighted with sorrow. "You will see, miss, and for that I am sorry."

Valerie followed him silently. Above, the sailors, perhaps sixty in all, gathered in small groups, eerily silent beneath the morning's heavy sky. At the edge of the quarterdeck, Bebain stood with his back to her. The first mate, Mr. Fevre, leaned uncomfortably into the railing, arms crossed, fingertips between his teeth.

Valerie's gaze sought her fellow prisoner. He stood alone, staring across the deck at Maximin. The sailor looked back at the priest, his eyes hard.

"Ah, my little beauty!" Bebain cooed, skittering across deck like a crab and lifting her bound hands to his mouth. The lowering sky set his long face in a halo of pale light, and his tanned skin shone dull in contrast to the dark men all around. "Now we can commence. We are gathered here today to celebrate a funeral." His voice lowered to a stage whisper. "Our diversions on board are few, and so we take advantage of every unusual occasion for a little entertainment. However, since a funeral is such a tiresome occasion, as occasions go, I have decided to enliven it by adding to it—ha!—the thrill of death."

A grotesque smile spread across his wide mouth, and his nostrils flared in tandem with the spark of madness in his pale eyes. He dropped her hands and gestured across deck.

A trio of sailors stood near a plank jutting from the railing above the moving waters. The men on either side supported the one in the middle. An iron slave collar hung around his neck like a fighting dog's tether, but there was nothing combative in the wretched figure. He was skeletally thin with skin the color of ash, nearly translucent as it stretched across the protruding bones of his face and body. His eyes were closed, his face devastated by long suffering.

Tears welled in Valerie's eyes. Her throat constricted, and she jerked instinctively toward the shackled sailor. An iron grip pulled her back. The giant's words came so quietly she barely heard them.

"He will kill you if you speak now."

Valerie tried to pull away, but Zeus lifted a broad hand and covered her mouth.

"God has provided for Ezekiel, *mademoiselle*. You must have faith."

She ceased struggling, her heart tearing at her own weakness. Zeus's hand fell away from her mouth.

Bebain warmed to his role as carnival master, prancing about deck from man to man, brandishing a long-handled knife. Finally he approached Ezekiel, and his right hand rose to the sailor's emaciated shoulders.

A voice rang out across the deck. Face filled with anger, Maximin shouted at Bebain in a language Valerie did not understand. Bebain only laughed.

"You mistake matters, Bebain." Etienne's assured voice cut through the madman's laughter. "Maximin is right. You put yourself at risk. Ezekiel is a sailor, not market goods. These men will not stand for such treatment of their own."

Lowering the knife, Bebain rounded upon the priest, astonishment creasing his features. He crossed the deck, his teeth baring, tiny and yellowed.

"Their own, you say, Father? Their own?" he shrieked and swept his hands around as he pirouetted in a swift circle. "These men have nothing of their own, as you so sentimentally put it: What they have is money, which I provide them with in sufficiency. They serve me, and if it is my desire that one of them die, then they serve me to see my desire met." He cast an eye upon the sailors supporting Ezekiel at the ship rail. Their expressions shuttered.

"You see, dear Father, they are obedient to me. I do not fear them because I am master over them, in complete control of their destinies." He began to turn away, then stopped and spoke again in clipped tones. "You, on the other hand, are an inconvenience."

"As you are to me," replied the priest.

Valerie's breath caught. She had seen the reaction on some of the sailors' faces when Bebain claimed them as property. They hadn't liked it. Anger boiled palpably across the deck. Etienne's taunting could only fuel Bebain's insanity.

Bebain's tapping boot paused and he brought his hands together behind him. Then, with one swift movement, he drew his knife in a quick arc and slashed at the priest. Valerie gasped. Etienne's bonds fell in tatters onto the deck.

"This is well," said the captain, moving to the gangplank. "I give you leave to do what you can to save this miserable fellow, I will do what I can to stop you, then we will see whether you are truly necessary to me, no?"

He laughed, raised the knife again, and sliced a long, dark line across his prisoner's shoulders, and another from the nape of his neck to the base of Ezekiel's spine. Crimson blood flickered onto the dying man's captors, but the sick man barely flinched. Bebain moved aside and displayed his work proudly. He had fashioned a perfect cross in the gray skin, surmounted by the black iron crown of the dying man's collar.

"Come, Father, aren't you even more enamored of this creature now?" he shrilled.

Enveloped in shock, Valerie slued her gaze to Etienne. He cast his eyes down, folding his hands.

Valerie's palms pressed to her face. She didn't know whether anyone spoke or moved. Her heart felt dead, the world she had once known a dream, the nightmare she now lived an endless misery.

She had thought she could escape it, imagined she possessed some power to save herself. But she was wrong. She never had power, for years. Nothing she had ever done mattered. This was only the end of it, the horrible, cruel finale she had been too naïve to even imagine.

With a cry, she yanked the rope from Zeus's hand and fled across deck, down to the shadowed haven of her prison cell.

Valerie moved around the cabin swiftly, her body shaking, hands cold. She didn't know how many minutes passed before the door swung open and the Jesuit crossed the threshold. His black robe was unfastened, revealing his shirt and breeches beneath.

Valerie's eyes narrowed, the angry look Maximin cast the priest upon deck coming back to her. The same emotion washed over her, despair and disillusionment sweeping in its wake.

"Ezekiel is alive," he said into the brittle silence. "Bebain spared him. He is resting now, but his time is not long. The disease will take him by tomorrow."

At the sound of the priest's voice, strong and soothing, Valerie's rage slipped from her tight grasp.

"If tomorrow ever comes," she uttered.

He closed the door, the latch's click soft.

"You should not have had to see that."

Valerie's eyes flashed wide.

"I should not have? None of us should. It should not have happened. But we stood there and let it happen. We let that madman tor—" She stumbled upon the words.

Etienne took a step toward her. She thrust out a palm and turned her face away.

"No. Don't come near me. I cannot look at you. I don't think I will even be able to look at myself again."

"Valerie—"

"Do not say my name." She could not bear the rich cadence of his voice, his bewildering nearness. She wanted to hate him for letting Bebain torture that sick man, as she hated everything else she had known over the past three days, an eternity of confusion. "Please," she begged. "Do not speak to me."

"Of course I will speak. Bebain is mad and he will pay for it, but you cannot hold yourself responsible for what happened. Your intervention would not have mattered. It would have only fixed his attention upon you as well."

"You spoke to him. You angered him. He tortured that man because of your taunts."

The priest remained silent.

"Well?" she persisted.

"I would bear Ezekiel's cross if I could, Valerie. I assure you."

Valerie's heart constricted.

She shook her head, resisting the allure of his soothing words. It did not matter what he said. No comfort he offered now could undo what had happened, what would happen to her in the coming days, the nightmare that cast everything she had ever experienced into pitiful shade. She once thought her father's coldness was the greatest cruelty possible. But she had been an ignorant fool.

"He did not feel pain." Etienne leaned back against the door, closing his arms across his chest. "Ezekiel took laudanum this morning. A great deal of it. He was barely awake, and did not know it, or I suspect he would have refused." He paused, then added, "He will die with dignity."

"What do you know of dignity?" The words shot from her lips. Fury boiled inside her again. His words, meant to ease her distress, intensified it. She felt impotent and exhausted. She had suffered like this for far more than three days, though—for two long years—and she needed relief.

But the person she wanted to give her that relief did not need her. As her father had, this man found his comfort elsewhere, from a source with which she could never compete. She could try to seduce him, pretend she did it to secure his help, and she could feel her heart bleed like Ezekiel's body. But she would still remain alone.

"What can a coward possibly know of noble things?" she pressed on, the words stumbling off her tongue. "You insist that you do not believe in fate, but you behave as though everything is predestined, as though what happened here today had to happen."

"Fate has not determined this, Valerie. God has it in his plan." His voice sounded peculiarly tight. Her gaze sharpened. His strong jaw was locked. She was affecting him, after all. She could move him with her words if not her actions. The knowledge bit at her with sick triumph.

"Your God, it appears, expects meekness, doesn't he? You bent your head to pray when a man was being murdered in front of you. Dignity?" Her voice crept higher, matching the mounting fire in his eyes. "I don't think you know anything about dignity, or about any other subtle feeling. You don't want anybody except a God who does not listen or care when his creatures suffer. Because of him you scorn human touch—"

"What I deny myself, I deny for others." His golden eyes shone suddenly vivid with compassion, and something that looked like pain. Longing quivered through her and her anger faltered. As though he sensed her uncertainty, Etienne's gaze flickered bright.

Infuriated by her weakness, Valerie lashed out again,

infusing her words with all the contempt she felt for everything she had been and still was, despite her confidence that she could change.

"Look at you, Father," she spat out, "so proud of your funeral black, like some awful raven of death hoping to scavenge another's kill. You asked me what kind of man you would be to leave me to Bebain's cruelty? This kind of man, Etienne." Her voice caught. "The man you already are, who holds himself aloof so he does not have to suffer with all the rest of us pathetic mortals."

He moved toward her swiftly. She backed away, her hands flying up in defense.

He grabbed them and pinned them to her sides, the vision of his muscle-corded arms and the scar running the length of his torso coming to her as he flattened her against him.

She came alive. Everywhere they met heat assailed her, heady and delicious, sinking through flesh and bone. But she didn't want this now. She hated that her body reacted as though made for his touch. The disconnect of heart and flesh was too much to bear.

She swung her gaze up, and the air drained from her lungs. Etienne's eyes blazed with heat. His fingers twisted in her hair, pulling her head back until he looked down at her.

"Call me Steven." His voice was like gravel, completely unfamiliar.

Valerie's eyes widened.

"What—Why?"

"Say it. I want to hear you say it."

Valerie tried to shake her head, but his grip tightened, snapping at her hair. His gaze seared her. He was angry, as she had thought this man could never be, like a lion surprised from sleep. Suddenly, terrifyingly awakened.

"Steven," she whispered, not understanding, yet somehow knowing it was not a taunt, that it meant something to him.

His gaze scraped across her face, her eyes and lips, cheeks and brow, her mouth. His head bent closer and she struggled for breath. With a strangled oath, his mouth came down upon hers.

Chapter 12

His kiss was nothing like the fantasy of melting communion Valerie had so naïvely, hopefully conjured in her imagination. It was an assault, driving her flesh into her teeth, brutal and unforgiving. His mouth opened, forcing her lips apart as he pulled her arms around to clamp her palms against his back.

But Valerie needed no restraint. Curling her fingertips eagerly into the solid plane of his back, she opened her lips wide, finally taking what she had wanted for days.

He drew away and his gaze caught hers, glittering with need and question. She swallowed, every feeling overflowing into her eyes.

He lowered his mouth and possessed hers anew. But he kissed her differently now, the change echoing her own lightning shift from pain to desire. Hurtful in fury before, his kiss hungered, stroking her lips and tongue with eager, gentle caresses, as though he sought in her what he most needed to exist. She wanted to give it to him, to give him everything.

As though in a dream created from her own yearning, his hand slid up from her waist and covered her breast. A sigh broke from her throat, foreign and primitive sounding. She pushed into his touch, her body sizzling to life, nipples tightening.

He slipped his hand beneath her loose bodice, and aching relief washed over her.

No man had ever touched her. All the stolen kisses, secret rendezvous, and forbidden meetings over the years with inappropriate men—all to anger her father—had only amounted to innocent fumblings. Etienne was the first man to put his hands upon her so intimately. She had waited for him.

His caressed her breast's sensitive peak, hardening it, then circling, teasing before he flattened his palm over it. Heat twined between Valerie's legs. He stroked her again and again until she moaned aloud, dissolving into his touch. Wanting more. How could he do this to her? How could she allow him to?

She tore her mouth from beneath his. His molten gaze careened into her senses, hot with need so intense her knees buckled.

"Why are you a priest?" she whispered. "How?"

Emotion crossed his face like a riptide, swift and sharp. He took her mouth again.

His tongue slipped along the inside edges of her lips, and his fingers came together tighter around her nipple. She gasped and he stroked, caressing the underside of her breast, then its taut tip, devouring her mouth as though he could not get close enough. She reveled in him, aching to feel him everywhere. She parted her knees and clamped her thighs around his, sliding her throbbing need against his hard muscle.

His hands swept down her sides and around, cupping her bottom, then spreading her thighs wide and shifting her body to fit his. Her eyes shot open as he pushed hard into her, honeyed heat flooding her, deep and so good. He was fully aroused against her need. His hand tangled in her hair again, his mouth hovering over hers. She tilted her chin up and touched his lips, feathering kisses across his jaw.

"Valerie." Her name sounded like a plea. "Sweet heaven."

She must be imagining the longing in his voice, but she didn't care if it was not real. He was holding her, kissing her, taking pleasure in her. It was all she had wanted since she first saw him.

"Touch me," she whispered. "Touch me more." She rocked against him, trying to tell him with her body what she could not say aloud. She wanted him completely, no matter how wrong it seemed for both of them. It could not truly be wrong. Nothing this perfect could be.

He pushed her to the wall. A soft moan escaped her lips, shivers racing from her belly to her breasts as he crushed her mouth beneath his and moved against her, massaging her fevered flesh with his hard length. His hands swept down her back, molding her to him, gripping her hips to hold her still as his tongue commanded hers and his body pleasured her with firm, agonizingly slow thrusts.

Frantic with the need building inside, she grabbed his face, her fingertips alive on his whisker-roughened jaw. He turned his mouth into her hand, and his lips upon her palm spread sweet, desperate fire through her. She whimpered, unable to stop the sound.

With a smooth movement he slipped her gown off her shoulder. His lips and teeth teased her naked flesh, curling sweet pleasure through her breasts and between her legs. She clung to his arms, wanting him so badly it hurt. Her body cried out for more, for pleasure, for his arms around her, holding her, driving her to madness. He pulled her gown to her waist.

For a moment, he didn't move, his ravenous gaze heating her skin. Valerie felt no shame, only the need for him to touch her again. He curved his hand around her breast, the pad of his thumb covering and pressing into her nipple. Her eyes fluttered half closed.

"Beautiful Valerie," he murmured, breathless from the feeling of her satiny skin, the taut peak of her breast beneath his palm, his own insanity.

He had pretended to be a priest for years, celibate by sheer force of will most of that time, and only very carefully satisfying his needs when he was sure he would not be discovered. Yet he could take this woman in a moment. He could bury himself inside her so hard and deep, neither of them would deny it ever again.

She was lovelier than he even imagined. He caressed her exquisite breasts, milky white, soft as velvet, and tipped with perfect beauty hardened by his touch. From the moment he had grabbed her she did not resist. She was living desire in his hands. Sweet, passionate, willing woman, begging him to give her more.

He wanted to give it to her, to touch her everywhere, to fill his senses with her, in the same way he wanted to defend himself, for her to understand everything. In the face of her anger he had stood mute, paralyzed by the fierce, alien need for someone to know him for who he truly was. For this woman to know. The deeper that need burned, the harder desire pounded through him. He hungered for her, a consuming want his grandfather had foretold years ago, a destiny he was not meant to refuse. A yearning to end the eternal exile from his own soul.

But he could not have that. He had a duty to fulfill. Why else would he deny himself the very thing he wanted? Why else would he lie to everyone around him if he did not do it for them? To protect them. To save them. To save her.

He bent and took her nipple into his mouth, taut and

soft against his tongue and lips. She arched her back, groaning and moving into his caress. Urgency flooded his cock, and he stroked his tongue across her sensitive flesh. She gasped, thrusting her hips, spreading her legs more to feel him, to pleasure herself upon him.

Steven was a man of great control, but not by any means made of ice. He sucked on her, she ground against his thigh, and not a moment's doubt crossed his mind whether he would touch her where she wanted it most.

He slipped his hand between their bodies and caressed her through her skirt, teasing the contours of her body, her unique, beautiful womanhood. She moaned, and satisfaction swelled in him.

It wasn't enough. Her need throbbed through the gown's worn fabric, hot and hungry from his touch. He had to feel how wet he made her, to know he could do this to her, as though she were made for his hands.

She was not made for him, of course. Only fools believed in prophecy. But he needed to touch her.

He took her mouth, long and deep, cupping her breast, light-headed with the desire raging through him, growing harder with each caress of her hands upon his body.

"Lift your skirts, Valerie," he said just above her lips. Her breath fluttered unsteadily, but he knew she would do it. Her need called through her questing hands, her impatient mouth.

She tugged at the rough gown, pulling it up her legs. He slipped his hand beneath her knee and spread his fingers upon her silken skin, the caress of her soft, supple beauty shivering through him. She sighed and gripped his back, a sound of pure rapture as he moved his hand along her thigh, closer. He stroked across her sweet center and she shuddered into him. She was firm and liquid, ready for him.

Swallowing hard, Steven instantly realized his mistake. Now that he had felt her need in his hand, he must satisfy it. But he feared this woman would never truly be satisfied.

He kissed her again, her delicate tongue entwining with his as he spread her with his fingers and rubbed gently. She trembled, her breathing shortened, her soft moans growing tighter. He drank in the sugared flavor of her lips, their tender, willing eagerness, and he ached to make her moan louder, to make her cry out with pleasure as he took her fully.

He circled her entrance. She gasped and stilled. Then she pressed into his touch, inviting him inside.

He slid a finger into her. His cock ached to be where his hand was, encased in her. She was perfect, like no other woman. It didn't matter what he tried to tell himself. She was made for him. For him alone.

"Valerie," he groaned, his body rushing toward satisfaction as he caressed her pleasure, gave it to her. She clutched his shoulders, gasping, opening farther to him. He grasped at restraint. He told himself he did not do it for her. This was about satisfying his pride, about teaching her a lesson.

But it was all a lie. He should never have begun this, never put his hands upon her. He hadn't anticipated her passion. He had been a fool not to, but he could not resist. And now *he must stop.*

Chapter 13

Valerie moaned, weak with pleasure. He touched her where she never imagined a man's hand could be, where she wanted this man forever. Delirious pressure built, coiling upward, spreading then twisting back together again with each thrust of his finger, each caress of his tongue across her lips.

She wanted his tongue in her mouth, upon her breasts, even where his hand possessed her. Aching, struggling for air, she cried out as he drove into her harder, then grasped her bottom, pulling her against his hand. The delicious pressure inside her constricted, and she shattered from within. She whimpered, barely able to catch her breath as pleasure shook her body. She clung to him, throbbing, shocked at the sensations pouring through her. It felt so good, so intimate and real. So dangerous and safe. She wanted him to hold her forever, to bury herself in his embrace.

Etienne's hands fell away. He stepped back and her skirt tumbled into place.

Shaking and stunned, she lifted her gaze. He drew her gown to her shoulders, covering her breasts. Valerie gulped in air. He smoothed back the locks of hair that had spilled from her hairpins, and his fingers drifted along her cheek before pulling away.

She struggled to clear her head, clutching her bodice to her breasts and clinging to the aching in her core, trying to force her thoughts into coherence. Bewildered, she lifted her gaze again.

She groaned, this time in misery over her willful, foolish recklessness.

With one embrace, he had devastated her, changed her forever. Yet now he stood perfectly composed, his handsome face devoid of emotion. Except for the muted glimmer in his golden eyes and the torment inside her, Valerie might have imagined the entire thing.

Without a word, he moved away, turning to the cabin door. She watched his physical grace in painful awareness and her entire body wavered, yearning toward him as he paused at the threshold.

For a moment he stood perfectly still, his back to her, silent. Then slowly, deliberately, he fastened the buttons of his robe. Finally he reached for the door latch.

"I am a man, Valerie." His voice was a defeated shadow of itself, her name only a breath upon his lips. "But this is not what makes me one." He turned, and from across the room his gaze met hers. Regret clouded his amber eyes. He opened the door and disappeared.

Valerie sank to the bed, hurt jolting through her. Her eyes filled, the first tears since before her father's death slipping down her cheeks. Now she feared she would never stop.

She did not see another person for hours. Near dusk, Zeus appeared and beckoned to her. She rose numbly, offering her wrists. Only then she realized that when Etienne had entered earlier, he had been alone. He departed on his own too, his hands unbound. The wonderful, terrible lingering ache in her body testified to that.

She followed the giant blindly. All day she had been free to open the door of her prison cell and walk away. She understood now, though, that freedom meant little when surrounded by depths of ocean, or mountains of anguished memory.

Her chest tightened. Stifling numbness had returned, stealing deep and sure into familiar cavities of her heart. If she let that numbness finally take her, perhaps someday she would even cease breathing.

Zeus halted before the door to the captain's quarters.

"The good God will be with you," he murmured, and knocked.

Bebain answered. A ribbon bound his combed hair. His shirt, coat, and pantaloons looked crisp and fresh.

"My little beauty, good evening." He lifted her hands to his mouth. "Go, go." He shooed Zeus away. "She will be well cared for here." He swung the door wider and gestured for Valerie to enter.

Amid the day cabin's luxurious furnishings, a dining table was dressed for two, laden with silver, porcelain, and crystal. Covered dishes and an epergne piled with apples, dates, candied oranges, and marzipan rested at its center. Valerie stared at it, the aroma of roasted meat and the sharp perfume of newly uncorked wine tingling in her nostrils.

A key grated in the lock, drawing her attention back to the pirate. Her breath stilled.

Bebain stood with his back to the door. Beside him, Etienne sat bound with ropes at wrists and ankles to a chair bolted to the floor. From a raw wound above his eye, rivulets of blood curved along the angle of his jaw, a vivid line of purple staining their path. The edge of his shirt collar above his black robe shone red, saturated with blood.

"You two are already acquainted, of course," Bebain murmured urbanely, then succumbed to laughter. Hidden in the folds of her skirt, Valerie's nails dug into her palms.

The captain shrugged. "But you see, my sweet, I thought to have a private dinner here for the two of us. But our holy friend and I had something of a quarrel this evening. He stole from me, in fact. At the very least I should take him atop and flog him in front of the crew. But in my present mood I am hesitant to let him know he has piqued me."

He regarded the priest thoughtfully, his long lower lip protruding.

"Really, he is most unappreciative of my generosity," Bebain sighed. "Alas, for various reasons, I do not feel comfortable leaving him in the care of my loyal crew tonight. So we must suffer his presence as we enjoy ourselves, my beauty. I hope you will not mind it." He turned to Valerie, false resignation in his insipid eyes.

"I will not," she said. If she could only cease breathing . . .

Bebain motioned her toward the table. Dizzy with hunger, she wavered above the feast. Her gaze sluiced back to the priest.

During her shadowed hours in the cabin she had relived his rejection like a knife wound through her heart. She tried to convince herself that he wanted to teach her a lesson, to chastise her with her wantonness. But the pain in his eyes before he left hadn't been there for her benefit, and it confused her.

Now, beaten and bound, he conveyed only steady calm. Bebain was no physical match for the priest. He must have had him tied up before beating him. Yet nothing in Etienne's tawny eyes suggested defeat. Only peace. Valerie willed herself to take that emotion into herself, to let his inner strength become hers.

"Have a seat, little one, and I will pour wine to whet your appetite." Bebain's eyes glittered with meaning.

So her initiation as his mistress would be tonight, with the priest apparently as captive witness. But even that irony did not stir Valerie now. She sat, took up a glass, and raised it to her lips. The fine vintage hit her tongue like vinegar. The pirate watched, not touching his own wine.

"Captain." She drew a deep breath, Valentine's gift burning against her booted ankle. "It is awkward for me to eat with my hands bound." She lifted her wrists.

Bebain's eyes narrowed.

"Come now, sir," she said, "You have subdued that great big man. How can you imagine I could pose any threat to you?"

He pursed his lips and stood. She held her hands forward. He reached for her arms and dragged her to her feet with surprising strength. Grinning lazily, he moved his hands to her shoulders, his fingers seeking the edge of fabric and bare flesh.

Valerie willed away her gooseflesh and lifted her wrists higher. With a dramatic sigh, Bebain unfastened the tether. But instead of releasing her, he gripped. Her stomach rose in her throat as his nails caressed her palms.

"I have had to wait too long for you, little beauty. You have not, I hope, imagined I forgot you." One finger slid under her chin, tilting her face up. He chuckled. "How could I? You are beautiful, no? And as I am not a man to trifle with boys, I have waited for you like a faithful bridegroom since you boarded my ship."

Abruptly the pirate released her, and Valerie sank shaking into the chair. He moved around the table and placed an embroidered napkin upon his lap.

"A toast!" He lifted his glass. "To your new home." His smile was salacious, and as he tapped his crystal to hers, the cold crept deeper into her veins.

Valerie clenched her teeth and took in a slow breath. She did not want the numb helplessness, this living death urging readmittance into her soul. Not any longer. Two years of it sufficed. It would end, now, forever. This man might try to force her into submission as her father had, but she would never again go willingly.

She would rather die.

She fingered her fork as Bebain ate, placing neat portions of food into his cheek and chewing with deliberation. Hiding her disgust, Valerie looked past the carving knife at Bebain's elbow toward her own plate. Her gaze passed over an elaborately heavy candlestick. Crimson droplets peppered the silver and red stained the table linen at the sparkling stick's base.

Valerie's eyes narrowed, and her breath escaped in a soft gasp.

Blood.

Now she understood what the priest had stolen from Bebain. Laudanum. Pilfering it, Etienne had traded a dying man's comfort for a beating with a candlestick. Just as swiftly Valerie now knew what she must do. Air rushed into her lungs and she nearly laughed aloud. A lifetime of practice might finally be of real use.

As though accidentally, the fork slipped from her grasp and tumbled to the floor beside her foot.

"Good heavens, how clumsy of me. I suppose I am famished," she tittered, pushing her chair out and bending forward to retrieve the utensil. The bodice of her borrowed gown sagged, and Bebain ogled her breasts.

Valerie raised her gaze, hot and bright, to the pirate. Dropping the recovered fork upon the table, she plucked a piece of candied orange from the brimming epergne. She opened her lips, allowing her tongue to show against her teeth as she extended it slightly, tasting sugar. She nipped off a corner of the orange slice.

Bebain's narrow chest contracted visibly. "Do you enjoy the food I have had prepared for you, my little one?"

Valerie took another morsel of fruit and let the tip of her tongue slide across her upper lip. Her lashes swept downward. "Mm," she purred.

"And the accommodations I provided?" the pirate asked. "These have also been to your liking, no?"

She reached for an apple, stroked its shining red surface with lingering fingertips, and raised it to her open mouth. Without tasting, she drew it away, her lips remaining parted.

"Adequate." Her teeth broke the apple's skin. She surrounded the wound with her lips and sucked. Upon the tabletop, Bebain's hand flexed.

"Merely adequate?" His gaze shifted to Etienne.

Valerie allowed the apple to dangle from her fingertips before she placed it upon the table and rose. She moved past Bebain toward the priest, looking around the spacious cabin with appreciation.

"You see, Captain, I was under the impression that I would enjoy a change of quarters earlier than this."

Etienne met her gaze, indifference masking the pain she now saw etched upon his handsome features. His skin was paler than usual. Behind her, Bebain released a slow breath.

"Am I to understand that you have been unsatisfied with your sleeping arrangements, my little one? This imprudent fellow did not appreciate my gift as we hoped, did he?"

Valerie halted before the Jesuit. She extended her hand

and caressed his face from brow to jaw, passing through his blood. Her fingertips paused upon his chin, and she could not prevent their trembling.

She opened her hand and slapped him. Her palm came away streaked with red.

Etienne did not move. His gaze remained steady in hers. Valerie glanced at Bebain, then at the blood staining her. Running her hand along Etienne's arm, she grimaced as she wiped her palm clean across his sleeve. Her fingers slid over his hand, skin against skin. She turned to Bebain, scowling.

"Untidy and disappointing." She crossed to the table. "And a liar. Aboard the merchantman, he did not tell you the truth. I cannot pretend to know his motive, but you did not take aboard a virgin. At least, not one of us." She cast Etienne a brief, scornful look. "He is handsome and his body is strong and attractive, so I allowed it. But now I am weary of him. A man trained to celibacy is not truly a man, is he?"

She placed her hand upon the pirate's.

"But why didn't you tell me this when we spoke before, my lovely?" Bebain gripped her elbow and pulled her down. Valerie stumbled into his lap. Recovering, she curled her arm around his shoulder.

"Perhaps I was intimidated by the magnificence of your ship. It is quite beautiful. And powerful, no?" She smiled secretively, as though sharing a joke with him. "And perhaps I do not enjoy carrying on such conversations in the hearing of servants." She moved her lips near his ear, swallowing down the bile rising in her throat. "Perhaps I wished to prolong the displeasure so my relief would be that much greater when it . . . came." Her tongue flickered against his earlobe.

Bebain's fingers closed around her arm. He stood. Valerie fell against the table's edge and he grabbed her and yanked her close.

"Why have I waited?" he murmured in airy falsetto, his gaze running from her crown down the length of her body. "Why have I waited?"

"Again, I do not know," she murmured. "But you needn't wait any longer." Before she could think, feel, struggle for freedom, Valerie opened her lips and pressed them against Bebain's.

She began to count. As he clamped his arms around her, surrounding her with his long, wiry body, as he sucked on her tongue and nausea pummeled through her, as she moved her hands along his arms to distract herself from the pushing hardness between her thighs, as his hands grasped her buttocks, kneading, pinching, pulling her thighs apart, as she tried to breathe without releasing the sobs and screams—she counted.

She counted to sixty, then to one hundred, then higher as Bebain's sloppy mouth polluted her hair and neck. She counted as he rubbed her legs, as his fingers pawed her skirt and pulled it up.

Panic seized Valerie and she could count no longer. She pushed against his chest, instinct driving her strength. He grabbed her hands. Forcing herself to cease struggling, she looked up. Bebain's pale blue eyes glittered with dementia and the unmistakable thrill of power. His face moved toward hers again.

But her body would not accept what her mind insisted it must. She struck out again at the pirate's grasping hands. He warded off the blows and swung her against a high chair back, pinioning her arms against the chair.

"It is impolite to fight like this, my beauty," the Frenchman trilled. "I know you desire our ultimate union, but perhaps you enjoy it better like this, no? I am often unimaginative when a woman is so beautiful. Imagination is not as necessary then, is it?" His lust was palpable in the humid heat of his breath upon her cheek. "Eh, but I will play along to make you happy."

His arm snaked around her and his hand clamped on her breast, his nails driving into her soft flesh. Valerie shouted out with pain, and triumph crossed his features. She slammed her heel down upon his foot, and his eyes kindled in a flash of fury before the impact of his hand shattered against her face. Reeling, she felt her skirts sliding up her legs. She exploded against him, freeing a hand to pound at his face and jerking her knee between his legs.

Abruptly he released her, his eyes bulging. The marble-handled carving knife protruded from the side of his neck, blood soaking his neck cloth. A gurgling groan passed through his crimson-stained lips. His incredulous gaze shifted over her shoulder, then he stumbled across the chamber, slammed against the table and collapsed. Upon the floor, he twitched, a pool of blood gathering beneath his head, and went still.

Valerie pivoted away, her stomach churning into her throat. She swallowed hard.

"What took you so long?" Her voice came forth thin.

"It is a very small knife."

Improbably, a smile of hysterical release tugged at Valerie's lips. She turned. Etienne extended his hand. Valentine's lethal gift to her glinted upon his palm. The ropes that had bound him curled beneath the chair by the door like discarded snakeskins. He held one arm gingerly against his chest. Valerie's smile vanished, her heart pounding again.

"You are hurt."

He shook his head and moved forward, fierce concern coloring his eyes. Her breath caught as his fingers brushed tenderly across her cheek where Bebain had struck her, and his gaze slipped to her mouth. Valerie's lips parted. Slowly, one corner of his sculpted mouth curved. Relief, strong and sweet, washed over her.

A key rattled in the lock. Etienne tilted his battered face toward the entrance, but his gaze remained on hers. The door slammed wide. Maximin stood in the opening, brandishing a cutlass. Valerie backed away, but Etienne grasped her hand, gently solid, enveloping her fear.

"It is done," he said to Maximin.

The sailor's sword arm dropped. He cast a surprised glance at the dead pirate.

"Evidently not according to plan." He shrugged. "But it is better this way."

Etienne's fingers slipped from Valerie's. "For some."

Maximin snorted, then smiled. Valerie stared at him in wonder. Then she took a deep breath.

"He is injured, though I doubt he will admit it."

"As usual," Maximin replied. "But as there is much to celebrate and also much work yet to do, we must see that he heals without delay."

Chapter 14

Welcome to the *Blackhawk, mademoiselle*. It is a pleasure to have you aboard."

Daggers of sunlight shafted through dark clouds, casting short, inconstant shadows across the deck where Maximin leaned against the foremast's base.

"Good day, *monsieur*. Or is it one?" Well fed, bathed, and rested, Valerie allowed her fortified courage to propel her from the hatchway toward the sailor. She had not seen him since the night before, when Zeus drew her from the scene of Bebain's murder to her cabin, no longer a prison. She had slept alone for many hours.

"Call me Maximin. Indeed, it is a good day, Lady Valerie. There is nothing to fear here now."

"But you did not fear Bebain, did you? Etienne didn't either. I may not understand what happened here, but that is clear enough. He would not have allowed Bebain to beat him, otherwise."

"Ah, you are as shrewd as he has said." He quirked a brow. Something in the gesture reminded her of the Jesuit.

"How were you able to do it? Is this mutiny? Disloyalty is common amongst pirates, isn't it?"

A chuckle rumbled from his chest.

"Black's the white of my eye, ma'am. The *Blackhawk* is restored to her rightful master. If that is mutiny, then so be it."

"Her *rightful*—?" Valerie's mouth gaped, but consternation swiftly overcame her. "I know you do not expect me to understand your sailor's cant," she clipped. "And I have clearly misjudged the matter to think that now the madman is dead someone will offer me straight answers. How did you and Etienne conspire together?"

"Ask him yourself." Maximin gestured aft.

Nerves jangling, Valerie turned to see the priest emerging amidships from the gun deck. He climbed to the bridge with comfortable purpose. Only a breath of stiffness in his graceful movements revealed the toll Bebain's beating had taken upon him.

He turned to her, and their gazes met across the expanse of deck. Valerie moved forward. Her breaths shortened as she climbed the steps.

He had exchanged his Jesuit's habit for a sailor's shirt, waistcoat, breeches, and a broad-brimmed hat. The clothes defined his well-muscled thighs and accentuated his broad shoulders and narrow hips. He was breathtakingly masculine. Valerie's gaze flickered to the bandage over the wound beside his eye and the sling hanging from his shoulder, unused. He looked, absurdly, as she always imagined a pirate would, only infinitely more beautiful.

She shook off the foolish notion and squared her shoulders.

"Am I to understand that you are the true master of this ship?"

He tilted his head, studying her, his gaze enigmatic.

"Yes, although when I am on land Maximin captains the crew."

"How can that be? You were a prisoner. Or weren't you?"

"I was. Just as you."

"Aboard your own vessel?"

He nodded to a sailor standing nearby. The man took the wheel into his hands, and Etienne gestured for Valerie to walk ahead of him astern.

"And your crew?" Upon deck, the activity of sea travel continued as industriously as ever. But Valerie noticed a difference, a levity in sun-blackened shoulders, newly assured gaits. "Who are these men?"

"They are freemen. Haitians."

"You lied to me."

"Not precisely."

Valerie shook her head.

"Then you withheld the truth."

"An unfortunate necessity."

"There is no such thing."

"You are young, yet."

"And you are a wizened octogenarian?" she snapped. None of it made sense. "Maximin says this ship is called *Blackhawk*. Is it a pirate ship? Were you responsible for seizing Raymer's vessel?"

"You needn't concern yourself over Raymer. He will be compensated for his losses."

Valerie blinked her astonishment.

"What sorts of buccaneers compensate their victims? You offer me riddles rather than answers."

Etienne regarded her intently. He touched her arm.

"I regret that I have told you all that I am able."

She yanked away from him, as much to still the rushing of her blood as in irritation.

"In point of fact, you have not told me anything. Am I no longer a prisoner?"

"You are free. Twelve hours dead ahead is a ship that will take you to shore. There, transport to England will be arranged for you. You will be home in a month."

Valerie remained silent for too long. Waves broke against the hull, sails cracked, and above the sounds Steven's heartbeat raced fast and hard, ricocheting in his ears. It had taken all his hard-learned discipline to say those words. But she clearly would not accept her fate easily, as he had feared since the moment he met her.

"So, that is that?" she finally uttered. "I am to be sent away, summarily, without explanation?" She was trying to sound affronted. But hurt trembled in her words, echoes of remembered banishments, her father's cruelty. Steven clamped down upon his refreshed anger.

"My crew and I have business that cannot be delayed. You are safe. Do you need more security than that?"

Her eyes flashed.

"I don't need anything from you. What I wish is to know why a French priest captains a crew of Haitians, pillages merchant ships, and takes people hostage. Is this the sort of pressing business you speak of?"

"When required."

"It was not accidental that the *Blackhawk* seized Raymer's vessel, was it? What was that envelope Raymer's navigator gave you? Is he a spy for the French?"

Steven masked his surprise. She couldn't know how close to the truth she came. But she was a clever woman, too clever for her own good. And his. He remained silent, watching her fists clench in her skirts.

"Splendid," she said. "If you will not tell me that, tell me what sort of priest murders a man in cold blood."

Steven dragged his memory from the pirate's hands upon Valerie's body.

"Hardly cold."

She swallowed awkwardly, drawing his gaze to her

lovely neck, dark tresses pressed against milky skin in the breeze. Steven took in a hard breath, slipping back to her turbulent eyes.

"Then," she said unsteadily now, "what sort of priest murders a man at all? Is this what Rome teaches? Are you a cleric or an assassin?" Emotion lit her eyes. Anger. Frustration.

Betrayal.

"I am the man you know me to be, Valerie," he said quietly, speaking the truth with raw clarity. "Nothing more, nothing less."

Her brow creased, her wide eyes glistening. "Well, that simply does not suffice."

"Valerie, thank you."

"And I suppose you expect me to say the same to you?" she retorted. "I will not." She turned her back to him, then paused. "I will be ready when we meet the other ship. And believe me, I will be glad to be rid of this den of liars and thieves."

Without waiting for his reply, she strode across the deck and down into the shelter of solitude.

The sun slipped beyond the horizon, and the cool air settled upon Valerie's skin with chilling fingers. She did not take any comfort in the lavish dinner Zeus laid out for her, or in her empty bed. Peculiarly breathless, she sought the dark night upon deck.

Atop all remained calm. Only a night's skeleton crew skulked about the main deck, quiet in the dusky shadows. Valerie leaned against the forecastle rail. A silvered-almond moon waxed over the ocean, and breeze stirred the hair escaping her hood.

Footfalls sounded upon the planking behind her.

"The weather is clearing. You will have smooth passage to Savannah tonight," Etienne said, coming beside her at the rail.

"Savannah? I wondered whether you would tell me or withhold that information as well." He did not respond. Valerie shivered and closed her eyes. "I want you to kiss me."

She heard Etienne's slow intake of breath.

"Valerie, I cannot—"

"No, not like before." She turned to him. "It's not that I want— I—I need something to erase—"

"Come." He reached for her in the blanket of night. She went with a sob, pressing her cheek against his chest. His arms wrapped around her, his muscles contracting. Remembering his wounds, Valerie pulled back, but he drew her close again. His fingers cradled her chin, lifting her face under the glow of his tawny eyes.

The kiss was brief, a bare caress. Eyes open, Valerie released a tiny sigh.

He lowered his lips again, settling his mouth upon hers as though in kneeling prayer, humble yet certain, and fully willing. She slipped her hands along his arms, holding fast as his mouth moved across her cheek, into her hair, trailing sweet, slow fever in their wake.

As he put his mouth where the madman's had gone before, and his hands traveled the same path Bebain's had lurched across her flesh, she understood why he agreed to do this. In Bebain's cabin, as the tiny knife sliced its way through twisted hemp, Etienne had watched what Bebain did to her.

Now his certain, deliberate touch upon her body where the pirate had grasped at her felt like the sun, warming, comforting, reclaiming. His familiar scent of man and sea and lime enveloped her. She gasped in breaths of freedom as his mouth returned to her lips, tasting wine and blood, and nearly laughed aloud, edging at panic. But he would not allow it. Instead he urged her lips to part and his hands moved below her waist, following the curves of her body.

Valerie shuddered, desire and fear crowding each other inside her. She clung to him, mouth open, giving where she had been forced. His hands caressed her thighs, moving upward, unhesitating along her waist.

His breaths were hard against her mouth. She could feel his desire in his rigid arms, and against her aching body. She tasted him and pressed into him, wanting to feel her need against the hard length of his arousal again, wanting the delirious pleasure he had awakened in her the day before.

He lifted his head.

"Don't stop." Her voice was a heated whisper in the dark.

"No," he murmured. "No yet." Gaze in hers, he caressed her breast gently and so seductively she leaned into him. He covered her mouth again, harder, seeking as he had in the cabin. Her knees parted, his tongue stroking across her lips, and nothing was left of the pirate's touch in her body. She hungered for Etienne, for his hands upon her, his scent and arms and taut desire pressing into her flesh, making her ache to have all of him.

He pulled back with a deep breath. She sighed, a quavering sound, and his arms tightened about her.

"If you change your mind and choose now to thank me," he said in a low voice, "you realize, I will have to throw myself overboard."

A constricted laugh escaped her throat.

"Consider it a penance." Reluctantly, she released his shoulders.

He grasped her hands.

"I came to give you this." He pressed a book into her

palms. Valerie's fingers closed around the Bible's worn leather cover.

"But you need this. Why are you giving it to me?"

"Please, take it." Again his hand cupped her cheek. He tilted her face up. "Read it, sketch in it, use it as a paperweight. Do with it whatever you wish. But take it." The corner of his mouth rose in beautiful modesty. "I have little of my own that I value, and I want you to have it."

She ached deep, as though a fist gripped her heart.

"I cannot thank you for it, of course." An uneven grin tugged at her lips.

Etienne returned the smile, but only for a moment. He seemed to be about to speak. Gaze tangled with his, Valerie held her breath. She had never seen him uncertain before, never hesitant.

"Valerie." His voice was rough. "I do wish circumstances were different."

Valerie choked, the sound emerging like a bitter laugh from her throat.

"Circumstances." She clenched her hands around the book.

He stepped back.

"Zeus will come for you when we meet your ship."

She nodded.

"Good night, Valerie."

"You mean that as good-bye, I suspect."

His beautiful lips curved up at one edge in the smile Valerie would never forget.

"Never satisfied." He backed away. "*Bon voyage*, dear lady."

But not good-bye.

The thrum of funeral drums pounded heavily through the deck, rocking Valerie's cabin with eerily mournful passion, conveying Ezekiel's lifeless body into the ocean's depth. Heart too unsteady to trust, afraid of the quickening that every beat drove more forcefully through her veins, Valerie remained in her cell alone, listening in the darkness.

Toward the middle of the night the drums faded into stillness. Shortly after that, Zeus arrived to find her cloaked and prepared to depart. They ascended to the top and he gestured her forward to the rail. Below, a slip bobbed in the dark water. The giant took Valerie's hands between his.

"God bless you, *mademoiselle*."

"Stop flirting with the lady, Zeus, and move along." Maximin grasped Valerie's arm. "Zeus will escort you to the *Seafarer*. Follow him down the ladder, but take care. It is sometimes slippery." He gestured to Zeus and moved aside.

The giant seized the rail and stepped onto the rope ladder extending down to the water. He disappeared over the ship's side, and Valerie moved to the deck's edge to follow.

Warmth gathered between her shoulders. She turned.

In the lantern light, Etienne appeared like a god of old, fashioned of bronze and amber, his gilt beauty mellowed through ancient worship. He took her hand, and Valerie's body shivered with heat from the mortal man's touch.

He lifted her fingers and pressed his lips to them. A smile curved the corner of his mouth. Valerie tried to breathe, but she could not quite remember how. Without a word, he released her. She turned, grasped the rail, and descended into the dark.

"All is well now," Steven murmured into the lamplight.

"Never again for you, I suspect." Maximin looked away from the slip moving through the black water. The schooner beyond was visible only by lanterns in the distant darkness. He placed a hand upon Steven's shoulder. "But that, my brother, is your destiny."

"I do not believe in destiny."

"It sighs before you. You tease it, make love to it. Yet you deny it. You make a fine priest."

Steven glanced at his friend, but he did not smile.

"You have succeeded, Max. I am distracted by your idiocy, if not by your dire warnings. You can be certain of it now, I will not brood."

"More the fool you are, then," the Haitian rejoined. "You want her."

"I do. Like a blindness." Steven took a deep breath. "But she will return to where she belongs, unharmed. I promised her. It is all I can do."

"One needn't do anything to be given a gift."

At his friend's words, something new in Steven, something untested, constricted.

"Tell me what gift I have, Max," he said, ignoring the sensation, "that I have not struggled for, bled, fought, and labored after. I defy you to name one."

"A gift for which such efforts would prove fruitless, of course."

Steven's jaw clenched hard against the unfamiliar ache of doubt.

"She had to go. We must stop Hannsley. Bebain was only the beginning. You know it as well as I. We don't have time to waste entertaining a girl bred to fine aristocratic living. She's better sent off quickly to those sorts of comforts." His tone did not suit his words. He couldn't care. "She longs for home, Max."

"She is not alone in that desire, my friend."

"You are free to go whenever you wish."

"I was not speaking of myself. And I was not referring to a city or nation, of course. You are a well-educated fellow. You should recognize metaphor when you hear it."

Steven could not see the little boat any longer. He turned away from the *Seafarer*'s flickering, far-off lanterns.

"You have already dealt with Fevre, I suspect?"

"Our faithless mate resides incommodiously in the bilge, no doubt full of remorse for the poor choices he has made."

Again Steven didn't laugh.

"Come," he said, investing his voice with a composure he did not feel. "We will eat, and you will tell me how you managed to withstand Bebain's madness for so long. And then you will tell me more about myself, I suspect, hm? Is there any rum aboard, or did that lunatic drink it all? I'll need it tonight."

Chapter 15

October 5, 1810

CAPTAIN ETIENNE LA MARQUE
BLACKHAWK
PORT-AU-PRINCE, REPUBLIQUE D'HAITI

Dearest Godson,

The Captain and I received your communication of August 8. All is in preparation, invitations pending our return to town. We will do all we can. Hurry home. It would be delightful to spend time with you alone before the festivities begin.

Affectionately,
Margaret, Countess of March
Derbyshire, G.B.

Chapter 16

"You are not dressed for dinner yet, Valerie. Aren't you joining us at Lady March's salon?" The Countess of Alverston's honey-gold hair, swept up into a fashionable arrangement, glowed in the candlelight as she crossed the bedchamber.

"I thought I would stay home reading, if you and Valentine don't mind it."

"Well, this is remarkable. Five months back and already so bored with society you prefer a book to admirers? Your time abroad truly changed you, my dear." Anna smoothed Valerie's hair. Valerie tilted her head into the caress. Since childhood Anna had been like a sister, and now she truly was one. While Valerie had been at sea, her brother and childhood companion had married.

But now suspicion shone in Anna's warm brown eyes. Valerie slipped her book beneath a cushion.

"It will be a large party. No one will miss me."

"Everyone expects you. Lady March especially told me

she wished you to attend. And there are others who won't like your absence."

Valerie shrugged, but she already knew what Anna would say next.

"Darling, Valentine is concerned that you are not being honest with Lord Bramfield." Anna's voice was unaccusing and painful to hear. Valerie found censure infinitely preferable to compassionate understanding. She was far more accustomed to the former, after all.

"Yes, my brother mentioned that to me," she muttered.

"I am concerned too, but not on Timothy's behalf."

"My reputation is not yet mended, do you think?" A spark lit in Valerie's chest. "Two years of exile did not suffice to redeem me? Ah, the *ton* is horridly unforgiving." If they only knew of her escapade aboard a pirate ship, society would thoroughly cut her. But Valentine had used his influence abroad and his wealth to ensure that Raymer and the officers of the *Seafarer* would never reveal it. As for the rest, she hadn't told her brother anything, even the name of the *Blackhawk*.

"That is not my meaning," Anna said. "All is forgotten upon that score. I speak, of course, of your reluctance to respond to Lord Bramfield's suit."

"Oh, dear. I have been acquainted with him such a short time—"

"He and Valentine have been friends since Eton. You have been acquainted with him longer than with me."

"That does not signify. We were children then."

"You have had ample time to come to know each other here in town. Did something happen on that corsair, Valerie? Was there a man?"

The breath hissed from Valerie's lungs. In five months, Valentine and Anna had asked her almost nothing about her experience, seeming to understand her unspoken desire not to discuss it.

She forced herself to laugh lightly.

"What do you mean, silly? I told you everything about that horrid vessel. My quarters were sufficiently comfortable and I was largely left to my own devices. At the time it was harrowing, of course, not knowing how it would end. But then the *Seafarer* showed up, there was a great deal of horrid cannon shot, and then they saved me. Now I am here with you and Valentine. Honestly, the whole ordeal barely registers as a bad dream to me now."

Valerie narrowed her eyes, infusing them with a teasing glint she had long ago perfected in this very bedchamber's mirror.

"Anna dear, have you been reading gothic novels? I used to think you were far too intellectual for those, but perhaps you are the one who has changed." She uncurled from the chair and went to the armoire. From the corner of her eye she saw Anna draw her book from beneath the pillow and study the binding.

"A Bible?" the countess murmured in astonished tones. "In French, no less." She brandished the volume like evidence. "Valerie, you are simply outrageous to imagine Valentine and I will continue to ignore this sort of thing. This is absolutely unlike you. You cannot possibly think I would believe you learned this from your stuffy Boston cousins, can you? Something must have happened upon that ship you haven't told us."

Valerie rifled through the row of gowns.

"I will wear the pinstripe muslin tonight. Lord Bramfield remarked upon my beauty twice when I wore it last." She called her maid to help her dress, maintaining a steady stream of inane chatter all the while. Anna tapped her fingers upon her lap. Finally, she rose.

"Do not be too long." She crossed to the door. "Valentine called the carriage for nine o'clock."

When Anna had left, Valerie barely noticed what her maid buttoned her into. She could not bring herself to care. Still, Lord Bramfield seemed suitably impressed with her looks when she entered the crowded drawing room of the earl and countess of March's town residence.

"Your loveliness is especially refreshing when it shines amidst so many grizzled countenances and blue-stockinged ankles, Lady Valerie." Timothy's blue eyes twinkled. He gestured to her companions engaged in animated discussion. "How you can endure this prattle, I cannot fathom. Give me the theater or a ball any night over this prosing on effete topics."

Valerie allowed herself a slight smile of appreciation. The viscount's coat of sky-blue superfine suited his animated eyes and shining copper hair styled forward in the latest fashion.

"If you do not like the conversation, my lord," she whispered, "why are you here?"

His gaze sparkled.

"The company drew me."

Valerie held her smile.

"You should attend to this particular debate. It is not precisely elevated. They are discussing horses."

"My greatest apologies. I became distracted by your beauty. But I will now attend more enthusiastically if you wish." He grinned and, raising his strong voice, entered the conversation. "I disagree entirely, Fredericks. That criminal Bonaparte rides an Arab, doesn't he? A little mount like that would be too delicate for our august prince. You are a horsewoman, Lady Alverston. What mount do you imagine would best suit a prince regent should our nation find itself, as it were, saddled with one in the coming months?"

The others laughed. A hand touched Valerie's elbow

and she pivoted. Lady March stood beside her. With a smile she drew Valerie from the group, and they settled upon a nearby sofa.

"I have wanted to chat with you for weeks, Lady Valerie. I hope you do not mind me dragging you away from your beau."

Valerie suppressed a sigh of frustration. All of society seemed to know Lord Bramfield had courted her since her return. The match was a done thing to everyone but her.

"No need to apologize, my lady. My friends were discussing horses."

The countess grinned conspiratorially, her six decades resting about her eyes in appealing crinkles.

"I cannot tolerate the beasts, myself. You don't admire them either, dear?"

Valerie shrugged. "I prefer boat travel."

"Ah, yes." For a moment it seemed that Lady March's gaze sharpened. She placed her hand upon Valerie's. "I hope your preference will not prohibit you from coming to our home in the country later this month. The Captain and I are gathering a party at Castlemarch for the holiday. I have already invited Lord and Lady Alverston, but I wanted to proffer the invitation to you personally."

"Thank you, ma'am." Of course Valerie would attend. She would go anywhere to avoid returning home. Valentine might be lord of Alverston now, but for Valerie the corridors and chambers of Alverston Hall would forever reverberate with the late earl's condemnations.

"I think our little gathering will be well suited to your taste," the countess added. "There will be a great many interesting people in attendance, including my godson, who, like yourself, has just returned from travels abroad."

Valerie smothered another exhalation. The countess must be yet another fond sponsor of a gentleman hopeful of finding a well-dowered bride.

"I will be pleased to make his acquaintance," she responded properly. Always proper. She ached to shout, scream, dance upon her forehead in the middle of the floor, simply to do something improper. She'd thought returning home would cure her long unhappiness, her numb loneliness. She had the daily affection of Valentine and Anna now, and she loved them so dearly. But she had never felt more alone and restless, not even in Boston.

She missed him. She missed a man she barely knew, whose gaze and touch and the fire he ignited in her blood would remain in her memory forever.

"I am so glad you will come. Oh, dear, there is the Captain looking for me. What could he want?" Lady March rose hastily. "Dear girl, I look forward to seeing you at Castlemarch in a few weeks."

Valerie stood to rejoin Anna, and nearly ran headlong into a white satin waistcoat.

"Ah, Lady Valerie. As beautiful as ever." The Marquess of Hannsley took her hand in large, smooth fingers and lifted it high to his lips.

Valerie had met the wealthy duke's heir at an earlier salon. Later that evening, the marquess was expelled for calling out his cousin over a quarrel concerning mercantile taxes, a minor upset, but apparently not uncommon at the Countess of March's political gatherings.

"Good evening, my lord." She tugged at her hand, but he held it fast. He was extraordinarily tall, and bent to come close to her.

"A lovely lady like yourself must crave more suitable entertainments than listening to a group of overly opinionated politicians."

"Oh, I don't mind it so much." It kept her mind too busy to dwell upon memories.

The marquess's thick, overtly sensuous lips curved down at the corners.

"I could not be mistaken, could I?"

"Mistaken, my lord?"

"You were speaking intimately with Lady March just now." He peered at Valerie. "But you do not know the purpose of these salons, do you?"

Valerie shook her head.

"My cousin hosts these gatherings hoping to dredge up support for insurgents and criminals, celebrating the cause of revolutionaries." Hannsley studied her from beneath heavy lids.

Valerie hadn't known about Lady March's radical interests. But given her own spotted past, she didn't much care. In any case, the Marquess of Hannsley seemed disturbed enough for the both of them. His hooded eyes looked downright threatening.

"Such plain speaking, my lord," she said, a sticky chill gathering at the base of her neck. "Are you certain I do not share Lady March's views?"

Lord Hannsley smiled reassuringly.

"Of course not. I must have suffered momentary madness to think you would concern yourself with such matters. A beautiful woman's head is never filled with more than the lightest of concerns."

His smile widened. Valerie stared, at once mesmerized and repelled.

"Some ladies like to ponder weightier topics," she suggested. Some ladies could not avoid it after spending days aboard a pirate ship crewed by revolutionary former slaves.

Hannsley shook his head, as though gently chastising an errant child.

"Not if their husbands control them as they should."

"I regret to be the one to tell you, Hannsley, but certain ladies will not be controlled, and certain gentlemen are glad of it," Lord Bramfield boomed at Valerie's shoulder.

Lord Hannsley drew a silver snuffbox from his waist-coat pocket and lifted a pinch of tobacco dust beneath his nose. With polite contempt, he sniffed and sneezed.

"A gentleman, Bramfield, would be played for a fool if he allowed such behavior in his woman. Please excuse me, madam." The marquess bowed and sauntered away as the butler called the announcement for dinner.

Valerie met Timothy's unrepentant glance. He offered his arm into the dining room.

"Do you think I should have called him out for saying such an outrageous thing to me?" He chuckled.

Valerie smiled, an odd sort of tight relief settling in her.

"I think you delight in disturbing people's composure, my lord."

"Hannsley is a pompous popinjay. And I know at least one lady who has historically taken great pleasure in the same kind of behavior of which she now accuses me."

"How uncivil of you to mention that, sir."

"I confess I have no justification for such behavior," he admitted as he pulled her chair out before a hover-ing footman could act. Against her neck Timothy's breath stirred the tendrils of hair cascading from her coiffure. "Unless it is that I have indeed become a fool for a certain lady who refuses to be controlled."

Valerie laughed lightly in response.

Hours later, as she lay cold and rigid upon her feather bed, sleep came slowly.

Chapter 17

Not far from its well-preserved medieval village, the red-and-gold brick Elizabethan mass of Castlemarch rose solid and square around an ancient keep, the remainders of its architectural origins. Stocky columns supporting a shallow porch above an entrance stair rose to rows of mullioned windows, the entire building topped with intricately fashioned crenellations. The Alverston carriage drew up behind a brace of elegant vehicles clustered in the broad, curving drive. Grooms tended cattle, and smartly liveried footmen bustled about with trunks and bandboxes, wisps of snow twisting in the frigid air.

Valerie entered the castle's ancient hall behind her brother and Anna. Across the broad chamber, the Earl and Countess of March moved from a group of guests and came forward to greet them.

"Welcome, ladies," the earl said. "What a great pleasure to receive you here. Alverston, you lucky fellow.

Your travels must have been enjoyable with two such enchanting companions."

"My sister fidgeted throughout the entire journey. But we made do." Valentine winked. Valerie pinched her brother's sleeve.

"I cannot believe that of such a seasoned traveler," Lady March said. "How beautiful you look after so many hours in a carriage, dear girl." She took Valerie's arm. "Most of our guests have already arrived. Before long the castle will be full, just the way the Captain and I like it best for the holidays." She patted Valerie's hands fondly. "You and Lady Alverston must wish to refresh yourselves after the long carriage ride. I will have the housekeeper show you to your rooms. May I send up my companion, Amelia, to help you unpack? She is a delightful necessity to me. Helps me remember where I have put my head sometimes."

The countess's acute gaze belied her claim of forgetfulness, and her voice sounded peculiar, but Valerie smiled as expected.

"My maid is following in the carriage behind us. But thank you, ma'am."

"Fine, fine. Today is too far advanced already for any interesting out-of-doors activities, I fear. But tomorrow we will have a foraging expedition in the woods for greenery to fest the castle. I need the help of younger people to make the place suitable for Christmas. I do hope you will join the party, Lady Valerie."

"Oh, wonderful. I will take my brother along."

"Why so eager, sister mine?"

"Darling, you cannot imagine that your inelegant complaint about my company will go unpunished? And so much snow needs a good purpose, don't you think?"

Valentine quirked a smile.

Lord March chuckled. "Never cross a clever lady, Alverston. She will always double-cross a fellow in return."

Anna and Valerie laughed at her brother's nonplussed expression. Lady March's gaze slued abruptly to Valerie, strangely sharp again as she seemed to study Valerie anew.

Valerie's grin faltered. "My lady?"

"Oh, yes," the countess chortled belatedly. "Gentlemen can be so blind, can't they, my dear? Now I have just recalled a matter I must attend to." She turned their party over to the housekeeper and hastened away.

Valerie's shoulders tingled with unease as she followed the housekeeper to her bedchamber. Knowing her hostess intended to attach Valerie to her godson, she had not really wished to come to Castlemarch. But she did not particularly wish to be anywhere else for the holiday, and certainly not without her family.

A mere six months home, and the rest of her years stretched out before her like a dreadful eternity. Nothing, not even gay Christmas festivities, could enliven that.

Near the cliff, from the shadows below, voices called out. They seemed to be inside the waves crashing against the sheer rock face.

Her hands were bound, tied to the people in front of her and behind. The man walking toward the cliff just ahead was huge and uncannily familiar, but he seemed likewise helpless in his bindings. She was cold too. Only a thin lace night rail covered her nakedness. But she felt no shame, only helplessness as they marched toward the wind-buffeted cliff's edge.

A man appeared at the rim, one hand in his waistcoat pocket and the other lifting a pinch of snuff to his nose. He stood casually, watching the line of people disappear over the cliff's edge. He was very tall and well dressed, and she knew a moment of hope when she realized he must be English. He could save her and the others if only she could open her mouth and force the words out. As she struggled to make her voice heard, he turned and she saw his face. As she recognized the hooded eyes and aristocratic features, his full lips parted in a toothy smile.

Valerie awoke gasping, covers strewn to either side upon the canopied bed. She sat up, shaking her head free of the dream's vivid images. Gathering the goose-down blanket to her, she curled up in a ball beneath it.

Even as a prisoner aboard the *Blackhawk* she had not dreamed in such horrifying images, and she rarely played such a significant role. Squeezing her eyes shut, she shivered under the warm covers.

The Marquess of Hannsley was arrogant and opinionated and looked at her as though he owned her. But plenty of English noblemen fit that description and she did not invent sinister roles for them in her dreams. The night before, discovering the marquess as a guest at Castlemarch hadn't bothered her, but now she could not banish his ghastly grin from her mind.

Her hand stole from beneath the covers, seeking the bedside table. Soft leather smoothed beneath her fingertips. She took in a long, steadying breath of cold morning air, pulled the Bible forward, and turned onto her side.

She cracked the volume open, releasing the scent of old leather and incense. The incense might be in her imagination, but it suited her notion of the exotic, alien world so distant from hers now. Each tissue-thin page was marked in the margins with notes in a hand too abbreviated to read for the most part. It was the same with nearly all the pages. In the six months since Etienne gave it to her, she had studied the entire thing from cover to cover.

Reluctantly she placed it again upon the table and lay

back. She closed her eyes. The cliff loomed behind her eyelids, dark bodies falling from it.

She sat up and shoved away the bolster. Fools depended upon prayers and memories. Activity would drive the dream from her mind, as it always did. Without busy activity, the past months would have been a slow torment, both night and day.

Three quarters of an hour later she sipped the final drops of a cup of tea in the morning salon. The little chamber overlooked the frost-touched, terraced gardens that cascaded down behind the castle to a frozen lake and woods beyond. As she stared out the window at the crystal white and blue day, a rider emerged into view from the woods, cantering up to the stables along the north side of the house. She leaned forward and peered through the glass, the window's frost cooling her skin.

The big, rawboned bay was not attractive, but his lope was as graceful as the seat of the man astride him. As she stared at the rider, a peculiar tingling of familiarity skittered across Valerie's shoulders. She shrugged, trying for the second time since rising to dispel unwelcome feelings.

Stepping away from the window, she set her china cup upon the sideboard as a gentleman entered the chamber. He bowed rigidly.

"Good morning, madam."

"Good morning, sir."

He stared at her, his brow furrowed under a Brutus-cut thatch of curly brown hair.

"Please forgive my presumption, ma'am. I feel we have met before, but I am ashamed to disremember where and when I had the pleasure. I am Alistair Flemming. It is my aunt's and uncle's home in which we enjoy Christmas this year." He bowed again.

"I am pleased to meet you, Mr. Flemming. I have attended your aunt's salon in town. Perhaps we met there."

Mr. Flemming's smile rested uncomfortably upon his face.

"You are Lord Alverston's sister, then. I understand you recently lived in the United States for some time."

"I returned from Boston in July. Are you interested in America?"

He poured out tea. "Somewhat. I have business concerns there."

"Really? My cousin has as well. A mercantile company. What about you, Mr. Flemming?"

"Oh." He waved a hand, as though regretting that he had introduced the topic. "My aunt's interests, you know." His cheeks turned pale. It was not the usual bluster of a gentleman defending his investments in trade and industry, and it struck Valerie as odd, especially in light of what Lord Hannsley had said about the Countess of March's political leanings.

"Mr. Flemming, you are Lord Hannsley's cousin, aren't you?"

His eyes narrowed, and the awkward smile creased his face again. He nodded.

"I presume you were at my aunt's salon the evening he called me out."

"And yet you are both present here," Valerie said. "Whatever came of the duel?"

His smile vanished. "It is remarkable to meet a lady who does not already know about it. The feminine sex often seems to take such pleasure in gentlemen's violence."

Nausea tickled her stomach.

"I fear I haven't attended carefully to gossip lately." But the hideous image of Lord Hannsley in her dream taunted anew. "Was it a draw?"

The gentleman shook his head.

"Hannsley's grandmother, the duchess, forbade the

duel. Her interference infuriated him, but he retracted the challenge."

"I thought Lord Hannsley was independent." The marquess was one of the wealthiest men in England, and his wealth would only increase once he inherited his grandfather's duchy.

"Hannsley's income is considerable, it's true. But reputation means more to him than money and title combined. If he lost the duchess's favor, the *ton* would invariably cut him." He paused before continuing. "It was fortunate for me she intervened. Clifford is very handy with both sword and pistol." Mr. Flemming's mouth slid into a tight line, as though he wished to end the conversation. Valerie reached for her shawl.

"Will you join the party gathering greenery in the woods this morning, Mr. Flemming?"

"Unfortunately I have business to attend to in the village."

"Then, good day, sir."

He bowed. "Good day, madam."

None of the other guests was abroad yet, and Valerie wandered the castle's empty corridors until she discovered the library. She spent a comfortable hour reading before the others roused, and finally a group set out to brave the cold in search of holly and fir branches.

The outing restored Valerie's spirits and banished the horrid dream from her mind. When the party straggled back into the hall, greenery-laden, smelling of sweet pine and tart spruce, bedecked with the snow now falling in swirling gusts, she felt almost like herself again. The others swiftly shed cloaks and gloves and headed for the drawing room's fire and the lunch laid out there. Valerie lingered in the hall to change her half boots into indoor slippers, appreciating the moment alone as she never would have two years earlier. Anna was right, she had changed in so many ways.

Lady March and Mr. Flemming appeared across the great hall and Valerie went toward them.

"Dearest Lady Valerie, I am so glad you and my nephew became acquainted this morning." The countess placed her hand lightly upon Valerie's cold cheek, and Valerie had the sudden thought that Mr. Flemming must be her godson. How the countess could ever imagine he would compete for any lady's attentions with a man like Timothy Ramsay, Valerie could not imagine. But mothers, even godmothers, were wont to be prejudiced.

"You have clearly been out gathering with the others, despite the snow and wind," Lady March said. "Have they all returned and gone off to the drawing room without you? We will go together and find something to warm you up." She took Valerie's arm and gestured for her nephew to follow.

The doors at the other end of the hall opened in a bluster of cold. A gentleman entered, shrouded in snow blowing in upon the wind. His many-caped greatcoat billowed about him and a footman hurried to shut out the elements.

The countess squeezed Valerie's arm. Mr. Flemming broke from them to move across the hall as the gentleman offered his coat and hat to the waiting footman.

"Ashford, you have finally returned," he said.

The stranger swiveled around, his face lighting into a smile.

"Indeed, I have finally returned." His voice was rich and tempered with the perfectly modulated accents of an English aristocrat. His sunlit gold hair was cropped short and slightly tousled from the curly-brimmed beaver hat he had removed. As he held out his hand for Mr. Flemming to grasp, he moved with the grace of a great cat.

The room spun around Valerie.

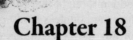

Chapter 18

For an endless moment, only Lady March's arm held Valerie up.

It could not be. It must be some trick of the light, some devilish play of her imagination. She'd heard that everyone had a double somewhere in the world. A perfect twin.

Mr. Flemming stepped back. Lady March laughed warmly as the newcomer turned to her, a smile upon his breathtakingly handsome face.

"Steven, how good of you to come before the snow begins in earnest." Gently, she released Valerie's arm and moved forward. "We were concerned the weather would stall your arrival until after Christmas. But now here you are, safe and sound, just in time to complete our gathering."

"Dearest godmother, I would not have missed joining your party for all the world." His long strides brought him gracefully to the countess. He grasped her hands and kissed her upon both cheeks. Still smiling, she freed a hand and reached back to Valerie.

"Lady Valerie, come meet my godson, Viscount Ashford," she said, taking Valerie's cold fingers and drawing her forward. "Steven, this is Lady Valerie Monroe, sister to the Earl of Alverston."

Perhaps his features arrested for an instant. But when Etienne La Marque's tawny eyes met hers with nothing more than courteous interest upon the surface of their expressive depths, Valerie's heart stopped.

He bowed elegantly. "Your servant, ma'am."

Valerie's heart reeled into life again at the sound of his voice addressing her, the voice she had heard in her memory every day for months, that she thought to never hear again. It sounded as warm and caressing now in impeccable English as it had in his beautiful French.

He raised his golden gaze to her eyes again, and Valerie's throat closed. He filled the silence.

"I am delighted to see, Godmother, that you keep company with ladies whose beauty complements your own so admirably," he said in playful tones, holding Valerie's gaze now with unveiled appreciation. "It says so much for your generosity, not to mention your most suitable self-confidence." He turned to the countess.

Confusion flooded Valerie. *It simply could not be.* This teasing English nobleman could not possibly be the same man whose strong, tranquil gaze had borne her through the worst moments of her life.

Lady March laughed. "Come now, Steven, you will not turn my head with pretty phrases, no matter how successfully you make the young ladies blush." She took Valerie's arm and moved toward the passageway to the drawing room. "Do not pay any attention to him, dear girl. He always had an angel's tongue, and he still insists upon plaguing me with it though he knows I am too old and wise to succumb to his flattery."

"La, Godmother," he said lightly. "You cannot depress

my spirits with your chastisements today. I am home in time for Christmas. I have been storing up my pretty words and good humor for months, and I fully expect to apply them all before this season of joy is over, whether you approve of it or not."

A pair of liveried footmen pulled the drawing room doors open. Lady March turned to her godson, poised to respond, but he bowed, grasped her hand, and raised it to his lips. From beneath snow-sparkled lashes, a mischievous glint lit his golden eyes.

"Of course, I would much rather have your approval," he murmured.

A grin curled the countess's mouth and she pulled her hand away. He released it with an airy sigh.

"Scamp," she said, and turned her attention to making introductions.

Valerie stood frozen in place, her mind awhirl and heart twisting as she watched the man she had dreamed of for six months move about the chamber greeting the other guests. He prettily complimented each young lady, deferred to the older gentlemen, presented a casually comfortable manner to his peers, and gently cosseted the elderly females, while to the matrons he was pleasingly attentive and ever so subtly flattering. Each person he spoke to seemed captivated by the attractive combination of easy manners and excellent breeding he radiated.

He made no effort to speak with Valerie.

By the end of an hour, her stomach burned like a pit of fire, and she did not remember anything anyone said to her. Her mouth was dry, her mind blank with incomprehension.

Cursing herself for weakness, and him for the confusion that tortured her each time she stole a glance at his beautifully unique profile, she finally set down her untasted cup of mulled wine and made her way out into the hall. Cold tingled upon her cheeks. She touched them and her fingers came away damp with tears.

Anger engulfed her, hot and painful. She fled to her bedchamber.

Sitting upon the edge of her bed, tearless, Valerie did not shrug off her anger. She turned it upon herself. She should never have dreamed of him, made him in her imagination some kind of hero. Long ago she had learned no man was that, but still she allowed herself to be a fool for this one.

And what a fool she had been! She believed him to be a Catholic priest, for pity's sake. She even dreamed of returning to America, of searching him out, and—

It did not bear thinking on now.

Of course, he hadn't given her any cause to believe he was not actually a French priest. But some natural feeling should have warned her. She should have known, listened to her desire for him, not to his lies.

But perhaps he was a priest, and a Frenchman as she had thought, his skills at dissembling so accomplished he was able to pass himself off as an English lord. Perhaps he was a spy, and she was the only one clever enough to discern it.

Despite her black humor, the idea made Valerie laugh, but the sound came from her mouth like a consumptive cough. Of course he could not fabricate his relationship with Margaret March. That lady was above reproach. Whoever else he might be, he was undoubtedly the countess's godson.

Whoever else.

Valerie wanted to convince herself he was a double, a twin lost at birth, one raised by English parents, the other by French. A romantic tale, but certainly common enough in lending-library novels.

But his eyes were unique. No other gaze could fill her

with such profound yearning. She longed to believe that for even a fraction of a moment in the great hall she had seen something familiar in them. Even masked in his efforts to charm the Countess of March and her guests, his eyes were the same.

He had lied to her, and his behavior in the hall and later did not encourage Valerie to think he intended to tell her the truth now. He lied to his godmother too. Valerie had seen him riding up behind the house toward the village earlier that morning. She felt him. But he allowed Lady March to believe he had arrived from town just this afternoon.

She released a groan, clutching the bed linens in her fists. Somewhere in the house the others were now busily decorating in holiday spirit. Valerie did not feel a spark of interest in the project. But she took a deep breath, smoothed out the creases in her gown, and walked to the door.

Her maid appeared from the dressing room.

"Miss?" the girl's voice tested. "Won't you have a bite of these biscuits the cook sent up? I am sure they're very tasty, and I expect you haven't eaten a thing since breakfast."

Valerie pasted a smile onto her lips.

"Don't concern yourself with my fidgets, Mabel. I am feeling much better now that I have rested. I see you have fetched tea too. You should enjoy it instead, and the biscuits, if you wish."

"Milady, I've news to tell you. If this is not a good minute for it—"

"Now is as well as any time, Mabel." No news could surprise her now. Or ever again.

"It's probably nothing, milady. While you were out in the woods this morning, I went below to press the silk you'll be wearing this evening. Lady Cassandra's girl was already using the iron, so I came back up in a trice, and there was someone here."

"Oh? Who?"

"I wouldn't trouble you with this if it were the coal maid. But it were Lady March's companion, that Miss Brown. I thought it a little peculiar and all, knowing as upper servants don't usually do little chores about guests' rooms."

"Yes, it is odd that Miss Brown would be here, but I daresay she had some reasonable explanation for it."

The girl nodded. She had clearly given the matter considerable thought, no dull-witted Harriet, this lady's maid.

"I tried to ask her what business she had in your bedchamber, but she stuck up her pointed nose and glided out of here like she was the Duchess of Devonshire. Wouldn't say a plumb word to me."

"I appreciate your concern, but you mustn't speak of Lady March's servant in such a manner." She should reprimand her maid, or at least take interest in Amelia Brown's intrusion into her chamber, but her mind was far too preoccupied. "Thank you for telling me about this, but no doubt Miss Brown was here by accident, or perhaps seeking me out for Lady March." Hollow nausea roiled in her stomach and she pressed a palm to it.

"Please, milady. Have a sippa tea before you go."

A hard smile thinned Valerie's lips.

"I had begun to think, Mabel, that we were well suited for one another. But if you continue to pester me I will be forced to admit that we will not get along, after all."

Valerie left the bedchamber before her smile faded. She would search out the decorating party and distraction. Distraction. Always distraction. And now more than ever, with her head so clouded with confusion she could barely think.

She came to the end of the east wing and passed the

library's closed door. The innocent enjoyment of her early morning hour reading seemed to mock her from within. Resolving to regain that feeling of calm before seeing him again, she reached for the door handle.

A gentleman stood across the chamber facing the window. His stance was rigid, hands clasped behind him. His broad shoulders, narrow hips, and long, muscular legs made a silhouette against the white of the falling snow outside.

Valerie's heart lurched. The shape of his body was as achingly familiar to her as his voice and eyes.

He turned.

"I expected you would find me sooner or later," he said, "although I thought sooner, truth be told. You do have a tenacious nature." He barely glanced at her before turning back to contemplate the curtain of white. His voice was as frosty as the winter scene without, at odds with the charming nonpareil he had played in the drawing room, and at odds with the heat sluicing through Valerie's blood.

She stared at him, openmouthed.

"You expected that I would find you here? You must know that I left the drawing room to escape you."

"Really? How gratifying." He pivoted fully around. "Still, it's not quite the thing for an unmarried lady to be alone with a man like this, and with the door closed." He gestured carelessly.

"Then why did you wait for me here?"

He shrugged, a negligent shift of his elegantly clad shoulders.

"It is your reputation at stake, not mine." He moved toward the fireplace. A blaze threw heat into the chamber, but Valerie did not feel it. Her body had grown numb beneath his cold stare.

"Who are you?" She barely mouthed the words, but he

heard. He bent his graceful form in a deep bow, indolence flowing from the gesture.

"Steven Frederick Ashford, Eighth Viscount Ashford, ma'am. It is a great pleasure to see you again. If I were wearing a hat right now, I would doff it for sure."

He might as well have hit her, in her belly, her chest, her face. She felt as though someone were shaking her awake, but the nightmare would not release her.

"How dare you—"

"Oh, I dare very well, thank you, *mademoiselle. That* is the whole idea." He spoke with silken assurance.

"Why are you speaking to me this way, and to the others as you did before?" she choked out. "What are you doing here?" Her voice halted, sudden clarity skittering through her. With it came memory like a knife's stab.

Steven. Just before he kissed her upon the ship that terrible day, he told her to call him Steven. Mind whirling with confusion, she stared into his mocking eyes, struggling to make sense of what she knew.

"The alias you used . . . Marque," she said, seizing upon the safer thread of memory. "It means brand. Like a slave brand. But why—" She halted, tensing. Without allowing herself to quail, she moved quickly across the chamber. He stood perfectly still as she neared, grasped his wrist, and wrenched back his coat sleeve.

That night when she had awoken to discover him bathing in their cabin prison, she had glimpsed the black mark. Clearly visible now, it slanted across his forearm, burnt into his golden skin. A *fleur-de-lys*.

Shock paralyzed her. Everyone in America knew how French colonial royalists persisted in marking criminals with King Louis's symbol, even years after the Revolution overthrew him. But for an English peer to bear the sign was scandalous.

"Marque," she said, looking up at him. "Like a criminal's brand."

Eyes dark and inscrutable, he drew his arm from her grasp. He stepped away with languid ease.

"Yes, well, you are very clever. Congratulations." He slanted her a derisive look. "But then, you are not the first woman to discover my little secret. Merely the most naïve."

Valerie's hands trembled again as frigid emptiness invaded her. In the months since her return to England, she had believed that her experience aboard the corsair prepared her for any cruelty she might encounter from the *ton*. But the Jesuit's steady, peaceful confidence had been essential to her sense of strength even long after she left America behind. She hadn't known that until now.

Betrayal spiraled through her. She took a step back and breathed in sharply, trying to steady herself. She could play his game. She had played games her entire life with an opponent just as formidable as this man. The difference was that Steven Ashford did not have any control over her life.

"Answer my questions, and I will not come looking for you again."

One brow rose lazily. "What do you wish to know, my lady?" He spoke her title with slight emphasis.

Valerie resisted the shame grabbing at her. "Why are you here? And I will not believe it if you tell me your godmother's gathering alone brings you to Castlemarch."

"Whether or not you believe what I choose to say is of little concern to me." The detached, feline acuteness of his golden eyes glittered in the firelight. Valerie's skin prickled. She had only ever seen him look at Bebain that way.

"I have business matters to arrange," he said. "The people with whom I must negotiate are amongst Lady

March's party and will remain here throughout the holiday, after which I will depart. Next question?"

Valerie hid her fists in her skirts, clenching them to still their quavering.

"You know what my next question is."

He shook his head, the slight, mocking grin slanting his lips again.

"Are you a priest?" she blurted out.

He hesitated. Heart racing, Valerie willed her breaths to come evenly.

His grin hardened. "Not any more than you are, my dear." He fell silent, watching her as the minutes ticked by on the library clock. Finally he drew his gaze away and leaned his broad shoulders against the mantel. Lifting a hand, he polished his manicured fingernails against the lapel of his indigo-blue coat, a coat that fit him to extraordinary perfection.

Valerie's traitorous body quivered with heat that had nothing to do with her consternation and rising anger. She could not look away from him. Her flesh and heart fought to reject what her head was screaming for her to believe, that despite his familiar, handsome face and rich, warm voice, this man was a complete stranger.

She dragged air into her lungs, backing away.

"I suspect I needn't be concerned about the remains of my good reputation," she said. "You clearly have no intention of making our previous acquaintance publicly known."

"Surprisingly perceptive," he drawled. "You outdo yourself, ma'am."

"Stop this! You do not need to play this part with me." It took all her effort to keep her voice steady. But the earl was dead. She would never again allow a man to deal her this kind of cold cruelty. Not even this man. "I am not the imbecile you wish to paint me, for God only knows what reason, to insult or offend me I cannot fathom. I don't know why you bother now, anyway. You have already done so with the mountain of lies you gave me when all I wanted from you was truth."

"Was that all you wanted, dearest Lady Valerie?" His suggestive tone sliced across her distress, the sound of her name upon his tongue twining intimately into her insides. He wanted her to feel ashamed that she had desired him despite his forbidden status.

She clamped down upon her trembling lips and gripped her fists tighter, stilling the tremors through force.

"If you are treating me this way to encourage me to leave Castlemarch, I won't. You cannot make me leave my family and friends."

"Why on earth, ma'am, would I care a fig whether you are here or upon the moon?"

Lead seemed to clog Valerie's ears, her blood running frantically through her veins. She gritted her teeth.

"I don't need this paltry display of contempt to repel me—"

"Paltry? Why, my dear Valerie, now who seeks to insult?"

"Leave me be," she said, ignoring his thespian pout, "and I will leave you to prey upon others more gullible than me. Only hear this, harm my family and I will make you suffer for it ten times greater than that which you have made me suffer."

This time he did not respond. With impenetrable eyes he stared at her, backlit by the fire's licking flames.

Valerie strode to the door. She prayed as she reached for the knob and flew into the corridor that he could not see the trembling finally overtaking her.

Chapter 19

Steven stood immobile long after the door closed. Staring blindly down at the toes of his outrageously expensive Hessians, he saw nothing but Valerie's pale, lovely face. He hadn't thought he could be so successful in hurting her.

He was an actor. He had been one for as long as he could remember, taking on parts to suit the need, like the Jesuit disguise. Wearing the black robe and mantle, he had taken advantage of the missionaries' freedom of movement in the Americas, and the intimacy of priestly ritual helped him learn things other men would never hear. The clerical collar gained him trust.

Trust he rarely deserved.

He had first come upon the Jesuits while searching for his life. Even as a boy he knew the chains of the English aristocracy would prevent him from becoming the man he could be. His impure blood guaranteed society would continually throw up barricades before him. His father's family scorned his mother as a savage, and he had burned to conquer their ignorance. When he finally escaped the stultifying world of the English *beau monde*, he never looked back.

Yet here he was in England, where he never thought to be again.

Peculiarly light in the head, he lifted his gaze, noticing the furnishings of the comfortable chamber for the first time since entering it. Tiring swiftly of his own farce in the drawing room, and with work to do, he had gone in search of paper, pen, and solitude to think. Then she appeared, and Steven realized he hadn't done any planning during his time spent alone, only thinking. Of her.

He could not clear his mind of her ocean-blue eyes filled with accusation and confusion. The fever running through his veins since the moment he saw her in the great hall bore upon him even harder. When she grabbed his arm to reveal the brand, the heat in his blood urged him to respond to the hunger in her gaze, to touch her, to feel her again beneath his hands and mouth, to finally take satisfaction in her and damn the consequences to her and everything he held dear.

The library door cracked open, then closed again with a soft click. Steven's well-trained senses told him who entered without his needing to look.

"Does she suspect?" his godmother asked.

"That I am the greatest scoundrel since Judas Iscariot? Most certainly." He ducked his head. The shine upon his Hessians glinted up at him like silver pieces.

"My dear boy, you know very well that is not what I meant." Lady March glided across the library, the fabric of her gown a breath's rustle as she lowered herself into a chair.

"Godmother." He turned to her. "I regret correcting you, but I feel I must remind you that I am no longer a boy." He had ceased being a boy the moment he left Castlemarch nineteen years earlier.

"You will always be my dear boy, Steven."

"And my godfather will always be your *gallant*, I suppose." He smiled.

"Of course. Now, quit quizzing me and tell me what that lovely girl knows. She is quite lovely and unique. I cannot wonder that you succumbed to her charms. But so it was with your father and mother."

If Steven were a man of less necessary restraint, he might have rolled his eyes. He refrained.

"She knows nothing, of course. She feels betrayed and angry, which should keep her out of my business." Anger would hold her distant. Safe. He counted upon it.

"She is an inquisitive girl, isn't she?" the countess said thoughtfully. "Alistair said she was full of curious questions for him at breakfast this morning."

"No doubt. Her mind is rarely idle. I daresay Alistair acquitted himself impressively, though."

"Mm, yes. My nephew is very clever. Not quite as clever as my godson, though." Lady March's gaze sharpened. "Amelia told me you spoke with her in London."

"Do you mind that I have gone behind your back with your servant?"

The countess's lips pursed. "Of course not. I trust you had your reasons for it, as you do for everything. Otherwise I would not have penned invitations for this gathering to every name upon a guest list with which you provided me without any explanation."

"Now, Godmother, many of them were your recommendations." Steven allowed himself another smile.

"That horrid Bertram Fenton was not my idea. If you are searching for a scoundrel, that lad is an excellent candidate. And there are several other unsavory characters here that the Captain and I would rather not ever have cross the threshold of Castlemarch, including one or two ladies." Her tone suggested she hoped for explanations.

Steven bent and kissed her upon a powder-dusted cheek.

"My dear, you and Godfather are infinitely kind to lend me your home, not to mention your patience, for my little project—"

"Don't start playing your charming games with me, Steven."

"—but do not for an instant imagine that I will tell you more than the very minimum you must know to assist me. If you want to blame someone for my methods, point the finger at my godfather. He set me upon my nefarious path, after all." He turned toward the hearth, placing himself directly before the giant gilt-framed mirror above the mantel. "The individual I wish to deal with is present. I will not say more to you about it unless necessity requires it."

"Was it required, Steven, that you tell me about Lady Valerie being taken aboard your ship, when you might have simply included her upon your guest list without note?"

"And as that mistake has led you to make an extraordinarily inappropriate comment—"

"But not inaccurate, I'll merit."

"—I will not be foolish enough to make such an error again." His voice chastised, but his eyes meeting hers in the mirror revealed a hint of amusement. He cleared his throat. "As I was saying when interrupted by your gracious self, it is my fondest wish to avoid causing you and my godfather distress from my endeavors here. I will see to it that no breath of scandal rests upon your fashionable salon. After all, some of my best operatives come to me through Godfather's and your recommendations."

"Young Machiavelli." Lady March chuckled.

Steven reached into his silk waistcoat pocket and drew out an intricately wrought watch on a chain to check the time against the clock upon the mantel. He slipped it back into place, then glanced up again, arrested by his unfamiliar reflection.

"Hm. How did those boys say it the other day in St. James's?" His lips curved up at one edge. "Bang-up-to-the-nines."

The countess laughed. "Are you admiring your appearance, my dear? I would not have thought it of you, although it is certainly deserved."

Steven turned away from the mirror.

"I am simply appreciating the material advantages of my exalted state. The coat is somewhat tight to suit my tastes." He fingered his high collars and starched cravat. "These monstrosities are ludicrous, but I am glad to be shaved every day and to have my hair cut. Much easier to control the nits, you know."

"Heavens, Steven. Must you?"

He grinned. "I quiz, dear lady. Even in the wilds of America we have bathing water." America had gently bred young ladies too, but he hadn't partaken of them while acting the part of a priest. Except once. One reckless tryst with a willful beauty, and far too brief.

In his new role, of course, he was expected to lavish attention upon aristocratic maidens. In truth, it was all a vast novelty. He had never before been to an event like his godparents' Christmas gathering. Since his accession to the title five years earlier, he had usually been acting the part of a renegade French priest in the Americas. Before that he hadn't been welcome among the *beau monde*. At least his mother had not.

Steven frowned at his newly adopted reflection, running his fingertip over the lid of the gold watch in his pocket carefully monogrammed in a previous century with a scrolling capital A for Ashford, the estate and title that rested so uncomfortably upon his shoulders now after years of pretending it did not exist.

He turned from the mirror.

"My dear godmother, I must now abandon your delightful company and be off to work."

"Of course," came her quick reply.

Steven made his way to the library door.

"By the by, Steven dear, do you plan on interviewing Lady Valerie in private again? I ask, you know, because it is not quite acceptable *ton*. You must realize that, though, don't you? You see, I would not want such a lovely girl to suffer unnecessarily. Society being what it is, one cannot be too careful."

As Steven's hand came to rest upon the bronze knob, he saw again Valerie's straight shoulders and high chin when she left the library. Earlier, in the drawing room, amid people who had once scorned her and confused by his arrival, she still radiated composure and grace. She was remarkable—sharp, proud, with a will of iron, and blindingly desirable. His memory had not mistaken anything in the insufferably slow months since he had seen her last.

He laughed, pretending to make light of his godmother's comment. The sound echoed hollowly.

"No, Godmother. I would never wish the lady to suffer upon my account."

"Your spirits seem improved, Valerie. I'm glad."

Valerie flashed a smile at the Viscount of Bramfield across the tea table.

"Thank you. Yesterday's long journey wore me out." After the horrible conversation in the library she had spent an hour alone in her bedchamber, explaining away her solitude to Anna the same way. Anna looked skeptical. But Valerie had chosen to lie to her family months ago. It wouldn't do any good to tell them the truth now.

Timothy, fortunately, believed her without question. He hadn't any reason not to. For all his appreciative smiles and compliments, he knew very little about her. The *real* Valerie.

"I am pleased the snow did not upset your journey." Her voice was less animated than she liked. She could practice every dissembling art she and her maid knew to appear fresh-eyed and fascinated, but she could not sham enthusiasm. Her heart was far too raw.

Timothy waved his hand in dismissal. "It was minimal until we came close to Castlemarch. Mother and my sister insisted they could not bear being stranded in some dingy inn on the road, condemned to share Christmas dinner with farmers in a taproom. They would have us drive through a blizzard rather than hazard that." He laughed cheerfully. "I would have too."

Valerie forced a smile. Timothy's eyes sparkled with admiration as she leaned forward to pour out tea.

Looking well on the outside hadn't helped the confused misery of her insides during dinner either. She had chatted and laughed her way through the living hell of remove after remove of delicacies, but now she barely remembered the faces of her dinner partners. Every fiber of her attention was wrapped around the Viscount of Ashford flirting with the women to either side of him. When the ladies had retired to the drawing room for Christmas carols on the pianoforte, Valerie breathed a lungful of relief. After taking port, a handful of gentlemen joined the ladies. The others had gone off to the billiards room, the Viscount of Ashford, apparently, along with them.

Timothy, of course, had instantly sought her out. Offering him a cup now, Valerie watched him from beneath lowered lashes.

Anna's wisdom reigned upon so many matters. Timothy Ramsay had become an attractive, decent man, a far cry from the rowdy youth Valerie had known years earlier. Tonight he seemed infinitely dear. He was uncomplicated, and he had been a loyal friend since her return from America. She cared for him.

"Have you yet had opportunity to tour the gallery, my lord?"

His gaze met hers with frank surprise. "Not in the four hours since I have been here. But I would be very glad now to see the old curmudgeons of March ancestry, if you will show them to me."

Valerie took the arm he offered, and as they left the drawing room he chatted lightly. She barely attended. By the time they reached the long gallery, lit dimly by wall sconces, she was regretting her invitation. The way she felt tonight, it seemed too much like a test, of Timothy or herself, she could not be certain.

He drew the door closed and joined her in the narrow, high-ceilinged chamber.

"Quite a few of these Marches, aren't there?" he remarked. "Look at this fellow, in his helmet and gauntlets. Why, he looks like he goes right back to when the Picts painted themselves blue and the Scots didn't yet know Latin."

She tried to laugh, but couldn't manage it. Gripping her fingers tight in her skirt, she searched inside herself for signs of stirring nerves. Candlelight flickered off mirrors placed at intervals between paintings. It was the perfect setting, dimly lit, sparkling, private.

She felt nothing.

Timothy placed his hands upon her waist. His mouth touched hers, then pressed closer as she accepted his advance. The kiss lasted a few moments, allowing Valerie time to feel his firm shoulders beneath her hands and take in his sandalwood and wool fragrance before he released her.

She stepped back. He drew in a deep breath before speaking.

"Valerie, you are uncertain of your feelings for me."

She stiffened, but he continued in an unusually sober voice.

"You know my feelings for you. I assure you, I will not demand of you similar sentiments at this early date. It would not be honorable of me, given the difficult few years you have been through." He took her hand, and his amiable blue eyes creased at the corners. "I am happy to wait for your return of my affections with hope." His mouth relaxed into a light smile. "You will not, I trust, make that wait too difficult for me?" His fingers tightened.

Eyes widening, Valerie tugged her hand free. She never thought of Timothy that way. But he was a man, with a man's desires. She simply did not reciprocate them. Instead, she felt them for someone else, a lying, wicked, confusing man she merely had to glance at to grow weak with longing. Guilt churned in her stomach.

Timothy chuckled and reached for her fingers again, trapping them in the crook of his arm as he led her back to the gallery doors.

"Do not fret, dear Valerie. I am well accustomed to waiting. I will not fall to pieces at the slightest touch of your lovely hand." They exited the gallery into the corridor toward the drawing room.

"Then you are a damned fool," Steven said into the stillness of the empty gallery. Stepping from the shadow cast by a mounted marble bust of some long-dead and best-forgotten Roman consul, he watched the pair disappear down the corridor and released a breath. It was almost ten o'clock. His informant would arrive at any moment.

He paced the length of the chamber, not bothering to glance at the dark portraits to either side.

She had invited her suitor to the gallery. That much was clear from her unusual coyness, Bramfield's easy manner, and his quick action. But she had kissed him without enthusiasm. Steven hated that he was actually savoring his satisfaction.

The Viscount of Bramfield was a well-favored, well-heeled, and well-liked fellow. He was also her brother's closest friend, and apparently had courted Valerie for months. Steven had learned all of this since witnessing their warm reunion in the drawing room before dinner. She was a fool not to respond to the fellow's suit. And Bramfield was doubly a fool if he did not make that beautiful woman his as soon as she would have him.

No. Tonight she was not merely beautiful. She was breathtaking, more vibrant and sparkling than Steven thought possible for mortal woman to be. And she had offered herself to Bramfield upon a plate.

Steven tugged at his high-pointed collar, the skintight coat his valet had buttoned him into constricting his chest. He couldn't blame his discomfort on clothing, though. He knew the name of the biggest fool at Castlemarch, and it wasn't Bramfield. The fellow might be an amiable dupe, but he was a careful one.

Taking another deep breath to clear his head, Steven saw a servant's door open at the end of the chamber. Moving forward in the dimness, he went to work.

Chapter 20

Valerie waited impatiently, kneeling in the snow while her brother tied the steel blades onto her half boots.

"You are coddling me. I am perfectly able to do this myself," she said, gazing over the treetops around the lake to the blue sky. Surrounded by tall, snow-bedecked pines, willows and nut trees, the broad expanse of frozen lake sparkled and the air smelled of fresh, sharp snow.

"Let a fellow coddle," Valentine said, climbing to his feet and casting a glance at his wife donning her skates. "God knows you've had little of it in your lifetime."

Valerie's throat tightened. "Oh, pish," she mumbled, and moved away. Valentine and Anna were looking at each other again in that knowing way. She didn't want any part of it. Their love was everything to her now, but she wished they would not worry. If they looked too closely, they might see something she did not wish to reveal.

Servants had swept the ice, laying out rugs along the sloping bank, arranging benches and lighting fires to warm spiced wine and cider. Privately, Valerie thought the advance preparation was a travesty, like a pretty girl using stays to enhance her figure. But the sensation of her body moving free and swift as she set out across the lake made her smile for the first time in days.

"This is the most perfect Christmas I have ever enjoyed," Alethea Pierce breathed as she approached. "The scenery is perfect, Castlemarch is perfect, the festivities are perfect." She glanced at Valerie with a playful look. "The gentlemen are perfect."

Behind them, young, flaxen-haired Lady Cassandra Fredericks giggled.

"I agree." She took Alethea's arm. "Are there always so many unmarried gentlemen present at house parties of this size? If so, I will ask Papa to bring me to many more."

Alethea laughed, but Valerie only shrugged. She hadn't really noticed the gentlemen at Castlemarch. Except one. And her brother, of course, but he did not count.

Familiar guilt prickled at her as she glimpsed Timothy at the edge of the lake. He did count, however. At least he was supposed to.

"Mr. Fenton is heavenly, isn't he?" Alethea said upon another sigh as their skates furrowed a path around the edge of the lake, away from the other guests. "And I nearly swoon every time Lord Michaels walks into the room."

"Your brother is absolutely delectable, Lady Valerie."

Valerie started at the sound of the throaty voice. Sylvia Sinclaire skated forward to join their group.

"But, of course, he is already claimed. What a pity." The girl turned her golden head to glance at the Earl and Countess of Alverston. A few locks of shining hair spilled around the edges of her hood.

"It is improper for you to say such a thing, Sylvia," Cassandra chided softly, glancing at Valerie.

"But accurate," Sylvia replied with a wide, thin smile.

Valerie knew that look. She had once been foolish enough to play at being wicked as Sylvia did now, before she had seen the face of true wickedness.

Alethea's grip upon Valerie's arm tightened. "Look. There is Lord Ashford. He skates as divinely as he flirts."

Valerie's heart turned over. She followed Alethea's gaze. Not far ahead, he skated figure eights with the nursery boys and girls, their maids watching attentively from the bank. Like mice to the piper, three boys followed his lead, trying to copy his movements. One of the girls practiced the lesson too, while others moved around the group coyly, calling out praise and casting shy smiles.

"Ah, the most mysteriously delicious man of the lot," Sylvia purred. "Isn't he magnificent, Lady Valerie? And all the more so since it is rumored he spent most of his life in the wilds of America."

Valerie's spine stiffened. She must accustom herself to this sort of thing, at least for as long as he remained in society. But something foolish and weak inside her wanted to keep him secret, to believe he was her dream, a memory that tarts like Sylvia Sinclaire could not share.

That dream, of course, had nothing to do with the man now present at Lady March's skating party.

"He is certainly handsome," she replied, keeping her voice even with effort, "and an excellent skater."

"I wish I were still in the nursery," Cassandra giggled into her gloves.

Sylvia grunted her contempt and headed toward the viscount and his youthful admirers.

"Forward baggage," Alethea muttered as the beauty arrested Ashford with a delicately gloved hand upon his shoulder. Stomach tightening, Valerie turned away. He was not her secret. Not even her dream. She did not know this man. She never had.

They had already far outstripped the other guests. Back at the other side of the lake, chilled skaters clustered by the fire. Accompanied by chaperones and gentlemen escorts, a handful of ladies pirouetted demurely about the carefully swept ice near the bank.

Valerie's eyes narrowed. Sylvia Sinclaire might be a forward baggage, but she did not own a monopoly on provocative behavior. Valerie could still defy convention, if somewhat more gracefully than before.

"I'm off for a little skate, ladies," she said to Alethea and Cassandra, and without another backward glance pressed her blades to the ice. The wind snapped at her cheeks and her fur-lined hood as she pushed out onto the open field of snow. Lengthening her stride, frigid air hissing against her chest in enlivening eddies, she was almost able to forget her aching heart for a minute. Immersed in the sparkling cold, the heartbreak of Etienne La Marque's sudden appearance at Castlemarch seemed less catastrophically painful.

Lost in her thoughts as she made the final, arcing turn of the lake to rejoin her friends, she didn't notice the alarm written upon Alethea's distant face until the moment just before the collision.

Valerie's breath exploded from her lungs and she lurched forward. Instinctively she threw her arms wide, her skates sliding out from under her, the cold, hard ice rising swiftly.

Strong arms seized her beneath the shoulders and hauled her upward, turning her in the direction of her scrabbling feet. Clutching on to the support, Valerie jerked up her chin and came nose to nose with the Viscount of Ashford.

She could not have been more closely pressed to him.
But not even the embraces they had shared aboard ship
had revealed to her what the vibrant, frozen brilliance of
the day did now. His golden eyes shone bright, his sculpted
cheeks flushed from cold, and his mouth, nearly hidden
by the crimson muffler wrapped about his neck, curved
wide in surprised laughter. He radiated beauty and joy so
intense it sucked Valerie's breath. She lost herself, sinking into the tangled warmth that connected them, that had
since the moment they met.

For a suspended moment, he held her against him, still
and silent, gazing down at her. In the sliver of space between them, their plumed breaths mingled.

"My lady." The words sounded husky in his throat.

Valerie's limbs went weak.

Abruptly, his smile vanished and he released her. She
wavered and slipped, nearly tumbling to the ice before
she righted herself.

"I beg your pardon, ma'am," he said contritely, backing away and bowing with a flourish. "I was moving too
quickly and not attending to my direction. It was terribly unsportsmanlike of me. Please accept my sincerest
apology."

Fighting for breath, Valerie watched, stunned at his instant transformation as he bent and picked her fur muff
from the ice. He dusted it off and made a gallant show of
proffering it to her. She heard the approach of others, and
her heart constricted. He meant this show for their audience. Another act. Another deceit.

She snatched her muff from him and turned away.

"Think nothing of it, my lord. It is already forgotten."
Her frosted words crackled in the air. She hoped he took
their double meaning. Heart pounding, she set her skate
to move away. Then, despite a voice inside warning her
not to, she glanced back.

He stood motionless, staring at her, lion eyes blazing with heat to melt the ice beneath them.

In an instant, the look disappeared. He laughed lightly and headed toward the far edge of the lake.

Throat constricting, Valerie turned to Alethea and Cassandra. Timothy followed, smiling. They reached the bank, and Timothy offered to help Valerie and her friends remove their skates. She declined, finishing the task herself, willing her heart to beat evenly, her thoughts to calm. Timothy knelt at Cassandra's feet, the girl's hand resting lightly upon his shoulder as he unfastened the blades from her stylish boots.

Valerie stood up, her gaze slipping away from the intimate tableau to the other guests gathered near the fire, then to the figures coming off the ice.

Far across the lake, the last skater made his unhurried return. He moved gracefully, his body as beautiful as his face, strong and powerful enough to save her from falling to the ice moments earlier. The same as when he had held her intimately, his muscle and sinew pressed to hers, the heat of his desire for her unconcealed. She watched him now, her skin tingling where he had touched her aboard ship, and the fire his burning gaze kindled inside her grew.

"You admire Ashford's style upon the ice, my lady?"

Mr. Flemming's voice startled her out of memory. Out of unwise reverie.

"He is a man of many talents," he continued without waiting for a reply, "and polished at all of them." His eyes seemed oddly intense though his lips smiled. "When we were children, I used to envy him for his looks and charm. I was jealous of his ability to do everything he wished with ease and aplomb. But we were just boys then, and I suppose envy is always a part of growing up, isn't it?"

Valerie's brow creased. "Perhaps."

"But not you, Lady Valerie. I suspect you never envied others, did you? Of what, after all, could you have been envious?" His flattering tone rang false.

"None of us were perfect children, Mr. Flemming. Especially not me."

"But perfection is in the eye of the beholder."

"Sir, you flatter me." Prickling heat crept across Valerie's shoulders. Mr. Flemming was too intense. Too unhappy, Valerie realized abruptly.

"A beautiful lady deserves flattery."

"But we were speaking of character attributes, sir, not appearance."

"And appearances can so easily deceive." His glance flickered to the ice again. "In your case, however, I suspect loveliness is more than skin deep."

"Thank you," she said, anxious to finish the conversation. "I wish, though, that my boots were as warm as they appeared."

Mr. Flemming smiled, seeming to shake off his pensive humor. "Shall we join the others returning to the house, and to less superficial warmth, my lady?"

Valerie nodded, twining the laces of her skates around her gloved hand and turning her back upon the lake. Upon a breathtaking man and futile memories.

Chapter 21

S wiping flour from her cheek with a sticky hand, Valerie suspected there must be a tidier way to avoid the Viscount of Ashford.

Her gaze traveled around the kitchen, taking in the table spread with sugar, egg whites, spoons, cups, flour, molasses, and mounds of biscuit dough; two squabbling children; Cook's toothy smile and brawny arms; and the pair of turtledoves tucked at the table's far corner.

Lord Michaels and Alethea Pierce seemed to have entirely forgotten that they simply adored making holiday biscuits. At least they had insisted that while trying to convince Valerie to join them and the pair of children for the task. Now they seemed much more interested in flirting than baking.

Valerie grinned ruefully. She'd gone along with them even guessing how it would be, certain that at least here she would not encounter the erstwhile French priest. After only two days sharing the vast estate with Steven

Ashford, she was beginning to think even Castlemarch not large enough to insulate her from the effects of his charming and much sought-after presence.

A war raged inside her. She feared seeing him, yet she longed to. She could not entirely avoid him, of course. The party gathered for dinner each evening, and other entertainments drew them all together, like the ice skating outing the day before. Recalling how his eyes had shone as he held her briefly on the ice, and his beautiful smile, weakened Valerie with yearning.

But he clearly did not want to be with her, and she refused to give him the satisfaction of knowing he disturbed her.

Swallowing a sigh, Valerie pulled her hands from the sticky dough and tucked an errant lock behind her ear. She glanced at Alethea, shoulder to shoulder with Lord Michaels and chuckling at some witticism the baron uttered. Valerie smiled. How lovely it would be to have an innocent flirtation like that with a kind, sincere gentleman.

Of course, she had thought Etienne La Marque was that sort of man. He felt like the same man. When she had touched him in the library, she touched the same delicious, warm, strong man she knew aboard ship. He hadn't spoken a word, remaining perfectly still, as though the contact affected him the same way it did her. Then on the ice, that could not have been an act. His pleasure had seemed so real, his reaction so unguarded at first. And his eyes . . .

Valerie rested her chin upon a doughy hand and drew in a long breath of warm, sweet, nutmeg-scented air. Distractedly, her gaze slid to the pair of children across the table, covered up to their elbows in flour.

"I have baked ginger men before, Cook," Beatrice Sinclaire insisted, her soft brown gaze resting seriously upon the woman. "I did so last Christmas with my sister Georgianna, so I know that Guy is incorrect. It does not require quite this much flour to roll out ginger men."

Guy Fredericks's tongue shot out from between his pouting lips so quickly Valerie giggled, surprised at how good it felt. She hadn't laughed since the day the Viscount of Ashford arrived at Castlemarch.

Cook's bracing arms, bared and floured, rolled the pin back and forth across the dough with unflappable ease.

"Master Guy, listen to your elders like a good boy and don't argue matters you know nothing about."

Beatrice was nodding in sage accord when a mist of flour settled upon her shoulders like Christmas snow. Guy's hand was sunk deep in the flour bin.

"Guy Fredericks, you little monster," the girl uttered. "Don't you dare—"

Flour flew in every direction. Valerie laughed as her gown and hair rapidly became a powdered mess and Cook scolded.

Abruptly, Valerie's neck and shoulders grew warm. Her breath caught. Only one thing had ever caused her that animal premonition. One person. Her gaze darted to the kitchen door and her stomach tumbled over.

"Ashford, have you come to help us make biscuits?" Lord Michaels greeted the viscount.

"It appears you have much more appealing assistance than I could ever hope to be," the viscount responded from the doorway, casting an appreciative glance at the baron's pretty companion. Alethea's cheeks turned pink. Valerie nearly choked upon the hard shaft of jealousy that sliced through her.

"Thank you, my lord," Alethea said with a lovely smile.

Valerie scowled. She did not wish to feel jealous of her friends. The viscount's amber gaze shifted to her, lit with unfeigned pleasure. Valerie's frown faded, her entire body flushing with heat.

"Dearest Cook," he said, turning to the kitchen's mistress and bowing with a flourish. "My godmother sent me here in search of chamomile flowers. I am terribly sorry to interrupt your, ah—undertaking, as it were. But what clever little men you are contriving, Miss Beatrice, Master Guy." He bowed to the children, a twinkle in his golden eyes.

Valerie could not breathe.

"It's over in the pantry, milord," Cook said. "The scullery maid will fetch it for you. Penny!" she bellowed.

A smocked girl peeked out from a doorway and bobbed the viscount a quick curtsy. He smiled.

"Thank you, Penny," he said gently. "I appreciate your assistance, and so will your mistress."

He turned to Valerie again, and his gaze glowed with amusement as it passed over her whitened coiffure. Then a glint of hardness appeared in it.

"My lady." He bowed to her. "You appear to great advantage in the style of our grandparents. It needs only a velvet patch upon your cheek to complete the image." He put a hand to his chin, seeming to study her, but his eyes glittered flinty. "It's too bad my godmother has not planned a masquerade ball for a sennight hence, rather than the simple fête she intends. You would have your costume at the ready." His words played, but his tone mocked.

Valerie's insides ached. She dragged her gaze to the children.

"If there is a masquerade, my lord, I daresay you will have the best costume. Beatrice, let me have that shape and we will show Master Guy how a man really ought to be cut."

Ashford's low, alluring chuckle tangled in Valerie's senses like new wine, sending heat through her again, this time focused beneath her tight belly. Where he had once touched her. Where he had been inside her. Her cheeks warmed. From the corner of her eye she saw him advance into the kitchen, gracefully nonchalant.

"Indeed, my lady, I do not wish to interrupt your creative project. Though, from all reports, God dealt more mercifully with his clay than you with your flour and molasses." Steven lifted a brow.

"Ashford," Lord Michaels said through a mouthful of biscuit. "Have you heard? March is making up a tourney for us tomorrow."

"Ah. Saber or épée?" Steven chose a biscuit from a tray, hoping he would not actually be required to eat it in order to remain in the kitchen for another few minutes. Little Guy Fredericks's hands were deep in the dough, and his nose was dripping fiercely. But Steven could not leave just yet. Walking into the chamber was like walking into a dream. Valerie's shining hair, dusted with flour, tumbled from its pins. Dough smudged her cheeks and gown, and her face was lit with laughter. She truly was not mortal. Rather, a goddess.

He lifted the biscuit toward his mouth.

"Épée," Michaels replied. "March is fixing the roster now. Will you have a go at it with me?"

Steven grinned at the eager young nobleman. "The books at Brooke's and Waiter's account you the best swordsman in London."

"Not at White's? I suppose Hannsley has that honor, the old stiff rump."

Miss Pierce giggled. Michaels cast the girl a pleased look. Steven felt Valerie's gaze upon him like a caress.

"Whatever the case may be"—he gestured with the ginger man—"you are a renowned blade. Why would I voluntarily place myself at your mercy?" The heat upon his skin where Valerie stared at him sank deeper. If he allowed himself to look, her eyes would be luminous sapphires full of question and rebuke.

"Oh, well," Michaels demurred with a grin. "You've practiced sword craft with masters all over the world. A man like you is bound to have secrets none of us here know about."

The baron's words seemed to echo through the kitchen chamber. Steven had to look at her. He simply could not resist.

Her sea-blue eyes did not question, no hint of censure coloring them. Instead they sparkled, radiant with heat, and perfectly aware.

He had to leave. Or eat the blasted biscuit.

"How have the ginger men turned out, my lord?" she asked, her voice deceptively light.

He allowed himself a smile. But he played with fire. He had to leave more than the kitchen. He should leave Castlemarch. He should complete his business and get as far away from Valerie Monroe as possible. He wanted it to be a game with her, a game they both won. But it could never be. Her gaze laughed and sought, a miracle by all accounts considering how he had treated her. But she could face real danger if the smallest detail of his plan went awry, if his enemy merely suspected her involvement, even as slight and unbeknownst to her as it was.

Steven simply could not allow that. He had spent nearly his entire life saving people he did not even know. He could not bear it if, because of him, harm came to the one he—

The one.

His heart stilled, his breath failing as he looked into her shining eyes. He placed the biscuit upon the table.

"If you seek a partner, Michaels, I am honored to

oblige," he said, turning toward the door as Penny appeared from the pantry, tin in hand. He smiled, bowed, and took it from her. "Only avoid killing me by accident, will you?" he added over his shoulder, struggling not to look at Valerie again. "I have a strong desire to continue living."

More and more each day.

Valerie escaped. It was cowardly and not at all like her. But the encounter in the kitchen had nearly undone her. Lord Michaels made that comment about secrets, and she practically choked upon her elation.

He was still her secret. He knew it too. His eyes told her. At the very moment his cold foolery surfaced and she rushed to harden herself to it, he looked at her so directly, his amber gaze warm with meaning and shared memory, and Valerie had felt like singing.

But he was a liar, he hurt her intentionally, and she betrayed all her convictions when she let herself feel something other than indifference for him. It was all far too confusing and raw. She could not bear another encounter like that in one day.

Eschewing luncheon, she dragged her maid from a cozy gossip above stairs, tied on the new half boots she had bought in London, and set out on the long wooded walk to the village. By the time they arrived, her toes ached and her heels sported blisters from the stiff shoes. But the winter sun shone warm on the soggy high street as she limped along. It could be worse. Steven Ashford could still be casting her expressive, bewildering glances.

A mounted party clattered onto the high street. Valerie turned toward it and her stomach flopped over. Grabbing Mabel's arm, she pulled her into the nearest shop.

"Are we purchasing chocolates today, milady?"

"Hush, Mabel." Valerie drew her maid to the back of the confectioner's shop. She smiled at the proprietor and pretended to admire the colorful displays. But her attention fixed upon the front window.

The party from the castle dismounted directly across the street. Viscount Ashford, with Mr. Flemming at his side, encouraged their companions to walk on ahead. The two men moved close to each other, a quick change coming over each as they spoke. As Mr. Flemming's stance grew stiffer and his mouth moved more quickly, the viscount seemed to relax. Finally Flemming's face reddened and his fists clenched at his sides. He pivoted away and strode across the narrow street toward the tavern.

Ashford turned toward the confectioner's window. Valerie darted deeper into the shop. Peeking around a display of Christmas marzipan, she waited until he sauntered out of sight. Then she hurried Mabel down to the church. A squat little Norman construction, barrel vaulted, silent as a tomb, and smelling of beeswax, it seemed the safest hiding place. Valerie took a seat in a wooden pew with Mabel at her side, and sat stunned and slightly trembling, the irony of hiding in a church from a man who pretended to be a priest not lost upon her.

When she finally felt certain the party from the castle must have left the village, she woke Mabel. They set out toward home, Valerie hobbling down the path through the woods, their boots crunching upon the thin layer of snow atop musty needles of pine and spruce.

"I didn't mind visiting the church, milady," Mabel covering a yawn, "though we stayed quite a lo didn't we?" She cast Valerie a curious look.

Valerie pursed her lips. "You are imper Probably the reason they suited.

"Yes, mum," the girl said lightly.

Valerie allowed herself a smile and relaxed her brow.

"You will not convince me our stop in the chocolatier's disappointed you."

Mabel bobbed a curtsy in mid-stride. "That Mr. Flemming, he is a queer fish, though, isn't he? What d'you think he and milord Ashford were arguing about?"

"I am sure it is none of our concern." Valerie's tone lacked conviction. She'd spent the entire time at the church wondering the same thing. Ashford and Flemming were childhood friends, raised nearly as brothers. But Flemming's animosity had seemed so strong just now, and his bitter words about his old friend during the skating party came back to her.

Laughter and hoofbeats resounded through the woods behind. Valerie moved to the side of the path, heart racing as a half-dozen horses cantered into view around a bend in the wide path. In the lead, Alethea's father was the first to see her and Mabel. He reined in his mount.

"Good afternoon, Lady Valerie," he greeted as the others slowed to a halt in his wake. "We have just been to the village to complete our gift gathering."

Beside him, Cassandra gave Valerie a gentle smile. Her pale pink skirts flowed gracefully over her mare's haunches.

"I wish you had been with us, Valerie. Alethea refused to give me her opinion on the ribbons I found for Anna. I know you would not have been so stingy."

Alethea cast an arch look at Cassandra as she pulled up, reaching out a hand to clasp Valerie's.

"Fortunately your brother happened into the shop while we were there, and he was happy to help. It seems the sunshine has driven everyone to the village today. Why didn't we see you?"

Perhaps the lady had your gift in hand when we arrived, Miss Pierce." Viscount Ashford's voice sounded smooth from atop his rangy bay. His gaze narrowed. "I suspect she hid so that you would not discover the chocolates she purchased on your behalf."

Alethea laughed, but Valerie knew why he said it. He wanted her to know he had seen her watching his conversation with Mr. Flemming. He enjoyed taunting her, making her feel uncomfortable around her friends. He wanted her to be unhappy. She stroked the horse's neck to steady her nerves.

"You have ruined my surprise, my lord. Now I must eat the chocolates myself and contrive something else for my friend."

"Oh, don't, Valerie," Alethea exclaimed, "or I will never forgive you or Lord Ashford." Her horse danced atop the white-powdered needles.

"Daughter," Mr. Pierce chided, "if you do not take care, that animal will have your neck, and Lady Valerie's as well."

"Yes, yes," Valerie said in relief. "You should not remain here any longer upon my account."

Mr. Pierce nodded and spurred his mount ahead. Alethea and Cassandra waved as Lord Michaels and Mr. Fenton urged them forward, tipping their hats to Valerie. Only the Viscount of Ashford remained. His mount stood tranquilly, taking cue from his master's calm.

Valerie returned his stare coolly. She'd frozen her bottom and sore feet hiding in the church, but she was through with that. The recollection of Mr. Flemming's anger sparked hers again. How this man treated her, or what he thought about her, or even what they had shared were all inconsequential. He had hurt her intentionally, just as he continued to try hurting her. It didn't matter that for a moment in the kitchen Valerie thought she spied something familiar, something of the man he had revealed aboard ship. If given the opportunity he would be cruel again.

She simply would not allow him that. She dug her hands into the sleeves of her cloak and squared her shoulders.

"Why don't you go as well?"

His mouth lifted at one side, nearly undoing her brittle composure. "So direct."

She took a hard breath and set off up the path. The horse fell in beside her.

"How did you like the church, my lady? Were you suitably impressed with its eleventh-century pilings and gallicized vaults?"

He wanted to put her off guard again by telling her he knew she had hidden from him. Despite what he'd said in the library about not caring what she did, her confusion pleased him. Dull anguish bloomed in Valerie's belly, fanning her anger.

"I was impressed," she clipped. "The French had a way with beauty and elegance." She paused. "At one time."

"I have no such loyalties, Valerie. You have missed your mark."

Sweet tension rippled through her. He said her name as he used to on board ship, with French intonation, smooth and intimate.

"If you intended that as a pun," she managed, "it was poorly done."

"I am almost ashamed I did not."

"Do you also not intend to plague me? If so, you should be ashamed at your failure at that too."

"Plague you? Why, that sounds positively medieval."

Valerie couldn't bear it any longer. She did not wish to trade mild insults with this man, not for another minute and certainly not for another fortnight. She wanted nothing from him.

No. Now she lied to herself. She wanted everything.

She halted, wincing as her boots pinched. He drew his horse to a halt.

"Why don't you hurry along?" she demanded. "You are not wanted here, and you will lose the way home if you do not keep up with your party."

"It is unlikely. I misspent the better part of my childhood in this wood, you know."

"How on earth could I know that? You haven't told me a jot of truth about yourself since the moment we met. You are probably lying now."

"Nonetheless, I appreciate your concern for my welfare," he continued as though she hadn't spoken. "But the others are more likely to miss you than me. I would be nobler to loan you my mount for the return."

"Oh, no, my lord." The words formed themselves upon her tongue without effort. "Nothing could possibly succeed at ennobling you, whatever exalted title you bear."

His gaze hardened. Valerie's breath failed. Alarm wrapped around her.

"Now whose gibe is poorly executed?" His voice pitched low.

"Does it bother you to have your noble worth challenged?" she said, grasping at words as a buffer from the cold seeping into her veins. "You didn't seem to have a care for it last summer."

"I hadn't a care for much of anything then."

Valerie gasped, but she bit back her protest. He had cared for her. She had seen it in the priest's compassionate gaze, felt it in his touch, and again in the kitchen, the something that kept her dwelling upon him. Rage boiled beneath her skin, directed at herself now for wanting him despite his heartlessness.

"Leave me be." She turned and set off swiftly along the path.

"Mabel? That is your name, isn't it?"

Valerie swung around. He had dismounted and approached her maid. Mabel curtsied. Beneath the force of the nobleman's golden gaze, the girl seemed speechless.

"Mabel, dear girl," he said, taking her hands and pressing an object into them. "Be your mistress's and my own greatest friend and allow us some distance to speak privately. Do not, however, take your eyes off her." He smiled conspiratorially. "A gentleman needs a chaperone when in the presence of such a beautiful lady."

Valerie watched dumbstruck as Mabel curtsied again, grinned at the coin in her palm, and walked in the direction of the village a dozen yards.

She rounded upon him. "What do you hope to accomplish with this?" Her heart raced as he moved toward her.

"I hope to encourage you to accept the offer of my mount," he said, drawing the horse forward. He glanced at her feet, hidden beneath the hem of her gown. "You seem uncomfortable."

Valerie's heart turned over.

"Thank you for your inelegant concern, but a few blisters will not kill me," she said, infuriated at how shaky her voice sounded. "My God, you must think I am an absolute fool. Oh, how stupid of me. I know you think I am a fool. You have already made that clear."

"Valerie."

"Don't say my name." She shuddered. It was too achingly familiar. "You have not earned the privilege."

"Then what should I call you? 'My lady' suits every woman in that drawing room. It is common." His golden eyes shone bright and sharp. She didn't understand his meaning. He narrowed the space between them and Valerie sensed his heat, his scent, everything she had longed for, for so many months.

"What are you doing?" She should move away. "What is this game you are playing now? Is it new, or simply part of the old game, more deceit and pretense?"

She gasped as he slipped his hands beneath her cloak and around her waist. Ready for her body's trembling betrayal, she did not anticipate her heart's tight lurch. His hands upon her felt like heaven. Like coming home.

"No pretense," he said, his grip firm. "Only what I have said very clearly." In one smooth movement he lifted her onto his horse's back. Valerie wavered, then grabbed onto the beast's mane. His hands dropped from her waist and he moved to his mount's head.

"Tristan is not a pretty fellow, but he is gentle. He will treat you well." He extended the reins to her.

Valerie stared, bewildered. No emotion colored the man's amber eyes, nothing she could read or understand, not even mockery. He had shuttered his thoughts.

She grabbed up the leather straps and gripped the saddle bow. He curved his gloved fingers around the horse's bridle ring and started them down the path. The animal's gait proved smooth, like his master's lies. Silence filled the chilly air, disturbed only by the sounds of boots and hooves upon the hard path and the calls of winter birds, the air crisp with pine and sun.

"You hurt me." The words popped through her lips.

"Your defenses were inadequate." He did not turn, his shoulders rigid.

"I never thought I would need any."

"Ever the excuse of the aggressor."

Valerie's insides quavered. Why had she told him the painful truth? He must know it already.

"I was frightened."

"I would wager gold upon the certainty, madam, that you have not been frightened a day in your life."

Valerie could insist that she had been consumed with fear every moment aboard ship. But it would be a lie as bold as his. She had not been frightened with him.

"You let me believe a lie," she persisted. "You knew I was torn with guilt."

He turned, drawing the horse to a halt. His eyes shone like polished crystal.

"I had no idea of your guilt, only your opportunism. As that was—by your own admission—your usual style of action, I didn't pay it any attention."

Valerie couldn't breathe, and she could not believe her foolishness. She was still searching for the man she knew briefly at sea, hoping and yearning for him. But this man with the cold eyes and sharp tongue was a stranger. She released the saddle and pushed herself off the horse's back. Ashford moved swiftly and his hands cinched around her waist as she dropped.

"You have nearly a mile to walk to the castle yet," he said. "You do not appreciate my gallantry with sufficient grace, I think." His hold upon her tightened. Valerie's body flooded with heat. His strength and rigid reserve burned into her through his touch.

"Take your hands off me," she said, her words coming out like a breath. "Take them off now."

His beautiful lips curved up at one edge. Mocking again, it seemed, but she stood too close to be certain, to even think. He did not release her.

"Why are you taunting me?" She tried to make her voice firm, but inside she foundered. If he asked, she would give herself to him, however he wanted her and for however long, let her reputation be damned a final, irredeemable time. She had wanted him for so many months, yearned for him when she thought she could not have him. Now her need was beyond measure.

"What do you hope to gain from this?" she said in a strangled whisper, tears prickling in her throat.

Slowly the hardness slid away from his eyes, replaced by something else, something familiar. Warm, deep, and real. Valerie's universe stilled.

"You are the same man."

Steven slipped his hand up along the gentle slope of Valerie's waist. Her sigh mingled with the whirlwind in his head, telling him to take her now, to answer the hunger in her sea-clouded eyes.

He wanted to. Dear God, how he wanted her, far more than he had wanted any woman. Just as he wanted her while aboard his ship, from the first moment he saw her, with a yearning greater than physical need. It had only grown with each encounter, her sincerity and passion for life delving into him like dagger thrusts.

He trailed his hand along her neck, reveling in the sweet curves of her body as he cupped her lovely face. Her lips parted, exquisite. He could already taste her, remembering her flavor and the eager caress of her mouth so well. For six months he had dreamed of kissing her again, this time to feel her mouth upon his body, to fall deep into her ocean eyes and allow himself to remain there.

He brushed his thumb across her lower lip. Frozen air curled between them.

She was wrong. This moment was a ruse, but not to trick her. To fool himself. He needed to be with her, to linger in her presence. To feel fully alive. To make this his reality.

He released her and backed away. She gasped, stunned. But she did not speak or challenge him, and that proved worse than his frustrated need.

Unable to look at her longer, he took up the reins again. "No doubt you wish to call your maid," he made himself say in his most insouciant aristocrat's voice, as though his blood weren't rushing like a tidal wave bent upon destruction. He put his foot in the stirrup and vaulted atop Tristan's back.

"I asked you what you hope to gain from this." Her voice was taut. "At least tell me that, so I can understand for once."

"Why, dearest Lady Valerie," he drawled, readjusting his hat as though its positioning were of utmost importance, "my own amusement, of course."

He glanced behind him, making certain her maid approached. With a touch of his fingers to the brim, he spurred his horse forward, back to the house, to warmth and camaraderie and all the inanities he cared nothing about as he left his heart upon the path behind.

Chapter 22

Valerie, your fingers are drilling a hole in that chair arm. Lady March will not appreciate needing to have it mended." The Earl of Alverston's voice came across the sunlit parlor in a mellow rumble.

Valerie snapped her gaze from the fire to her brother. He reclined in a chair, sunshine spilling through the paneled window onto him. His eyes were closed, hands clasped around a journal propped upon his chest.

Valerie pursed her lips. "I thought you were asleep."

"I was asleep until you woke me with that drum honor. It lacks only a fife to make me long to stand and march." He didn't even flicker an eyelid.

Valerie grinned. She'd joined him to avoid playing cards with the other guests in the drawing room. The day was frigid, so she had to scotch her plan to avoid the Viscount of Ashford by taking her horse out. When Valentine announced he would eschew more party games in favor of stealing off to read *The Times* in Lady March's little blue parlor on the opposite side of the castle, Valerie went along.

Her brother fell asleep within minutes. He and the other gentlemen, it seemed, had lingered late at billiards the night before. Valerie knew this because she knew everything the gentlemen did if the Viscount of Ashford was part of the group. She was dying to ask Valentine if he had spoken to Ashford. But if she asked, he would wonder about her interest. Valerie would not be able to tell him, because she did not know.

Her body burned each time he came near, and his touch in the woods left her trembling for the remainder of the day. It was as though he could not help but touch her, as she longed to be touched. He haunted her thoughts, her very blood and bones. Her mind and heart were a chaos.

"Why don't you go practice, sister dear?" Valentine mumbled. "I hear Margaret keeps a fine pianoforte in the music room."

Valerie glanced at her nervous fingers. She wasn't overly fond of playing. But at least it would give her mind and anxious hands something to dwell upon other than the mercurial Lord Ashford and his changeable, fire-flecked eyes.

She stood up. "Do you plan to fence this afternoon? Lord March scheduled the tourney for after luncheon."

"Mm-mnh."

Valerie walked over to her brother and dropped a light kiss upon his brow. He grunted, and she patted him upon the shoulder.

"I am off to practice, then."

A footman directed her toward the castle's west end and Valerie discovered the passageway to the music room. Raised voices issued from an open door.

"I do not wish to speak to Ashford, Alistair." The Marquess of Hannsley's deep tones carried into the corridor. "I am under no obligation to you, and I have no wish for any commerce with him."

Valerie stepped toward the wall and pretended to study a small painting there. She had to stretch to hear Mr. Flemming's voice, quiet and conciliating in tone.

"You may find that he has a proposition to tempt you, Clifford. Since the law changed, you cannot be so satisfied with business affairs to pass up such an opportunity."

"My business affairs are none of yours," Lord Hannsley countered. "How is it that I have never heard of Ashford's illicit activities before this?"

Valerie's eyes flew wide. Mr. Flemming's voice seemed to shrug in response.

"Perhaps you don't know everything there is to know about the trade, after all, cousin. He has rather widespread interests. You limit yourself to too narrow a field. The East has a great deal to offer, and Ashford's business puts him upon coasts that are nearly untapped. Unpatrolled waters . . ." Mr. Flemming uttered the final words rather too casually.

Valerie waited.

"What do you know of Ashford's ships?" Lord Hannsley finally asked.

"I have access to some papers, and maps as well. They would be of no interest to you, of course, a man whose business is already so successful."

Footfalls approached the door. Valerie jumped back. But Lord Hannsley's words halted Mr. Flemming.

"What do you want for it, Alistair? And understand that if you agree to this it will not go well for you if you play me false. I will expect to learn everything."

Valerie held her breath through the long pause.

"Five thousand. I have too much at stake to risk it for less."

Lord Hannsley chuckled derisively. "You are a fool, Alistair. You will have your paltry five thousand when you have delivered me Ashford's interests."

"Upon a silver platter, Clifford."

Valerie didn't stay to be discovered, ducking past the door and running the rest of the way to the music room. She spent the next hour moving her hands across the keyboard, but whether she played she didn't know.

Mr. Flemming clearly planned to act as a spy against the viscount and as an informer to Lord Hannsley. Flemming had meant his words of entreaty only to whet Lord Hannsley's appetite for acquisition, not partnership as he initially suggested. He was double-dealing, and the marquess agreed to it.

Valerie suspected five thousand pounds was a tidy sum to pay for information. It must involve the black market. Often enough her Boston cousins complained of how illegal trade undermined honest merchants' work. Added to that there was danger involved in that sort of trafficking.

Then Steven Ashford was the perfect man for the job.

Valerie stood up and started out of the music room, but her steps faltered. An image arose in her memory, the Jesuit manacled and beaten for stealing laudanum, yet not vanquished.

He was a criminal. She'd seen the brand burned into his arm. But she had also touched him and felt warmth deeper than the temperature of his skin. And, at moments, she glimpsed the compassion in his eyes when he did not mask it with disdain or foolery.

Valerie paused, holding on to the doorjamb to steady her quivering hands. It must end. She could not bear these feelings of helplessness and confusion. And she would not stand being shunted aside. Not again.

What had he called her, naïve? At one time she might

have been. But that was long past. Now she had information she suspected Etienne La Marque would dearly wish to possess. She knew precisely the price she would exact for it.

Servants carted away furniture, rolled up rugs, and swept the great hall in preparation for the afternoon's swordplay. The medieval keep made a fitting backdrop for the fencing. Broadswords, longbows, lances, and other weapons of ancient lineage lined one wall. Footmen arranged chairs along the edges, and Lord March opened up an Elizabethan balcony above for the faint of heart.

Too agitated to sit, Valerie stood upon the ground level, only half an ear on Alethea and Cassandra's murmurs of appreciation as the gentlemen, garbed in fencing gear and bearing weapons, took their partner assignments. With a smile, she watched Anna tie a discreet ribbon around Valentine's arm.

Her pulse tripped as the Viscount of Ashford entered the hall with Lord Michaels and Sylvia Sinclaire. Lord Michaels offered a pretty bow to the golden-haired girl and kissed her fingers. Casting a tolerant glance at the flirtation, the viscount drew a leather gauntlet onto his right hand and started across the floor.

Valerie stared. He looked for all the world like Apollo consorting with mortal men. His gilt-embroidered tunic of pristine white and tight shirtsleeves fit him to perfection, the buff breeches hugging his muscular legs like a second skin. His blade flashed like sunlight as he tested it comfortably, and his hair shone gold beneath the chandelier.

Lord March announced the tourney under way, and the gentlemen commenced fighting. Valerie tried to be attentive to the other bouts, but her attention kept straying to the false priest. He fought well, besting two opponents before Lord Michaels, the recognized champion, beat him by a point.

When Lord Hannsley approached him, they greeted each other with casual interest, sweat-dampened hair and clothes marking their earlier efforts. But neither looked particularly weary as they drew their sword tips obliquely to the floor and raised the épées in salute to each other, then to the president of their bout, Lord Fredericks.

Ashford's voice came across the floor, quiet and low. "Let the event be what it will."

Lord Fredericks's brow furrowed, and the marquess narrowed his eyes. Ashford's cryptic words must mean more than they suggested.

Hesitantly, it seemed, Lord Fredericks spoke the ready alert, the fencers set their stances, and he gave the command to begin.

As with all the other bouts, the two opponents began by testing for openings with careful moves, swords sparkling in the light from the crystal chandeliers. Valerie willed her stomach to cease clenching. It was simply a game, played in the midst of dozens of people. What she had heard Lord Hannsley and Mr. Flemming discussing that morning didn't matter. Nothing could happen here.

Still, she could not quite draw a full breath.

"That maneuver is called an *une-deux*," Mr. Fenton said to Alethea after Hannsley dipped his sword tip toward Ashford's chest. The viscount's blade caught Hannsley's with apparent ease.

"Ah, a conservative riposte," Mr. Pierce remarked close by.

"Almost too casual, wouldn't you say?" another gentleman replied. The marquess pressed forward in short, quick steps to capitalize upon the opening. The viscount gave way.

"They seem a little tired." Alethea said. "Are you worn from your own contests, Mr. Fenton?"

"No doubt this will be a quick finish to round out the numbers. Ah, here come Michaels and March from their bout now."

Valerie's gaze slipped to the other pair of fencers as they shook hands to end their bout. Metal clashed and her gaze swung back.

Silence echoed throughout the hall. Hannsley and Ashford stared at each other from less than an arm's-length apart. Their swords, joined at the hilts, locked in a V pointing to the crystal chandeliers above.

From the direction of Lord Fredericks's frown, it was clear Hannsley had dealt the illegal hit. As he opened his mouth to reprimand the marquess, Ashford's lips curved into a one-sided grin. With a graceful step back, he disengaged.

"Brave and fierce is their action and their movements quick and light. At least mine had better be, hm, Clifford?" he called laughingly across the floor, winning a scowl from Hannsley. But he had also adroitly deflected Lord Fredericks's reprimand away from the marquess. There could not be a simple reason for it. He and Hannsley must have a grudge to settle. Valerie couldn't doubt it.

"Lord Ashford, maintain silence," Lord Fredericks commanded. The viscount offered an apologetic nod to the president and another swift smile to his opponent. The spectators seemed to relax.

He engaged the marquess anew, this time with a series of swift, simple thrusts to Hannsley's chest that the marquess seemed to anticipate with equally rapid parries and ripostes. Lord Fredericks called the points. Hannsley was already far in the lead, yet the viscount's fighting continued light, nearly insubstantial.

Valerie darted a glance at Hannsley's face, the effects

of his opponent's insouciant approach clear. His lips were compressed, his deep-set eyes intensely focused, and his color heightened. He was furiously angry.

Laughter lit the viscount's eyes and shaped his mouth. But beneath his handsomely smiling façade gleamed cold, hard calculation.

Ice shivered up Valerie's spine. She could not be imagining it. Didn't everyone see it so clearly? The two men mock-fighting wished to kill each other.

Murmurs stirred through the group, but Valerie barely heard the comments over the sliding of steel and the din of her racing heart. After every few parries, without actually disengaging, Ashford effectively broke contact with the marquess, refusing to riposte and forcing Hannsley to continue one long, pressured attack.

"Ten to one he has a *botta segreta* up his sleeve," Lord Michaels said to Mr. Fenton in a subdued voice. "Been all over the world. Must've learned some move he is waiting to use to impress us all. Why else would he let Hannsley carry the bout? He has the openings."

Mr. Fenton's response came upon an uncomfortable laugh. "Why would Ashford waste a coup for this sort of thing? This isn't a duel. He won't kill Hannsley."

Valerie couldn't draw breath. He would not kill Lord Hannsley. He *could* not. Their blades were blunted, and the rules of honor forbade it. Common sense should too. But there was nothing common about Steven Ashford. She wished she could trust her intuition, the voice inside her insisting that the man she once knew would not kill another when honor bound him to fight according to the rules.

But Steven Ashford was a murderer. She had seen him cut a man's throat.

Hannsley quit his forward attack, casting wrist-driven jabs at the viscount's chest, metal swishing and clanking as the blades met. Ashford reacted more carefully now, no longer allowing Lord Hannsley to monopolize the offensive, but his eyes sparked flintlike beneath the gold light.

Something had changed.

Hannsley's blade whipped out from his elbow, slashing toward the viscount's left shoulder. Ashford's hand crossed his body, deflecting the cut as it flicked against his arm. Valerie's gaze darted to Lord Fredericks. His eyes widened, but he remained silent. If the viscount's parry had not succeeded, the blow would have wounded.

Still Ashford did not counterattack. Gasps sounded around Valerie as Hannsley lunged, his long legs carrying his blade point-forward to Ashford's chest. The viscount jumped back, leveling a slap across the marquess's protected ribs. Its impact rang throughout the cavernous chamber, and shouts of relief sounded from the uneasy spectators. But Ashford again did not press his advantage.

A metallic clink sounded upon the stone floor.

"Lord Hannsley, your blade is compromised," Lord Fredericks called out. "Cease fencing, my lords."

As though he did not hear, Hannsley's feet left the ground, the splintered tip of his sword flying fast toward the viscount's chest. Ashford's wrist shot upward, his steel deflecting Hannsley's thrust. Lunging again, the marquess leaped, propelling his body forward as his blade untangled from Ashford's, arcing to swing close around the viscount's head.

Lord Fredericks shouted, a lady screamed, and Ashford twisted around and drove his weapon back.

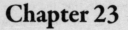

Chapter 23

S word arm wide, the tip of the Viscount of Ashford's weapon quivering against his throat, Lord Hannsley stood like stone. His eyes flared with impotent fury.

Slowly, Ashford drew his blade down.

With an odd calm, Lord Fredericks said, "The bout goes to Lord Ashford." No one needed him to add that the marquess was disqualified for wielding a dangerously splintered blade. The day's play was over.

As though shaken out of trance, the spectators seemed to breathe a common sigh. Applause filled the hall, conversation erupting among the party. Valerie watched Steven turn and extend his hand to his opponent. Lips tight, chest rising and falling heavily, Lord Hannsley shook it in silence then strode off the fighting floor.

Cassandra and Alethea talked in Valerie's ear. She did not hear it. In the shock of relief, she saw only Steven Ashford watching his opponent leave the hall. He dropped his gaze and stared, long and thoughtfully, at his right hand, palm open upward.

Then he looked up and directly at her. Valerie shivered, meeting his gaze steadily. Finally he shifted his attention to several gentlemen approaching. She took in a fast, deep breath.

Anna's slender hand slid around her cold fingers.

"Come, darling. Let us go dress for dinner."

Nodding, Valerie followed.

"You two favored us with quite an exhibition today. I'll wager you are both riddled with bruises." Lord Fredericks spoke down the length of the dining table. A dozen gentlemen reclined around it. Smoke from lit cheroots circled through candle flames, the musty scent mingling with the aroma of strong wine.

No one had yet mentioned Hannsley's broken blade. Steven assumed it seemed best among everyone present to pretend the marquess hadn't known of it. Or to actually believe that. Astounding. But he'd never really understood the rules of the English aristocracy. One moment they were prosing on about honor, the next protecting villains within their exalted midst. The latter was the very reason Steven had to gather every piece of proof available before he publicly accused Hannsley. Without hard evidence, the marquess's peers would never condemn him, a member of Prinny's set, one of the wealthiest men in England.

"Ah, yes," he said lightly. "One must continually strive to impress the gentle lords and set the gentle ladies' breasts aflutter. What, hm, Clifford?" He raised a crystal goblet of port toward the marquess.

Hannsley bared his teeth in a grimace that might have been a smile. Steven laughed, flicking an errant fir needle fallen from the table's centerpiece to the floor beneath his finely clad feet.

"Since the ladies are not present, I challenge these two to admit who could best the other when they were boys," Bertram Fenton said. "You were schoolmates at one time, weren't you? I'll lay blunt upon the chance, Hannsley, that you beat this frippery fellow soundly every time."

Steven raised a languid brow at the younger gentleman, then allowed his mild gaze to slide to the marquess. Hannsley's eyelids were nearly closed. Smoke streamed from his distended nostrils.

"Memory fails at present," Hannsley murmured.

"Tiresome modesty," Steven said upon an exaggerated yawn. "I, for one, won't prevaricate. You would win your pony, Fenton, for I don't believe I ever bested my lord before today. It was remarkably good sport, but I shan't attempt it again. Too taxing by far, don't you know." He rose, glancing at the Earl of March. "Hope you don't mind me usurping your privilege, God-*père*. The ladies await."

The earl nodded and stood. The others followed, stubbing cigars and gulping final mouthfuls of port before leaving the dining chamber. As they strolled along the sconce-lit corridor to the drawing room, Alistair fell in beside Steven.

"All is prepared," Alistair said. A pair of gentlemen passed them, and he waited before continuing in a hushed voice. "I made the offer, and he seems agreeable to it. I expect a positive outcome to our plans."

Steven glanced aside. Alistair's coat was open, his fingers tucked into the tiny waistcoat pockets. He held his chin tight to his chest.

"Are you quite certain? Today's display of martial enthusiasm does not inspire confidence that our friend is sincerely on board with us."

The color waned from Alistair's hollow cheeks. "He tried to kill you, didn't he? And to make it look like an accident."

"Indeed he did," Steven drawled, watching his companion's reaction. "It is fortunate that he did not manage it, as then you would be obliged to complete our task alone, wouldn't you?"

"What are you saying?" Alistair's white face turned red as his head snapped up. "Do you think I would wish for that monster to injure you? And I suppose you think I would sacrifice Aunt Margaret and Uncle Robert as well?"

"I haven't a notion as to what you can mean, my dear Alistair. I merely lamented a would-have-been. I have a proclivity for drama, don't you know."

"I would not want them harmed." Alistair's voice was stiff.

"I have every confidence in your loyalty to my godparents."

"And to you? Do you trust me, Steven?" He paused at the open drawing room doors, a staying hand upon Steven's sleeve. Steven glanced at the fingers wrapped around his coat sleeve, then at his old friend's face.

"As I trust my own heart." He shrugged out of the man's hold and crossed the threshold. "Ah, Godmother, you outdid yourself with dinner tonight. A fine, delicate aspic, the rémoulade positively delighted, and the ducklings . . . like butter upon the tongue. Absolutely succulent, weren't they, Alistair?"

"You know I don't have anything to do with the aspic and ducklings, Steven. You are a scamp." The Countess of March laughed as Steven kissed her hands, then dropped them abruptly.

"Ah, then another deserves my caresses," he exclaimed. "I must go and make love to Cook instead. Or should my object be your housekeeper? Perhaps both. Do not wait for me. I expect I will be some time below stairs." He turned to make for the door.

A slender hand halted him.

"My lord, you must remain upon two accounts." Miss Sinclaire's heart-shaped face tilted toward his, her lips parted to reveal the glistening edges of perfect teeth.

He bowed. "I am all ears, ma'am."

"In the first case, if you depart now, we will suffer so greatly from losing your company that you will owe us recompense."

Steven chuckled, nearly amused by the coquette's effrontery. But not quite.

"I do not relish the weight of such a debt upon my shoulders, it is true," he replied.

Her appreciative gaze slipped across his coat, lingering. "A pity," she murmured.

He could bed the girl. She declared her willingness with every batted lash and whispered sigh. Her figure was ripe and her eagerness especially appealing. He had no doubt that indulging himself with this young beauty would bring him momentary relief.

But she was not what Steven wanted. Not now. Not ever. What he wanted carried a price he was unwilling to pay. Merely knowing his desire remained alive and safe must suffice.

Across the chamber, Valerie's face remained averted. She hadn't looked at him since he entered. Whenever she trained her gaze upon him he felt it like a brand, like the hot iron once pressed into his skin. Each time she glanced his way, the heat of her gaze rocked him, setting his blood afire.

Now he only felt the cold.

That cold made him seek her out, speak to her, tease her despite his resolution not to. But with each encounter, indifference and disdain grew harder to pretend. For only the second time in his life of masquerades, his façade was slipping—with the woman who had stripped it once before. Briefly, but completely.

He lifted the golden-haired beauty's hand beneath his lips. "And the second account, ma'am?"

"We begged Lord Michaels, but he will not reveal to us the origin of your astounding maneuver today, the one that decided your bout with Lord Hannsley."

Steven released the girl as though reluctantly, clasping his hands behind him.

"Ah, yes. Well, I cannot say that I recall it." His voice trailed off.

"I told them you would not give it up, Ashford," Michaels said laughingly. "A gentleman never reveals the source of a *botta segreta*."

"Muscovy?" Steven considered as though he had not heard. "No, no. That amiable Turkish prison guard, perhaps? Hm." He looked up. "Yes, that's it. A Bedouin chap taught me that little trick. Ah, what an adventure. White sand as far as the eye could see, curdled milk for breakfast, roasted goat for dinner, and the fellow had the most astounding number of wives—"

"Oh, no, my lord!" Miss Pierce giggled.

Steven turned a grin upon the girl as he moved toward the tea table. A quick glance told him Valerie's attention remained locked against his idiocy. All the better.

"I advise you not to listen to a word my godson utters, Miss Pierce," Lady March cautioned as she poured tea. "He invents all his stories to shock and amaze."

Steven perched upon an ottoman at her feet. "Ah, Godmother, how you do spread blight upon my merriment."

The burning began then, searing beneath his skin like living coals. His hand remained steady upon his cup as he lifted it to his lips. Ever in control, no matter what the price, as he long ago conditioned himself.

"Was she always such a damp spirit when we were children, Alistair?" he quipped, his throat dry despite the strong brew.

"I do not recall her ever being anything but kind and generous," Alistair said. "And indulgent. Especially to you."

Valerie's sharp attention shifted to Alistair, then returned to him. This time Steven could not resist the sweet temptation. He lifted his head. Their gazes sought, met, and melded. He allowed her ocean eyes to hold him, awareness shimmering in their depths.

"Yes, rather too indulgent, I suppose," he murmured, and turned to Lady March. "Godmother, I fault you for spoiling me outrageously. Such lush liberality can only result in depravity."

"My dearest boy, I could not have known that at the time, could I? Now, Alistair, you have the cards already, I see. Perhaps you will begin a game?"

"No chicken stakes tonight, Flemming." Fenton complained as several guests moved to sit around a table. Steven took another sip of tea and the cold invaded him.

Chapter 24

When dawn crept through Valerie's bedchamber draperies, her eyes were already open. They had barely closed all night. Her mind was too busy, her body too agitated.

At least she had not dreamed. She had, however, come up with a plan. She would entice him into serious conversation with hints of what she had learned from Lord Hannsley and Mr. Flemming's conversation. Then, as payment for hearing everything she knew, she would demand that he treat her with respect, and tell her the truth.

Valerie wrinkled her nose. Not a perfect plan by any means. But it was a start, and it did not require seducing anyone, certainly a change from her usual method of getting her way with men.

In the woods, he had taunted her about that method.

She was determined to show him how wrong he was about her. She simply must find him alone again. Her lips creased into a smile. Determination felt good, fresh and uncluttered. With renewed purpose, she pushed away the bedclothes, pressed cucumber slices to the puffy circles beneath her eyes, and went down to breakfast.

At the dining room door, she stopped short. Near the end of the long table the Viscount of Ashford sat in indolent solitude, a journal in his hands and a cup of coffee at his elbow. He looked up. After a pause, he inclined his head in greeting.

Valerie drew in a shaky breath.

"Good morning, my lady!"

She swung around to the voice at the other end of the chamber. Standing by the sidebar laden with breakfast foods, Lord Bramfield smiled wide. He held a plate of fish, eggs, and muffins, and a pair of serving tongs.

Releasing her pent breath, Valerie went toward him. "Good morning, my lord."

"Did the sun waken you as it did me? It seems brighter today," he continued, clearly not requiring a response. "These fellows"—he gestured toward the footmen standing to either side of the buffet—"say it is already less frigid out than yesterday."

"Perhaps Lady Cassandra's plan for a sledding expedition will come about." Valerie glanced at the breakfast display, but her appetite had fled. The back of her neck felt warm.

Frustration chafed at her as Timothy piled another rasher of bacon atop his food. Being thwarted now in her desire to talk with Ashford was unendurable.

"Before other activities begin, we must take a ride over to the lake," Timothy said, gesturing her to the table. "I thought to go right after breakfast. I would enjoy your company very much." Honest, affectionate entreaty brightened his blue eyes. He always looked at her that way, except when she had taken him to the gallery, briefly pulling him into her life of game playing and wickedness.

Slowly she nodded. "I would like that."

"What do you say, Ashford?" Timothy said pleasantly. "Care to join us for a ride?"

The viscount folded his journal and stood.

"Delighted to be asked, Bramfield." He tucked the paper beneath his arm. "But I will allow you to enjoy this lovely lady's company exclusively." He moved toward the door. "If given the same opportunity, after all, I certainly would not have asked you to come along." He grinned, a mischievous curve of his lips that set Valerie's heartbeat flying. Then he sketched them a quick bow, and left.

"He's a pretty mannered fellow, isn't he?" Timothy said, chuckling.

Valerie dragged her gaze from the door, but she did not reply.

Returning to her bedchamber a few hours later to change out of her riding habit, she heard a thump as she opened the door. A woman whirled around to face her.

"Oh, Lady Valerie! How do you do?" Lady March's companion dropped a curtsy. She was well beyond the first flush of youth, with dark hair pulled back in a chignon and a fine though subdued gown.

"Miss—"

"Amelia Brown, my lady."

"Of course, Miss Brown." Valerie laid down her hat and approached the woman. "Has something happened to my maid?"

"Oh, no, I do not believe so," Miss Brown said with extraordinary composure for an intruder.

"I am relieved to hear it. But then how is it that I have the pleasure of your visit?"

"Gracious me, you must think me a scatter wit. I was—"

The woman's words froze as Valerie's gaze fell upon the Bible, cracked open on the floor beside the bed table, pages crumpled beneath. Valerie bent and picked up the book, and set it again on the nightstand.

"How singular. I thought I left this on the table. Perhaps Mabel knocked it off when she straightened the bed this morning."

"It was my fault, my lady," Miss Brown said quickly. "I came searching for a brooch Lady March lost. She thought perhaps she dropped it when she came here to see you several days ago."

"Have you had any success in finding it?"

"Unfortunately, no. Your maid is out—"

"Yes, I sent her to the village upon an errand."

"When I found you weren't here, I took the liberty of entering in search of the brooch. Then I saw the Bible, and could not help but glance at it. I neglected my prayers this morning, you see. Lady March is resting, so I thought . . ." She barely faltered as she lied. "I was so startled when you entered that I dropped it. I hope it has not suffered in the fall."

Valerie schooled her expression. "Oh, I shouldn't worry about that, Miss Brown. It has undoubtedly suffered worse." Her gaze went to the Bible. "Do you read French, then?"

"French, my lady?"

Valerie cocked a brow. "Why, yes. This Bible is in French translation."

Miss Brown stared at Valerie, eyes unblinking.

"But perhaps you did not have time to notice that before I startled you?" Valerie said, pasting a gracious smile upon her lips. "Do tell Lady March I am devastated her brooch has gone missing. I will inform Mabel, and if we come across it I will return it immediately."

The woman moved toward the door. "I apologize for having disturbed you, my lady."

"It's nothing, Miss Brown. Do not mind it a bit. I am glad to have met you, in fact. Lady March sings your praises. Good afternoon." Valerie shut the door.

She dashed to the night table and grabbed up the Bible. Her fingers shuffled swiftly through the thin pages, searching.

Trembling seized her. She threw down the book and gripped her hands into fists. There was nothing there. He had given it to her as a gift, pure and simple.

Valerie turned to the wardrobe. Drawing in a deep breath, she reached into the press and drew out a gown of sheer white silk shimmering with silver embroidery and tiny sequins. She laid it out in her dressing room beside a note for Mabel to press it for the evening.

But first, if she was to truly shine tonight, she needed sleep. Drawing off her riding habit, she went to the bed and curled up beneath the covers.

The sword sparkled in candlelight, suspended above the gray granite altar. She grasped the hilt, smoothing her fingers along the cold steel, gripped, and swung the blade downward. Metal reverberated against stone, but the blade remained whole, the altar unblemished, and she felt nothing.

She swiveled to face her opponent. Above his black, concealing mask, his hair shone like gilded bronze in the candle's glow. Her sword arm rose again with deadly purpose. He mirrored her movements, lifting his blade tip to shoulder height. Then he laughed and pulled off his mask.

She screamed, and the madman laughed again, the sound echoing across the hillside as his pale blue stare drew her forward, his clawlike fingers curling in anticipation. Upon his shirtfront a stain soaked outward from

*the skin, arcing in a crimson crescent from his heart
across the pristine, starched white fabric to the hilt of the
carving knife embedded in his belly.*

Valerie's sobs woke her. She opened her eyes wide, staring at the canopy and willing away the horrifying images.

Her dreams had grown worse since coming to Castlemarch. She wished she could talk to Valentine about
them, or Anna. But she hadn't told them about Bebain.
Not the truth, at least, and nothing about Etienne. They
would not understand about the dreams. They would
think she was mad.

She wanted to tell the man she had known aboard the
corsair. She longed to talk with him, to truly talk. Damn
his changeable self, she longed for him. Etienne. Steven.

On the ship that day he demanded she call him by his
real name, then he held her in his arms and touched her
with a hunger she'd never felt from any other man. In
her confusion of pleasure she barely wondered why he
wanted her to speak that name.

Valerie gulped back the tightness in her throat and sat
up, dashing the tears from her cheeks. Tears were for
foolish girls. She must remain clearheaded.

She climbed from bed. At the mirror she studied the
drawn skin beneath her eyes before meeting her gaze.
Need stared back at her.

She did not care who or what he was, or what he called
himself. She was in love with him. She had loved him
for months and she still wanted him, with a desperation
beyond bearing. Not because of who he was or wasn't, his
lies or subterfuge. He could be the local country vicar, a
highwayman, or the king himself and she would still want
him until the day she died.

He did something to her, stirred a passion in her soul.

In those fleeting moments when his mask faltered, as in the drawing room after his battle with Lord Hannsley, she saw a hunger in his eyes equal to her own. Hunger that went far beneath skin, beyond flesh and blood.

He might try to push her away again. But tonight, she would not let him. And if he resisted, she would bribe him.

Chapter 25

December 22, 1810

THE RIGHT HONBLE. THE VISCOUNT ASHFORD
CASTLEMARCH, DERBYSHIRE

My lord,

I have discovered information regarding Mr. F's debts to The Gentleman that I must relate to you. It would not be advisable to convey this by the post. Additionally, a messenger from Saint-Pierre awaits your instructions. Can you come to London immediately?

Bernard Farthing, Esq.
Farthing and Cooper Solicitors
Fleet Street, London

Steven placed a steadying hand upon the marble mantel of his bedchamber hearth. An unusual gesture for him, to be sure, but the news was not what he hoped for, although unfortunately what he suspected.

Anyway, he needed the support. He'd drunk too much brandy after leaving his dinner largely untouched. Insanely foolish of him, given the circumstances, but too tempting not to indulge.

Tonight she had been radiant.

Throughout the evening, when he managed to tear his gaze away from her, Steven had watched the other men watching her. One after another they sought her attention, finding ways to be near her, to touch her under pretense of some gallantry or necessity. Even the married men came under her spell, casting her appreciative looks behind their wives' backs. Only her brother had regarded her with something less than pleasure. He looked worried. Steven had noticed that and refilled his glass.

Despite the attention she received, Valerie did not show special interest in any one man. She was friendly with Bramfield, but not markedly so.

Steven's fingers pressed into the mantel's edge.

The Honorable Timothy Ramsay, Viscount Bramfield. Genial, stalwart bastion of the English aristocracy with nary a blemish upon his clear white skin or pristine noble lineage.

As at breakfast, Bramfield's gaze had followed Valerie all evening. Steven guessed the fellow's thoughts, how her sea-blue eyes glowing with affection and trust could enchant a man. Once she had looked at him that way, at the priest he pretended to be. Then he betrayed her.

He glanced down at the missive from his solicitor. He must go to town, to leave her again, if only for a day. Merely a foretaste of what was to come, a preview of his eternal, unwelcome reprieve from madness.

A metallic click sounded on the other side of the chamber. Steven stilled, his muscles tensing, gaze flickering to the sword propped against a chair, close enough if needed. The bronze doorknob glinted in the firelight as it turned. A crack of light from the corridor lit the threshold. Valerie slipped inside and closed the panel behind her, pressing her back against it and turning the key in the lock.

"You are here," she said, her voice breathless but level. Of course it was level. She was no shrinking violet, especially not when engaged in a daring escapade.

Steven commanded his racing pulse to steady. Her color was high, her shimmering gown taut across her perfect breasts, her eyes luminous in the firelight. If only he had a knife handy. It would be easier, after all, to cut out his heart right away than to endure the torture he suspected was about to come.

"Indeed I am," he said coolly, leaning against the mantel. "It is half past one at night and this is my bedchamber. The issue, however, is not whether I am here, but that you are."

She moved forward a step. Her gaze shifted around the chamber, then to the dressing room door before returning to him squarely. "Are you alone?"

"What are you doing here?" His voice was hard, but Valerie expected that. He stood in his shirtsleeves and trousers, the creased page of a letter in his hand. The fire illuminated the chamber with wavering light, gilding his hair and casting his skin in a warm glow. His eyes were icy.

"The door was unlocked," she said, heart slamming against her ribs.

"That hardly gives you leave to enter uninvited."

"It seems careless of you not to lock it."

"Your presence here proves it. What do you want?"

Valerie had silently practiced her speech all evening, searching out the opportunity to give it to him. When the party dispersed, she determined to see it through even if it meant this. But now that she was here, with him before her, breathtakingly handsome in the firelit intimacy of his bedchamber, her thoughts tangled. The only honest answer she could give was that she wanted to be in his arms.

"I want the same thing you want."

He hesitated only the briefest moment before replying, "Do not presume to know what I want."

But the missed beat sufficed for Valerie. Now the Marquess of Hannsley, Alistair Flemming, and the entire underworld of villainy would have to wait. This was not the opportunity she had sought for a day, but the one she had ached for since she first laid eyes upon Etienne La Marque.

She took a step forward. "I know you don't want Sylvia Sinclaire."

One brow lifted. "We have been attending to the endeavors of others, have we?"

"Don't use that tone with me."

"You invade my private chambers in the middle of the night, then hand me orders? Your breeding is not what I imagined, my dear. Nor is your judgment."

"You don't care about my breeding. You don't care about anyone's breeding." She moved toward him, pulse pounding in her throat where he must see it. "And my judgment is perfectly fine. I recognize desire in a man's eyes."

"Do you also recognize words upon a man's tongue? Words such as leave now."

"No." She gulped in a breath and halted before him. His body was rigid. Steeling herself, she laid her hand upon his chest. Warmth stole through her, exhilarating. She slipped her fingers beneath the loosened laces of his shirt. He did not move.

"Give me what I want," she said, unsurprised at the husky quality of her voice. Her fingertips were alive with

pleasure, darting deep through her. His body, smooth and
taut, intoxicated her. His heart beat hard and fast against
her palm.

"Ah, I begin to see." His tone was silken. "The scandalous young maiden has not yet given way to the respectable society matron she hopes to become someday." He
lifted a hand and traced a finger along her jaw to her lower
lip. It was the barest touch, but sizzles of honeyed pleasure swirled up Valerie's legs, twining in her core.

"You are talking to hear yourself speak," she gasped as
he trailed his fingers to the edge of her bodice, his touch
burning her skin with sweet fire even as it remained light.
"I don't need words now."

"What do you need, then, my lady?"

"I need—"

His hand slipped beneath her bodice, bringing her
nipple to a quick, tight peak. She sighed and leaned forward. His touch felt even better than her heated memory
recalled, as though her flesh had been made for him alone.

He bent his head and whispered against her cheek,
"You need what Bramfield will not give you until he has
put a ring upon your finger." He grasped her waist and
dragged her to him. His body was unyielding, his arousal
hard against her abdomen. Valerie's throat closed. She
nodded, entirely awakened to him, heat flooding her.

"He fears to lose you." Steven's voice came close at her
ear. "He fears his passion will not match yours, and that
you will tire of him before you are safely his by law."

His hands slipped down, curving around her bottom
and pulling her flush against him from shoulder to knee.
Valerie grabbed at his chest, twining her hands in the soft
linen shirt as sweet sensation coursed through her, dipping between her legs in hot coils of anticipation.

"He fears you have not changed." He stroked her thighs,

slow, measured caresses to her waist then down again. "He fears that even if he wins you, once you speak your vows, you will cuckold him."

"I would not," Valerie uttered upon a ragged breath. "He is a decent man."

"Then what are you doing here? Why aren't you with him right now?"

She looked up, and his eyes seared her.

"Because I—"

He dipped his head, brushing his cheek against hers.

"Because you want this?" He pressed his fingers between her legs. She moaned, clutching at his shirt.

"Yes."

He cupped her, stroking her through the thin gown and shift, sending pleasure skittering everywhere inside her. "Yes," she sighed. She tilted her face up, leaning toward his mouth.

He did not kiss her.

Valerie needed to be closer, needed the tenderness he had shown her aboard ship and in the woods for that brief moment. Her hands sought his waist, grasping his shirt-tail and pulling up the garment. He shrugged out of it.

Her limbs went weak. His body was breathtaking, raw male from taut belly to the sheer power of lean muscle in his chest and shoulders, even more beautiful than she remembered. Her gaze slipped to the scar curving up his ribs. She reached to touch it.

Steven gripped her wrists with a strong hand and pulled them behind her. Frustrated sound rose from her throat as her sensitized breasts pressed against his bare skin.

"You are a wanton, Valerie Monroe."

"I said don't speak to me like that," she whispered as his palm covered her again. His thumb passed firmly over her nipple, and rich shivers seized her deep inside.

"I speak only the truth." He caressed her and it was madness, but she wanted to be naked beneath his hands again, forever.

"You mean to hurt me," she breathed. "But I won't be hurt again. I know what this is."

His fist tightened around her wrists at the small of her back, pinning her to him. He moved against her and her body sank into his, her lashes fluttering.

"What is it?" His voice was low, unsteady. Valerie's heart constricted.

"Nothing I have ever felt before," she whispered. "Nothing you have ever felt."

He did not deny it. His tawny gaze fixed hard upon her mouth. Valerie willed him to meet her gaze, to admit to the truth. If he admitted to this, he must admit to more, to what he felt beyond the primal heat between them. To the longing that burned so deep.

He swept her into his arms and carried her to the bed. His hands worked quickly, unfastening the tiny buttons down her back, the lacing on her corset, the ribbons of her shift. He pulled the garments to her waist, pressed her down, and without hesitation took the peak of one breast into his mouth.

Valerie's back sprang off the mattress. She moaned, struggling to free her arms trapped within the sleeves of her gown.

Steven grabbed her hands, stilling them as he leaned to her face.

"Do not fight it." His breath feathered across her lips. "The moment you touch me, Valerie, this will end, I promise you."

Valerie's mouth fell open. But he was already drawing away, his hands still tight around hers. Panic, strange and coarse, scuttled through her. Wide-eyed, she nodded.

Holding her gaze, he grasped her skirt and drew it up

her legs. His hand came around her calf, slipping slowly toward the junction of her thighs. She trembled, aching everywhere he touched her, and where she knew he intended to touch her. She held her breath, willing him not to stop, wanting so badly to feel him, it hurt to hold her hands flat against the mattress.

He was still looking into her eyes when his fingertips grazed her damp, aching flesh. She arched her neck, sucking in breaths as he caressed her. He was gentle at first, teasing, drawing out her pleasure. But it was not enough. She lifted her hips, urging him to stroke her harder, astounded by the violence of her need. She wanted more than even this delirium. She wanted all of him.

She choked. "Please, Steven—"

His finger came inside her. Her hips bucked off the bed, ecstasy swamping her as his mouth again found her breast, his tongue flickering against the nipple, his teeth teasing. She groaned, pushing against his caress, moving her body frantically, feeling herself close around him and still wanting more.

She was heaven in his embrace, beautiful, pliant woman answering his caresses as though created for them. From the moment she had first touched him, Steven had known it and tried to deny it. This time he could not, but he could not allow her to touch him now. If she did he would be lost, and he would drag her along with him, into the black danger of his life.

Instead he touched her, served her with his mouth and hands, giving her what she most needed. She moaned, her eyes half closed in primitive rapture, her satin-dark hair spilling over white linen. He traced a fingertip around the taut, dusky peak of her breast, and she whimpered, thrusting her hips against his hand, urging him deeper.

"More?" he murmured, disguising the need in his voice with tight control.

"Yes." She tossed her head. "Yes."

He pressed a second finger into her. She was exquisite, wet and so tight, better than his memories and infinitely better than his countless fantasies.

"More," she begged. "Now."

He nudged her soft, supple thighs apart, bent, and tasted her.

She gasped, digging her hips into the mattress, then lifting to meet him, her hands clutching the sheet. He took her fully, gripping her hips and holding her as he slipped his tongue along her swelling womanhood, dipping into her, filling his senses with her musky beauty. He caressed her firmly and steadily, knowing no man had ever been here before. In this, she was his alone. Her gasps grew faster, higher as she strained against his hold, her body shaking, her voice whispering his name over and over.

"Now. Oh, please." She writhed, on the cusp of ecstasy. Her hips left the bed and he thrust his fingers into her again, fast and deep. She cried out, jerking against him, her breaths faltering as pleasure took her.

Steven's body pounded with hard need, aching to be inside her, to feel her encompassing him. He had never known such satisfaction, watching her face, her lips parted as release shuddered through her to her soft, high cries.

He moved between her legs, seeking her breasts with his mouth again, sucking hard and kissing her tender peaks until she cried out a second time. She gripped her thighs around his hips, forcing him against her, moaning, a helpless sound of want and fulfillment at once.

He threaded his fingers through her hair, willing her eyes to open. Her lashes fanned out, sea-blue pools swimming with need, the same need that forced its way through every fiber of his body, through his very soul. He drank in the sight of her desire, the flush upon her cheeks and brow, the cascade of satiny hair. In moments it would be too late to turn back.

Her lips parted, her voice wondering and infinitely gentle. "Why won't you kiss me?"

Steven jerked away. "*Chér Jésus.*"

He rolled off her onto his back, covering his face with his palms. "Go." The word tore from his throat like skin from flesh.

Beside him, Valerie did not move.

Steven dragged in a breath and pulled his hands away from his eyes. With an effort beyond reckoning he turned to her. Her gown was bunched about her hips, her silken legs pressed hard together. Her glittering eyes swam with confusion.

He laid his forearm over his eyes. "I said go."

"*What?*"

"Make yourself presentable and leave now, Valerie, before I pick you up and throw you into the corridor as you are." Before he made love to her and never let her go again. Before he told her everything.

She sat up, dragging her gown around her legs and over her beautiful breasts.

"But I didn't—I did what you required," she stuttered, her voice low. "I followed orders, for possibly the first time in my life, mind you, and it was not easy."

"Valerie—"

"You cannot do this, Steven! This will not simply go away. *I* will not. Who do you think you are?"

Steven stared. In her outrage, her face suffused with passion and eyes flashing, she stole his breath, his reason, his conviction. Good Lord, she *must* leave.

"I am the man telling you that if you do not leave now, you will come to be very sorry for it. Perhaps even sorrier than I will be."

"And you think I am not already sorry?" she spat out. But her voice quavered.

"Undoubtedly." Hopefully.

"Don't try to—" She halted. Her gaze fixed upon his wrist at the brand etched into his skin. She slid off the bed backward. "Did you want to kill him?" Her voice was abruptly tight.

Steven's heart raced but he remained perfectly still. "Which part of the threat I just offered didn't you understand?"

"I don't care about your threats. Did you want to kill him?"

He forced out an intolerant sigh. "Did I want to kill whom?" But he knew.

"Lord Hannsley, when you fought. You wanted to kill him, didn't you?"

"Why on earth would I have wanted that? You have an extraordinarily vicious imagination, madam."

She looked like she would strike him. Steven didn't blame her. She had seen him kill a man, and he did want to kill Hannsley. If Steven had his wish, the villain would be at the bottom of the ocean with the hundreds of people he had caused to die that way. Yes, certainly he wanted Hannsley dead. But he would not be the one to do it.

Her gaze burned. "What crime did you commit? How did you earn that brand?"

"How quickly you assume I committed the crime and was not merely wrongly accused."

"You haven't given me any reason to imagine otherwise. What was it?"

"This conversation quickly grows tiresome."

"What was the crime?"

"It hardly matters any longer," he said, investing his tone with the hated measure of indifference. It was like pulling nails from his fingertips. No matter how hard he tried, he could never be indifferent to this woman. Not in truth. Only in lies.

Her voice dipped. "It matters to me."

Dear God. *No.*

Slowly, Steven pushed up onto his elbow, steeling himself for what he must do.

"Then you are a greater fool than I had already thought you to be." Nothing stirred inside him now. No desire. No pain. Only emptiness. "Now go."

The color drained from her face, but her eyes remained fonts of determined, willful feeling.

"And you, Steven Ashford, are an even greater liar than I had thought." She crossed the chamber, unlocked the door, and with her garments gaping open at the back, disappeared into the corridor.

Chapter 26

C hristmas Eve seemed to last for weeks to Valerie. He did not speak to her throughout the interminable day. Valerie might have been content to sit in cozy conversation with Anna and Alethea as they wrapped gifts, to bedeck the castle with yet more greenery, to help prepare the spices for wassail, or to take part in any of the other diversions Lady and Lord March offered their guests. She might have even enjoyed the game of charades struck up in the drawing room after dinner, if Steven Ashford's very existence did not make a mockery of that particular diversion.

She saw him, aching at the sight of his beautiful face and body, warmed by his voice across a room. But he avoided her. When she entered a place, he left it—graceful and charming as always with their fellow guests—but permanently. She tried to catch his gaze before he fled, but he would not allow it.

In the bedchamber firelight, that golden gaze had heated with desire but so much more, something deep and unfeigned and thrilling in its intensity. With his powerful body pressing her into the mattress, she had craved his mouth upon hers, needing to consummate their intimacy with that simple touch. Then the cruelness returned. But different, as though he had to make an effort to drive her away.

At midnight, Valerie bundled up in thick woolens for the ride into Highmarch. In church she sat with her hands folded, prayers the furthest thing from her mind. Even the candles' glow and the hymns filling the sturdy Norman chapel failed to lull her into a suitably reverent state. She stared at Steven's broad shoulders and straight back in the front pew, filled with the memory—so fresh, delectable, and wickedly right—of the pleasure he had given her.

A sigh rose in her throat. She clamped her lips together. Dragging her attention to Vicar Oakley's sermon, she tugged her cloak more closely around her shoulders.

She did not relish the idea of another restless night. Steven obviously wanted her. But after an entire day pondering it, she could not think of a single reason he would deny himself what she offered. He clearly thought she intended to marry Timothy, but that hadn't dampened his desire. His business with Alistair Flemming and the Marquess of Hannsley still loomed mysteriously, of course. But that had nothing to do with her.

She needed a new plan. The one she had devised to gain his confidence had failed miserably. *She* had failed. He'd been her captive audience and instead of forcing him to tell her the truth, she forced herself on him, albeit with remarkably gratifying results.

A smile quivered across her lips and her gaze slipped back to the Marches' front pew. He was gone. Beside his empty place, Mr. Flemming sat stiffly, his chin tucked tight to his chest. She looked over at Lord Hannsley's place a few rows back. The marquess had disappeared.

Valerie's heartbeat tripped. Then it raced.

When the service ended, she hurried from the church ahead of Valentine and Anna. The marquess's carriage still waited in the yard with the others, the horses stomping in their traces, blowing plumes of smoke into the air.

Valerie looked around. Neither Steven nor Hannsley stood among the clusters of guests and villagers mingling in the snowy churchyard. Mr. Flemming climbed into a carriage, scanning the dark edge of the copse of trees that flanked the cemetery. His brow creased.

Valerie followed his gaze. The Marquess of Hannsley strode into the circle of torchlight alongside the graveyard's low stone wall, toward the carriages.

Valerie pivoted back to Anna.

"Darling, I left my reticule in the church," she said, tucking her tiny bag into her cloak sleeve. "I will go fetch it and return in a trice."

Valerie wanted to bolt for the copse, but she took her time walking toward the church. When she reached the shadowy edge of the pool of yellow illumination, she dipped into the darkness and stole around the graveyard wall toward the trees.

Within, lamplight flickered at a distance through the brittle dark. Snow sank into her kid boots as she hurried forward, heart pounding. She neared the light, and her breath caught. Steven crouched above a dark shape stretched upon the ground. Crimson stained the snow. The light of the lantern wavered, casting shadows over Steven's hand pressed hard against the bloodied man's chest. He lifted his head and his darkened gaze met hers.

"He is badly injured, Valerie," he said in a voice she had longed to hear for six months. "I cannot leave him, but I need help to carry him back to the vicarage. You must bring Oakley here, but do not alert any of the others." He regarded her for a silent moment, his face taut. "Will you do this?"

She nodded, turned, and ran back toward the graveyard. Stepping into the torchlight, she found the others much as she left them, as though the night weren't bristling with cold and they did not have a fire and mulled wine waiting for them back at the castle. She went to the vicar standing amid a group of guests and villagers, and touched his sleeve. His face crinkled into a smile.

"Mr. Oakley, could you explain to me an architectural curiosity I noticed in your church earlier? It's such a delightful building." She placed her gloved hand firmly upon his arm and smiled.

"It will be my pleasure." Conversation continued without him, and he went with her toward the church. She spoke in a quiet rush.

"A man is injured in the woods just beyond the cemetery. Lord Ashford is with him now, and he asked me to bring you, but to tell no one else of the trouble."

The vicar's face creased. "Who is it?"

"I don't know him."

His shrewd eyes studied her with sudden interest. He took her hand.

"Tell the others you are remaining with me to help me in a task, and that I will shortly convey both of us to the castle in my gig," he said with a calm certainty that amazed Valerie. "Then go to the vicarage, wake my housekeeper, Mrs. Hodge, and tell her what you know."

Valerie stood, dumbstruck.

"Go on now," the vicar said. "And keep your wits about you, my girl." He hurried toward the cemetery.

By the time Valerie reached Anna and Valentine, most of the carriages had already begun to depart.

"Darlings," she said with forced brightness, "Mr.

Oakley has promised to explain to me a lovely architectural feature of the church I noticed the other day. He will return me to the castle so that you don't need to wait. The poor horses must be miserably cold."

"The grooms walked them during the service," Valentine said, cocking a curious brow. Valerie ignored his silent question as he handed his wife up into his curricle.

"I will see you back at the castle," she said, fearing her tone sounded too breathy and trying not to cast anxious glances at the marquess climbing into his carriage.

"All right, dear. Do hurry, though," Anna said, pulling a rug over her lap and making room for Valentine beside her. "It's positively frigid."

Valerie breathed a silent sigh of relief and gave her brother a smile. He frowned, but he climbed into the curricle and snapped the reins.

As soon as the remaining vehicles faded into the darkness beyond the churchyard gate, she dashed to the vicarage. She let herself into the cottage and searched for the housekeeper's bedchamber, then gently roused the widow from sleep. Mrs. Hodge didn't seem at all surprised to be wakened in the dead of night, drawing on her boots, dress, and apron, as though this sort of thing happened frequently.

The vicar and Steven returned minutes later. The viscount carried the body into the parlor and laid it upon a sofa Mrs. Hodge prepared with thick blankets. Wordlessly, he stripped off the injured man's bloodied coat and shirt as the vicar piled coal onto the fire, releasing a flurry of sparks and smoke. Mrs. Hodge carried in a basin of water, bottles of iodine and another of clear liquid, and bandages. Valerie stood at the edge of the firelight, shivering as she watched the eerily silent goings-on.

"It is not as hopeless as I thought," Steven finally said, on his knees before the injured man. The clean cloths Mrs.

Hodge furnished him with returned to the housekeeper's hands red, and the water in the basin turned pink. "He lost less blood than he might have on a warmer night."

"Bless the merciful Christ child for bringing us a bitter Christmas," murmured Mrs. Hodge.

"He was not cut deeply?" The vicar's voice, so strong from the pulpit earlier, now seemed aged and worried.

"In the muscle. He will lose easy use of the arm, I suspect. But he will live. His arm deflected the intended blow."

"Your approach must have stopped his attacker from making a second attempt," Mr. Oakley said.

"Praise be to our good Lord." The housekeeper proffered a needle with a long tail of thread attached to it.

Steven sewed up the man's wound, Valerie's memory stirring as he worked. He had tended to the sick man on board the corsair. Later she realized that as master of the *Blackhawk,* that was his responsibility. But he had done it even while he was a prisoner aboard his vessel, acting as servant to his men.

Unbidden, images passed through Valerie's mind, his thoughtful presence in the church earlier that night, his evident enjoyment in teaching the children to skate, the sincerity of affection when he spoke with his godparents, the silent grief in his eyes that day aboard ship when he told her he would have borne the dying sailor's pain if he could. And in Bebain's cabin, the blood streaking his face, his trophy for stealing laudanum to ease another man's death.

With crystal clarity, Valerie understood the cryptic words he had uttered after he kissed her that horrible day in their cabin, about what made him a man. At the time she thought he meant to humiliate her. Now the words meant something entirely different. He believed that this— tending an injured man, caring for another as he had cared for Ezekiel aboard ship, acting with compassion—*this* made him a man.

He stood and backed away from his patient, wiping his stained hands upon a cloth. He spoke quietly with the vicar while Mrs. Hodge dressed and bandaged the wound. Valerie collected the soiled linens and water and took them to the kitchen. When she returned to the parlor, Mrs. Hodge was tucking the coverlet around the wounded man.

"Oh, dear, Lady Valerie," Mr. Oakley said. "I must get you to the castle at once, or they will wonder where you are. Steven, will you come along now?"

The viscount turned from studying his patient and fixed Valerie with a measuring regard.

"Yes, indeed, sir. But first we should introduce the lady to our visitor."

Valerie stepped toward the sofa.

"My lady," Steven said, "this is Jeremiah Trap, late of His Majesty's Royal Navy. Please do not be offended if Jerry fails to bow to you. No doubt he would in more favorable circumstances."

Ignoring the comment, Valerie looked down at the blanket-wrapped form.

"Why, he is merely a boy." She stroked the youth's bandaged brow. His skin felt warm. By morning he would be in a fever. She smoothed back his hair and tucked the blanket more firmly about his neck.

"Most of them are only babes when they are impressed into service." Steven picked up his greatcoat and hat. "But that is a story for another day. Mrs. Hodge will take good care of the lad tonight. We, however, had best be on our way before our absence is noted."

"The groom is off with his family tonight," Mr. Oakley said. "I'll have to fit up the cart myself. Allow me a few minutes." He rushed from the parlor as though relieved to be going.

Gesturing for her to precede him, Steven followed Valerie into the vicarage's narrow entrance corridor. As he reached for the door, she put her hand against it to stay him. He did not move. She could shift only the barest inch and be in his arms.

"Who is that boy, really?" she asked.

Drawing his arm away, Steven leaned back against the wall. Even garbed in a greatcoat and drawn with weariness, his masculine beauty robbed Valerie of breath.

"A messenger sent to me from an associate." His quiet voice filled the confines of the entranceway.

"From where?"

"Portsmouth. Before that, Martinique. He was a long way in coming here to be cut down like a common thief, wasn't he?"

"Who attacked him?" She knew the answer, but she wanted him to tell her. At least one truth.

"Why did you come into the woods?" he asked instead.

It was not the right time to tell him about Hannsley and Flemming. He would certainly refuse her more answers if he thought she knew something she should not.

"I was looking for you. I saw the light."

His gaze did not falter. "You were not afraid?"

"You know I was not. What good would that have done? Now tell me what business you are engaged in that your messenger risks assassination on Christmas Eve in the very shadow of a church."

He regarded her silently. Then, pulling in a deep breath, he replied. "I apprehend illegal traders in the Atlantic and her environs."

"Traders of what merchandise?"

"Human beings."

Valerie nodded slowly, shivering at the truth finally from his lips. He was not a criminal. But she had known that in her heart all along. Still, it didn't all make sense.

"It is illegal to enslave men out of freedom now, isn't it?"

"That does not stop some. The trade is lucrative. Much more gold can be made selling newly imported men than reselling the children of slaves born in the Americas."

"But the French and Dutch—"

"Still allow imports. It is not difficult for an Englishman without respect for the law to continue very successfully."

"Maximin, and your crew . . . You work for the king?"

"Not quite." His sculpted mouth looked as though he might smile. In the churchyard, a harness jangled and snow crunched under carriage wheels and the heavy hooves of the draft pulling it.

"Are you rogue abolitionists?" she persisted.

Steven cocked his head. "Not quite that either. We have powerful allies when we need them, and sufficient patronage when necessary." He pulled the door open and stepped back to allow her to pass into the cold night.

The vicar grasped her hand and pulled her into the gig's narrow seat. Steven jumped neatly up beside her, and Mr. Oakley clicked his tongue to set the horse into motion.

"Like Jerry, the vicar here is another soul dedicated to justice," Steven said. "We are very grateful for his work."

The cleric shook his head. "I fear I have become too old for this," he said. "There were times when Margaret and Robert could call upon me and I would be ready for any escapade. Now I feel my decades every morning when I wake up. I do not know how much longer I can be of use to you, Steven. But my house will always be open for souls like young Jeremiah, putting himself in danger to do God's work."

Mr. Oakley's words hung in the chill air. Valerie's mind whirled with the memory of Lord Hannsley's comment at Lady March's salon about the countess's radical political activities. Lord and Lady March were involved in Steven's work, and apparently had been for quite some time.

"Lady Valerie, you did a fine service this evening," the vicar said. "You kept your head and helped when needed. Few young ladies in your position would have been up to it."

"Indeed, we accompany a brave noblesse home tonight, Vicar."

He sounded sincere, but Valerie didn't know how to think of his words. A jumble of confusion muddled her, and from where she pressed against him, shoulder to knee, she burned in mingled pleasure and agitation recalling their bodies so close the night before. But the bewildering proximity did not allow her space to think, only to feel. Now, though, she needed clarity, to put the pieces together and fully understand. The parts Mr. Flemming and Lord Hannsley played seemed infinitely more menacing.

The gig clattered up before the castle, and the vicar threw the reins to a groom. Steven grasped her fingers to assist her down onto the icy drive then released her. Heart hammering against her ribs, Valerie took a decisive breath and extended her hand again. With an odd light in his eyes, he accepted it and placed it upon his arm, then drew her toward the stairs to the house.

"Mr. Trap will bear a scar from his wound, won't he?" She spoke to rein in her jumbled nerves.

"Most certainly."

"How did you come by yours?" She must know. The duel with Hannsley, her dream, the image of Steven's hard, scarred body in the firelight, all of it racketed about in her head, begging for explanation.

"When I was eighteen, I sought to assassinate a man," he replied without hesitation. "I felt no qualm about it.

My cause was just. He was guilty. To my ill fortune, he was also a master swordsman. Before I killed him, he wounded me."

Valerie's mouth was suddenly dry. They came to the foot of the stairs and she halted. Vaguely, she could hear the vicar still speaking with the groom behind them.

"I see," she said, looking up. Her blood stilled. The answer to her question from the night before shone in his eyes. The crime he now spoke of had earned him the brand upon his arm. "This assassination," she said slowly. "You had never before met with such a challenge?"

"I had never before tried to kill a man." He seemed to shrug. "Suffice it to say, I did not make the same mistake again."

"You are quite skilled with a sword now." Valerie's belly felt hollow, but she was a fool to be affected like this. She wanted the truth. She should be ready to discover anything, even that his work required him to assassinate other men. "Did you learn to fight well so you could kill more efficiently?"

"I learned to fight well so that I would not need to kill."

"Because your cause no longer required it?"

"Because life is sacred." He spoke to the snow-dusted marble beneath his boots. "A man may deserve to die, Valerie, but it is not my right to mete out the time or place of it." He lifted his gaze to her. "It is testament to my youthful foolishness that I was obliged to murder a man in order to learn that. Fear and power, on the other hand, are astonishingly effective deterrents."

"Your Jesuit preparation was real. Wasn't it? You actually trained to become a priest."

Steven laughed. The unexpected rustle of self-deprecating warmth sent Valerie's heart galloping into her throat. He drew her up the steps toward the castle.

"I studied with the Jesuits for a time. But I swiftly discovered I am not suited to the clerical life, even the Society's adventuresome variety."

Forcing an outward calm she was far from feeling, Valerie struggled to suppress the memory winding its way through her body of his hands and mouth upon her. No, Steven Ashford clearly was not meant for celibacy. But, no doubt, he meant that as a Jesuit he would not be free to kill.

"Then, your conviction not to take another man's life was short lived?" she ventured.

His mouth curved up at one edge. "No. That did not deter me from entering religious orders. My conviction upon that matter remains firm."

Valerie drew her hand away from his arm, doubt again filling her. "But you killed Bebain."

"He threatened my interests."

"Oh, of course. He had control over your men."

"He believed he did. Maximin and our crew knew otherwise."

"Then, your ship—" Valerie's voice snared in her throat. Steven's jaw had grown taut.

"My ship," he said slowly. "How did he mistreat her, then?"

Valerie's memory of the *Blackhawk* under Bebain's rule was clear as day: gleaming decks, bleached sails, perfectly coiled rope. The madman had treated the vessel like a treasured mistress.

Steven's property had not been in any real danger from Bebain, nor his men, apparently. Valerie had.

Chapter 27

In the sudden silence, Maximin's voice echoed through Valerie's memory, his peculiar statement when he found them in the captain's cabin. Looking at Bebain in the puddle of blood, the Haitian had commented that matters had not proceeded according to plan.

Valerie could not breathe. Steven hadn't wanted to kill Bebain. He did it to protect her. To save her tarnished virtue, the virtue she had been so eager to give to a priest.

Shame and astonishing regret sliced through her. She parted her lips, but no words came forth. He grasped her hand and bent his head. His touch was warm and strong, his breath stirring the fur trim of her hood.

"Thank you, Valerie, once more. But I hope not again. There is great danger in this business. You must stay clear of it. And you mustn't tell a soul." His golden eyes entreated.

She held his gaze. "You can trust me."

"I am certain of it." He released her hand as the castle door opened. Light from the hall spilled onto the drive along with voices of laughter and song and the revelry of Christmas come.

Christmas dawned white and sparkling. Winter sun glinted off crisp snow, throwing into relief every dark, leafless branch, emerald bough, and wintering bird dotting the crystal landscape.

Valerie rested her chin upon her knees and sighed. Even in her impetuous childhood she had not passed such a restless Christmas Eve. The night had endured black and cold without, but Valerie burrowed under the bedcovers, warm in her cocoon but unable to sleep. Her thoughts alone heated her. More than ever, she ached for Steven, for his nearness, his confidences, his body, the touch of his lips upon hers. She had not been kissed in so long . . . at least not on her mouth.

She started guiltily.

She had been kissed on the mouth, very recently. Trying now to recall the sensation of Timothy's embrace, all she could summon was the bliss of Steven's strong grasp around her hand and his tawny gaze filled with a plea as he insisted she stay clear of danger.

Warmth curled through her. He was still anxious for her safety. His worry could be the very reason he held her off, so that she would not be in danger from his intrigues.

Even more wonderful than his concern, he trusted her. With his sanction, the vicar spoke freely of Lord and Lady March's involvement, as though he assumed Steven had already taken her into his confidence. Valerie leaned her head back and her chin tilted aside, her gaze coming to rest upon the weathered Bible on the bedside table. Miss Brown's visit to her bedchamber flickered into her mind.

Comprehension came fast and violent, like a kick to her belly.

"Dear Lord, not again," she groaned, burying her face

in linen-covered down and cursing her memories. Where
Steven Ashford was concerned, none of them was sacred.
All his new confidences, all she believed she had learned—
his apparent honesty, compassionate honor—and still he
continued to lie to her.

Valerie sat up, her gaze piercing the leather-clad book.
She had already suspected the Bible was not what he said
it was, an affectionate gift. Now she knew for certain
it was something else entirely, sent with her across the
ocean for some devious reason. Steven had enlisted his
godmother to retrieve it for him, and Lady March had
sent her companion to do it. It was probably the reason the
countess had invited Valerie to Castlemarch.

The blood drained from Valerie's cheeks.

He thought killing was wrong, yet he had murdered a
man to assure her safety. The thrill that rushed through
Valerie at thought of it horrified her. But his deceits tangled so thickly between the past and present, she didn't
know whether she could even trust what she had seen
with her own eyes.

She pressed her palms to her face. She wanted to de-
spise him, to continue mistrusting him. All the evidence
argued that he told her the truth now, that the man he had
pretended to be for the past sennight was the lie and the
man he revealed to her last night, real. Despite that, and
despite Vicar Oakley's words, she wished she could shut
her heart to him and his pretty falsehoods.

Bitterly cold now, Valerie climbed out of bed and went
to the window, dragging her coverlet with her. Parting the
drapery, she let her gaze stray to the fields beyond the gardens. In the shimmering dawn light, a horseman mounted
the hill north of the lake, heading toward the village. The
animal was the same gangly beast she had seen from the
breakfast parlor the day after her arrival at Castlemarch,

the horse Steven made her ride when he had seen her pain walking.

Perhaps he was on his way to see Jeremiah Trap at the vicarage. Or perhaps to meet another shadowy contact. She would never know. He would never tell her.

Valerie pressed her forehead against the frozen glass. Horse and rider reached the forest and disappeared into the dark trees. Her heart went with them.

He could so easily have told her the truth. Instead, he ordered her to stay out of his business. But Valerie wasn't innocent either. She hadn't said a word to him about Hannsley and Flemming's conversation. She didn't trust him yet. Steven had said he could trust her, but he was not giving her enough reason to do the same in return.

Sitting back and drawing her feet beneath her, she saw what she must do now. First, however, she needed more answers.

"My godson has not lived a simple life."

The Countess of March rested in a cushioned window embrasure. The blue parlor looked out onto the estate's rear grounds stretching down to graceful willows hanging like ancient sentinels over the frozen lake and the Greek folly at its far side.

Valerie sat beside the countess, holding a loose skein of wool. With long, ivory needles Lady March fashioned the yarn into a nightcap. In the gardens beyond the parlor's frost-tinted windowpanes, children played in the snow, governesses and older siblings chasing them through white drifts. Ensconced somewhere inside the vast mansion, their parents relaxed after the morning's gift opening and the lavish Christmas breakfast.

Valerie was not in the least bit relaxed. Seated far down the table from Steven during the meal, she had barely managed to swallow a bite. Stomach tight, afterward she went straight to her hostess and requested a private interview. Soon enough, everyone in the castle would venture into the woods in search of the Yule log. This was her chance. It didn't even matter that as she left the dining room with Lady March, Steven's gaze followed her.

The countess's needles came to a halt.

"Why do you ask about him, my dear? Are the young ladies inventing stories about Steven, enshrouded as he is in mystery?"

"I have heard others speculating. I like to think my interest is more merited."

The needles again clicked swiftly. "And why is that, my dear?" the countess asked in mild tones. Valerie's brow lifted. Had godmother or godson taught the other to dissemble so masterfully? But she had an uncanny sense that Lady March's kindness was no ruse.

"We made each other's acquaintance last summer before I came to London. In rather peculiar circumstances."

"Peculiar circumstances? Yes, that sounds like him. And from what I understand, Lady Valerie"—her tone did not censure—"it sounds like you too."

"Perhaps at one time." Valerie could not bring herself to smile. "I would like to know why he went to America."

Lady March laid her knitting upon her ample lap. Valerie bore her assessing regard, the crinkled eyes wise.

"Steven has not actually been in Louisiana for most of his lifetime, as rumor has it, but only a scant seven years or so," the countess began. "He spent his childhood like any English boy of the nobility, upon his father's estate in Kent, his summers here with me and the Captain. For most of that time he was without a mother. His father had a wandering spirit." The countess's gaze strayed out the window.

"I remember Rory Ashford, full of Irish pride, set loose at an early age to explore the world. He was a younger son, you see, never expected to inherit and something of a black sheep. He pursued unusual activities and kept unusual company. He was terribly handsome, but there was no real mystery about him. The greatest adventure of his life was when his father sent him to take care of some business interests in the West Indies. Before returning home, he took a tour through the Louisiana Territory, and there he found a bride entirely unacceptable to his family."

"Who was she?"

Lady March's brows rose. "A native of that country, a Natchez Indian, though living with a Cherokee tribe at the time, I believe. Her name—her English name, that is—was Willomena, though the family never used it when they spoke of her. She was the daughter of a native woman and a Prussian fur trader. Rory Ashford fell in love with the girl and wed her as soon as he could find someone to perform the service. She insisted upon a priest. She was a Catholic, you see. Some renegade Roman priests, it seems, will condone such an alliance," the countess added with a sideways look that made Valerie's palms go damp.

"Rory gained the sanction of an Anglican bishop as soon as he could, and the marriage was made licit and valid according to the Church of England. He had broken society's rules plenty when he was a single man, but he knew them, and did not wish to take any chances with his children," she added.

"The couple spent a few happy years in America. But when Rory told his wife finally that he wished to return to England, she refused to accompany him. She gave birth to a son, and when the boy was only a year old, Rory said good-bye to her and sailed with the boy to England. So, you see, Steven has been traveling across the ocean since practically the day he was born."

Valerie studied the countess's face.

"He left her in America?" Her chest felt hollow.

"Rory loved his wife," the countess said, "and he suffered dreadfully without her. He was never quite the same after he returned. But his love for his homeland was too strong. Bless him, for good or ill, Steven did not inherit that particular trait from his father, or from his mother, for that matter."

Valerie found her tongue. "She never joined them in England?"

"Eventually, but only when she learned her husband was dying. She wished to see him again, and she wanted to have the care of her son." The countess's gaze drifted once more across the parlor, unfocused.

"I met her shortly after she arrived, two years before her death. She was magnificent, beautiful beyond what I ever imagined a woman could be." She glanced at Valerie, a distant smile in her eyes. "I was young then, and she was majestic, elegant, with raven hair and golden eyes. It was not difficult to understand what Rory saw in her. She was a strong woman too, and clever. One of the few surviving people of her tribe, she had learned at an early age to fight for what she loved. When Rory died, she battled the Ashford family for her son, standing up to their cruelty and ostracism until they relented and gave her the management of Rory's house and the care of her own child. Steven was still under the legal guardianship of his grandfather, but he would have no other keeper. She won his heart instantly, as she had won his father's."

The countess nodded, as though conjuring up memories with the gesture. "She also won the Captain's heart, and mine. When she died of fever just shy of Steven's tenth birthday, the family made plans to send him off to school. Instead, the Captain took him under his wing and together they set off for Paris."

"Paris?" Valerie murmured. "During the Revolution."

"Indeed," the countess said soberly. "The Captain and I had become betrothed that season, and he promised to marry me after he returned from I knew not where, then." She lowered her voice as though the very air might overhear her. "You see, at the time he was engaged in some diplomatic activities which he did not see fit to share with me, the silly man." She waved away the memory. "When he left in '91 he took the child with him. Steven's grandfather and uncles did not protest. He was so far from the title, and they were so little interested in their mongrel relative that I think they would have been happy to learn he perished on the Continent.

"Instead he thrived. The Captain found a home—homes, actually—in which Steven was more than welcome, and the boy flourished in the excitement and intrigue of revolutionary Paris." For a moment Lady March's gaze lingered upon Valerie's warm cheeks.

"My lady?" Valerie's fingers twisted together. The story could not be over yet. She never wanted it to end. She wished to know everything about him, to entangle herself in the intimacy of his life. Her anger had faded, replaced by need and burning desire to understand him, and to trust him.

"The Captain returned from France for the final time without Steven," the countess said. "It was 1796 and he was only fifteen. The Captain and I had been married for several years by then, and his work was complete. He told me Steven decided not to return to England ever again."

"But he is here now." Valerie struggled to keep her voice steady.

"Indeed. He is here now," Lady March folded her hands

in her lap. "He appeared upon our doorstep in London just over a month ago. Oddly enough, it was five years to the very day he succeeded to his uncle's title. We have heard from him regularly over the years, of course, but had not seen him until then. He remained in town with us only a few days, then went off again to I don't know where until he arrived to join our party here."

The countess looked at Valerie in frank appraisal.

"I suspect, Lady Valerie, that your curiosity is not yet satisfied." Her tone held a light challenge.

"Not entirely, no." Valerie set down the yarn and reached into her reticule. "I believe you have been searching for this, my lady." She extended the worn French Bible.

Lady March glanced from the book to Valerie. "Are you certain you wish to part with that, my dear?"

"Fairly."

"He may never tell you why."

"I know."

The countess took the book and slipped it into her knitting bag.

"Now, dear girl," she said louder as a footman opened the door to admit other guests to the parlor. "You have tarried here long enough listening to an old lady's stories." Her needles paused and the shrewd eyes pinned Valerie again. "I wish you good fortune in your quest for answers, and when you have found them, the wisdom to know what to do with them."

Chapter 28

Rousing his guests, Lord March announced that the search for the Yule log would begin immediately. With only half a heart for the activity, Valerie joined the others for the trek into the woods, following her host and a burly footman bearing the Yule horn.

The merriment included a large quantity of alcohol concealed in pocket-sized flasks. As they left the yard and wended their way through the pristine green, gray, and white forest, Valerie spotted her maid sharing a bottle with a fine-looking footman. Closer at hand, Lord Michaels's valet produced two flasks.

"I will not be outdone by my own man," the baron exclaimed, drawing an embossed silver flask from his pocket. He offered it with exaggerated courtesy to Alethea.

"Thank you, my lord." She laughed, drank, and coughed, but managed a smile, then handed the liquor to Lady Alverston. Anna chuckled and took a sip before passing it along. Another pocket produced another flask, and yet another, and within minutes Valerie found a bottle in her hand.

She didn't want to drink. Her thoughts were sufficiently tangled already. But she raised the flask to her lips. Beyond her hand, not four yards away, Sylvia Sinclaire leaned upon Steven's shoulder. He tipped his face toward hers and she whispered in his ear. He smiled.

Valerie choked, then gulped. The liquid burned, curling into her clenched stomach. She sputtered.

"Dear me, Valerie," Cassandra said upon a girlish giggle. "If this is your first taste of spirits ever, I will be terribly disappointed."

Valerie wanted to scream. Turning from the sight of the golden-haired beauty hanging upon Steven's arm, she pasted on a grin and pressed the flask into her brother's hand.

"As for her first drink, my lady," Valentine said to Cassandra, "she took it at the age of twelve. Bramfield and I were home from school, and late one night we foolishly left a bottle unattended. It turned up empty the next day, and none saw my sister abroad until dinnertime."

Valerie pursed her lips, certain she deserved her brother's teasing and equally unimpressed with it, as Viscount Ashford seemed to be. His attention was all for the ruby-lipped coquette at his side.

"Lord Bramfield, is it true?" Alethea asked with a grin, "or is Lord Alverston simply trying to put his sister to the blush?"

"Alverston." Timothy smiled. "You should not spread unsavory rumors about the lady."

"I wager the lady herself does not consider the incident so unsavory." Steven stepped into the small circle and Valerie's heart tripped. He rested his glimmering gaze upon her. "Do I mistake it, ma'am?"

Alethea chuckled. Anna threw Valerie a curious glance. Valerie screwed her lips into a playful scowl, her heart pounding fiercely. With one mischievous statement he claimed to know her better than Timothy, the man everyone present knew had courted her for six months.

Of course, the faithless cur was right.

Stealing a glance at Timothy's benign expression, Valerie forced a grin to her lips and made herself look at Steven.

"Don't throw away your guineas, my lord. I am deeply ashamed of the episode. I took the bottle for my educational betterment. Miss Shockley's Academy for Young Ladies offered no curriculum in spirits, you see. I was obliged to augment my education where I could." For the sake of her audience, Valerie peered with theatrical curiosity at the flask in her mittened hand.

"I do believe that this contains some new beverage as yet altogether unknown to me. I suppose I must test it too." She sighed and put the bottle to her mouth. The others laughed. Eventually some moved away, continuing their stroll through the woods in search of the Christmas log. Valerie released a thin breath of relief.

The level of intoxicated hilarity grew louder and cheeks turned rosy. When her head started spinning, Valerie realized she had drunk more liquor than she intended. And her wool-wrapped mind had attention for only one object.

Accompanied by Sylvia's cascading laughter as they strolled among the snow-draped trees, he was easy enough to locate. Every nerve in Valerie's body tingled at his nearness, though her head argued that her nerves were widgeons. She certainly knew more now about the mysterious Viscount of Ashford, but that did not mean she understood him any better. Or trusted him.

Foolishly, she had hoped to find him changed overnight,

but her hopes were in vain. He did not flee her presence as he had the day before, but the sharp-witted nobleman had returned, and he was acting the part diligently now.

Sylvia's laughter trilled through the trees, followed by his warm chuckle. Swallowing bile, Valerie squared her shoulders and moved toward Anna and Alethea. A dramatic exclamation of delight stalled the party's progress. Everyone turned to the sound.

Sylvia stood beside a tall oak, staring into the boughs above. With both hands she grasped one of the capes on Steven's greatcoat. Her crimson cloak perfectly matched his cashmere muffler, and her golden curls brushed his shoulder as she turned her face inches from his.

"My lord, I have told Lady March we cannot celebrate Christmas without mistletoe, and here I have found some." She cast a long-lashed glance at the others now gathering around. "Will one of you gentlemen climb up to gather some from that branch? It will make the holiday complete." Her pleading voice rippled.

Valerie's lips pursed. Of course, her disgust for Sylvia's provocative behavior had nothing to do with the fact that the flirt had made the Viscount of Ashford the principal object of her attentions. Nor that Valerie had witnessed Sylvia hang several bunches of mistletoe in the hall only the previous day.

"Dearest Miss Sinclaire," Mr. Fenton said, ambling forward. "This tree is simply too tall to climb without a ladder. Isn't that so, gentlemen?" He glanced about for corroboration. Lady Cassandra giggled and several of the others nodded. "I propose we modify the tradition to make it serve our wishes just this once."

He took Sylvia's gloved hand. She glanced at Steven with guilelessly wide eyes as Mr. Fenton drew her away to stand beneath the milky bunch of berries. "Mistletoe is mistletoe, after all, wherever it hangs," he said, and kissed her upon her ruby lips.

At the look of satisfied delight upon Sylvia's face and Fenton's smug grin, laughter erupted from the group. But instead of blushing and moving from under the berry-laden branch, she turned to her former companion.

In painful awareness, Valerie watched Steven step lightly to Sylvia's side. He lifted her hand with elegant grace, bowed, and placed a kiss upon her gloved fingers that would have sent Valerie's heart into the boughs of the giant oak. Instead, Sylvia's classically beautiful face wrinkled into a pout.

"Come now, Ashford, that's not at all how it should be done," Lord Michaels said cheerily, grasping Sylvia's hand. Drawing back her glove, he kissed her bared wrist. Sylvia's face instantly brightened.

"Are married ladies unfit for such antics?" Anna murmured to her husband. Valentine pulled his countess under the bough and kissed her upon the lips, but Sylvia was still waiting beneath the mistletoe. With a smile, the earl offered her a chaste kiss upon the cheek. Lord Michaels led Alethea from the circle of laughing onlookers to buss her soundly upon the cheek as well, followed by a less-modest peck from Mr. Fenton upon her lips, and a beautifully executed kiss on the forehead from Steven.

Caught up in the laughter, when it dawned upon Valerie that soon she would be drawn into the fray, she panicked. She might exchange bantering words with him among her friends, but nothing in the world could induce her to accept a public kiss of any sort from Steven Ashford.

A burst of rowdy laughter offered her opportunity to escape. Slipping past a cluster of watching servants, Valerie ducked behind a broad fir. Not far ahead, another group of revelers wandered through the wood, trailed by a pair of spaniels. Valerie clapped her attention upon the dogs' wagging tails and set off after them.

Steven guessed at the reason for her flight. All he had wanted since releasing her hand upon the castle's doorstep the night before was to drag her into his arms and kiss her.

Since the night before? Since July when she disembarked from his ship. Since June when he first saw her on the merchantman's deck and heard her name called. Since before he'd been born, it seemed. He had wanted her forever.

She knew who he was now, and he felt as though he'd been released from prison chains. He no longer needed to pretend disdain or even indifference to her. He could speak with her freely. Or perhaps not freely, but at least as he spoke with other ladies.

His mouth still tasted sour from his affected flirtation with the Sinclaire chit. A necessary evil. Valerie might know who he was, but the remainder of the party still thought him a frippery fellow without a thought in his head.

The longer they believed that about him, the better. He'd only been in society for a fortnight. Soon, when the party at Castlemarch dispersed, the rumors would begin. Speculating upon how he came into the title, someone would recall his father's death and his mother's arrival in England. Gossips would remark on how he left as a child, so far from the succession to the title it did not seem to matter what happened to him upon the Continent. By then it would be common knowledge that his mother was not of pure English blood, not even pure European blood. That she had been Catholic.

Gossip would flow. The typical aristocrat had little mind for anything more useful.

So Steven would continue to make pretty with the jades

and innocents until he got what he had come for and was free to leave the *ton* behind again.

He would regret only one loss. Profoundly.

Flirting with Valerie would not leave a sour flavor in his mouth. And kissing her would be sheer pleasure. But not in a crowd of drunken revelers, however chastely. Even a lifetime spent training himself to self-discipline could not overcome the fever that ran through him when he touched her. He trusted Valerie to keep his secret. He simply did not trust himself to keep his other one.

She wove her way through the snow-bedecked trees unsteadily. He had driven her to drink, perhaps by leaving her to chew all day upon their last encounter. If he hadn't gone to the vicarage to check on Jeremiah earlier, he would have already sought her out. Not to kiss her, of course. To talk with her and learn what she knew of Clifford Hannsley.

The villain mustn't discover that she meant anything to him. If Steven's suspicions about Alistair proved true, Hannsley would know to be wary of him, further reason to maintain his imbecilic flirtation with everything in a skirt. At least then, any attention he paid to Valerie would not seem marked.

Presently, however, Hannsley was closeted at the castle with Fredericks playing chess, and the others still giggled drunkenly over the weed hanging in the oak. Casting a glance about to make certain no one noticed, he moved off after Valerie.

He found her standing amid a cluster of ancient, thick-boughed fir trees. Her back was to him, her arm bent behind and hand lodged within her collar. Even in such an awkward pose, the sight of her took his breath.

"May I be of assistance, my lady?"

She whirled around. A sliver of ice fell from her fingers. She wiped her hand upon her cloak.

"You are too kind, Lord Ashford, but no thank you," she said in a dampening tone, swaying a bit.

Steven lifted a brow. She was foxed and piqued with him, an unpromising combination. But then, he didn't want her promises. He wanted her mouth, her hands on him, her body beneath his, her hungry gaze upon his skin.

He took her arm.

She stiffened. "What are you doing?"

"When I encounter a lovely lady in need, I feel compelled to assist her."

She jerked around, eyes snapping.

"Do not hand me flummery, sir. After last night, after everything"—her eyes flashed eloquently—"do you think I'm simple? I am not silly little Sylvia Sinclaire, to be easily distracted by your charming smiles and pretty words."

"Thank God for that," he murmured, her jealousy settling unreasonably well in his chest.

"And I said I do not need your assistance." She wrenched free and stumbled away. Steven grinned. Even inebriated she was determined, and exquisite.

She righted herself again and her chin rose in defiance. The movement was so slight, so unconscious, it grabbed at his gut. He wanted her. She knew him—better than she realized even now—and he was tired of holding her off. Tired of resisting.

"I would like to know what would distract you, dear Valerie." He moved to her. "Mistletoe, perhaps? Or like my words and smiles, is that winter treasure destined to be appreciated only by silly girls?"

He glanced up. Valerie's gaze followed. Her mouth fell open as she saw the modest bunch of tiny white berries nestled in a bough above. She looked back at him. Her eyes were wide and sparkling with longing.

In an instant, everything changed. Nothing—not a crowd of revelers, a ship full of pirates, or even Clifford

Hannsley's looming presence—could stop Steven from kissing her.

"Mistletoe is mistletoe, after all," he whispered, closing the space between them and bending his head, "wherever it hangs."

It was only a kiss. On the lips, with little else involved. Given that two nights earlier he had touched the most intimate parts of her body with his hands and mouth, Valerie should not find it remarkable.

But it was like nothing she'd ever experienced. Perhaps because she had longed for his kiss for six months. Perhaps because he had denied it to her two nights ago even while drawing her body to frenzied pleasure. Perhaps because of the effects of brandy upon her bewildered senses.

Perhaps because she was so utterly, desperately in love with him.

Ever so gently, he brushed his lips against hers as his hands slipped beneath her cloak and around her waist, holding her still.

Valerie's eyelids fluttered closed.

With the tip of his tongue, Steven traced her lower lip. Pleasure burst into warm, tingling life in her belly, spreading through her legs, to her fingertips, and into her breasts. Her nipples prickled. She sighed and leaned into him, tilting her face up and gripping his arms.

He kissed the corner of her mouth softly, lingering. She shifted to meet his caress and he caught her lower lip, tugging gently until hers parted upon another sigh. He barely touched her, yet every iota of her being felt him, sensed his warm, masculine scent, his hands firm around her waist. A sound rose in her throat, of need laced with desperation.

He took her mouth fully, and Valerie fell into paradise. With confident, delectable pressure he opened her farther, filling her with heat, kissing her as though her mouth was all he wanted, all he needed. His tongue stole along the inside of her lips, washing frissons of pleasure through her. His big hand cupped her head beneath the fall of her hair, and he deepened the caress until nothing remained but his mouth and strength holding her so close, captive, driving her mad with yearning.

It ended much too soon. Through her foggy senses, the laughter of the others came to Valerie. Her eyes fluttered open.

Steven's gaze focused upon her face. His fingers came beneath her chin and he bent and touched his lips to hers again briefly, with infinite tenderness. He stepped away and took a breath, as though struggling for composure.

"Sweet Valerie." His voice was low and not in the least bit level. "I have wanted to do that for months."

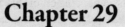

Chapter 29

A spiral of nerves spun through her. "You have?"

"Indeed, I have." His eyes shone warm and astoundingly candid. The voices of their companions, full of spirits and merriment, were close by. She had run away trying to escape this man's effect upon her, and now he was looking at her as though he didn't want her to run, as though he wanted to take her back into his arms and kiss her again.

She could not believe it. He lied. The only truth was that once more he had made her his prisoner, without offering anything for her to trust other than her reckless desire.

She stepped back, wavering upon wobbly legs before jamming her heels into the snow.

"Then why didn't you kiss me the other night, Monsieur le Prêtre?" she demanded. "I certainly gave you ample opportunity to do so."

Valerie stared, the breath knocked out of her as a grin split across Steven's handsome face.

"You are angry," he said, his tone lighter. "And you are somehow even more impossibly beautiful than usual when you are in a passion." He adjusted his tall-crowned hat, setting it at a rakish angle atop his shining gold locks.

"Passion? Of course I am in a passion," Valerie exclaimed. "I am foxed."

"I noticed that." The corner of his beautiful mouth curved up again. Valerie's insides responded as though he touched her there. She groaned.

"Is that why you chose now to finally kiss me?"

"Not very gallant of me, to be sure." He shrugged, still grinning.

Valerie shoved her fists into her hips.

His eyes sparkled. "It seems I could not prevent myself," he murmured.

Valerie gulped in a breath. "But what if I do not remember it once I am sober again?" Oh, Lord, had she really just said that? A pox on brandy. A pox on her heedless heart. A pox on noblemen-priests with heated amber eyes.

He stroked her cheek. "I will remind you." His voice was unmistakably husky.

It took every ounce of her will not to throw herself at him. Beyond his shoulder, Valentine and Lord Bramfield stepped into view from around the trees, the remainder of their party following. Steven pivoted with an open, easy countenance to the others. Dizzy pleasure still coiling through her, Valerie took a deep breath and cast a bright smile toward her friends.

"They found the Yule log, Valerie," Cassandra announced with spirit. "We are on our way there now. Didn't you hear the horn blow? None of us realized you wandered off."

Even intoxicated, Valerie could tell that Cassandra and the rest of her friends were in a similar state. Everyone except the Earl of Alverston, it seemed. As Valerie linked arms with Cassandra, her brother caught her eye and frowned.

Valerie snapped her gaze away, pulling her hood over the curls escaping her chignon with trembling fingers. She gripped Cassandra's arm and tried to walk steadily. She feared nothing would ever be steady now that Steven Ashford had kissed her again.

Valerie peered at her elegant reflection in the mirror. She was no longer foxed. In fact, no trace of the muddle-headed, jittery-nerved, tangle-bellied ninnyhammer from the woods appeared to remain.

"You are like a princess, mum," Mabel breathed in awed tones over her shoulder. "Better than a princess, for all I've heard of them."

Valerie turned from the glass. She might look her best in the silver-shot gown of sapphire silk, but her insides still swirled in a mass of confusion.

"If I appear well, Mabel, it is due to your magic. I feel absolutely dreadful." Valerie lifted her train and accepted a silver-embroidered shawl and a fan of midnight lace sewn with sequins.

"'Tis just the drink complaining. I've a bit of the megrim myself tonight."

Valerie wished she had the heart to grin, but she knew full well the after-effects of brandy did not cause her heart's erratic beat. Her gown whispered against her legs as she moved toward the door, and she crossed the corridor to Valentine and Anna's chambers.

"Ah, here she is, my dear," Valentine said pleasantly as the door closed behind her. "Never more beautiful than when she has done something indiscreet." He stood at the mantel, dressed with impeccable elegance, twisting the delicate stem of a wineglass between his fingers. Anna sat at the dressing table gowned in rose satin. A knowing smile curved her lips.

"Oh, Valentine," Valerie scoffed, "you sound more like the earl each day." She squeezed Anna's hand. "How do you bear this old curmudgeon?"

The countess's warm eyes twinkled. "It's not always so difficult."

"I will have you recall, young miss," Valentine said as he set his glass upon the mantel, "I am the earl now."

"Valerie, you are a Diamond," Anna said. "Is there a reason for the particular brilliance of your toilette tonight, darling?"

Feeling pathetically transparent, Valerie looked from Anna's interested smile to her brother's lowered brow.

"Valentine—"

He raised a palm. "I will not pry into your affairs, sister dear, or even chastise you. I am not our father, and I will not behave as he did, as I have informed you many times. You are a woman, and you have spent too much time away doing God-knows-what for me to question your behavior now." He paused, adding, "Despite the fact that it may be construed wrongly by others."

"Oh, Valentine, it was not as you think," Valerie said uneasily. "And Lord Bramfield—"

"Bramfield, indeed." The earl moved toward his wife. "Timothy, I am glad to say, seemed to find nothing amiss with discovering you alone in the woods with Ashford." He picked up Anna's shawl and draped it over her shoulders. "Tim's intentions are not what concern me, though. I hope you will take care with gentlemen about whom we know very little. Do you know anything of Ashford's character?"

"Valentine," Anna said, her perceptive gaze still upon Valerie, "Lord Ashford is the soul of graciousness, and clearly endeared to Lord and Lady March."

"That speaks well of him." Valentine conceded, offering his arm to Anna and extending his other for Valerie.

She tucked her hand into her brother's elbow.

His look gentled. "Do you wish me to learn something of him? Give me the word, and I will see to it. I would do it without asking, but I'm afraid that if I displease you, you will disappear into America for another two years and refuse to write again."

Valerie smiled, tears pricking at her eyes.

"Thank you, but not at this time," she said thickly. She would never take him up on the offer. All of Anna's and Valentine's love and support could not help her this time. She must face this challenge alone.

The moment she entered the drawing room and her gaze met his, Steven saw that her anger still simmered. He smiled, making her a small bow. She turned her back to him.

He should not have kissed her. But it felt so extraordinarily good to do something without thinking it through first. He hadn't done that in years, and he could not regret it.

He wanted to be with her, and his control was disintegrating. It didn't matter how he tried to justify it to himself, or to her. He should not touch her, seek her out, need her like breath. Yet he'd done so since he arrived at the castle, drawn to her like tide to the moon, impelled into her sea-storm gaze, waking him up to dreaming at last. He had kissed her again, held her in his arms, made her siren's body sing with pleasure, and he craved more. He ached to caress her satin skin and take her to the edge of insanity, just as she did to him by merely walking into a chamber.

He was not free to do so, however, when that chamber also contained Clifford Hannsley.

Hannsley's hooded gaze rested upon Valerie now. Steven couldn't blame him. Half the men in the room were staring at her. Her shimmering gown clung lovingly to shapely curves Steven's hands burned to know again, silken tendrils of dark hair caressing her ivory neck.

He drew in a long breath. His fashionable unmentionables and cut-away coat were not exactly suited for his body's response to her beauty. He searched for distraction. Alistair slumped in a corner removed from the conversation.

Steven suspected what his solicitor in London would tell him about Alistair's debts. Still, he must make certain of his old friend's betrayal. Jeremiah had brought assurances that the marquess carried with him the documents Steven needed. Steven could not prove Hannsley's guilt without those. Short of breaking into his private chambers, there seemed to be no solution. The man's valet was a bloodhound, on duty at all hours and armed, according to Amelia Brown, who had subtly investigated Castlemarch's upstairs denizens. Steven could subdue such a fellow. But he'd sworn not to do anything that would implicate his godmother and godfather in illegal dealings, or anyone else at the castle, including servants. He must manage this some other way.

Now Alistair claimed to be upon the verge of acquiring the documents. Steven had a great many reasons to feel unease. But a single glance at the woman across the chamber undid that all.

The butler announced dinner. Valerie turned to her brother and Lady Alverston. A warm smile curved her lips and a glimmer lit her eyes as she took the countess's arm. Lady Alverston bent her head to Valerie's, and the two women laughed.

She seemed happy with her family. At ease. She had what she longed for now, a home and acceptance among the people she loved and who cherished her as she deserved.

Steven's chest tightened. For a moment he allowed himself to imagine what it would be like to dance with her. The gentry from miles around would attend the ball tonight, and he would do his duty among the maidens and matrons. But he would only have eyes for Valerie. To dance with her, to hold her without secrets or censure, for anyone to see, just an ordinary man dancing with a beautiful woman, that would be like nothing he had ever experienced.

He dropped his gaze and stared into his untouched glass. In the candlelight, the wine looked like blood.

"Lord Hannsley is watching you," Anna whispered.

Valerie shrugged, pretending not to care. It was not the first time. He'd been casting her admiring looks since her first night at the castle. But now with what Valerie knew about him and Flemming and Steven's work, the Marquess of Hannsley's stares rested upon her skin differently. They felt like oil, dangerous yet full of opportunity if one struck the correct match.

"Have you promised a set to him?" Anna asked.

"Yes."

"Ah, then he is anxious for it to begin. What about Lord Bramfield?"

Valerie nodded. She had promised dances to practically every other man in the hall too.

"And Lord Ashford?"

Valerie's belly clenched. She shook her head. Anna turned a look of consternation upon her, but did not speak.

"He has not asked, and please don't say another thing about it." Valerie looked around, flicking open her fan to hide her search. Steven stood among a group of gentlemen. He stepped away from his companions to a young lady from the neighborhood sitting with her mother. He bowed and extended his hand. She dimpled and nodded, and he led her into the set forming.

Valerie's stomach felt like twisted caramel. Her dance partner appeared and she struggled to paste a smile onto her lips, glad to be away from Anna's knowing looks.

Quadrilles and minuets and contredanses of interminable length and excruciating monotony passed. Valerie stood up with apparently every gentleman in the district. An agreeable interlude with a cheerful Lord Bramfield left her dumbfounded as to whether he had actually seen her alone in the woods with Steven. She was standing at the edge of the floor waiting for her latest partner to return with a glass of champagne when Steven's voice came quiet and assured at her shoulder.

"Good evening, *mademoiselle*."

A warm shiver of pleasure rippled up her spine.

"Quite a festive gathering, isn't it?" He clasped his hands behind his back, looking out at the array of dancers forming the next set. Valerie's insides turned to jelly. Evening finery suited him extraordinarily well. She let her regard linger upon his etched profile, welcoming the tingling awareness coiling through her.

She dragged her gaze away. She did not want to feel this tangled weakness for him. She wanted to feel strong, in control of something, even if only her willful heart. She swallowed down the ache in her throat.

"Good evening, *my lord*."

"You delight in emphasizing the title, don't you?" he said lightly. "It seems you have not yet relinquished the conviction that I lack nobility."

She turned to face him. "Are you here merely to tease me, or have you come to ask me to dance?"

His slow smile curled around Valerie's senses like sweet fire.

"I do not care to dance this evening. I wish to talk."

"Yet it seems you have asked every other lady in the hall to partner you upon the floor."

"I haven't." His eyes glimmered. "I have not asked Lady Agnes or Lady Dorsey."

"Lady Agnes is eighty years old and Lady Dorsey uses a cane."

"I might still have asked them."

Valerie wanted to laugh, and cry. She could not bear the way he made her feel, full of amusement and warmth and longing and frustration all at once. It hurt in the very pit of her stomach. In her soul.

"Why don't you wish to dance with me?"

The gold flecks in his eyes glittered. He bent his head, and his voice came low and intimate beneath the shimmering music.

"Because, Valerie, to touch you and yet not hold you would be beyond my ability at this time."

Heat flooded her from brow to toe. "A simple dance?" she said shakily.

"A dance in this society is merely a pretense of making love, and not a very satisfying one at that."

Valerie's knees went watery. This was exactly what she had wanted to hear from him, and now her tongue would not seem to untwist.

"You are mistaken," she managed. "It is a mild entertainment, or perhaps a gesture of admiration. At most it is an indication of courtship."

"All the more reason that I should not ask it of you."

Valerie stepped back, her stomach heaving. She felt like screaming. She couldn't believe she had let herself fall into the silken grip of his game playing again, or that he was still doing this to her, after everything. But it seemed he simply could not give without taking away again.

Pressing down upon her pain, she sucked in a breath,

words catching in her throat. Steven's golden eyes shadowed with disquiet.

"Valerie, I do not wish to—"

"Tell me what you are doing here at Castlemarch," she blurted out. "If nothing else, you owe me that."

He nodded, his face grave. "You are entitled to know something."

Valerie swallowed, holding her tongue.

"There is a man amongst the party here who illegally exports Africans to sell in the West Indies. My associates and I intend to halt his activities. To do this we need certain documents that will finally implicate him in this crime."

Valerie's heart raced. It all made sense now, the conversation between Flemming and Hannsley, the fencing bout. Hannsley and Steven were enemies, and Flemming was indeed double-dealing.

"Does this man know who you are? Your other identity?"

His gaze changed, studying her. "Possibly."

The hairs on the back of her neck bristled. "I see. And the Bible for which I was unwitting courier? What part does it play in your intrigues?"

"Hidden in its binding is a signed letter written by the master of the slaver's flagship. In it he admits to his employer's crimes."

Valerie clamped down upon the quaver in her throat. "It seems extraordinary that you put this letter into my possession. Only last night you told me to stay clear of your business."

"Raymer's navigator brought the letter to me. It had to reach England even if I did not. I sent it with you for safekeeping."

Hollow nausea stirred again in Valerie's stomach. He'd known she would not discard the Bible. He depended upon her infatuation with the priest, her yearning for adventure, and her desperation to cling to both once she was again in England. Like a love-starved child, she had not disappointed him.

"You used me," she said dully.

"I trusted you."

"I don't believe you."

"Believe me or not, it is the truth."

Valerie fought back anger and tears. She couldn't rant, but she could not cry either. Instead, she would think. Her heart was powerless against his pretty lies. Her mind must see her through, a mind that for years devised scheme after scheme to win the love of a man who died refusing it to her.

"Does this criminal have the documents with him here?"

He hesitated only a moment. "Yes. Jerry nearly lost his life yesterday bringing me that information. He was in this man's employ until he decided it suited his conscience to work for us instead."

"Why don't you steal the documents?"

Steven's expression grew guarded. "I will acquire them in due time."

Valerie wanted to ask whether he planned to acquire them before or after another near-fatal battle with his enemy. She clamped her lips shut. She would not reveal that she knew Lord Hannsley was his target. It seemed he already suspected Mr. Flemming was betraying him.

But Valerie knew something too, exactly how to wrest the precious documents from the marquess in a way that Steven Ashford, for all his clever disguises, could never attempt. Heart beating rapidly with newfound purpose, she wanted to be away to set out on her mission. But pulled like a magnet, her whole body seemed to resist leaving him.

"Is Mr. Trap well? I sent a message to the vicarage, but I didn't hear back. No doubt Mr. Oakley and Mrs.

Hodge were busy enough today without penning assurances to me."

"He is somewhat improved." His eyes looked oddly bright and his voice sounded strange.

"What is it?" She peered at him. "You regret having told me about your business here, don't you?"

"I make it a point to never regret anything." His words shivered through her like a touch.

"Then what is amiss?" He could not possibly know what she planned.

"You care about how Jerry goes along now."

"Of course. Why shouldn't I?"

He did not respond immediately, and Valerie's breath stilled as flame seemed to dance in his eyes.

"Valerie Monroe," he finally said in a low voice, "you are a remarkable woman. Fearless yet genuine, and so very lovely."

Valerie's tongue failed. For a fortnight he had flirted with every lady at Castlemarch except her. Now, in the middle of a ballroom full of people, he slayed her with one simple, beautiful compliment.

"Lady Valerie," a male voice said breathlessly behind her. "I offer my most profound apologies for my wretched delay in— Oh." Her dance partner stopped short, a glass of champagne in each hand. "My lord." He bowed stiffly to Steven.

The viscount bowed back. He lifted one corner of his delicious mouth, nodded, and walked away.

Chapter 30

Resolve high, Valerie made excuses to her next partner and went straight to the Marquess of Hannsley. He stood in the flickering light of the Yule log's blaze. Despite the warmth still coursing through her veins from Steven's words, she moved toward the hearth, letting her shawl slip from her shoulders. More quickly than she imagined possible, Lord Hannsley came to her side.

"Dear Lady Valerie, are you chilled in this cavernous keep?"

Valerie clasped her hands behind her, giving the marquess an ample view of her gown's revealing décolletage. She batted her lashes.

"The hall is rather frosty this evening, isn't it, my lord? Gentlemen have the advantage of current fashion on such evenings, while ladies . . ." She raised a gloved hand and fluttered it provocatively over her bosom. "We are not as well protected."

"A minor injustice, madam, when compared to the great delight such stunning fashions afford admirers."

His hooded eyes showed hesitant appetite, as though he was not certain of her intent.

Valerie brought the tip of her closed fan to her lips. "You are too kind, sir," she said upon a sigh that pressed her breasts further against her bodice.

"Kindness has little to do with it, my dear."

Valerie grinned, the cat at the cream pot.

"May I now claim that dance you promised me?" He extended his hand.

Valerie pushed out her lower lip. "I would be happy to dance, sir"—she pouted—"but my maid has vexed me horridly. I sent her to fetch my reticule ages ago, and she still has not appeared with it." She sighed and pinned the marquess with a sweet smile. "Aren't servants trying on one's patience? Not to mention disloyal. Why, only today my maid told me she would leave at week's end to serve in another household. What impertinence." She set her fingertips upon her chest, breathing deeply in false indignation.

"Indeed, my lady," the marquess replied, not bothering now to hide his interest in her swelling breasts. "When a man cannot trust those who serve him, he must take serious measures. In fact I have recently disciplined a servant who betrayed me."

Valerie's stomach twisted at the note of fresh anger in his voice. But his words and tone confirmed her conviction. He had attacked Jeremiah Trap in the woods to silence him.

She took another deep breath, her skin prickling as he gazed down at her with undisguised desire. It was an uncannily familiar look. She had seen it on Bebain's face, the look of a man whose anger fueled his lust.

"I have a splendid idea, my lady," the marquess purred. "We will outwit your worthless maid and fetch your reticule ourselves. Perhaps we will catch her frittering her time away instead of serving her mistress." He extended his arm.

Valerie took it, sticky heat crawling beneath her skin. She let him lead her toward the door to the great hall, casting a look back. No sign of Steven. A silent sigh of relief escaped her lips.

Lord Hannsley spoke little as they climbed the stairs to the castle's east wing. The corridor leading to Valerie's chamber was deep in shadow, lit by only a single lamp. The marquess grasped her arm and pulled her around to face him.

"Which door leads to your chamber, my dear? Show me and we will hasten to chastise your insubordinate servant." His voice was throaty, revealing his eagerness. Valerie felt sick with triumph.

She sighed. "Oh, my lord, I cannot allow you to enter my bedchamber." She matched his tone as expertly as any Drury Lane actress. "My maid would talk, and I do not want any unpleasantness with my brother. I am sure you understand."

Displeasure narrowed Hannsley's heavy eyes. His hand tightened upon her arm and he took her chin between his fingers, stroking her jaw with large, smooth fingers.

"What would you like me do, my lady? I am yours to command," he said silkily. His thumb stroked her lower lip, and a spiral of treacly sensation coursed through Valerie. She shivered. His eyes steamed.

"My brother and sister-in-law will miss me if I leave the ball early. But your valet would not reveal me to the other servants if I were to . . ." She looked up in pretty confusion.

"After the ball I will dismiss him," he supplied. "Once you have found your way to my chambers we will enjoy all the privacy we wish." He moved his face close. Valerie steeled herself, hiding her distaste behind a mask of muted fervor.

"Until then I wait impatiently, my beauty." He pressed his mouth against hers, his hand sliding from her arm to her shoulder and then down to her bodice. His lips slavered, his palm covering her breast. He groaned in frustration as she pulled away as though reluctantly.

She shivered again, and tugged her shawl around her shoulders, repressing the urge to wipe her lips.

"I will see you after all are abed, then," she whispered. She lowered her lashes and turned, making her way quickly down the stairs and to the great hall.

To her next quarry.

"Place a scant teaspoonful of the syrup in a glass of warm milk just before you lie down to sleep—"

"At least ten minutes before you lie down—"

"No, no, dear girl. My sister is incorrect. Forgive me, Agnes, dear, but you have got it all backward. Lady Valerie, you must drink the milk after you are abed, I assure you."

Valerie gazed earnestly at the Dowager Baroness Dorsey. With mirth bubbling up in her, it was hard to keep pretending she had a terrible megrim. But the conversation of the septuagenarian sisters only partially caused her giddiness. The rest was sheer nervousness.

Thank the Lord, at least Steven was not in the hall any longer. Valerie was vastly relieved. Subterfuge was difficult enough without his perceptive gaze upon her.

"Lady Dorsey," she asked, glancing at the vial of sleeping draught in the dowager's outstretched palm, "won't the cordial take effect unless I lay supine?" Her nerves jittered. If she must, she would go all the way to the bed with Lord Hannsley to ensure he passed out, no matter how much she dreaded it.

"Heavens, no, dear girl!" Lady Agnes exclaimed. "Its effect is quite sudden, in fact. My sister never drinks it until she is already abed for fear of falling short of her mattress before she dozes off." Lady Agnes slapped her hands upon her taffeta-clad knees and chortled. Her sister cast her a wrinkled glare.

"I see." Valerie nodded. "Ladies, I am so grateful for your help. I daresay I will sleep well after sipping this." She curled her fingers around the glass container and tucked it into her reticule.

"Very good, child. So glad we could be of help." The dowager patted her hand. "Now, remember, that vial contains enough for at least a sennight. I shouldn't have given it to you at all, but you are such a lovely girl. I do not want you to lose your looks over a frightful megrim."

No, Valerie thought grimly, she did not want to lose her looks either. Especially since she was counting upon them, as well as her wits, to ransack a nobleman's bedchamber momentarily. She left the sisters and went across the hall to Anna.

"There you are, darling." Anna took her arm. "The locals have all departed and the orchestra is packing up. Valentine has gone to play billiards with a few other gentlemen." She lifted her brows in question.

Valerie ignored the suggestion. If Steven was off playing billiards, all the better. Seeing him now would tax her too greatly, and she needed to focus. "Let's retire." They started across the emptying hall to the foyer and the stairs Valerie had climbed a mere hour earlier beside the Marquess of Hannsley.

Anna halted. "Oh, no. I have left my reticule in the drawing room."

"I will come."

"No, no." Anna waved her ahead. "You go on to bed. I will see you in the morning." She bussed Valerie's cheek and turned back to the hall.

Valerie's heart tightened. She so much wanted to share the truth with her closest friend. She still didn't know why she hadn't told Anna about Etienne. Steven. The man she had fallen in love with at sea.

He was the same man, from the flame in his lion eyes that weakened her with desire, his touch that melted her anger and frustration, leaving only longing, to the tender caress of his voice when for brief moments he ceased pretending he did not care for her.

She started up the steps and a hand wrapped around her wrist. She knew instantly who touched her, whose fingers slipped around hers, warm and strong, drawing her alongside the staircase and into the shadowed alcove beneath. Valerie would know him anywhere.

She should not allow this. She wanted to help him, but she could not continue touching him, kissing him, or she would go mad with wanting him, wanting more than he would ever give her.

Steven pulled her to the wall and closed the space between them. Valerie's lips parted, but refusal stalled upon her tongue. His eyes shone fever-bright. He bent and covered her lips. Aching swelled up from the deepest part of her, tangling in her mouth and throat, her belly and legs and along her skin as his hands curved around her shoulders and his kiss deepened. He parted her lips with a sweep of his tongue, and his body pressed hers to the wall.

She could die right away. Because she simply could not live through another moment of this torturous seduction of blazing passion followed by frost.

Barely mustering the effort, she broke free.

"What are you doing?" she whispered.

Steven's arm cinched her waist, his mouth trailing heat across her skin. His hand curved around her breast and his thumb passed over her nipple. The caress echoed inside Valerie everywhere, as though he touched her between her legs. She dug her fingertips into his shoulders. "What are you doing to me?"

"Kissing you. Touching you as I have wanted to touch you all night," he said against her lips, stroking her breast through gown and corset. The peak swelled, the ache he roused unbearable.

"Why?" She strained into him, shivers of pleasure springing from his touch. "Why now?"

"I cannot stop myself," he said, his voice low, urgent. "When I am apart from you, I crave the sight of you. When you are near, I think of nothing but holding you." He slid his cheek against her hair. "I told you before, I am unable to not touch you any longer."

Valerie groaned and sank into him. His words, his caresses could not be real. And yet the man she longed for with hunger so deep it clamped upon her lungs—that man held her now, touching her as though he truly could not prevent himself. And as much as she knew she must remain strong, could not bear his extremes for another day, she wanted him. Wanted his caresses, his lion's gaze heating her, his rich voice speaking breathtaking words to her.

She slid her hands beneath the fall of his pristine white cravat, then inside his coat.

"Then now you know a little of the torture I have endured," she whispered, smoothing her palms over contoured muscle, his heat infusing her through the linen.

"There is nothing little about it," he growled, trapping her fully to the wall and pushing her knees apart. His hips shifted against hers, his rigid need stroking her tender flesh. She whimpered, gazing up at him. He was so beautiful, sculpted cheeks, sun-gilded hair, serious mouth. She ran her palm up his chest over his cravat to his neck, sliding her fingers through his hair.

His fire-flecked gaze searched hers, then he bent his head and kissed her, deep and drinking-in, and she touched him. His jaw beneath her sensitive fingertips was rough with the day's golden whiskers. Her hand slipped to his sinew-corded neck, tenderly caressing his Adam's apple and halting his kiss, his throat working at the unexpectedly intimate caress. She found his pulse, fast and hard, and her body thrummed with awareness. He grabbed her palm and flattened it to his skin.

"Valerie." Her name was a breath only.

She tugged free and slid both hands inside his coat again, spreading her fingers across his heart, finding the reckless source of his pulse. His silk waistcoat and linen shirt gave no suggestion of the scar beneath, brutal and uniquely beautiful upon his muscular body. But she remembered it, knew the danger he had once lived, still lived. His scent filled her, hot and male, flooding her senses. She slipped her palms lower, aching to feel him, to revel in his closeness, his willingness, his need pressing into her, feeding her desire.

Through fabric, her hand closed upon him. Steven sucked in his breath and gripped her arms, but he did not push her away. Valerie explored, his flesh hard as bone but wonderfully supple. He wanted her. For the moment, the night, or longer than that, she had no idea. But he was not moving away, and she wanted to touch him more, to bask in the delirium of his nearness.

She curved an arm around his waist and pressed into him. Taut muscles flexed beneath her palm as he bent his head and covered her mouth. His body surrounded her, her whole being fusing into him. She gripped him tight, fierce need tangling reason and fear into uselessness, leaving only sensation and longing. If he did not force her to release him, she would never be able to.

"Sweet Valerie," Steven murmured, taking her mouth again, drinking in her beauty and warmth, her lips the color of autumn roses and the flavor of madness. Her hand slipped from between them around his back. In agonized relief he coaxed her lips open to his tongue, tasting her moist beauty, inside her again where he always wanted to be.

He had struggled to leave her earlier. He shouldn't have waited for her here, should not succumb to his desire. But he must feel her again, drown his senses in her if only for a fleeting heartbeat before he left for London. His blood pounded, the caress of her confident, tender hands making it impossible to think, to plan, to reason, only to feel what she did to him.

He threaded his fingers through her hair and crushed her mouth, urging truth into his kiss. Finally, the truth. For three decades he had ruled his life with iron control. She turned that iron to chalk and he wanted her to know it.

He was mad already. He had come to Castlemarch as though possessed, drawn by a fantasy, a mirage of what warmth and desire felt like entwined. He'd known that fantasy so briefly with her at sea. He never would again because his life—the godforsaken destiny he had mapped out for himself—would not allow another to share it.

She wrapped her arms around his shoulders, the intoxicating shape of her hips and breasts a living breath of heaven against his body.

It must end. He must leave now or risk everything. She knew he targeted Hannsley. After they spoke in the hall, she went straight to him.

Damn his weakness. He ached to tell her everything, but he'd held back. Yet still he revealed too much. Now, before she involved herself further, he must act swiftly. At dawn he would leave for town. After he returned, he would do whatever it took to get those papers from Hannsley. Then she would be safe and Steven could go back to his reality, so far from the family and home this woman cherished that it might as well be across the world, not merely an ocean.

Now was too soon, though. Fire burned in him, hotter with each caress of her lips, each soft sigh in her throat. In the darkness he pressed down her gown and the cup of her corset and shift, and stroked her tender flesh. The firm peak swelled at his touch. She moaned low in her throat and curled her foot around his ankle, cradling his erection intimately. She gasped and whimpered his name.

He crushed her mouth beneath his. He must have her, touch her everywhere. God Almighty, he had never needed to be inside a woman with this frenzied urgency. Only this woman. He ground against her and she arched to him, gripping his shoulders, her breaths rapid. He could give her pleasure again so easily. She was ready for it. But if he did not stop now, he would not be able to stop at all. He would have her here, beneath the stairs, against the wall, fast and hard and absolute.

He would finally make her his.

He lifted his head. Her ocean eyes shone hazy with passion, her lips glistening red and swollen from his kisses. It took every ounce of his will to loosen his hold.

"You must not involve yourself in this business, Valerie." He struggled for breath. "Leave it alone. Leave him alone. Promise me you will."

Her body convulsed as though with shock, then stiffened. She swallowed quickly, repeatedly, and her gaze lit with renewed betrayal.

"This seduction," she said raggedly. "This is to bend me to your will, isn't it?"

She could not have hit him physically with such force. Steven stared, astonishment and pain racing through him like wildfire. After thirty years, he finally knew how it felt to be damned for his sins.

Her arms slid from around his neck and she turned her face away. "I will never understand you. I don't know who you are or what you want. I don't even know what to call you."

A fist closed around Steven's heart. He surrounded her face with his hands, forcing her gaze to his again, need and sudden desolation coursing through his veins.

"But I know what to call you," he whispered, the words coming so quickly he hadn't the will or strength to stop them. *"Mon âme. Mon coeur."* His soul. His heart. She had been those and more for months already.

She trembled, her eyes wide. But she did not say a word.

"I must go to London tomorrow for the day." He stroked his thumb across her cheek, willing away the stunned doubt in her eyes. "While I am gone, take care, Valerie. Do not play these games. There is grave danger involved, and I want you to remain safe."

Disbelief colored her eyes. "You want me to—?"

"It is all I have ever wanted."

Chapter 31

Valerie choked down the sob rising in her throat. She ached to believe him. Every fleck of desire in his eyes, every gentle caress upon her skin, every tenderly spoken word seemed so real.

"I don't know whether you are lying to me," she said, swallowing hard. "But I think you must be."

"I have never lied to you, Valerie."

No. It couldn't be true. He had led her to believe untruths. He intentionally deceived her, over and over again. She wrenched out of his arms.

"Go to London. Go. Leave me in peace." She spun away.

"Promise me you will not involve yourself in this matter."

She rounded on him. "You lie more times than I can count, even about telling me the truth, and you still think you can give me orders?"

He gripped her wrist, his touch unyielding. "Promise me."

Valerie bit back on the desire washing through her. Even his rough handling filled her with yearning. She wanted him so badly it blinded her. But even as he said beautiful things, he still held her off.

What he had called her—his soul, his heart—it could not be the truth. Her heart could not bear it to be true and still lose him. He'd said it himself tonight, there could be no courtship between them. There might be passion, even warmth, but nothing else. He would never let her truly know him.

But if he believed she would cower under his demands, he did not know her either.

She threw back her shoulders. "I promise I will not do anything to compromise your mission."

Abruptly, the fire in his gold-flecked eyes receded. Cold resignation took its place. After his heated declaration, the icy response stole her breath.

He released her, and without another word turned and disappeared into the dark corridor. Valerie fled up the stairs.

"So, it's milord Hannsley you're going off to see now?"

Valerie met her maid's gaze in the dressing table mirror. "How do you know that?"

"Saw you with him earlier in the corridor."

"It is none of your business."

"His valet's got the look of a highwayman," Mabel said darkly.

A shiver of apprehension passed through Valerie. "And how would you know what a highwayman looks like?"

Mabel remained ominously silent.

Valerie turned to her maid. "Lord Hannsley possesses some papers that are valuable to me. I am going to get them." Mabel's brow drew down. Valerie guessed it would be a good idea if at least one person knew her plans. She certainly couldn't tell Anna or Valentine, and Mabel's shrewd look satisfied her. "I will dose him with a sleeping cordial, then search for the papers."

The girl's eyes widened. "Mum, you can't."

Valerie pinched her cheeks to bring color to them. She looked as pale as a specter. "You can keep this to yourself, Mabel, or, if I hear a word of it has gone above stairs, you can expect to be dismissed. But one way or another, I am doing it."

The maid's back went ramrod straight. "I will never tell a soul."

"Anyway, you owe it to me after the way you let Lord Ashford cozen you into obeying him on our walk back from the village the other day. Now, how should I carry this knife?" She frowned and handed it to her maid. "Keep it. It won't do me any good in my reticule." The small bag already contained the only essential item for Valerie's undertaking. Smoothing her hair a final time, she turned toward the door.

"Let me go instead, mum," Mabel said. "Or wait a day, and tomorrow I will make up to that nasty valet and sneak into milord's chambers that way."

"Thank you, but I have to do this myself." She took a steadying breath and pulled her shawl around her shoulders. "But you can remain in the corridor, just by my door here."

"If anything occurs, I will be ready to defend you." Mabel brandished the knife.

"I am persuaded it will not come to that," Valerie said with a great deal more confidence than she felt. She stole into the corridor and to the far end of the east wing, halting before the marquess's door. With a glance behind to see Mabel slide into the shadows, she knocked. The door opened immediately, and Valerie slipped inside.

Lord Hannsley turned the key in the lock.

"I trust you were not noticed, dear lady," he said smoothly, taking her arm and leading her toward the hearth.

"I don't think so. I was very careful." Careful to wait until all were in bed, and to stop herself from crying after she fled Steven so she wouldn't ruin her face before meeting the marquess. She'd also been very careful to repeatedly convince herself that this was the right thing to do, no matter how cold her hands and how twisted her heart.

A fire burned in the grate. The room was overly warm and heavy with the sticky scent of Lord Hannsley's cologne. She sank to the sofa as he sat down across from her. A decanter of wine and two crystal goblets were arranged on a silver tray upon the table between them. She extended her chilled fingers to the fire.

"Are you anxious, my dear lady? I cannot believe it of you. Perhaps you would care for a drop of wine?"

Valerie's nerves didn't sizzle in the way Lord Hannsley imagined. Six months earlier she'd lived through an adventure much more terrifying than this. Beneath the marquess's hooded gaze now, she could not bring herself to be truly afraid. Whatever else happened, at least he was unlikely to kill her.

Though, of course, he had tried to kill Steven.

Valerie pressed down upon her fear. It was simple. She simply must make sure the marquess had no idea why she had really come.

She accepted a glass. Lord Hannsley stood and sauntered to the window to draw together the thick red draperies. She seized the opportunity. Snatching the vial from her reticule, she poured its entire contents into the crystal carafe. The dark syrup dissipated into the wine, and an involuntary breath of relief escaped her.

The sound drew the marquess's attention. He returned and squeezed her shoulder.

"You are not weary after the long day of merriment, are you, my dear?" he purred, and rounded the sofa to sit beside her. Valerie shook her head, smelling cheroot as his thick thigh pressed against hers.

"No, my lord, I am well. But I would like you to answer a question for me."

"I am at your service, lovely lady." He stroked her cheek with the back of his finger. Valerie resisted a shudder of disgust.

"In the hall, you seemed to realize that I—mm— wished for your company this evening." She fluttered her lashes. "How did you know?"

The marquess splashed more garnet liquid from the decanter into his glass. He touched his goblet to hers and lifted it to drink. Valerie set her mouth to the edge of her goblet. His gaze settled upon her lips.

"My dear, you have me in a quandary. How am I to reply?" He sipped. "I cannot imply that your behavior was anything but modest by saying that you called to me with your delectable body when you entered the hall this evening."

Valerie's stomach knotted. He took another pull of wine, and his hooded gaze shifted to her breasts.

"And I cannot impugn myself by suggesting that I have enough experience to tell when a woman is desirous of an intimate acquaintance."

Valerie stared in amazement as the dark circles at the centers of his eyes widened. He drew another sip, but still his goblet remained half full. She tipped her crystal glass against his again.

"Then, my lord, shall we say that you simply had an intuition?" She tried to keep her voice low.

"Intuition, my beauty, and some knowledge of the sort of female you have been in the past." Wine funneled through his lips. With a deft movement he grabbed her glass out of her fingers and clasped her face between his huge hands. His wine-wetted lips came down open upon hers.

Stunned, Valerie forced herself to submit. Hannsley groaned, and his hand went to her breast, then without warning between her thighs. Sick, cold sensation jolted through her, and she tried to shift away from his groping fingers. He pushed onto her, sucking her neck, his fingers clutching at her through the gown.

Valerie clamped her eyes shut and forced herself to remember the reason she was again voluntarily submitting to a bad man's desires. This time, however, the success of her plan did not require Steven to commit murder.

His words from earlier still ricocheted through her, filling her with fever even as she tried to shut out the sensation of the marquess's onslaught. He had all but declared himself. Afraid of how he could hurt her, she had been unable to believe him then. But now exhilaration and renewed purpose crowded out fear. Steven wanted her, and she would do anything to help him. Any moment Hannsley would succumb to the cordial and she would be free to use her wits instead of her body to achieve her goal.

Hannsley bore her down upon her back to the cushions. Valerie struggled to free her lips.

"My lord," she gasped. "I cannot—"

"Temptress," he said heavily as his mouth shifted to the edge of her bodice. "You can for me, just as you have for others. My cock is primed for you already, vixen."

Valerie gulped in air and shoved at him. "My lord, please, I need a moment to prepare."

His grip between her legs released and his hold on her breast slackened. Valerie's heart leaped.

"Lord Hannsley?"

"Dearesht Lathy Vaalera, I cannosh sheem to—to—"

His slurred voice sounded like music as his chin dug into her shoulder. She pushed his chest hard and rolled him off her onto the floor. Springing up from the sofa, she gathered her skirts and looked down at the giant man sprawled upon the thick Persian carpet, his arms splayed at odd angles beneath him, his hip jutting up and face pressed into the floor.

Valerie knelt and pressed her fingers to the pulse at his neck. A breath of relief stole through her lips. He slept.

She looked about the bedchamber, for the first time fully aware of her surroundings. She scowled. A real intriguer would think to look around when first she entered a new place, to prepare. But it could not be helped now.

She hurried to the escritoire and filed through its meager contents: a stack of handkerchiefs embroidered with scrolling Hs, several vowels of unfortunate gentlemen, a high-polished snuffbox, and a container of cigars.

No papers.

Valerie didn't know exactly what the documents would look like or say, but she suspected Lord Hannsley would not travel to a country house party with such a great many papers that she could not recognize the important ones when she found them.

She moved through the bedchamber and into the dressing room, searching every nook. Finally, crowing quietly in triumph, Valerie discovered her prize, a string-tied bundle of correspondence tucked into the bottom compartment of the marquess's traveling trunk. Fingers trembling, she untied the knot and spread the papers upon the lid.

The documents were mostly written in English, a few in French, and others in Dutch, the script elegant. Her heart raced. These must be the papers Steven sought. Her gaze flew over the pages, picking out phrases and words.

> . . . *in our Interest to discontinue purchasing in the West and turn our attentions to the East Coast of the African Continent . . . fetch a suitable price for newly imported Males . . . unreasonable fear of detection by the Authorities . . . concerned with his own safety and not enough with the successful delivery of Cargo . . . unable to sail due to unsuitable Weather Conditions and the interventions of the ship* Blackhawk *under the command of the so-called Angel . . .*

Valerie's eyes flew open. Angel. As though it had happened hours earlier and not months, she remembered Zeus speaking of the Angel that first day aboard the *Blackhawk*.

Not Bebain, as she had thought, but Steven. Etienne La Marque.

Her heart raced as she read through the letter and moved quickly to the next. It was dated August 20, 1810, and signed by the vice governor of the formerly French colony of Martinique, now under English control.

> *It has come to my attention that the man they call the Angel, and his associate the Panther, have caused great damage to our trading Interests. We believe that at this juncture their activities must at all costs be stopped. There are no other Appreciable Impediments to continuing the Trade in imported Africans if these men are destroyed. When*

this is completed, we will with pleasure renew our offers of Assistance and Protection to your ships when in our waters, and our armed escort when we are able beyond the Sphere of our Jurisdiction . . .

Valerie didn't need to read more. She saw immediately the difficulties Steven would face bringing Lord Hannsley to justice. He must make accusations against the king's appointed governor as well as the marquess. These papers would allow him to do so with a hope of success.

Valerie's chest expanded with an unfamiliar sensation. It was not the shock of learning of treason at such high levels of the government, or even the sheer thrill of her success.

She sat back upon her heels.

Pride. She felt proud of Steven. Against impossible odds, he put his life at risk to help others. He was a good man. The papers in her hands finally, in some strange way, made that goodness real beyond what her heart had always told her.

Wonder swelled in her, powerful and pure.

Folding the papers, she carefully rearranged the contents of the traveling trunk and closed it. She smoothed her rumpled gown and returned to the bedchamber. Lord Hannsley still breathed slowly in deep sleep.

The crystal wine decanter hefted solidly in her hand. She poured the liquid into the simmering hearth embers, as well as the wine in the marquess's goblet, her stomach rumbling as she smelled the steam rise. She'd barely eaten all day. Heady with triumph, she picked up her own glass and with a salute to her success, took a drink.

Two sickeningly sweet swallows later, Valerie blanched. She gagged, spitting out the marquess's drugged wine. Somehow she had mixed up the glasses. How could she be so foolish?

Snatching up her shawl, she bolted for the door. She closed it as softly as her trembling hands allowed, and fled up the corridor, cursing her idiocy and praying she would reach her chamber before the drug took effect.

The corridor spun and her head grew heavy. Mabel emerged from the shadows. A man appeared in the passageway beyond. With her last thought, Valerie felt the papers sliding out of her grasp. She followed them to the floor.

Chapter 32

"Thank the Lord Almighty!"

Mabel's exclamation rattled through Valerie's head as though it came through a coal scuttle. Valerie tried to open her eyes, winced, and pulled a leaden hand from beneath the covers. She laid it across her forehead. Her mouth tasted woolen.

"What time is it?"

"Oh, milady, it's two already. Sore worried I was you'd never wake."

Through slitted eyes Valerie saw her maid hover into sight, face awash with relief.

"I haven't got a wink of sleep, afraid you killed yourself with that poison instead of His Lordship."

Valerie pushed herself up in bed. Sunlight streamed through partially drawn draperies.

"It was not poison, Mabel," she mumbled, "only a sleeping draught. And I never intended to kill Lord Hannsley." She shook her head, trying to clear her muddled thoughts. "It must have been terribly potent. I only drank a mouthful—"

She snapped awake entirely, the images of her last moments of consciousness crashing back. Her frantic glance scanned the room, her head spinning with grogginess.

"Who was the man in the corridor, Mabel? Do you have the papers?"

"I hid them in the window box, mum. I thought it the best place if someone came looking."

Guarded relief washed through Valerie. "But who was the man who saw me fall?"

"Mr. Flemming." Mabel folded her arms across her chest, narrowing her eyes.

"Mr. Flemming? Are you certain?"

Mabel nodded. "He helped me bring you in here. When I thanked him and told him it were better he left, he started asking about those papers, if he could see them and how you'd got them."

A cold shiver raced across Valerie's shoulders. "What did you say to him?"

"I told him it were your business and I didn't know; then I thanked him again and shut the door. Locked it too. Did I do well?"

Valerie forced a smile. "Very well. You are a born adventurer." She pushed back the covers and swung her legs over the edge of the bed, muddled but determined. Steven said he would be gone only for the day. Valerie wanted to be ready the moment he returned to Castlemarch. She didn't look forward to encountering Lord Hannsley, even though he could not possibly suspect her of stealing the documents. He hadn't any reason to believe she and the Viscount of Ashford had any particular relationship. At least Steven's diffidence toward her during the past sennight was good for something.

She swallowed down the thickness in her throat, and pushed away from the bed. "Mabel, please ring up a bath for me."

"Right, mum. But first you might wish to—that is—"

"What? Haven't you told me everything?" Valerie's stomach tensed.

Mabel took a visibly fortifying breath. "Nothing we can't do something about, milady." She shoved a hand mirror beneath Valerie's chin.

"Dear me," she muttered, cringing at the bruise smudging her neck just above the collarbone, a bruise the exact size and shape of Lord Hannsley's open mouth. "Do bring that bath up right away, Mabel. I feel the need to wash thoroughly." She turned toward the window box. "And lay out the green pinstripe muslin. I feel a chill in the air today. I think I will be most comfortable in a high-necked gown."

Sodden and pocked with ditches, the road from London wasn't any easier to negotiate under the afternoon sun than it had been in the icy gray of dawn traveling in the opposite direction. But Steven urged Tristan along it as though the hounds of hell chased at his heels.

Alistair was betraying him. Men all over town held Alistair's vowels, some men of honor, but most of them not. Steven's solicitor, Farthing, had discovered that Alistair was in debt to at least fifteen thousand pounds, and he owed the largest debt to Clifford Hannsley.

He had borrowed money from Hannsley for more than a year to pay his gambling losses. He'd even performed a few unsavory tasks for the marquess in some of London's rougher hells. The most damning piece of news Farthing found, though, was that Hannsley had recently sold Alistair's debts to the sharks. The seedy loan agents were preparing to collect, already looking to the Earl and Countess of March as surety.

Tristan's hooves skidded across an icy patch. Steven steadied the horse, then urged him faster. Time was short. He would return to Castlemarch and force Alistair to tell him what Hannsley knew. Then he would blackmail him into turning on the marquess. The threat of Lord and Lady March discovering their nephew's villainy would be enough to make Alistair succumb. Dirty business, but necessary.

As the road rushed by beneath him, Steven made careful calculations, figuring every detail, every word, every gesture that would assure him success. But for the first time in his life filled with such scripting and staging, his thoughts kept straying.

The truth gripped his belly. His urgent need to be back at Castlemarch had little to do with Alistair, or even with bringing Hannsley to justice. All of that could wait until the holiday party drew to a close. It would be safer for his godparents that way, and easier not to disturb any of the other guests.

Steven needed Valerie. He needed her more than air, more than freedom and destiny and wisdom combined. And when he had her with him again, he would tell her everything.

She was fearless, passionate, and quick-witted, with an open heart despite the hurt she had suffered for so many years. Steven could not bear wounding her again, and he would not be without her for another day. The hours since he had held her in his arms felt like thirst upon the ocean. He could not resist any longer.

It was time to find out if she could accept him for who he truly was.

Lord and Lady March invited their guests to help distribute Boxing Day gifts to the servants. Valerie went out in a carriage to the tenant farms, relieved the Marquess of Hannsley was not present. But impatience skimmed through her blood. Steven would return within a few hours. It could not be soon enough.

As though waiting for her to return, Mr. Flemming stopped her in the hall as soon as she entered the house.

"I hope you are well, my lady." His sober face creased with concern.

"I am glad to meet you here, sir," she spoke her words smoothly. "Thank you for your assistance last night. My maid told me you appeared at the precise moment she needed help. I am grateful."

He bowed. "I mean no disrespect, ma'am, but you seemed to have an air of haste about you. I am concerned you might have been fleeing something—or someone—displeasing to you." The pupils of his eyes were pinpoints of intensity. "May I offer assistance?"

Valerie forced a smile. "How valiant you are, Mr. Flemming." She laughed. "But I assure you, fiendish pursuers are not threatening me. Rather, I am in danger of Lord March's potent Christmas punch. I drank far too much and lost my way in the corridors." She lowered her lashes as if embarrassed. Then she smiled, wished him a pleasant day, and fled.

Dropping into a chair in the library, she slapped a trembling hand over her brow and drew in a breath. Remaining calm under Alistair Flemming's skeptical gaze took all her powers of dissembling. He had looked at her so peculiarly, as though he knew what she had done. But he couldn't know. How could he?

Valerie glanced at the mantel clock. It was not yet four o'clock, hours until Steven was likely to return, if he indeed made it back to the castle at all before the end of the day. In the meantime, Mr. Flemming might seek her out again, or she might meet Lord Hannsley.

Her neck prickled. She tried to rub it off, but the sticky feeling of helplessness clung. She wanted Steven back quickly, but not so he could protect her from the danger in which she had willingly put herself. She was foolish not to have planned her next maneuver.

She felt vulnerable waiting for Lord Hannsley's interrogation, and the same waiting for Steven to put his stamp of approval upon her accomplishment. She despised feeling that way. And she hated that even though he said he trusted her, he was not acting upon it now. When he might have asked her for help, he told her not to get involved yet again.

Nausea swirled in Valerie's belly as she pressed back the horribly familiar sensations, the same pathetic feeling of irrelevance she had suffered each time she tried to win the earl's attention.

She stood up abruptly. She would devise a new plan, one that would not depend upon a man. This time she would rely upon her own talents entirely.

The Countess of March sat at her dressing room secretaire, a pug nestled in her lap, when Valerie found her.

"Do come in, Lady Valerie. I hope you are enjoying the festivities." She gestured Valerie to an upholstered chair.

"Oh, yes. I suspect your other guests feel the same. In fact," she plunged on, "I have come to ask you about one of those guests."

The countess quirked a brow. "My godson still eludes understanding?"

"Well, perhaps a bit. But he is not the man who piques my curiosity at this particular moment. Although he does hold my interest at most others."

A smile twinkled in the countess's eyes.

"My dear girl, you are priceless. No other young lady would dare say such a thing to me. But you have no fear and, I'll merit, no falseness in you either." She sat back. "Now, who must you know about this time?"

"Lord Hannsley." Valerie chose her words carefully. "You see, I do not think I trust him."

"Why on earth would you expect to?" came the instant reply.

Valerie stuttered, "Well, he is a gentleman, and a guest in your home."

The countess studied Valerie, stroking the pug's wrinkled neck.

"I suspect you already know that not all of the Captain's and my guests come with our endorsements of character approval, don't you?"

"I had guessed."

"And what else have you guessed, clever girl?"

"It's not so much that I have guessed, as I have seen and been informed about Vicar Oakley and Mrs. Hodge, and your involvement with Lord March in certain activities that would not be looked upon with sympathy in certain polite circles."

"Certain polite circles, I like that. You turn a pretty phrase, Lady Valerie. No wonder I have heard so many accolades of you." The countess chuckled, then her regard sharpened. "Let's have no more talking around the matter, my girl. What do you want of me and how is Hannsley involved?"

Clearly Steven had not told his godmother about the marquess and the documents. Valerie took a breath and clasped her hands. For this piece of her plan to succeed, Lady March must know more than Steven wished. But that would simply be his price for having mistrusted her.

"It seems that last night Lord Hannsley made—shall we say?—unwelcome overtures toward my *maid*. She was somewhere she probably should not have been, seeking certain documents that really are not any of her business, but for truly admirable purposes, rest assured. In any case, she chastised him suitably, then acquired the papers without his discovery."

Lady March's eyes narrowed. "Did she? And?"

"Well," Valerie went on, "at the risk of behaving in a shamefully *outré* manner—"

"A risk which you are more than willing to take," the countess murmured, a smile lifting the corners of her mouth.

"—and offending my hostess, I wonder if one might somehow encourage Lord Hannsley to prematurely depart from Castlemarch? For the protection of my maid, of course, not to mention the documents she borrowed from him."

The countess's look remained blank for a moment. Finally she spoke.

"I suspect that another gentleman here at Castlemarch may consider a dismissal of that sort to be inconsistent with his own desires."

"The gentleman to whom you refer is absent for the day, and in any case does not yet know the full extent of my maid's involvement. My lady," Valerie added with a lift of one brow, "perhaps you are familiar with that irritating characteristic of so many of our noble gentlemen, their tendency to underestimate us."

"Both our courage and our competency," the countess clipped, setting a decisive pat upon the pug's head. "The Captain will never see reason where a woman's capability is concerned, especially his wife's. Something about a man being in love clouds his better judgment."

Valerie caught her breath. The countess's knowing gaze sparkled.

"Tell me your plan and what you have already accomplished, my girl," Lady March said. "Be quick about it. If I understand correctly, I suspect we've little time to see that matters go as you wish, and not as our fine marquess does."

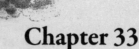

Chapter 33

My lord,

The Prince has discovered your treasonous business interests in the Colonies. He has sent a spy to your present location to find you out. You may expect her in the guise of a lady's maid.

An Interested Party
London

The butler took furlough for the servants' holiday, so the task of collecting the wine for dinner fell to the Earl of March. Descending into the castle's cellars, he offered his guests a guided tour. Dark and cool, the long, narrow corridors of golden Chablis, rich Burgundies, ruby-red clarets, strong ports, and dark Highland scotches wound in labyrinthine twists and turns beneath the medieval core of the castle, illumined by wall sconces.

"My ancestor devised this system of tunnels during the reigns of King Henry VIII and Queen Elizabeth," the earl explained animatedly to his small audience as they wandered through the bottle-lined corridors. He gestured to a nook in the wall. "These little chambers were used then as priest holes. They hid monks and priests fleeing their monasteries and churches, as well as a number of prominent noble sympathizers."

A low voice spoke at Valerie's shoulder. "The earl seems to take pleasure in the misfortune of others. Though he is not the only one, I think." The words drove icicles up Valerie's spine. She turned to confront the marquess's hooded eyes.

"My lord, I am relieved to see you well," she breathed. "I have been concerned about you all day."

The party continued along the corridor, but the marquess's large hand circled her elbow, forcing her to a halt.

"Vixen," he whispered huskily, a trace of anger in his hushed voice, "I will not be duped a second time. You have chosen the wrong man with whom to play your little games."

Valerie wanted to pull away. Instead, she touched his arm.

"I don't understand. What games?"

His expression turned suspicious, but at least the spark of fury disappeared from his heavy eyes.

"What did you slip into my wine last night, Lady Valerie? Laudanum, or something stronger?"

"I don't know. I have had an awful megrim all day," she answered peevishly, then widened her eyes. "But, what do you mean, I slipped it into your wine? You cannot believe I drugged us?"

Hannsley considered her cautiously. "You resisted. Women sometimes change their minds."

Valerie looked away, screwing her features into an expression of delicate distress.

"My lord," she whispered, "I came to you willingly. I was only momentarily uneasy." She glanced up at him. "I am not so practiced in these matters that I can school my every emotion."

"Forgive me, my dear. I must have been misinformed."

Valerie's belly tightened as she remembered Steven's words about Timothy's fear of her passionate nature. Her reputation might still be tarnished, but she had changed, even if men like Hannsley and Timothy didn't believe it. She no longer wished to use men temporarily to gain anyone's attention. She wanted only one man, forever.

She tugged at Hannsley's grasp, frowning.

"You should have explained your concerns to me," Hannsley said, kneading her upper arm. "I would have put your fears to rest."

Valerie could not hear the voices of the other members of their party. The passageway seemed to close in upon them.

"I did try to tell you. The drug overcame me then, and you too, I think. Didn't you receive my note explaining?"

"Note?"

"I sent it to your room with my maid this morning. She told me your valet informed her you were still abed and could not be disturbed. He gave it to you, didn't he?"

The marquess shook his head. "He gave me nothing. My dear, do not lie to me. I will tell you only once more, I am not a man who forgives lies easily."

Valerie pretended indignation. "My lord, you are unkind." She held her breath.

"I received no note," he finally said. "You seem to have been drugged as well. Who would wish to incapacitate us both?"

Valerie's insides unwound. She grasped his arm with renewed excitement.

"Your valet, of course! He must have filled the wine decanter, didn't he? He probably still has my note, or has destroyed it. He wants you to believe I am deceiving you and has nearly been successful in doing so." She clasped her hands to her breast for dramatic emphasis.

"Impossible. Jones has been with me for a dozen years, and I filled the decanter just before you came into the room."

"Did you leave it unattended? Did you step into your dressing room for a moment, giving him a chance to—" Valerie halted. She stared in alarm at the marquess's paisley waistcoat. "Oh, dear me! How could I be so foolish? And now she has—"

"What is it? What have you done?" Lord Hannsley gripped her shoulders.

Valerie bit her lip and bowed her head, her voice a declaration of shame. "My maid drugged us. You see, I asked her for something that would prevent—well . . ." She fluttered her hand. "You understand, I could not risk— She gave me a cordial. She said if I put it in my wine I would not . . ." Her voice trailed off. "Oh, my lord, what a foolish widgeon I have been. Especially now, when it is too late."

The marquess stared down at Valerie for a considering moment. "You merely lack the necessary suspicion of inferiors, my dear. You should know better, but I will not chastise you for it now."

Valerie grabbed his hands and clung to them. "You are too forgiving."

"I think it best we lay aside recriminations and consider what motive your maid had to contrive such a thing."

Valerie dabbed at her tearstained cheek. "I don't understand. She could have drugged me any time during the past months. I don't know why she chose to do so when I was with you."

The marquess's eyebrows came together. "She must have wished to access my rooms, and took advantage of your visit last night to do so. I had released my valet for the evening, as planned. No doubt she learned that in the servants' quarters."

Valerie nodded miserably. "She has undoubtedly robbed you. Do you have any jewels?"

"She must be the one," he muttered. Valerie's pulse leaped.

"Which one, my lord?"

"Occasionally, Lady Valerie, I am involved in business of a sensitive nature. Only an hour ago I received a message from an informant. It told me that a French spy currently hides in this house, an agent in disguise seeking to uncover information regarding issues of importance to England's welfare. The spy is believed to be a lady's maid. Undoubtedly yours."

Valerie did not pretend her wonderment. It amazed her that Lord Hannsley accepted Lady March's forged missive so easily, then swiftly fabricated the story about a French spy, even going so far as to share the information with her. He must truly think she had cotton batting for brains. Awe and disgust mingled in her, overcome quickly by tingles of triumph. Lady March's instinct to play upon the marquess's fear of being discovered had been a good one.

Voices sounded in the tunnel beyond, signaling the others' return.

"I must speak with your maid immediately," the marquess said. "Take me to her now."

"But that is what I was saying before." Valerie nearly cringed at her shrill tone. "It is too late. She has disappeared."

"Disappeared? When?"

"I don't know. She was gone when I looked for her to press my gown. She left a note saying she was leaving for London. Oh, we must catch her. Perhaps she has found valuable information in your rooms and has fled to Napoleon with it. England could be in danger!"

Hannsley's lips whitened. "I will not allow it to go that far, my dear," he said between tight teeth.

Footsteps sounded in the corridor and Valerie pivoted, stepping away from the marquess as the earl's party appeared around the corner.

"Lady Valerie?" Lord March exclaimed. "Have you been waiting here for us all alone? I am so sorry to have left you behind."

The marquess had disappeared. Chill slithered up Valerie's back.

"Dear me," she said, "I should apologize for lagging. I was simply enraptured by this priest's hole here and did not know you moved on." She willed a pink flush into her cheeks.

"Think nothing of it, Lady Valerie. I am glad we have found each other again." The earl tucked her hand into the crook of his arm and drew her along. Behind, Valerie heard someone mutter the marquess's name, followed by a deep chuckle and a girlish titter.

So be it. If society saw her as depraved, she would use it to her advantage. She was not afraid of what the world had to say about her.

No fear and no falseness, Lady March had said of her. At least the former was accurate. Lately she was making a real habit out of the latter.

Steven cursed the slippery road. He cursed the carriage-and-six that careened around the corner in the dusk light, keened over like a sloop in a gale, and tumbled halfway down the embankment at the side of the road fifty feet in front of him. He cursed the driver and postilion, both so overset by the accident they could not manage to unhitch their frightened horses from the traces, or calm the distraught tradesman, his wife, and daughters within the carriage. He cursed bad weather, unfit stables, useless grooms, and simpering innkeepers. Though at least the inn's proprietor sped the task of settling the merchant's family in a private parlor and sending a boy for a carriage maker.

Mostly, though, Steven cursed himself for leaving Castlemarch that morning. As the gray sky turned black and Tristan stood cooling down in the inn's stable, dread crept stealthily up his spine and into his chest.

Valerie was in trouble. He knew it the same way he knew he was in love with her, in his blood, the marrow of his bones, the very breaths he drew.

Finally extracting himself from his grateful charges, he slung atop Tristan's back and set off on the last fifteen miles to Castlemarch, wishing his body was already where his heart had been all day.

Snow fell lightly around the marble pillars of the Greek folly at the far side of the lake. A soft, white haze shrouded the frozen vista in the gathering dark. Valerie huddled closer into her cloak. She could strangle Alethea for proposing the ridiculous plan to visit the little faux temple at night.

But she was too harsh on her romantically inclined friend. She had accompanied the group willingly enough. Lady March had hidden Mabel away in an unused upstairs chamber, and Lord Hannsley had already departed for London, so all was well on that score. Valerie only hoped to avoid another private interview with Mr. Flemming. The outing to the folly with the others seemed just the solution. Then at the last moment Mr. Flemming came along. But she couldn't let that worry her. Steven could be back any moment. She must remain confident.

She flexed her freezing toes and listened with half an ear to Alethea's flirtation with Mr. Fenton. Finally several of the others began to stamp their feet too. Someone mentioned a warm fire waiting at the castle.

"Lady Valerie," Lord Michaels said, stepping toward her, "we have just decided to walk through the gardens to the house rather than await the carriages. Bramfield and Lady Cassandra report that a path skirts the lake before ascending the hill. They walked it yesterday and assure me it is not such a long way."

Valerie avoided looking directly at Timothy, smiling at all three.

"An excellent suggestion, my lord," Mr. Flemming said as he appeared at her side. He turned to Valerie. "May I offer to escort you, my lady?"

She laid her gloved hand upon his arm. "Thank you, sir." He could not possibly try to interrogate her among the others, after all.

The group set off, but within moments Valerie realized she was again acting the fool. Flemming deliberately slowed their pace. The group moved away from the trees and onto a section of path where the snow fell more thickly. Soon she barely saw her friends a few paces ahead.

Willing herself calm, she finally spoke.

"Mr. Flemming, I would be much happier if we remained within sight of the others." She turned a confiding smile upon him. "It is a dreadful night to be separated from one's friends."

"You needn't to concern yourself, Lady Valerie. You will be safe with me as long as you tell me what I wish to know." He forced her to halt, heavy flakes gathering upon the hat brim above his fevered eyes. Valerie's heart constricted. He had the look not of a curious man, but of a desperate one.

"I beg your pardon?" she said, tugging away her arm. He gripped it tight and his gaze took on a penetrating gleam.

"Come now, my lady, we both know you have involved yourself in business that is not yours. Tell me now what you have learned, and I will be very grateful for your immediate compliance."

Valerie steadied her voice. "Mr. Flemming, I assure you, I don't know what business or information you are referring to. It is wretchedly cold, however, and I wish to return to the house." She yanked free again.

His hand clamped upon her shoulder and he whirled her around to face him.

"You cannot deceive me with your well-rehearsed looks and words. I have seen you speak with Ashford and know you went to Hannsley's room last night. I would threaten to make that interesting piece of information public," he uttered, "but I suspect even that would not persuade you to tell me what I need to know." He shook her, his fingertips driving through her cloak. "Hannsley is gone and I need answers. Tell me now, or it won't go well for you."

Valerie's whole body went cold. She had dreadfully misjudged this man. But he was Lady March's nephew and Steven's childhood friend. She hadn't imagined he could betray them both so fully. She prayed Steven had not underestimated him too, that she was the only fool.

"I don't see how my private affairs are any concern of yours, sir," she said as firmly as she could. "Now unhand me this instant."

The wind whirled the icy snow around them. A flicker

of uncertainty crossed his eyes. Then his lips twisted in distress.

"You have played your last game, my lady. If you will not tell me what you know, you will not tell him either."

He pushed her hard. Valerie stumbled back and her foot stepped into emptiness. Flailing, she grabbed his coat. He pried her hands loose, and she tripped again, tumbling down the icy embankment. Her head slammed against the ice, and pain sliced through her before blackness descended.

Most of the guests were already abed when Steven finally arrived at the castle. Thrusting Tristan's reins into a groom's hands, he barely paused to throw off his hat and greatcoat before bolting up the stairs to the east wing. No answer met his knock upon Valerie's bedchamber door. He tried the handle. Unlocked. The rooms were empty, neither lady nor maid preparing for sleep. Panic gripped him.

He searched the castle and found Michaels and Fenton in the billiards room finishing a bottle. They greeted him and asked laughingly if he passed Hannsley on the road to London. The fellow had left Castlemarch that afternoon as though Napoleon's entire army chased him. Fear clutched tighter at Steven's gut.

Casually, he inspected their game, twirling a cue in his hands as though he meant to play, and asked what entertainments he had missed. Fenton scowled as Michaels mentioned charades, and then a stroll to the Greek folly after dinner.

"Flemming stole your march on the lovely Lady Valerie at the lake, didn't he, Michaels?" Fenton taunted as he took his shot. "Didn't see either of them in the drawing room later either. Guess she prefers the quiet type." He snickered.

Michaels cast Steven a careful look and said something noncommittal, but Steven had heard enough. Extricating himself, he vaulted up the stairs to Alistair's bedchamber.

His childhood friend slouched before a dead fire, an empty bottle of brandy in his hand. As Steven walked toward him, Alistair lifted his drink-fogged gaze, blinked several times, and seemed to recognize him. His eyes pooled with fear.

He shook his head. "I didn't want to do it," he slurred, clutching his fingers around the bottle. "She knows, and I had to. I—I—"

Steven grabbed his neck cloth and dragged him up.

"Where is she?"

Alistair continued wagging his head. Spittle ran down his chin.

"I will see you hanged, Alistair. Don't doubt me," Steven ground out, twisting his grip. "Where is she?"

"The lake. The f-far side."

Steven released him, swinging back toward the door.

"I didn't mean to— Didn't want—" Alistair's protests faded behind him as he ran down the corridor.

Chapter 34

Valerie swam into consciousness, waking into icy cold penetrating her senses. She floated, a sea of soft, stinging snow enveloping her, urging her to return to slumber. Dull pain echoed through her head and she could not feel her hands or feet. Distantly a muffled voice whispered that this was dangerous, but she greeted the idea with apathy, slipping again toward soothing oblivion.

Out of the blackness a shadow rose above her, reaching for her, taking her up. Her eyelids fluttered and soft fabric cradled her face. As her eyes drifted shut, she smelled the sea.

She was light in his arms despite the ice coating her cloak. The snowfall slowed, and Steven could see the gamekeeper's cottage ahead, tucked into the trees where the forest came near the lake's edge. For now, the modest shelter was the closest place of safety.

He whistled for Tristan, pulled the saddle off, and settled Valerie atop the exhausted horse's warm back. With a knife from his saddle pack, he pried the cottage door's lock open. The dwelling was small and rustic but clean-swept, a pile of wood stacked against one wall.

Steven drew horse and woman into the cottage and set to starting a fire. Heat soon snaked into the frigid air. Lifting Valerie from Tristan's back, he carried her to a straw pallet before the fire. With quick fingers he unclasped the fasteners upon her cloak and removed her sodden muffler, gloves, and boots. Her damp gown and stockings followed, as well as the snug corset he sliced open with his knife. Wrapping her in a blanket, he tucked the edges of it around the mattress.

Staring down at her pale cheeks and lips, Steven willed his heartbeat to slow and his hands to cease trembling. Dragging his gaze away, he turned to his horse. Swiftly, mechanically he rubbed down the animal with a rag and draped a blanket over its back. Then he filled a bucket with snow and set it by the hearth to melt.

When no more tasks remained, he crouched beside Valerie and placed his palm upon her brow. She was far too cold. The fire burned steadily, but its warmth was insufficient, and he could not move her closer to the blaze without danger of igniting the straw ticking.

Without further thought, he stripped off his boots, coat, cravat, and waistcoat. Then, answering a months' old wish, he slipped onto the pallet behind her and drew her inert body against his.

Half an hour later he added wood to the fire, offered water to his horse, and returned to Valerie. Tucking her again into his embrace, he breathed deeply. She was warm, at least for the time being. Steven closed his eyes, praying that her temperature would not now climb, and finally allowing himself to sleep.

* * *

The snap of a burning log woke Valerie. Then she heard a different sound beneath her ear, low and regular. A heartbeat.

Feeling and awareness returned slowly. She did not stir. Her head throbbed, but she was warm, blessedly, deliciously warm. Without opening her eyes, she knew that a fire blazed nearby and that she was in Steven's arms.

Breathing in the scents of burning wood and horse and the unmistakable remnants of limewater, she cracked open her eyelids. Firelight danced across her sight, slicing pain through her head. She clamped her eyes shut.

They were not in the castle. But it didn't matter where he had brought her. He had come for her and remained with her, holding her in his arms as she had yearned for him to hold her.

Sleep ran through her head and behind her eyes and she struggled to hold it at bay. She might want the delicious fantasy of Steven's embrace to last forever, but it would end. Until it did, she must stay awake for as many stolen moments as possible.

She opened her eyes again and focused upon her hand resting atop his chest. Not far from her fingertips his shirt buckled enough for her to see a glimpse of skin beneath. Stretching her sore lungs in another deep breath, she let her fingers stray to the closest tiny button. It came open easily. Another, and a few more, and she pushed the linen aside and laid his chest bare.

Heartbeat pounding in her aching head, she slipped her palm over him, trailing her fingers across his hard belly and passing with a feather's touch over the line of hair that ran beneath his breeches. She stalled as her fingertips discovered the uneven, silky smoothness of his scar. Holding her breath, she traced the length of the old wound across his waist and ribs.

His iron grip seized her hand.

"Stop." His voice was incongruously soft.

Valerie let out her breath slowly. "Why?" Her throat scratched. "Aren't all pirates made of salt and leather so they can withstand the rigors of life at sea?" She tugged. He released her and she moved a fingertip lightly alongside the scar. He flinched.

"I told you once before, I am not a pirate." His conversational voice rumbled beneath her cheek. "This sailor, however, is made of flesh and blood, and that flesh is rather prone to ticklishness in some spots."

Valerie's eyes widened. She flattened her palm over his ribs. Gooseflesh spread across his warm skin in the wake of her touch.

Relief bubbled up in her and she raised her head. Her smile faltered. His gaze was dark, firelight flickering in his lion eyes as though to warn her off. Valerie swallowed hard, her throat raw and pulse racing.

"Is that why you wouldn't allow me to touch you the other night? Because you are ticklish?" She tried to make her voice light, but it sounded hoarse.

Steven took her hand and lifted it to his mouth, setting his lips to each fingertip, one after the other. Warmth tangled with sweet tension inside her.

"No." His voice was low. "I did not allow you to touch me, Valerie, because if you had I could not have stopped myself from making love to you." He leaned up on his elbow and his hand curved around her cheek. "What did Alistair do to you?"

Valerie shook her head. Her mind and heart spun. She didn't want to think of Alistair Flemming's desperate glare as he pushed her onto the ice. She wanted to gaze into Steven's golden eyes and lose herself forever.

She spread her palm upon his chest. His rapid heartbeat sent delicious pressure gathering in her belly. She smoothed her hand across his lean muscles, and the eager ache spread.

"Where are we?"

"The gamekeeper's cottage at the far end of the lake."

"And the hour?"

"Past midnight, only."

She stroked a finger across his flat, brown nipple and watched it harden. Leaning forward, she surrounded it with her lips. His fingers gripped hers again. He felt wonderful, so firm and male and him, the man she had loved forever, it seemed. She flicked her tongue against his skin, tasting salt and heaven.

"I am touching you now," she murmured.

His chest rose upon a tight breath. "So you are."

She kissed his body, lingering with her lips open. "Well, Father La Marque?"

"Well what, wanton?"

Valerie tilted her face up and her breath caught. Steven's eyes sparkled with heat and, amazingly, laughter. She went perfectly still, only her heart galloping wildly. She loved him, so painfully and so completely.

"Steven, I have longed for this for months," she whispered. "Beneath my skin—" She broke off, not knowing how to finish.

"You have not been alone in that longing, dear lady." His lips brushed hers in the gentlest caress. She leaned into him. He took her completely, first her lower lip, then both, flooding her with heat as he opened his mouth over hers and pressed into her.

Valerie melted against him. No one had ever kissed her the way he did, claiming her as he caressed, demanding until she gave him everything. Shivers of satisfaction washed through her as he nipped at her lower lip, then slipped his tongue along it ever so lightly. But she wanted so much more. She sank into his mouth, moving along with him as he pulled away.

"No. Don't stop." She gripped his neck to draw him close. "There is no one near."

"No pirates, priests, or polite society?" He chuckled, a rich sound of pleasure. But his gaze seemed hesitant. Valerie pressed her lips to his again, wanting to feel his mouth on her entire body.

"Or fear," she said.

Steven's arms encircled her, turning her onto her back as he moved atop her. A whimper of pleasure escaped Valerie's throat and she welcomed his hard body between her legs, against her aching. His firelit gaze searched her features as his hand cradled her battered head.

"I don't want to hurt you," he whispered, his voice beautifully husky, golden eyes questioning.

Gulping back the thickness in her throat, Valerie touched his face, caressing the sculpted planes of his brow and jaw.

"Then don't," she said. "Don't."

Steven's mouth came down on hers hungrily, instantly seeking. His hand moved along the curve of her waist and he pressed his hips into hers. Pleasure rushed through her, and Valerie moaned, opening her mouth to his tongue. A growl of satisfaction rose from his chest, and his kiss changed, deepened. She wrapped her arms around his neck, responding with her mouth and hands, telling him silently what she couldn't dare say to him with words. Not yet.

She trembled as he pushed aside her shift and curved his hand around the underside of her breast. Lightly he caressed the arc of her waist, then up again. Valerie shivered, her breaths shortening as he traced a circle around her tight nipple, then played it lightly. Her lips parted on a silent sigh of need. He cupped her and passed over the tender peak again, his touch dipping deep inside her, his hands adoring her. She sucked in air and he caught her gasp, drawing her tongue to his with wickedly teasing caresses until she shifted in want.

As though sensing her need, he slid his hand around the side of her face and tilted her chin up, kissing a trail of wild pleasure along her throat. She arched her neck, pressing into his hand, nerves strung with drunken anticipation as he dipped down the valley of her breasts.

"I have no dramatic scars to make this especially interesting for you," she whispered shakily, aching beneath his touch, running her hands along his arms and back, memorizing the feel of him.

"I assure you, my love," he murmured, his voice deep. "You are sufficiently fascinating *sans cicatrices*."

Valerie's breath seized as though a fist grabbed her lungs and heart and lifted her upward. Steven's tongue crossed her nipple. She moaned, moving into his kiss. Her heart would never begin beating again. This ecstasy could not be real.

His love. It must be a dream. But his gaze was so familiar, his strong arms holding her fiercely and with powerful tenderness.

"Make love to me, Steven." She struggled for breath. "Now. Please make love to me."

His eyes glimmered as his fingers curved delectably around her breast, tormenting her arousal. He traced the seam of her lips with his tongue as his hand slid down her body, drawing the gossamer fabric of her shift up her legs.

Without warning he touched her need and Valerie gasped. The gasp turned into a groan as he stroked, gentle and firm. For a moment she lay breathless, paralyzed with pleasure. But she could not bear the sweet torture of anticipation. She shifted her hips, pressing into his touch as she gripped his shoulders. Everything in her strained toward him, gathering, stealing her breath, her thoughts, all but her desire.

"I need you," she uttered against his mouth. "I need you inside me."

Chapter 35

He burned to possess her, to make her his the same way she owned his heart, his body, his very soul. He tasted her lips and teased her inflamed flesh, damp with need. She was radiant, soft and hot in his hands. Choking down on his rising heat, he slid his finger into her slowly and she sighed. Her velvet-tipped breasts rose upon quick breaths as he stroked her, feeling her sweet beauty, forcing himself to wait.

"Valerie," he whispered over her mouth.

She gripped his arms, arching into his touch. "Do not refuse me," she uttered, eyes half closed.

"I must know if you are a virgin."

She reached down and grabbed his wrist, stilling him. Her eyes opened, luminous in the firelight. Her chin rose.

"Will it make a difference to you?"

Through the crush of need, satisfaction skimmed along Steven's senses. She would not be bested, and she would not be denied. She was more woman than he had ever known.

Weaving his fingers through her satin hair and tilting her head back, he laid his mouth upon hers again, savoring her flawless lips, her alabaster and sable perfection. He drew back slightly.

"Only in the particulars," he said, unable to stop his mouth from curving up at one edge.

Valerie's ocean eyes widened, vulnerable, and his grin faded. She nodded.

Steven swallowed hard, without breath. She was an innocent. For all her passionate nature and scandalous past, Valerie had never given herself to a man. But even if Steven's mind had not been entirely certain, his heart had known it for months already. She had seduced Bebain, risking rape for his life. Unable to offer herself to the priest he pretended to be, she had offered him that gift instead.

Now she was giving herself to him, and this time he would take her. Forever.

Gently, reverently, he shifted between her silken thighs, unfastening his breeches and kissing her tender lips and the perfect curve of her neck. Her hands pushed his shirt over his shoulders, her touch light and sure, exploring, searing. He cupped her face, still wanting to protect her from the hard pallet and from his own urgent desire. But his hand shook maintaining harsh control, and when she parted her lips against his palm, slipping her tongue across his skin, it jolted like fire through him. He pressed into her, her body opening to him.

"Please," she whimpered, and he claimed her mouth again. Slowly, with steely restraint, he entered her.

She was beautiful, pure woman, her lips parted and her breaths coming hard, her thighs spreading farther, opening fully to him. She shifted beneath him, and he tasted her mouth with his tongue, widening her inside. Tight and

hot, she urged him deeper, hardening him beyond endur-
ance. He pushed in, meeting her barrier.

"Don't stop," she uttered and thrust her hips up, sinking him in abruptly. He groaned, and a cry tore from
her throat. Her eyes flew open and her hands scrabbled
against his shoulders.

Embedded in her taut beauty, Steven ached to drive into
her. Calling up every ounce of his strength, he went perfectly still. Her eyes darkened, filled with confusion.

"I—" Her voice was strangled.

"Come with me, my heart," he whispered, touching her
cheek, willing his eyes not to reveal the consuming fever
he knew now that he was inside her. He kissed her brow,
drawing aside her hair and breathing in her scent, the
scent of desire and woman and unique, perfect Valerie.
"Come now, love. You are safe." As he was, remarkably,
finally safe within the woman he loved. Home for the first
time in his life.

She nodded, her eyes trusting. Despite everything,
trusting.

He moved in her, tasting her soft lower lip, the arch
of her neck as her brow relaxed and her pain subsided.
Caressing the sensitive peaks of her perfect breasts, he
watched her pleasure mount, her throat working, her sea-
colored eyes growing hazy in passion. With burning need
he felt her accept him fully, drawing him in eagerly as her
lips parted and her breathing grew shallow. She arched
her neck and shoulders to welcome his kiss, the artlessly
sensuous movement of her hips and legs suiting her body
to his rhythm inside her.

Finally, drinking in the flame-lit curves of her face,
Steven drew a deep breath, swept his hands down, and
pulled her hard to him.

She moaned, grasping his face between her palms and

covering his mouth with hungry kisses as he thrust into her—once, then again, and again. She threw back her head, eyes closed, and her hips twisted, engulfing him deeper. She jerked and gasped, a startled sound. Slowing, Steven slipped his hand to her face, urging her eyes open.

Valerie's lashes fluttered, and her breaths came fast. "How many more times must I tell you not to stop?" She pinned him with a desperate stare, but beneath the outrage her eyes sparkled.

Laughter and desire swept through him.

"Never again," he promised, stroking steadily into her depths, catching her moan in his mouth.

She shifted, her lips parting beneath his, and she was everywhere in him, around him, whimpering higher, shorter, fusing her hands to his skin and twining her legs around him as he plunged into her so he didn't know where her flesh ended and his began. He wanted all of her at once, her sweet, tight womanhood, her supple, clinging legs, her perfect breasts, and her seeking mouth. He covered her body with his hands, touching everywhere, unable to get enough, wanting more, her heart, her soul to bind with his as their bodies were bound.

He said her name, pressing his lips to her brow and mouth as he thrust harder into her. He said it again, whispering the call of his heart through the syllables. Then a third time, "Valerie."

She cried out, a euphoric utterance as her eyes flew open, her gaze embracing him as she convulsed around him. Steven's body gathered, surged, and came apart.

Valerie rose against him, her cries straining as Steven's thrusts came faster, the sounds of their entwined bodies moving together luscious and erotic. Wishing it would never end, aching everywhere, she rocked against him and gasped, shudders seizing her anew. His mouth claimed hers and his muscles hardened beneath her hands and against her legs. She clung, holding him, drowning in the pleasure sweeping from his body into hers, in her fierce longing for it to never end.

She shook as he eased against her, pleasure curling through her, deep and solid. She smoothed her hands around his arms and beneath his shirt, needing to touch him. His powerful body quivered as his breaths slowed, and her heartbeat pounded. His gaze met hers, intense and dark, holding her immobile. Then his lips curved into a delectable half smile. He lowered his mouth and kissed her with infinite gentleness, as though for the first time.

Valerie trembled, in her hands and lips and arms and where he remained inside her, binding them together. Delicious aching warmed her. But it felt different from the desire he always aroused. Now in her chest and throat and behind her eyes echoed profound, ecstatic happiness.

He drew away from her lips, holding himself lightly atop her. His fingertips grazed her face and his gaze lingered upon her cheeks.

"Tears." The word came as soft as his touch as he wiped moisture from her skin. "Dew upon a velvet tulip, or perhaps raindrops upon rose petals?"

Astonishment pushed aside exhaustion as her memory brought back the moment upon the merchantman when she first stood beside him. He had held her hand and, rather than a flower, he called her summer rain. Even then he knew her better than anyone else ever had.

"You remember," she whispered.

"Every word. Every touch. Every glance." His face was beautiful, lit with a tender smile as he dipped his mouth to hers again. This time his kiss was solemn and devastatingly earnest, a certain, eloquent acknowledgment of mutual possession. Valerie clung to him, fighting the sobs seeking to escape. She did not know why she should cry. She had never felt so complete, so sated and filled with life. So safe.

Her eyelids drifted shut as he kissed her.

He circled his arms around her and settled her into his embrace. Raw where they parted, she burrowed into his warmth and he held her tight. As though already dreaming, she felt him grasp her hand and bring it to his lips. Breathing his name, she descended into sleep.

She stared up beyond the trees where they meshed into a canopy in the darkening sky. The hawk's eyes stared back at her, watching, waiting for her to reveal herself. Her heart raced and she was frightened, more frightened than she could ever remember.

Her foot shifted forward in the carpet of leaves and dry needles, crackling into the shadowed silence. The black eyes widened. Panic flooded her and her feet moved again, dragging her ahead to uncertain shelter. Nestled in the underbrush, they were hidden from sight, heedless of the rest of her body, naked to the alert stare of her predator.

Chapter 36

Valerie's eyes snapped open. The fire had burned down to embers and Steven crouched before it.

Her heart tripped, then eased. She drew in a slow, steadying breath as he placed a log upon the coals and prodded it into flame.

Gradually the vision before her erased the images of her dream. Once before she had watched him in flickering firelight, her desire stirring as her gaze traced the shape of his body. This time, though, she would not drift again into sleep, satisfied with a brief glimpse of his beauty. This time he was more than a remote mystery, tantalizing in his aloof appeal. He was warm and real, and her body still thrummed with passion he created.

She swallowed dryly, her head throbbing as she blinked. Steven turned. Reaching forward, he placed a cup beside her.

"Drink this." He sat back on the bare floor.

Valerie hesitated, her gaze shifting to the cup and then again to his face. Silhouetted by the firelight, he was in shadows now, but his mouth curved up at one side. Transfixed, she did not move.

"It's water," he said. "Melted snow." When she remained motionless, his smile faded. "Believe me."

Taking another steadying breath, Valerie raised herself to sit and her fingers curled around the cup. The cool liquid slipped down her parched throat.

"I thought we were past misrepresenting the truth," he said quietly.

Her gaze shot to his, her heart jumping. "Are we?"

"I am."

Valerie set the cup upon the floor and stared. He sat with his knees up and his arms draped over them, hands clasped loosely together. His shirt, open and tucked into his breeches, hung carelessly upon his broad shoulders. He was wrinkled yet still impossibly elegant. She lifted her gaze.

His eyes were the color of dusk in the flickering shadows, his look enigmatic as it had been aboard ship, when he held her off to keep her safe from Bebain. When he killed a man to save her. When he sent her away from danger, keeping her at a distance, always at a distance, to protect her.

Protecting her because he loved her? All along?

Valerie's heart stilled. Her body leaned forward, a shadow of movement.

He saw it, and his eyes changed.

She rose to her knees and he came to her, wrapping his beautiful, warm hands behind her neck and waist and pulling her against him. His kiss demanded, his tongue delving into her mouth as she dragged his shirt from his shoulders. Her body was aflame, her nipples tightening against his chest, constrained by the fabric of her shift. With explosive satisfaction, she welcomed his desire pressing against her through their clothes, driving her hunger higher.

"Let me touch you," she said as his mouth went to her neck, scoring her with delicious heat. "Nothing between us." She didn't know if she meant between their bodies or hearts, but Steven's hands gripped her, then grabbed up her shift and yanked it over her head. She dragged his shirttail from his breeches, and he pulled off the garment and crushed her body to his again as he claimed her mouth.

But Valerie hadn't finished undressing him. Dizzy from the sensation of his skin brushing hers, his warmth and lean strength capturing her, she wanted to see all of him, and to touch him. Sliding her hands down his waist, she hooked her fingers in the band of his breeches and tugged.

"You will need to unfasten them first," he murmured. Frissons of delight skittered through her where his tongue teased the sensitive edge of her ear and his big hands covered her back.

"You would not believe it, but I haven't much experience with this sort of thing." She found the buttons, released them, and her hand curved around his hardness beneath. She paused, reveling in the feeling of his satin, solid length, hearing his quick intake of breath as she grasped gently and stroked upward then down again, mimicking the motion of their lovemaking with her touch.

"I would and I do believe it," he said roughly.

Valerie stiffened. Even if he had found her deficient before, he would not say it this way. Not the man she knew him to be now.

"Do you mean—?"

"That I am the most fortunate of men to be the recipient of your extraordinarily capable inexperience?" He touched her chin and drew her gaze to his. His eyes were ablaze and his chest rose upon a hard breath. "Yes. Now hurry along your self-education, my lady. I grow impatient."

She grinned in satisfaction and wrapped her hand around him fully. Steven's grasp on her arms tightened. She caressed his marvelous length, the damp tip, his body responding to her touch thrillingly. The power she had over him shivered through her, tightening her own arousal until its throbbing was nearly pain.

"Valerie," he whispered harshly, his cheek pressed to her hair. "I need to be inside you. Now."

"Yes." She tugged his breeches down impatiently. "Sit back." She pushed at his hips, her swollen nipples stroking his chest as she moved against him, driving her fever higher.

"You will note that there is still a garment present," he said, falling back onto his heels.

"It won't bother me." Urgent, she slipped her thighs around his hips and guided herself onto him. "And it would take too long—*Ohh*!"

She took him in quickly, pulling him deep, and the heat of her desire and Steven's heart became one. He breathed hard against her brow to steady himself, needing her but for the first time in his life frightened.

While she slept, he had time to think on why Alistair wanted her dead, time to stare at the bruise on her neck, to admit finally, fully, that he had dragged her out of a world of comfort and warmth into the constant turmoil of his life—a life he willingly chose but that was hers to bear through sheer accident upon the capricious sea. Time to decide that he could never again put her in danger because of what he must always do.

"What happened to nothing between us?" he said, pushing away the unfamiliar fear as she moved on him. Her fingertips dug into his skin, her breaths coming short and eyelids fluttering closed as her hips circled, drawing him in, enveloping his need, mounting it.

"There is nothing between us now." She wrapped her arms around his shoulders, her naked body supple, slender, beautiful, her sensuous thrusts artless, stealing his control.

"And yet everything," he whispered.

Her eyes flew open.

He gripped her hips and lifted her off him, opening her wide and sinking back in again, repeating it, taking her harder each time, faster. She moaned her pleasure, her skin glistening with the glow of heat rising in her body, and her dark hair tumbled about her shoulders as she shook her head like a wild horse upon the plains of America. The land he would return to, far from everything she called home. Here in England, surrounded by the people she loved, she was as free from fear as she said. Free to be full of passion and desire.

Steven caught her mouth and drank her in, certain that no matter how much he wanted her, he could never bind her, even if now she thought she wanted those bindings. He would die before making her a slave to his blasted destiny, no matter how willingly she came to it at first.

"Oh, Steven," she gasped, "I never knew—" She faltered, pressing to him, and he gripped her tight, pulling back on the abrupt onrush her words provoked, waiting, aching, needing to fill her, to be complete.

She came abruptly, clutching his shoulders as she shuddered, and he let go, driving into her tight, pliant body. It felt so right forcing his way deeper until nothing remained in him, only her hands and breath caressing his skin. He covered her mouth, and she wound her legs around him, still hungry, seeking more. He reached between them and caressed her, and when her release rose again, she cried out, gasping as pleasure shivered through her.

She grabbed his hand, entwining her fingers with his and pulling it to her lips. Her mouth pressed to the brand upon his wrist.

"Take me, Steven," she whispered raggedly.

Steven's universe stilled. He swallowed hard, recognizing the moment at once for what it must be. She forced it early with this order, but it would have come soon enough. Now he must go forward or risk destroying everything that meant anything to him—her life, her happiness.

"Your demand comes a bit late, my dear," he replied with a half grin he did not feel. He was already growing numb even as she rested in his arms for the last time.

"You know I don't mean my body." Her fingers tightened around his, her quavering voice urging its way into his soul. "Take me, Steven. I cannot be another man's."

"And yet," he forced himself to say, lifting his hand to trace the dark smudge above her delicate collarbone, "It seems you have been another man's quite recently."

Chapter 37

Valerie's chest pounded. She stared into Steven's cool amber eyes, disbelieving as pain sliced through her foolishly unguarded heart. It hadn't been a minute since he made love to her; for God's sake he was still inside her. But his voice sounded as cold as the day he arrived at Castlemarch.

She choked, backing off him. He knelt and drew up his breeches, fastening them with perfect calm. But his composure must be affected, and she knew the only way to discover the truth of it.

"I have gotten Hannsley's papers for you." Her voice shook, but she couldn't care. She'd already laid her heart bare to him. Nothing he said or did now could change that.

Flame flickered in his eyes. "What?"

A chill spun up Valerie's spine, but she would not let him frighten her. He must love her. Even if he tried to put her off again, she must believe that.

"He thinks my maid is a spy. He has gone to town in

search of her and the stolen documents she supposedly carries. Mabel is safely hidden with Lady March at the castle, of course, as are the marquess's papers."

Steven's features hardened, his eyes deadly sharp. "Last night you went to him, when you promised you would not?"

"I never promised that. And why should my word be any more sincere than yours?" She gestured between them, unable to remain still beneath his searing regard. "You are through with misrepresenting the truth, are you? How many minutes ago did you say that?"

He reached out and grasped her arm, his grip unforgiving. His other hand went to her neck, thumb stroking hard against the bruise.

"Is this how you acquired the documents? You bribed him for them?"

Paralyzed by the white heat in his eyes, Valerie struggled for breath.

"Of course not. I put a sleeping draught in his wine. While he was unconscious I searched his belongings. The documents I found detail the buying and selling of Africans under the protection of British officials in the West Indies. They mention you—the Angel—and Maximin, I think, and the threat you pose to their operations."

He stared at her, not moving or speaking. She jerked from his hold, grabbing up her shift and pulling it before her as she stood. The room seemed to tilt.

Steven came to his feet and took her arm again, this time to steady her. She tried to pull away, but he held her fast.

"You are indeed remarkable, *lalkupi*, a strong woman." His voice was low, pronouncing the foreign word like a native. "My grandfather prophesied well."

Staggered, Valerie could not speak.

Hard purpose set upon his handsome face.

"Alistair is working for Hannsley. I went to London to

confirm that. How did he learn of your assignation?" His gaze flickered to her neck but his tone was cold again. Valerie resisted the urge to cover the bruise. Hurt careened through her.

"Does it bother you? His hands on me, his mouth?"

"This is not a game of coquetry, Valerie."

"I have not played games since the day I learned my father died," she bit out. Blinking back the prickling behind her eyes, she clenched her jaw, seeing the same resolute resistance in Steven's eyes. He held himself in harsh control again. Valerie longed to break him, to banish that control with her forever. "It bothers you that he touched me, doesn't it?"

"You know it does," he ground out. "Now tell me what else you know."

"Why should I? You have what you desire now. In the meantime you have had everything else you desire as well." She couldn't breathe. "Run off to London now, Steven, Etienne, whoever you are," she said, her mocking tone echoing through clouded ears, so hollow that the words seemed to reach through to her heart. "Follow your villain there, or across the ocean, wherever he takes you. But don't tell me the truth, never the truth, and certainly do not allow me into your intrigues. I am not adequate enough to—"

He gripped her arms, halting her speech as he bent his head to her, his body rigid. He spoke just above her brow.

"You want the truth? Hear this one then." His voice scraped like gravel. "When I was no older than you, I went to live with my mother's people. You spoke to my godmother. You know of my parents, of my mother who died too young of fever because she left her home to care for the man she loved, and for her son."

Stunned by his abrupt turn of words and stark tone, Valerie could only nod.

"I lived with my mother's people for four years. After a time, they gave me a name they believed suited me. To the Natchez I am *wī'dan kapa'htia*."

Valerie's heart beat fast and thick. "What does it mean?"

"Lone Hawk." Steven's gaze burned into hers. "It is not a name I would have chosen for myself, but it is what they discovered me to be. Because it is who I am, Valerie, a man who must live alone, hunt alone, and die alone."

Valerie's head spun and her heart rose into her throat. She swallowed back panic, images from her dreams sluicing through her memory. So many times, on the ship and since returning, she dreamed of the hawk watching her, hunting but never coming close. Always at a distance.

She shook her head, trying to deny it. Dreams meant nothing. It was a mad coincidence, a peculiarity of whimsy, irrational for her to refine upon. As irrational as her father's rejection of her after his wife's death. As irrational as Valerie's own defiant attempts to win his affection. As irrational as her suspicion, nurtured carefully over years, in England, Boston, at sea, that no man could ever love her. When she had returned to England, to her brother and Anna's warm welcome and Timothy's constancy, she had flirted with the idea that perhaps she could find what she always wanted. But her heart lingered with the French priest, yearning for him so powerfully.

Now he was here, telling her he did not need her the way she needed him.

But she simply would not believe that. Neither he nor her wretched dreams could convince her otherwise after everything that had passed between them.

"Give yourself whatever name you will," she said, the words thick in her mouth. "I will not—" Her dry tongue faltered, exhaustion scoring her limbs. She blinked, and shivers gripped her. It seemed like a tremendous effort to part her lips. "You cannot—"

"Valerie, we must get you back to the house," he said close with concern. His palm curved around her brow, his other grasping her arm. "You are fevered."

She nodded, fumbling with the garment in her hands. Steven took the shift and dressed her. Valerie tried to assist, but her fingers would not function properly and her head grew heavier each moment. She might have spoken to him, but she didn't know what she said, perhaps that he was a rogue for breaking her heart, but that would have been too close to the truth, and there could not be any truths between them, could there?

He placed her atop his horse, climbed up behind her, and wrapped her in his arms. The wind drove the snow against her. Weary and chilled to the core, Valerie slipped in and out of awareness as the horse picked his way to the stables. Steven dismounted and drew her down, moving aside to slide open the stable door.

An arm snaked around her and hauled her to the edge of the lantern light. She struggled, icy metal pricking her neck as Steven swung around.

"Don't move, Steven," Alistair Flemming's voice came at her ear, harsh and halting. "If you do, I—I will cut her."

Valerie's heartbeat stalled, her vision swimming.

Steven reached into the saddle pack and drew out a pistol. With calm assurance, he cocked it and pointed it at them.

"Harm her, and I will kill you, Alistair." He tilted his head, as though considering. "In fact, if you do anything but release her instantly, I will kill you."

"You would kill her instead. You don't have a clear shot." Bluster laced his tight voice.

"Are you quite certain of that?" Steven's eyes narrowed. His hand around the pistol remained still as stone, the snowflakes settling upon his greatcoat sleeve like fleece upon a nighttime meadow, eerily peaceful.

A desperate whine erupted from her captor's throat and he threw her forward. She stumbled on the ice, and Steven caught her, pressing her cheek into cold, wet wool.

"You cannot do any worse to me than what I have already done to myself," Flemming hurled out, backing up. Staring at the knife in his hand, his eyes went wide. He threw it down and ran, slipping across the snow until the whitened darkness swallowed him.

Trembling seized Valerie, setting her teeth against each other frantically. She pulled out of Steven's hold, pivoting around to him. His eyes were aflame, lit with something she had never seen in them before. Fear. Anguish.

He would have killed his childhood friend to save her. Killed again. For her.

Small wonder he did not want her. Small wonder.

She lurched back, but he caught her. His arm came around her and the pistol thudded to the snow-covered ground. He sank his fingers into her hair and brought his mouth down upon hers. His kiss was hard, like the first time aboard ship, when lies stood as barricades between them, in her heart and upon her lips and in everything he thought he must do. She sank into him, clinging.

He released her abruptly. Valerie opened her eyes and his gaze was impenetrable.

"A Catholic half-breed is at least as scandalous as an impoverished Italian violinist," he said in a gravelly voice. "A fine addition to your list, I should think, my dear."

The words hit her like a blow. She gaped as he drew the horse into the stable and, without a word, moved away in the falling snow toward the house. Numbly, she followed.

They entered through the kitchens. Dawn had not yet broken, and the castle remained quiet. Valerie trailed Steven's quick strides through narrow servants' passageways and staircases. Without glancing back, he led her to her bedchamber door and opened it. Amelia Brown rose from a chair, ashen-faced in the firelit room. She hurried forward and grasped Valerie's frigid hands.

Steven closed the door.

"Where are the papers?" he said to the woman, and then sharper, "Quickly."

Amelia dropped Valerie's hands and moved swiftly across the chamber. She returned with the packet of documents clutched between her palms and gave it to Steven.

"Call a maid and wake your mistress." Steven's deep voice came through Valerie's fogged senses. "Lady Valerie is ill."

Amelia moved toward the bellpull.

He grasped Valerie's wrist, searching her face, no mockery in his golden eyes now.

"Sleep now. Sleep long and dreamless, dear lady," he said, his gaze holding hers barely a moment. He released her, opened the door, and disappeared into the dark corridor.

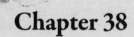

Chapter 38

December 27, 1810

M. MAXIMIN PANTHÈRE
Blackhawk
TERCEIRA ISLAND, AZORES

Task completed. Make berth at Portsmouth by month's end. Will sail for Elmina weather permitting.

Etienne

Chapter 39

No one stirred within the castle. The day sparkled without, the winter sun glinting with brilliant abandon off each crystal of new snow, the air mild. Servants rested after the holiday excesses and the nobles were abroad, some in the village, others sledding.

Only Miss Pierce lingered after lunch in the drawing room with the Earl of Alverston and his wife, waiting for the physician's report. After the doctor pronounced Lady Valerie remarkably sturdy given her fever, they seemed to relax. From his position at the far end of the chamber, Steven watched his godmother shoo them outside, assuring them that if the patient worsened she would alert them instantly.

For a moment Alverston paused upon the threshold, turning to fix his hostess, then Steven with a sober look. Steven bore the man's stare without expression. Finally, the earl continued out. Without a word or a glance at her godson, the Countess of March followed.

Her snub did not bother Steven. He felt no guilt. He only needed to know that Valerie was safe, and he must see her once more before leaving.

He climbed the stairs. Outside Valerie's bedchamber door he stood motionless. He pressed his palm against the panel, then his brow.

He didn't care if anyone saw him. Soon he would be gone to chase down Clifford Hannsley and to set the man's destruction in motion. None of these scions of the *ton* would ever see him again. His presence at Castlemarch would be forgotten quickly, as well as any interest he took in a particular lady.

Steven nearly laughed aloud in self-mockery. For days he had kept Valerie at a distance to protect her. Now, with his minutes in England numbered, he longed to spend every one of them at her side.

A faint sound came from inside the bedchamber. The knob turned as he stepped back, and his godmother appeared. She studied his face, then pulled the door wider for him to enter.

Nestled amid white linens, Valerie slept the unwaking sleep of unconsciousness, her breathing shallow and quick and her cheeks flushed in the thin rays of sun slanting through partially drawn draperies. Amelia Brown sat in a chair on the far side of the bed. The countess gestured, and Amelia stood and went into the dressing room, closing the door.

"Have you gotten everything you wished?" the countess said.

Steven suspected she meant more than the stolen documents. He moved to the bed and gazed down at the single reason for every one of his heartbeats now.

"Alistair betrayed you, didn't he?" his godmother asked. He nodded.

"He is gone today, without even a note," she said. "His valet told me. I love him in his own way. He is my flesh and blood. But I knew he would turn on you one day. He hasn't the integrity for it."

"There seems to be a short supply of that virtue around here lately," Steven murmured.

"Not upon that bed."

"No." He glanced at his godmother. "I was not speaking of her, of course."

"I certainly hope you were not speaking of yourself," she clipped, her brow drawn. "You were never one to whine, even as a child. I would be surprised if you began now."

He lifted a single brow. "Naturally I was speaking of your neighbor, Clifford Hannsley." He paused. "Thank you for your help, Godmother."

She fixed him with an intense look. "You are leaving again, aren't you?"

Steven turned toward Valerie. Behind opaque lids, her eyes flickered in frantic dreams.

"Shortly," he said.

"Will you return?"

He shook his head. But the response apparently was not sufficient for his godmother.

"Does she know this?" she asked.

"I suspect she has guessed it."

"Steven, I adore you. You know I do, and the Captain and I would do anything for you. But you are a fool."

He pivoted to meet her censuring gaze. "Thank you, Godmother. Your expression of affection warms me, especially since you offer it despite my flaws."

Her lips pursed tightly. "You are head-over-ears in love with that girl, and she is with you."

"She will no doubt survive the misfortune."

"And you?"

"That, Godmother, is not particularly your concern."

The countess drew in a voluble breath. She moved to the door.

"Lock this behind me. It would not do for a servant to enter unannounced and see you here." She shook her head as though to clear it and moved to the door. "Alert Amelia before you leave."

Steven lowered himself to the edge of the bed and took Valerie's hand. Her limp flesh burned. Even so, touching her felt like heaven, and he cradled her fingers in his palm. Her lips moved and her eyelids fluttered, but Steven knew she would not wake. He had seen too many victims of fever. She would remain unconscious for many hours to come.

He smoothed back the damp hair clinging to her skin. Unable to resist, he bent and pressed his lips to her brow. Valerie's fingers tightened around his.

Heart lurching, Steven drew back. Her eyes opened, heavy with fever, the black centers huge.

"Don't leave me." Her words came like sand slipping across a windy beach. "Please don't."

Breathless and mute, Steven watched as her eyes closed again and her features slackened. Her fingers loosened within his. Once more he touched her face, caressing her cheek as his heartbeat gradually slowed. Then he tucked her hand beneath the linens, stood, and went to the dressing chamber door. Amelia came out quickly. Without another glance at the bed, Steven left.

In the drawing room two days later, Miss Pierce cheerfully announced that Lady Valerie's fever had broken. Awake and alert, she had taken some food and drink, and the doctor pronounced her to be convalescing successfully. The other guests greeted the news with smiles and

compliments to Lady Valerie's lovely character and gracious manners, as well as her great beauty.

Within fifteen minutes, after making a quick visit to
the servants' quarters, Steven set off upon the road to
London.

Everyone walked upon tiptoes.

First, the maid hovering over Valerie's bed tiptoed. She
did this after beaming and declaring that milady's fever
had broke. Then she bit her tongue and hurried off to
inform her mistress of the news, leaving Valerie drenched
in sweat with a head full of dreams of Steven making love
to her, his strong hands, beautiful eyes, his mouth and
body giving her pleasure.

When Lady March came to call, she tiptoed too, in a
manner of speaking. As usual she spoke directly, apolo-
gizing for her nephew's villainy and assuring Valerie
that Mabel was safely tucked in a little chamber on the
castle's top floor, and that by all reports Lord Hannsley
still searched for her in London. But Lady March did not
mention her godson, although Valerie knew he must have
left Castlemarch.

Valentine and Anna visited next, and in their own
loving way minced around too. Valentine stood stoically
at the end of the bed, looking grim but relieved, while
Anna combed Valerie's hair and encouraged her to eat
the broth Cook sent up. They did not say a word about the
Viscount of Ashford either.

Four days into her convalescence, wearing a dressing
gown and sitting in a chaise by her bedchamber hearth,
Valerie finally wished to scream. At Alethea or Cassandra, either would do. Both tiptoed too.

"Lock me in the attic and discard the key," Valerie muttered after a quarter hour of cosseting and expressions of

delight over her quick recovery. Alethea cast her a curious look. Cassandra's gaze dropped to her lap. Valerie bit her lip and folded her hands upon the coverlet.

"I would like to know what everyone is doing these days," she said as smoothly as she could. Her throat was still raw, but her energy had returned. Nevertheless, the doctor, Lady March, and Anna all insisted she spend another sennight in bed. She had looked forward to her friends' visit, hoping it would distract her from the ever-present ache in her chest. But if she must endure another insipid interview, she would truly begin to wail. That seemed unjust, since the individual who truly deserved her haranguing had left Castlemarch days ago.

Alethea shrugged. "In all honesty, Valerie, nothing worth note has gone on. We have been rehearsing *Twelfth Night*," she said without enthusiasm. "But really everyone is still talking about your—" She halted, casting a quick look at Cassandra. The flaxen-haired girl continued to stare at her own hands.

Valerie's insides clenched. Her scandal? Did they all know?

"My what?"

"Your rescue!" Cassandra's chin came up, her eyes glowing. "It is the most romantic thing any of us have ever heard."

Valerie swallowed back the lump in her throat and pushed her quivering hands beneath the coverlet.

"Is it?" she said in a strangled voice, hoping her friends would put it off to her illness.

"Of course it is," Cassandra exclaimed. "Lady Alverston told us all how it happened."

"Really?" Valerie's insides trembled too, now. "What did she say?"

"She told us how she and the earl looked everywhere in the castle for you that night, and how at the very moment they were telling Lady March of their worries, Lord Ashford returned from town and went straight out with your brother to search for you in the snow."

Valerie struggled to catch her breath. Anna and Valentine knew everything, yet in four days they had not said a word to her about it. Instead, they invented a story that protected her reputation and still included Steven.

"And then?" she managed to utter.

"You must know it already." Alethea grinned.

"Oh, yes." Cassandra sighed. "How Lord Ashford found you upon the ice where you had fallen and carried you back here. Of course, Lady Alverston did not need to tell us the rest." She smiled sweetly. "We all saw it ourselves."

Valerie heart raced. "What did you see?"

Alethea tilted her head. "How Lord Ashford remained at Castlemarch until the moment your fever broke. He left for London only minutes after I told everyone the news. It seems he had important business there he put off until he felt certain you were well."

Valerie forced herself to blink. She had been unconscious for two days, two days during which Steven had delayed in pursuing Hannsley. Two precious days that could mean the success of his plans or their failure.

"I see," she managed to utter.

"Lord Ashford will certainly be missed," Alethea said slowly, peering at her with undisguised interest.

Cassandra's pretty pink lips turned down in a scowl. "Mr. Flemming, however, will not be missed at all."

Alethea's astonished gaze shifted to the girl. Cassandra's chin seemed unusually firm.

"Well, he won't. He is as dull as dishwater and it was his fault you were injured, Valerie. If he hadn't forgotten his hat and told you to walk on without him, you would not have slipped and fallen onto the ice. He should have at least inquired after you when he arrived back at the castle, but he did not. I don't like him above half."

"Yes, Cassandra dear. It was unforgivable that Mr. Flemming left off escorting Valerie." Alethea said carefully. "But it obviously does not please our friend to hear this now, so let us speak of something else."

A crease appeared upon Cassandra's brow. "I am only sorry Valerie is ill on account of our negligence at the folly. If Lord Bramfield and Lord Michaels and I had paid closer attention, Valerie would be with us now in the music room practicing her role for *Twelfth Night* instead of languishing here."

Valerie did not wonder at her friend's guilt. Cassandra's eyes were all for Timothy that evening by the lake, as his were for her. At the time, Valerie considered it a blessing that Timothy seemed less interested in watching her.

"Cassandra, please do not chastise yourself. I am fine now so all is well." She smiled, took a breath, and plunged forward. "Tell me, how do you like Lord Bramfield's courtship?"

The girl's eyes went wide. "I— But—" she stammered, her cheeks washing with color. "But he has not—He— You—"

Valerie leaned forward and patted Cassandra's slender hand.

"He is a very good man, you know, and a dear friend. He deserves a wife who will truly appreciate him."

Cassandra's face grew even pinker, but she smiled as her lashes fluttered down.

Anna and Lady March finally allowed Valerie to move to the blue parlor. She was reading with only half an eye on the page, the other half on the far side of the frozen lake, when Timothy entered. With a twinkling smile, he sat upon a chair beside her chaise. He grasped both her hands and kissed her fingers lightly.

"You look well, Valerie. Your usual, lovely self." His eyes glowed with familiar appreciation.

"You flatter me, my lord. I do feel better today, thank you," she lied for the tenth time since waking. Her physical pains were nearly gone. But she still ached, and inside a part of her gaped like a cavern.

Timothy's fingers tightened around hers and he glanced about the empty chamber.

"I hoped we might have a brief word." Disquiet shadowed his usually merry eyes.

"Of course." Valerie folded her book on her lap.

"I care deeply about you, Valerie, as I have told you before. I said also that I would wait for you to care about me in the same manner." He looked down for a moment, and when his gaze met hers again, resignation colored it. "I do not believe that day will ever come."

Valerie opened her mouth, but he continued.

"I hope you won't deny it. I am not an overly observant man, but in these past days, before your accident, I noticed a change in you." He squeezed her hands, and his words seemed to make him uncomfortable. "You are more beautiful now, more alive and vibrant than ever before. I've never seen your eyes sparkle as they did on Christmas Day, Valerie. But you see, I don't think I could bear to see you look at me every day for the rest of our lives without wishing I could inspire the same radiance in them."

Valerie could not respond.

Timothy pulled back, his fingers tightening briefly again before he let hers go. He smiled, a gentle look of acceptance.

"I wish you great—"

"Don't wish me happiness, Timothy," she hurried to say, unable to bear the sentiment. "Instead, let me wish it to you."

His brow furrowed.

Valerie let herself grin. "How does Lady Cassandra go on these days?"

A smile cracked his lips and he reached forward to take her hands again.

"Valerie, you are a jewel beyond all treasure. Ashford is a lucky man, indeed."

Chapter 40

January 10, 1811

THE LADY VALERIE MONROE
ALVERSTON HALL, KENT

Dear Valerie,

Cassandra and Lord Bramfield are to be wed! They announced the engagement last night before dinner. Lord Fredericks made a lovely toast and we all kissed the bride-to-be, except for Mr. Fenton and Miss Sinclaire, who were absent at the time.

Other than that, everyone here has been very dull since you, Anna, and Lord Alverston left last week. Today The Times *arrived, so at least there is some talk of another much-missed member of our dwindling party. The journal reported that Lord Ashford has let Ashford House for five years to an India nabob—an unknown tradesman. It is astounding!*

They say the viscount plans to return to America for good. But perhaps you already know this?

I return to London on the 28th. Will you go up to town once you are fully recovered? I should very much like to see you there, for, in truth, Valerie, I am in need of company.

> *Your abiding friend,*
> *Alethea Pierce*
> *Castlemarch, Derbyshire*

Chapter 41

*T*he deck echoed empty beneath lowering clouds. Above, dozens of white sails billowed in the wind, sending the ship cutting through green water. No hands hauled the lines, no sounds met her ears but the creaking of seasoned wood and the wind's hum. She stood alone, shackled to the mainmast.

Across the waves, another vessel moved under half sail. Standing stiffly erect at its helm, an elegantly clad gentleman with iron-gray hair stared at her benignly as the wind carried his ship away.

She sniffed the breeze. It smelled like salt and life.

She looked down. Around her feet, the pool of blood widened.

Crimson stained the wrinkled bed linens.

Bleary-eyed, Valerie stumbled to her dressing chamber and the basin of water the maid left warming over coals. She washed, then affixed the uncomfortable straps about her waist and wadding between her legs, pulled on a clean nightshift, and returned to her bedchamber. The maid had already changed the bed. Everything operated with smooth, disciplined care at Alverston Hall. Except her heart.

Valerie slipped in and curled into a ball.

It was the last day of her courses, but she still ached, from heart-soreness rather than cramps. All she had left now of Steven Ashford were confused memories.

Her hand slipped to her abdomen, palm flattening. Her memory was so strong, she could practically still feel him inside her, driving her into ecstasy. Her menses seemed to heighten her body's memory, making her tender, making her want him as she had wanted him for weeks. Months.

She pressed her fists into her eyes, willing tears away.

A knock sounded upon her bedchamber door, jarring her.

"Come," she uttered.

Anna entered upon light feet. "What's this? Still abed?" she said brightly.

Valerie covered her head with the pillow. "For someone in your delicate condition, you rise like a farmer's wife."

Anna sat upon the edge of the bed. "It is nearly midday. I rose hours ago. The doctor tells me I will again begin to feel absolutely wretched about two months from now, so I am taking advantage of this hiatus. After all, I have just gotten over casting up my accounts every morning, noon, and eve. Anyway, nothing tastes the same now." Lady Alverston's hand strayed over her still-slender waist. "I have news for you."

"If it concerns vomiting or eating, it will have to wait until after I have slept a bit more. I was awake till the small hours."

"Doing what?"

"Reading."

Anna pulled the pillow away from Valerie's head. "Oh, not dreaming, then?"

Valerie pushed the hair out of her face and sat up.

"Leave me alone, won't you? I have really endured just about all I can of this cheerful concern. You and Valentine will drive me to wit's end. I warn you, I may do something drastic just to spite you. I've got plenty of practice at that sort of thing, you know."

"Ah, yes," the countess nearly hummed. "In that case, old Jasper recently hired a fine, young stable hand. He's strapping, appealing in that rustic sort of way you once admired. I suspect he would be agreeable with very little encouragement."

Valerie lay back, wrenching her arms around her waist again.

"Sounds lovely. I will slip on my riding habit and dash off to have a go at him."

"You have become absolutely vulgar, darling."

"And you are no pristine innocent either. But you haven't a sennight spent aboard a pirate ship to justify your vulgarity, do you?"

Anna smiled fondly. "My news still awaits. In fact, she awaits in the corridor as we speak."

Valerie's brows shot up. She jumped out of the bed, reaching for her dressing gown.

"Oh, mum!" Mabel said, coming through the door. "It's surely a great pleasure to see you looking fit and— Faith, but you ain't been sleeping, have you? Or eating. Aren't you well?"

Valerie squeezed her maid's hands. "More importantly, you are."

Anna was looking at her oddly, but Valerie could not hide her relief. For nearly three weeks she suffered an anguish of worry over the part her maid played in Hannsley's duping. Safely hidden at Castlemarch with Lady and Lord March, Mabel hadn't been in any real danger. Still, Valerie's insides were twisted with anxiety over her. She had put Mabel in danger, after all.

Suddenly, like rain clearing away a fog, understanding blazed in Valerie.

She swung around to Anna, abruptly wanting to tell her everything. Valentine too. Well, perhaps not exactly everything. But the important parts.

"Pish-tosh, mum," Mabel said cheerily. "It were indeed a great trial to sit day in and out in my very own chamber stuffing my mouth with sweetmeats and looking at fashion plates when I should have been working." She grinned. "And there weren't no insisting from you, not that I remember. I like a bit of adventure. Now here's a letter from Her Ladyship for you."

Valerie plucked the envelope from Mabel's hand and tore it open.

January 18, 1811

THE LADY VALERIE MONROE
ALVERSTON HALL, KENT

Dear Lady Valerie,

I hope this missive finds you well.

You should know that my nephew Alistair has disappeared without leaving word. The Captain believes he has gone to America, but I suspect he fled to the Continent until our godson is again gone. While Steven has made certain that the Other Transgressor will be duly punished, he refuses to pursue Alistair, which is probably imprudent, but

*he can oftentimes be unwise when it comes to mat-
ters of the heart. He always has been. I suspect he
realizes he has met his match in you and simply
does not know how to go on now. He has spent a
lifetime alone, and bad habits are difficult to break,
of course.*

*He sends word that he sails from Portsmouth on
February 2.*

*Fondly,
Margaret, Countess of March
Castlemarch, Derbyshire*

Valerie lowered the letter. Mabel and Anna stared at her.

Valerie swallowed hard. "I love him."

Mabel nodded vigorously, bouncing up on her toes.

Anna smiled. "But of course you do, darling. What will
you do now?"

Valerie's heart pounded so rough and fast she could
barely breathe. He had left her, and it didn't really matter
what anyone else said about his feelings. If Steven did not
want her with him, Valerie would not force him to have
her. She was through with insisting upon her worthiness
to any man. She knew her worth. If he couldn't recognize
it, then he did not deserve her. She'd told herself that for
three weeks already.

But she wanted him so much.

"He sails in less than a fortnight."

"Sails?" Anna's brows went up.

Mabel sprang to the wardrobe. "I'll start packing, mum."

"What do you mean he sails, Valerie? Where is he
going? Back to America?"

Valerie looked at Anna and a new ache sliced through
her. She grasped her hands.

"Oh, dear friend," she said upon a ripple of pleasure and pain. "There is so much I need to tell you. He is not at all what he appears."

Anna nodded. "I suspected as much. He could not be to have captured your heart."

Warmth bloomed in Valerie, spreading through her belly and limbs. A knock came at the door and a maid entered carrying a silver dish bearing a calling card.

"Milady, a gentleman is here to see you. Mr. Sibble sent me up to you right quick." She curtsied and ducked from the chamber.

Valerie clutched the card in shaking fingers, disbelieving the name she saw embossed there.

"Well, that's unusual of Sibble to hurry a caller's card up like that," Anna murmured, peering over Valerie's shoulder. "Who is it? Would you like me to ask him to return later? You are hardly dressed for visitors, and you haven't yet answered my questions about Lord Ashford."

Valerie caught up her breath. "But, Anna, I still have questions about him myself, and this gentleman is the one person who can answer them for me."

The ramshackle carriage once belonging to a baronet long since in his grave blotted the London street corner like a plague pustule. No one bothered the hackney coach, though. It lacked a driver, and it had been parked for well over an hour already. A pair of swaybacks slumped in the harness, no longer bothering to stomp their impatience to be back at the mews.

Dusk dropped and shadows lengthened across Ewer Street's narrow confines. The wooden placard above the plumber's door swayed. The proprietor locked the bolts and hurried to make his way up the street, away from the hackney and away from Steven leaning like a dark specter against a wall opposite.

The old fellow was the last. Shop fronts along the street all stared blankly, unwelcoming in the deepening gloom of urban twilight.

Steven moved toward the coach, the hem of his greatcoat brushing boots worn thin from such use. One never knew, after all, what fluids one might find upon one's footwear following the sort of interview Steven anticipated. Reserving a special pair for certain occasions had always seemed wise, at least since he'd discovered himself to be despicably wealthy.

He opened the coach door, pulling back upon the rickety hinge and steeling himself for the bullet's impact.

"Get in, fool."

"Now, now. Sticks and stones, Clifford." Steven stepped lightly up and bent himself into the cab. He closed the door. The air inside was fetid. Stale sweat and urine mingled with skin-soaked liquor and the pungent, unmistakable odor of defeat.

Hannsley's hooded eyes barely registered his presence. Slumped against the torn squabs, he held a snuffbox open in one hand. Gray dust littered his neck cloth and waistcoat. A turtle-shell embossed pistol balanced upon his thigh.

"You deserve the name. Fool," the marquess repeated, his voice slurring. "You should be ashamed of yourself. But tainted blood makes for simpletons. I wager pretense is all you have, though. Isn't it?" For an instant his eyes cleared, glinting momentarily cruel. "Polite society's doors are open to you now because of Margaret March, but they won't be for long. You may as well accede the title to perdition. A gentleman would not have you for his daughter, and a Cit would be too afraid to ally his house with yours, you half-breed papist. A viscount, and you can't even cross Parliament House's threshold. Hunh?"

"Can't say I'd much wish to if you were there, old

fellow. Anyway, I don't have the taste for politics. Too untidy." Steven kept his tone light. "I do have plenty of blunt, though. That *is* the reason you arranged this little back alley assignation, isn't it? In dun territory? Hard to imagine, with all your ready. But a fellow's expenses are his own business, I always say. How much do you need?"

Hannsley's eyes dulled again, but his fingers slipped toward the pistol.

"My patience is thin, Ashford. Cease this stupidity."

"If it's not money you want, Clifford, then I haven't the foggiest notion why you called me to this dreadful place. But I don't think I shall stay." Steven drew back, considering the other man. "You know, old fellow, I believe you're foxed. Won't blame you. Present accommodations are dismal, don't you know." He looked about with exaggerated distaste, drawing his hand away from the seat cushion to wipe it upon a handkerchief.

Hannsley's grip encircled his wrist. "I could kill you now," he snarled, jerking his chin toward the pistol. "I don't need this thing to do it. I could kill you with my bare hands for what you have done."

"It would be fascinating to see you try. Again," Steven drawled. "Nevertheless, I think I will pass. Now, remove your hand from my person, if you please." Above his pleasant smirk, his eyes warned.

Slowly, the other man's fingers loosened.

"Your confidence is undeserved," Hannsley muttered. "That slave spawn Fevre was my man. He bought his freedom with your betrayal, whimpering like a whelp as he took the money. But you know that already, don't you? Learning that tidbit of information must have burned like lamp oil. You thought you were omniscient. Thought you had everything in hand. But you never did."

Steven remained silent. Though impressively lucid,

Hannsley was indeed disguised. In Steven's view, responding to a drunk's taunts was not a worthy pursuit.

"You know, after I realized it was you, I almost wanted you to discover Fevre." The marquess laughed in satisfaction. "S'why I didn't kill that boy, showing up at Castlemarch on Christmas Eve like he did. Too many coincidences. Tipped your hand. Oh, I will admit Flemming was convincing. But I am not the trusting fool you are. Though . . ." He paused, and his fingers slipped to his thigh, caressing. "I didn't see the girl coming. Not even after she stole the letters. Must've been her after all." His heavy gaze swung to Steven's face. "Well done, my boy. Little trollop passes herself off nicely as a la—"

Steven's thumb and forefinger pressed an inch deep into Hannsley's throat before the marquess saw him move. Snuffbox and pistol both clattered to the cab floor. Hannsley's eyes protruded. After a moment, his hands flailed around Steven's outstretched arm.

"Insult me all you wish, Clifford. But do not, in my presence, impugn the honor of a lady."

He released his grip. The marquess gulped in breaths.

"Th-that's the w-way it is, is it?" Hannsley coughed, gingerly massaging his crushed cravat. "She won't have you, you know. At least not for long. Whatever she does with her nights, she'll have to wed carefully to salvage her reputation."

Steven stilled, clarity washing through him like cold seawater. He was, indeed, the greatest fool alive. It almost made him laugh to realize that Clifford Hannsley, of all people, was the one to finally show him how foolish.

Valerie did not belong in Hannsley's world of unbending codes of behavior and status, the one Steven had left behind so many years ago. She would die in it.

She belonged with him.

Abruptly restless to be away, he straightened the capes on his greatcoat. "I would like to be able to say that this little interview has given me great pleasure, old friend, but I simply cannot. So I will take my leave—"

"Is it decided, then?" Hannsley's hurried voice halted Steven's hand upon the door latch. "Prinny won't return my messages. Turned me away from Carlton House." Desperation laced his tone. "It's coming, isn't it? They all know?"

Steven wished he could feel pity. Honesty, for once, would have to suffice.

"What do you wish me to say, Clifford? With a shovel of gold you have dug the graves of thousands. Your own tomb now awaits you."

Steven's hand turned upon the latch and the cab door swung open. He stepped down, closing it behind him. As he crossed the street, his boots echoed upon the uneven cobbles, obscuring the muffled pistol shot within the carriage.

Valentine and Anna offered Maximin a tour of Alverston Hall and the nearby grounds of the estate, including the stables and hothouses. A lavish dinner followed, and tea in the drawing room afterward. They went out of their way to welcome the man who helped save her life the previous summer, extraordinarily gracious despite the fact that they were obviously mad with curiosity and concern. Valerie knew she should be grateful.

She wanted to throttle them.

Finally they withdrew from the drawing room, leaving the door open. Maximin swirled the brandy in his glass, and a smile crept across his handsome face.

"Your brother is uncertain whether to thank me or throw down his gauntlet," he said in French. He wore a cutaway coat of finely tailored English wool, and his top-boots shone with the glow of a valet's effort. A gold pin glimmered in his starched cravat, and a single gold ring glinted upon one finger. He looked nothing like the sailor she'd met at sea, but his grin still teased.

"He is only concerned for my welfare."

Maximin's dark gaze narrowed. "As is another dear to both of us, *mademoiselle*. Which, of course, is why I have come here."

Valerie waited mutely. She had ached all day to ask him a hundred questions about Steven. Now that the moment arrived, her tongue tangled.

"Last April I was obliged to go ashore to arrange certain matters," Maximin said. "During my absence our first mate, Fevre, intentionally lost the *Blackhawk* to Bebain at cards. Bebain came aboard with additional crew members of his own. We had learned that Bebain was Clifford Hannsley's man, and when I returned and found circumstances as they were, I saw this as opportunity. After we met with Raymer's ship as planned, Etienne was not as pleased. Naturally, this was because of you."

Valerie's brow puckered. "It was not my idea to be kidnapped."

"I believed Bebain's men could be more easily subdued with him dead rather than captive," Maximin continued as though she hadn't spoken. "Etienne disagreed with me, as I expected him to. More importantly, he disagreed with me concerning nearly everything since the moment you came aboard our ship."

"That's why you seemed so angry with him that day on deck, wasn't it?"

"It was."

"You have no love for me, do you?"

He cocked an amused brow. "Are you so greedy for it, *mademoiselle*, that you insist upon both of ours?"

Valerie's heart sped. "I disrupted your plans."

He stepped toward her. "I have known Etienne since we were boys. We have battled side by side for justice. We are bound through those trials more than any who share the same parents."

Valerie tried to nod, but apprehension paralyzed her.

"In October it came time to send our associate here to complete the work we began long ago," Maximin said, "to retrieve Hannsley's documents and put the letter which Lady March was meant to have taken from you into the appropriate hands. At this time, contrary to our plans, Etienne told me he would come here himself. He told me he had been given a responsibility for others with his title of nobility, and that he must make arrangements before he was free again to continue our work."

Under the Haitian's steady regard, Valerie shivered, waiting.

"Until then," Maximin finally said, "he never told me he was an English lord."

Valerie stood still as a sail on a windless day.

"But he left me," she whispered.

"He believes you wish to remain in this world of comfort with your loved ones. He seeks to protect you from danger, and he wants your happiness. My friend is wise in many things, *mademoiselle*. But sometimes he can be a great fool." A gentle smile played upon Maximin's lips. "We sail for America in two weeks' time, but I do not travel with a whole man on this journey. On this island that is no longer his home, he leaves behind his heart."

Chapter 42

The Earl of Alverston nodded at Maximin. "The carriage should make good time on muddy roads, *monsieur.*"

Tears rolled down Anna's cheeks but she smiled gamely. Valerie took her friend's hands and drew them to her cheek.

"Oh, dearest," she said. "Do stop crying. I promise I will visit someday. I must meet my nephew, after all." She drew back, her own smile wavering. "Or niece."

"God forbid it's a girl," Valentine muttered. A grin creased Maximin's mouth. Anna choked upon another sob.

Valerie put her hands into her brother's and let him draw her into his embrace.

"Godspeed, dear sister," he said gruffly. "I expect you will get into a great deal of trouble and have many adventures. But you may as well do it on the other side of the ocean as here. I will miss you." When he released her, tears dampened Valerie's cheeks. She turned quickly away from her family and toward the waiting carriage.

Portsmouth stretched out in the spectacular array of a kingdom at home upon the sea. Ships dotted the harbor. Dozens of others rested in berths along the quay, active with the business of loading and unloading cargo, and uniformed soldiers were everywhere. The salty wind whisking across the water buffeted Valerie as her gaze sought the only vessel that mattered to her.

Maximin touched her arm. She turned to follow his gaze. Not far along the quay, a familiar, sleek ship sat abreast the dock, two banners waving from its mizzenmast: one white; the other blue and red, its center emblazoned with cannon, palm trees, flags, and words she could not decipher from the distance.

As though he read her thoughts, Maximin said quietly, "The motto upon the flag of the Republic of Haiti reads *L'Union Fait la Force*. Our union makes our strength." He turned to her. "Go, *mademoiselle*, and make strength."

Taking a deep breath, Valerie strode up the dock toward the *Blackhawk*, her heart pounding. Mounting the gangplank, she didn't hesitate, sending herself up to the spar deck and scanning the ship swiftly as she went. A handful of barrels and crates littered the boards at the hatchway amidships, waiting to be hauled below. A pair of hands worked at the lines stretching to the bow.

A man in a neat overcoat approached.

"Good afternoon, ma'am. I am Sainte, first mate on this vessel. May I be of assistance?"

"I am looking for your master."

"Ah," Sainte shook his head. "You have just missed him. He has already departed."

"Departed?" Valerie's breath left her. "But where—"

She swiveled around to look for Maximin, and her gaze met Steven's.

Like that first moment in Boston months earlier, he stood upon the dock staring up at her. But this time there was no trace of the priest about him, or even the nobleman. In buckskin breeches and a dark coat, with his shirt open at the neck and his hair shining like gilded bronze in the winter sunlight, he was all sailor.

Valerie's heart turned over so hard her knees buckled.

"Ah, there he is." The mate bowed and continued across the deck.

Valerie gazed at the man upon the dock, no longer a stranger, but achingly, deliciously familiar. Her entire body trembled with anticipation as Steven looked at her for what seemed endless minutes. Finally, he climbed the gangplank and stepped onto the deck.

Valerie stretched out her palm and swung. He caught her wrist and pulled it between them. A breathtaking, one-sided grin curved his lips.

"You may well have the right to strike me, dear lady. And more." His rich voice tumbled through her, his touch filling her with warmth. "But not on my ship and in front of my men."

Valerie took a breath and squared her shoulders. "I am coming with you."

His smile broadened. "I have wished for nothing else."

"You what? *What*?"

Steven's brow wrinkled. Valerie had never seen consternation upon his face. It looked beautiful, as everything did.

"Do you doubt it?"

"Of course I doubt it," she exclaimed. "You insulted me then you left me. *Again*!"

"I had business to see to."

"Business?" Valerie spluttered.

"Indeed, I have been considerably occupied," he said with exasperating calm. "You know perfectly well that I needed to secure matters regarding our friend the marquess."

"Yes, but I don't see why you could not have—"

"I was also very busy trying to convince myself that I could live without you."

Valerie's heart stopped. Steven's strong grasp slipped around her hand, his fingers lacing through hers.

She swallowed. "And did you—convince yourself, that is?"

His gaze was fierce, the gold flecks in his eyes lit with fire. "I am sorry I hurt you, Valerie. More sorry than you can possibly know."

For the first time in a life filled with daring escapades and scandalous adventures, Valerie's courage deserted her.

"Your mate says you are leaving," she managed. "Where are you going?"

Steven's hand tightened around hers. "To retrieve you."

"To retrieve me?"

"No doubt you are happier to have come by your own choice." His half smile flickered again as he reached to untie her bonnet ribbons. "I have never met a woman more in possession of her own will."

"What are you doing?" she asked dazedly. He drew her into his arms. Valerie's whole being sang to life, tingling everywhere she fit against him.

"Removing this ridiculous thing." He dropped her bonnet to the deck. "I am going to kiss you now in full sight of anyone passing by."

"I will be compromised," she whispered, her hands slipping to his shoulders. "Ruined. Finally."

Steven bent his head. "I depend upon it," he murmured,

and met her lips. Valerie sighed, melting into his kiss. He deepened it, and his arms tightened, as though holding her against escape. But Valerie didn't want to escape, she never had.

"But, Steven." She gasped in a mouthful of air, smiling. "Not on your ship and in front of your men."

"My ship and my men be damned," he said huskily against her brow, then kissed it, and her eyes, cheeks, and mouth again. His lips lingered and his hands upon her back held her firmly against him. "How did you know I was here, my sweet Valerie?"

She drew away only enough to trace the planes of his face with her gaze, to assure herself she did not dream.

"Maximin came to Alverston Hall." She turned. Mabel stood alone at the edge of the wharf. The maid grinned and came up the gangplank. Valerie made a sound of protest when Steven released her, but he kept his hand wrapped around hers as he turned to Mabel.

"Good afternoon, *mademoiselle*," he said, bowing. Mabel returned it with a curtsy and a blush. She held out a folded piece of paper.

"Mr. Panthère said he had to be off, but that I was to give you this, milord."

Steven took the paper from the girl's grasp. His gaze remained on hers a moment longer. A quick, wordless communication passed between them before Mabel shook her head. Then she curtsied again and moved away, her eyes widening as she looked about at the ship. Grinning, she dropped her bandbox upon the deck and moved toward the sailors at the bow.

Valerie stared in amazement. "What on earth did you two just say to each other?" she demanded, trying to pull her hand from Steven's.

He gripped her fingers and drew her back into his embrace. Her body quivered as awareness dawned upon her lovely face.

"You employed my own maid to spy on me, didn't you?" she exclaimed.

Steven smiled in sheer satisfaction. This woman would never be deceived again, and he could not be happier about it.

"Yes," he replied, "although I would not quite phrase it that way."

"Aha. The truth so quickly offered?"

"Always, now."

She smoothed her fingers across his cheek, and her gaze sought his, brimming with trust. "No more lies," she whispered.

Relief washed through him. He slid his hands down her back to feel her body, to claim her again.

"In the spirit of truth, Monsieur Sailor," she murmured against his jaw, "what would you have done if I had not come here, and Mabel reported to you that I was increasing?"

"I would have forced you to wed me." He kissed her. Her soft lips and questing tongue tasted like sea air and desire. Trailing caresses across her brow and the bridge of her nose, he drank in her scent, every silken curve of skin and bone of this perfect woman. His woman, finally.

"And what will you do now that you know I am not?" she said as he kissed her neck and his body hardened, wanting her as he always did.

"Force you to wed me." He pulled her hips against his.

"There need be no force about it, my lord." Her body shivered in his hands as her mouth opened beneath his. He slipped his tongue between her eager lips. She pressed into him, twining her fingers in his hair.

When he drew away, her eyes were bright with desire, but a hint of challenge flickered in their sea-blue depths.

"Why did you leave me?"

He took her defiant chin gently between his fingers. "To protect you."

"From what, more pirates?"

"From me. From the horrors of the life I lead."

Her brows rose. "You thought I would prefer the horrors of *haute société*?"

"I will always protect you, even from myself. Valerie, I—"

"I do not need protection from you, Steven. I love you." Her voice was firm. "I loved you when I knew I should not, and I love you even more now that I know what you are. Who you are."

He stilled. He did not deserve this woman. He certainly did not deserve to have had so many chances to claim her. But this time he would seize her and hold on to her forever.

"My brother sends his greetings, by the way," she added with an unusually hesitant smile, "along with the message that if you ruin me and leave me he will hunt you down and put a bullet through your heart."

"I am relieved to learn he is so conscientious." He kept his tone sober, despite the pounding in his chest. He needed her so powerfully he could not conceal it. But he needn't any longer.

Valerie's eyes glimmered. "You have been very foolish, believing you could make decisions for me. Didn't they teach you any better in seminary?"

"My education has lacked a great many things, I fear." He kissed the corner of her luscious mouth.

"And yet you are so successful at what you do. How is that?" she gasped in surprise as his hands moved beneath her cloak, curving around her bottom and dragging her to him.

"Luck. Fate," he murmured, his voice taut. "Valerie—"

"You don't believe in Fate," she whispered.

"I most certainly do now." He took her mouth hard, instantly demanding, urging her to open to him. His arms wrapped around her waist, holding her tight. Hungry for his touch, for everything, Valerie sank into him.

He pulled back, his lion eyes afire.

"I love you, Valerie. You know I do," he said roughly, his gaze sweeping her face, raw and thoroughly unmasked. "More than my life. I did try to stop loving you. I had always succeeded before at everything I attempted. But—" He broke off, searching her eyes. "With you, for the first time in my life, I am home." He kissed her long and deep, with a warmth that stole Valerie's breath.

"Say it again," she whispered against his mouth, twisting her hand in his shirt to hold him close.

"I love you," he replied promptly, raining sweet kisses upon her cheeks and the corners of her mouth, so delicious her limbs went weak. He paused and whispered into her ear, his voice a tender caress, "I love you."

She clutched his shoulders. "And you want me to be with you."

"I want you in every way you can imagine. And several you cannot, I suspect, but we will soon remedy that."

Desire flooded her. Valerie laughed aloud, joy and sweet anticipation crowding her senses.

Steven drew back, smiling. "What is it?" he said, his lips tracing the line of her cheek, sending tingles of delight skittering through her awakened body. She pressed closer to him.

"I have been thinking." She tried to sound serious, but her lips twitched up at the edges. "I will accept my role as your counterpart if you choose once more to play the dashing ship captain or English lord." She paused. "But if you adopt clerical robes again, Steven, honestly, I think I would quickly come to find convent life a dull bore."

His laughter resonated through her. Valerie's insides melted, his happiness as seductive as his touch.

"I daresay," he murmured, setting his mouth just beneath her ear. She sighed and wrapped her arms around his neck. "Rather than a nun's habit, jewels and silken veils would better suit your beauty." He brushed her lips. "I have a bit of work to do in the East, you see." He kissed her again, this time slowly, lingering and deep, sealing their union with a promise of even more to come.

Finally he released her mouth and cocked a roguish smile. "How would you like to visit India, my love?"

Author's Note

Amid scandalous accusations, in 1773 when the powerful Society of Jesus was disbanded, the order did not fade away as its enemies hoped. Jesuits continued to work undercover for the day when they were finally reestablished with all honor in 1814. This made Steven's ruse possible; in 1810, no official Jesuit authority existed to chastise him for his masquerade. As a group, the Jesuits had an appreciation for and acceptance of native cultures unequaled in the colonial world.

While violent persecution of Roman Catholics in England came to an end in the seventeenth century, Catholics still experienced repression of various sorts due to their allegiance to what frequently amounted to a papal monarchy. Catholic peers were prohibited from taking their seats in Parliament until 1829.

As for the Atlantic slave trade, as a result of slave insurrections in its Caribbean colonies and abolitionist fervor, the fledgling French Republic abolished slavery in 1794. By the end of the decade, however, those dependent upon the lucrative trade and plantation economy were lobbying for slavery's reestablishment. Napoleon Bonaparte supported the anti-abolitionists, overturning emancipation in France and its colonies in 1802. Thousands of freed men, women, and children were reenslaved. The former slaves in the French colony of Saint Domingue, a plantation society whose inhabitants had briefly tasted freedom, violently revolted and in 1804 overthrew their French governors. Renaming itself the Republic of Haiti, this nation became the third free republic in the world (after the United States and France, the latter which had meanwhile succumbed to the emperor). The Haitian flag still bears the motto *L'Union Fait la Force*, "Union Makes Our Strength."

At the forefront of the abolitionist drive, England outlawed the importation of slaves from Africa in 1807 and finally abolished slavery altogether in 1833. France followed suit in 1848. Within all the colonial European nations, however, many like Clifford Hannsley used their positions of power to continue the trade illegally.

In the seventeenth and early eighteenth centuries, Natchez (pronounced "Nah'chee") people in Louisiana welcomed escaped slaves and other refugees into their communities. The relationship between Natchez people and French colonists ultimately proved tragic, though, resulting in the decimation of the tribe in the 1730s, including the forced enslavement of Natchez of noble status and relocation to the island of San Domingue, where they were put to work in the cane fields. Natchez who escaped this fate found homes with other native tribes. The Natchez language no longer exists in spoken form, and only sketchily in written renderings. The words Steven speaks represent my humble attempts at reconstruction, assisted by Charles D. Van Tuyl's wonderful lexicon and Jim Barnett of the Mississippi Department of Archives and History.

My heartfelt thanks go to Father L. F. M. Radrigues of the Institutum Historicum Societatis Iesu in Rome, Dr. Leslie Marx and Alex Beguinet of Duke University Fencing, Dr. Christine Daniels, Mari Freeman, Nancy Gideon, Dr. Anne Brophy, Noah Redstone Brophy, Mary Brophy Marcus, Dr. Diane Leipzig, Georgann T. Brophy, and wonderful Kimberly Whalen for falling in love with this book.

And now a sneak peek at
KATHARINE ASHE's
next thrilling novel,
coming in 2011
from Avon Books

Many were the men whose cities he saw and whose minds he learned, and many the woes he suffered in his heart upon the sea, seeking to win his own life.

—Homer, *Odyssey*

G or blimey, Cap'n Redstone. Cut off his head already."

With his long, leather-clad legs braced upon the pitch-sealed deck, Alexander "Redstone" Savege stared down at the cowering form, his broad-brimmed hat casting a shadow over the figure. The whelp's skinny arms encircled his head, his pallor grayish from a dredge in frigid coastal waters. He wasn't more than fourteen if he were a day. Far too young to be living such a wretched life.

Alex rubbed his callused palm across his face, sucking in briny air laced with the scent of oncoming rain, his gray eyes shadowed. He gripped the hilt of his cutlass, a thick, inelegant weapon, long as his arm and meant for only one purpose, the same as the ten iron guns and pair of agile pivots jutting from the *Cavalier*'s sleek sides, all at rest now but easily primed for battle.

Violence, the hell's ransom of a pirate. Once mother's milk to Alex, now a curse.

He cast a glance at his helmsman, a hulking, chestnut-skinned beast sporting a missing earlobe and a leering smile. Big Mattie was always eager to see blood spilled. The faces of the five dozen sailors clustered around showed the same gleeful anticipation.

Alex withheld a sigh. He'd brought this on himself. The lot of them knew, after all, the swift ease with which their master's blade could fly.

"Nip his knob right off, Cap'n," cackled a sexagenarian with cheeks of uncured leather. "Or slice his nose and ears."

"Stick 'im in the ribs, just like you did to that Frenchie wi' the twenty-gun barque we sunk in '13," an ebony sailor chimed in.

Alex repressed a grimace, his hand tightening around the sword handle. He fixed the grommet with a hard glare.

"Are you ready to die for your crime, Billy?" he grumbled in his deepest, scratchiest voice, the sort that never saw the inside of a St. James's gentlemen's club or a beautiful lady's Mayfair bedchamber. The sort that his mother, sister, and most of his acquaintants would be shocked to know he could affect.

The Seventh Earl of Savage never cussed, rarely swore, and only in the direst circumstances raised his voice above an urbane murmur. Handy with his fives, expert with saber, épeé, and pistol alike, he never employed any of them, to the eternal vexation of not a few cuckolded husbands. He preferred perfumed boudoirs to malodorous boxing cages, and the elegant peace and quiet of a fine gaming establishment to the dust and discomfort of a carriage race.

But each time Alex stepped aboard the *Cavalier*, he left the Earl of Savage behind.

"Blast and damn, Bill, are you trying to fob off a whisker?" He glowered. Several of his crew members echoed his discontent with mumbles.

"I didn't cackle, Cap'n. I swears it," the youth mewled. "You can't kill me for not telling them nothing, can you?"

Alex took a long breath, steadying the blood pounding through his veins fueled by a dangerous cocktail of anger, frustration, and pure cerebral fatigue.

"I can kill you for soiling my ears with that sound," he grunted. "What's that coming from your throat, a plea or a girl's whimper?" He tapped his sword tip to the boy's bony rear and nudged. "Stand up and let me hear if you can speak like a man instead."

The lad climbed to his feet.

"On my mother's grave, Cap'n, I didn't tell any of them smugglers about our covey. I didn't."

"Your mother is still alive, Billy, and happy you've nothing to do with her any longer, I'll merit." Alex sheathed his sword.

The whelp's eyes went wide. "Then you ain't going to kill me after all?"

"Not today, but you'll scrub the decks for a fortnight," Alex growled. "And caulk that crack on the gun deck at the bowsprit. Caulk the whole damn deck, for that matter. The rest of you get back to work."

Nothing stirred atop but the fluttering banner, gold rapier upon black undulating in the fresh breeze.

"Now!" Alex bellowed.

Billy jumped, and the crew scattered like grapeshot. Alex moved toward the stair to below deck. Big Mattie lingered.

"You ain't gonna even strap him to the capstan for a day, Cap'n?" he prodded. "But he gave up our covey to those curs at the tavern in the village. Got to make an example of him. What do you want, for the rest of these lilies"—he gestured around the ship—"to go spouting their mouths off?"

"Stubble it, Mattie, or I'll stubble it for you," Alex

warned without breaking stride, hand still upon the metal at his hip. He forbore grinding his straight, white teeth, the only bright spot on his polish-blackened face except the whites of his eyes.

"Big Mattie has a point, Captain," his quartermaster said quietly, falling in beside him, matching stride for stride. Jinan stood a mere inch shy of Alex's considerable height, of similar build though somewhat leaner in the chest like his Egyptian ancestors.

Alex met Jin's steady blue gaze, the intelligence glinting in it reminding him as always why he left his ship in this man's hands for most of the year.

"Big Mattie has an unhealthy thirst for blood, like his master," he muttered, swinging down the steep steps to the gun deck, leaving the gray of the spring day behind. "We don't need to worry about the smugglers. They'll keep to their own if we keep to ours." From habit his gaze scanned the cannons as he ducked beneath the beams, moving aft through the open space.

They entered the day chamber. Appointed in Aubusson carpets, with brocaded upholstery sheathing walnut and cherrywood furniture, a crystal carafe cradling French brandy upon the sideboard, a silver and onyx writing set upon the desk in the adjacent office, ivory bookends supporting leather-bound volumes of Greek verse, and the finest linens in the bedchamber opposite, they looked like the private rooms of a lord of the realm. Unbeknownst to all aboard except Alex and his quartermaster, they were.

Jin closed the door and affixed the shutters of the windows letting on to the deck. He folded his arms.

"Thirst for blood, my arse. Mattie might gripe, but your mercy stands you in good stead with the men, as always. Even when they're itching to be ashore."

"Lilies, the lot of them, just like he said." Alex waved a

dismissive hand. "They ought to be ashamed to be weary of the sea after a mere seven weeks abroad."

"They're not weary, only looking forward to a lick at the grog we took off that Barbadian trader." Jin shook his head. "You're right about the smugglers, of course. But, Alex, the hull won't clean itself. We've got to careen the ship."

"Which you should have done before the last cruise."

"I couldn't heave to for that. Not after the *Etoile* challenged us off Calais."

"And left you twiddling the sweeps when the wind died and she failed to show for the fight. Jin, I did not give you permission to go after that blasted privateer. We are at peace with France now, or hadn't you noticed? Even if we weren't, that is not our purpose."

"The men think it is, at least since you put French merchantmen off limits after the treaty last November."

"You sound as though you agree with them." Alex moved into his washroom, pulled off his sash strung with dagger and pistol along with his leather waistcoat, and hung them upon a hook. His sweat-stained linen shirt came next. "Have you finally become greedy for pirate's gold after all these years, my friend?" He drew on a fresh garment.

Jin scowled, marring the aristocratic lines of a face that mingled the blood of English nobles and eastern princes.

"Don't insult me. But after our run-in with that American frigate last week and the quick repairs, the crew deserves a break." He paused. "And so do you."

"Have a yen to take the summer cruise without me? Are you hoping to storm the Channel and win a fat French prize despite my prohibition?" Alex chose a dark, simply tailored coat from his compact wardrobe and took up a wrinkled cravat. Tubbs would have his head for donning such a rag. But Alex did not answer to his valet, or to anyone else.

"Of course not," Jin replied. "If you say we mayn't take merchantmen any longer, we will not. The boys got accustomed to it after three successful years, though."

"The war didn't last long enough for some."

"Long enough for you to take out a half-dozen French men-of-war," Jin murmured.

Alex ignored his friend's look of measured admiration and wound the linen about his neck. It smelled of salted fish, but that was a good sight better than plenty of the other aromas upon the *Cavalier* at the end of the seven-week cruise. Jin was right. Both ship and crew needed a break before the next trip out. And, according to the note Billy brought back from his trip ashore last night, Alex had business at home.

He wrapped the cravat about his jaw, stretching it over his nose and tucking it fast at the base of his skull. With the black face paint and a concealing hat, the disguise had not failed him in eight years. It still astounded Alex that, despite the *Cavalier*'s repeated visits to the north Devon coast of late, no one among the *bon ton* connected the notorious buccaneer Redstone with the Seventh Earl of Savege. With a vast, prosperous estate stretching miles of remote Devonshire coastline, the earl was far too busy in London whoring and gambling away his fortune to set foot at home often.

Alex took some pride in Redstone's mysterious identity. His brother, Aaron, positively delighted in it. Blast him.

"Last autumn the men grew richer than bilge rats should," Jin said.

Alex dropped a nondescript hat atop his head and tugged it low over his brow.

"Then they should be content this season with an occasional English yacht. In the meantime, allow them ashore, north as usual. But for God's sake tell them to behave and stay clear of those blasted smugglers. I don't want them getting mixed up with that bunch of miscreants, or being mistaken for them."

"The locals know the boys well enough by now." Jin frowned. "But Billy didn't like the looks of the *Osprey*'s crew, and he brought back news." He shook his head, bracing his stance against a sudden sway of the ship. The far-reaching eddies of the Bristol Channel were friendly enough in gentle weather, but rain beckoned. Alex could feel it in his blood as he felt sunset, moonrise, and the ebb of the tides.

"What have they done?"

"Seems they roughed up a girl."

Alex's gaze snapped up. "Roughed up?"

"Aye." Jin nodded. "A group of them."

"What girl?"

"A dairy maid. Did it right under her brothers' noses. In a barn."

"They took a girl from a barn and no one challenged them?"

"*In* a barn—"

"No." He lifted his hand. "I understand. The farm sits upon the shore, doesn't it?" Weeks ago he'd come upon the smuggling brig out of a fog and had a good look at it. Well armed and deep in the draft, the *Osprey* was an impressive vessel. Even if she sat too far off shore for the cannon shot to reach land, sailors' cutlasses and pikes could readily best a farmer's pitchforks and axes. The girl's brothers could not have saved her virtue, much as Alex's brother could not have saved their younger sister's years earlier.

Alex headed toward the door. "Why did you wait until now to tell me this?"

"You always say you don't wish to know the business of

English smugglers. Let them go their own way. But this is a nasty one. Captain goes by the name of Dunkirk."

"I don't care about the *Osprey* or her captain. Only—"

"The pleasure boats of spoiled English nobles. I know."

Alex set an even gaze upon his friend.

"If you object to the *Cavalier*'s purpose, you are free to find other employment. I've made that perfectly clear many times, and you must have enough gold stored in London banks by now to buy yourself a fleet. You owe me nothing."

Jin returned his steady stare. "I will decide when my debt to you is repaid. And you need me, now more than ever."

Alex refused to bite at that bait. He reached for the door handle.

"What about Poole, then?"

Alex paused, a hot finger of anger pressing at the base of his throat once more. But it did not spread to fill his chest as it had for so many years. Now it merely lapped at his senses, taunting him with what might have been. Revenge was sweetest served hot, and eight years had in truth cooled Alex's thirst for blood. Now the sole reason he pursued his present course sat in solitude at Savege Park awaiting his return.

Unforgettable, enthralling love stories,
sparkling with passion and adventure
from Romance's bestselling authors

At Avon Books, we know your passion for romance—once you finish one of our novels, you find yourself wanting more.

May we tempt you with . . .

- **Excerpts** from our upcoming releases.
- Entertaining **extras**, including authors' personal photo albums and book lists.
- Behind-the-scenes **scoop** on your favorite characters and series.
- **Sweepstakes** for the chance to win free books, romantic getaways, and other fun prizes.
- Writing **tips** from our authors and editors.
- **Blog** with our authors and find out why they love to write romance.
- **Exclusive content** that's not contained within the pages of our novels.

Join us at
www.avonbooks.com

AVON *An Imprint of* HarperCollins*Publishers*
www.avonromance.com